Rave reviews for Jilly Gagnon

'Classic Agatha Christie goes meta in this wish-we'd-thought-of-it premise: a real whodunnit set against the backdrop of a 1920s-themed murder mystery weekend. Think *Knives Out* all dolled up as *The Great Gatsby*. This is a super-fun pastiche with a wicked smart plot peppered with clever clues and compelling characters'
Ellery Lloyd

'When a couple attend a 1920s themed murder mystery weekend to save their marriage, they find themselves in a real-life whodunnit after one of the actors disappears. Jilly Gagnon's well-crafted maze of clues and shifting realities is the perfect read for fans of Lucy Foley . . . mind-bending fun!'
Wendy Walker

'Gagnon invites readers inside one seriously wicked little game with this utterly satisfying mystery. I didn't stop second-guessing myself until the very last page'
Kieran Scott

'With a deliciously creepy setting and juicy interpersonal intrigue, deftly weaves the search for a missing woman with a nuanced exploration of a marriage on the brink'
Sarah Zachrich Jeng

'*Clue* meets Shari Lapena's *An Unwanted Guest* . . . I felt as if I was in the middle of a murder-mystery game and playing along with the characters. Such a fun read!'
Georgina Cross

'A clever mystery . . . Becca's sardonic first-person narration sparkles. Lovers of both golden age and contemporary whodunits will have fun'
Publishers Weekly

JILLY GAGNON's humour writing, personal essays, and op-eds have appeared in *Newsweek*, *Elle*, *Vanity Fair*, *Boston magazine*, *McSweeney's Internet Tendency*, *The Toast*, and *The Hairpin*, among others. She is the author of the young adult novel *#famous*. She also co-writes the *Choose Your Own Misery* dark comedy series with Mike MacDonald.

Website: **www.jillygagnon.com**
Facebook: **/JillyGagnonWriter**
Twitter: **@jillygagnon**
Instagram: **@jillygagnon**

By Jilly Gagnon

#famous
The Murder Weekend
Scenes of the Crime

SCENES
OF
THE
CRIME

JILLY
GAGNON

ACCENT

Published by arrangement with Bantam,
an imprint of Random House, a division of
Penguin Random House LLC.
First published in the United States in 2023

First published in 2023
by HEADLINE ACCENT
An imprint of HEADLINE PUBLISHING GROUP

Cataloguing in Publication Data is available from the British Library

ISBN 978 1 0354 0040 9

Book design by Virginia Norey

Offset in 10.67/14.65pt Legacy Square ITC Std by Jouve (UK), Milton Keynes

Printed and bound in Great Britain by Clays Ltd, Elcograf S.p.A.

HEADLINE PUBLISHING GROUP
An Hachette UK Company
Carmelite House
50 Victoria Embankment
London EC4Y 0DZ

www.headline.co.uk
www.hachette.co.uk

*To all the women who have taught me about friendship:
both what it can be, and what it shouldn't.*

SCENES OF THE CRIME

1

I'D MADE IT ABOUT THIRTY PERCENT OF THE way through the most glaringly inane round of script notes known to man when a ghost walked into the coffee shop.

Actually, let's back up about five minutes. As a screenwriter, I should know to set the scene at least *slightly*.

I closed my eyes, breathing deeply in through my nose, out slowly through my mouth, trying to let the white noise of the coffee shop fall away, let my mind go blank, keep my focus on the breath moving through my body, all the way down to my fingertips, weaving through my leg muscles on its way to the soles of my feet, slithering along my vertebrae and pooling in my tailbone, whispering up into the tips of my eyelashes. *Calm. Lower your vibrations and be* calm.

It would be weird anywhere but LA.

But eventually I had to open my eyes again, and that same idiotic script note was still staring back at me, maddening in its Feedback 101 simplicity.

Motivation? Why is she still here? Let's dig deeper.

She's still *here* because this is an episode of *Back of House*, the broadest of network comedies, a slurry of gender stereotypes, cheap sight gags, and plotlines so dull they couldn't even cut the mental mashed potatoes we've been serving up *for five seasons now, Mike.* She's here because the loving but slightly exasperated wife character—literally, in early versions of the pilot her name was *Wife*—exists *exclusively* as an eye-rolling sounding board to her husband's constant string of wacky mishaps in the restaurant they run together.

And not for nothing, you don't need motivation to stay when the A story for the episode is "Hector accidentally locks himself and Maria into the staff bathroom before an all-important VIP dinner. But Maria's new get-fit focus on hydration means soon she's gonna have to go . . . when neither of them can go anywhere!"

I could feel a thin layer of my molars sanding away as I tried to cling to those "breathe deep" vibes. Useless. *Say goodbye to your enamel, Emily*.

I reached for my brownie, breaking off a large corner and stuffing it into my mouth as I sank into the too-deep armchair I'd set up in for the day, letting the chocolatey goodness do what meditative exercises alone couldn't manage. I looked out over the coffee shop, my favorite in LA not only because it was walking distance from my Los Feliz condo, but because the dim, windowless, sagging-velvet-upholstered-furniture ambiance seemed to scare off some of the would-be actors perpetually posing for the candid shots no one was taking of them. Instead, it attracted my people: the huddled screenwriters actually eating the indulgent baked goods, the bluelight glow of their screens only highlighting the vampiric pallor, unkempt hair, and smudged eyeglasses that formed their personal rebuttals to the famous promise of carefree SoCal sunshine. I always came to Grandeur in Exile when it was my week to write the script. It was impossible *not* to get work done surrounded by so much hushed intensity.

And occasionally, like now, someone so unexpected would appear that it revived that tiny flame deep inside me—perilously close to snuffing out after five years in the *Back of*

House writers' room—that flickered with *What's that abouts?* and *Wait, reallys?* and in this particular case, a *What's she doing in* here? The tiny moment of not-quite-rightness that feels pregnant with an untold story.

The woman at the counter had the elongated proportions of a designer's sketch, all willowy limbs and swanlike neck, its slim length accentuated by the sharp line of her near-black bob. Even I could tell that her outfit—trendy black booties and a long-sleeved raw silk sheath, the demure hemline seemingly contradicted by the way it clung to her slim figure, highlighting every curve—was expensive, in a Beverly Hills way you rarely saw in this part of town. And she was carrying a fricking *Birkin*. What was someone like that doing in this dungeon—albeit a dungeon with plush amenities and excellent wifi—for creatives?

And then she turned to glance toward the heavily curtained windows and I almost choked to death on gooey chocolate.

It was Vanessa. But it couldn't be.

Vanessa had been gone for fifteen years. I should know. I was one of the last people to see her alive.

And it was possible I was the one who had killed her.

EXT. PRECIPICE WINERY—NIGHT (15 YEARS AGO)

OPEN ON the rear of a large lodge-style home, its details reduced by the heavy mantle of night to the suggestion of a roof, shimmers of plate glass reflecting the strong moonlight, and a flagstone patio dotted with furniture, all ghostly gray. A darker shadow moves around the edge of the house and one of the motion sensor lights flickers on. The shadow—now just barely identifiable as a slim young woman—stops short, waiting for the light to flick off before moving out of its range to continue skirting the perimeter of the building's luminescent defenses.

The camera follows the girl away from the building, until she's a few yards shy of a jagged cliff's edge, where a spindly staircase is set into the rock face. She holds a wine bottle by the neck with one hand. Glancing back over her shoulder, she pulls out her phone with the other. The glow carves out her beautiful, slightly sharp features, accentuated by her choppy short dyed-blond hair. This is VANESSA MORALES. She nibbles the edge of her lip as she stares at the screen, then takes a large swig of wine.

                    VANESSA
                 (whispering)
         Are you really doing this, Vee?

She stares at the phone a few beats longer, then, seeming to make a decision, types out a quick text. In CLOSE-UP we see her finger hovering over the send button.

                    EMILY (O.S.)
          Vanessa?

Vanessa startles visibly, glancing over her shoulder as the other girl approaches, and clicks the phone dark, slipping it into a pocket. It's EMILY FISCHER, Vanessa's close friend. She's shorter, and curvy, with more of a girl-next-door look, especially when contrasted with Vanessa's angular beauty.

                    VANESSA
          Jesus, Em, you scared me.

                    EMILY
          Sorry. Where have you been? I
          haven't seen you since Paige and
          I went into town. Brittany didn't
          know where you'd gone either.

                    VANESSA
          Around. I . . . needed some alone
          time.

Vanessa runs a hand through the hair at the back of her head, wincing slightly, but Emily doesn't notice in the dark. She offers the bottle and Emily takes a sip, then passes it back. Vanessa takes another large swig, clearly working herself up to something.

                    VANESSA (CONT'D)
          Can you . . . not tell anyone
          that you saw me?

                    EMILY
                 (dubious)
          I mean, sure . . . but why?

                    VANESSA
          It doesn't matter, just don't
          tell the others about this,
          please. Or anyone else after. You
          have to promise me.

                    EMILY
          You're being weird, Vee.

Vanessa grips the other girl's arm, eyes
intent.

                    VANESSA
          Promise me, Emily. Promise you
          won't say anything to anyone. No
          matter what happens. The last
          time you saw me was this morning,
          you understand?

                    EMILY
          Okay, geez, I won't say anything.
          But Vee . . . what do you mean
          "no matter what happens"?

Vanessa gazes out over the cliff's edge,
considering, then sucks in a deep breath,
seeming to have made another decision.

                    VANESSA
          I can't go into it right now, I
          just need you to do this for me.
          Promise me? You're the only one I
          really trust, Em.

                    EMILY
          I already said I wouldn't tell.

Emily's clearly unsettled by Vanessa's intensity. Vanessa is never unsure of herself, but now she seems . . . almost scared.

                    EMILY (CONT'D)
          Vanessa, what's going on?

                    VANESSA
          Nothing.

                    EMILY
          C'mon, it's *me*. Just . . .
          tell me.

Vanessa swallows hard, tears springing to
her eyes.

                    VANESSA
          It'll all be okay soon. I know
          how to fix this. I have a plan.

She rubs her eyes roughly with the back of
her hand.

                    VANESSA (CONT'D)
          But Emily . . . if anything hap-
          pens to me . . .

                    EMILY
               (shocked)
          If anything . . . What are you
          talking about, Vanessa?

                    VANESSA
          Nothing. Sorry, I'm just being
          dramatic.

She shakes her head, takes another swig of
wine. Emily leans in, clearly concerned.

                    EMILY
          Do you need me to call someone?
          Your grandparents, or . . .

                    VANESSA
                (sharp)
          No.
                (takes a breath, collects her-
                self)
          No, I'm okay, really. I'd never
          do anything like *that*, I swear.
          Just . . . don't tell anyone you
          saw me. I need to work through
          some stuff on my own. You promise?

                    EMILY
          I promise . . . if *you* promise
          you'll tell me what the hell is
          going on once we're back at
          school.

Vanessa smiles grimly.

                    VANESSA
          Deal.

                    EMILY
          I'm gonna try to squeeze in a
          power nap before dinner, last
          night totally destroyed me. You
          coming?

> VANESSA
> In a little. But remember, you—

> EMILY
> Never saw you. Don't worry, Vee,
> I remember.

Emily squeezes her friend's shoulder and turns back to the house, quickly disappearing from view. Once she's gone, Vanessa turns back to her phone, clicking it on again. This time we can see the message, though not who it's intended for: <u>I can't keep your secret anymore. I have to tell the truth.</u>

PAN OUT as Vanessa clicks send, then responds to the messages that quickly come in as she makes her way toward the cliff's edge. Glancing one last time at the house, she walks onto the staircase and descends . . .

FADE OUT

INT. PRECIPICE WINERY BEDROOM—THE FOLLOWING MORNING

Emily winces as the light hits her eyes, reaching up to rub at her temples. She blinks owlishly, worry seeping in as she tries to piece together the night before.

CUT TO

INT. PRECIPICE WINERY DINING ROOM—LAST NIGHT

The light is hazy over the table, and there's a distorted quality to the image Emily recalls: herself at the head, laughing as she raises a glass of wine to her lips, drinking deeply. We see the suggestion of other women around the table but their faces are obscured, it's only Emily in the frame, eyes too bright, laughing too loudly.

                                    CUT TO

INT. PRECIPICE WINERY HALLWAY—LAST NIGHT

Emily stumbles down the hall, leaning heavily on the wall for support. Her phone buzzes in her pocket and she pulls it out, swaying slightly as she looks at the message. She looks around, checking that she's alone, before slipping through a door to her left. It seems to lead to the front of the house.

                                    CUT TO

EXT. PRECIPICE WINERY LAWN—LAST NIGHT

Emily sways on the same patch of grass where she encountered Vanessa some hours before. She squints at her phone again, then looks around the dark landscape. She has the glassy-eyed look of the extremely drunk. She looks over her shoulder, then—

    CUT TO BLACK (hold for several seconds)

                                    CUT TO

INT. PRECIPICE WINERY BEDROOM—THIS MORNING

Emily swallows hard as she tries to piece together her fragments of memory. She can't seem to form a picture out of them. She fumbles for her phone on the nightstand and clicks into her text messages. The most recent chain is with Vanessa. Emily frowns as she reads it.

VANESSA: Meet me on the beach

VANESSA: It's urgent

EMILY: Whats going in????

VANESSA: We need to talk abt what happened with Alden

VANESSA: I'm not okay with what we did to him I can't keep your secret anymore

EMILY: My secret??

VANESSA: don't play dumb emily we both know what you did

VANESSA: he is threatening to go public and if he does I'm not going to protect you

EMILY: Okat on myway

VANESSA: Are you close?

EMILY: Where are you?

VANESSA: In the cave on the beach

VANESSA: You have to hurry the tide is coming in

VANESSA: NM I see you outside

Emily blinks at the phone, anxiety cutting deep creases into her forehead. She looks around the room for clues, but her last-night clothes slung over the back of a chair, her bag spewing out shoes and crumpled outfits in the corner, don't reveal anything. She scrolls through the late-night texts again, and it's clear she has no memory of them . . . or of any visit to the beach. Licking her lips, she clicks the phone off and climbs out of bed, unsure what to do.

                                        CUT TO

INT. PRECIPICE WINERY KITCHEN—DAY

Emily stands at the coffee maker, squinting at the buttons on the front, nibbling at her lower lip and glancing at her phone on the counter every few seconds, like it's a bomb about to go off. She presses a button just as rapid footsteps approach. It's LYDIA KEHOE, her dark hair mussed by sleep, oversized T-shirt and pajama pants only accentuating her Dickensian urchin slightness and pallor. Her large eyes are wide with disbelief.

                    LYDIA
          I can't believe you're up. You
          seemed like you were getting
          after it last night.

                    EMILY
          Oh, well . . . spring break,
          right?

LYDIA
I guess. Personally I was still
too destroyed from the night before.

Emily shrugs, attempting a weak smile.

LYDIA (CONT'D)
What were you doing on the beach,
by the way?

EMILY
(tense)
What?

LYDIA
I saw you heading to the stairs
down to the beach last night. I
almost followed you, I mean . . .
you were pretty out of it. But
you'd made it all the way across
the lawn by the time I spotted
you, and I was already in bed.
And obviously you made it back in
one piece.

EMILY
Oh. Right. I, uhh . . . just
wanted to dip my toes in the
water.

LYDIA
Seriously? The water's freezing.

EMILY
What can I say? Drunk logic.

Emily grimaces and Lydia laughs. After a few moments the coffee maker beeps. Lydia gestures for Emily to go first. Emily pours herself a mug and moves to the table as Lydia pours two.

> LYDIA
> I'll be back in a minute. With Tylenol.

> EMILY
> You hero.

Emily sips at the coffee tentatively, the shaky clamminess starting to wear off slightly. She's gazing out the window at the ocean, frowning as she tries to dredge up any memory of going down to it the night before, when Lydia reappears, both mugs still in her hands. She sets them down on the breakfast bar, frowning.

> LYDIA
> Have you seen Vee?

Emily pauses for just a moment before she shakes her head.

> EMILY
> Not since yesterday at lunch. Didn't she say she had stuff to do?

> LYDIA
> Yeah . . . but I haven't seen her since then either. And she's not in her room.

                    EMILY
          Have you tried calling her?

                    LYDIA
          It goes straight to voicemail.
          And her bed hasn't been slept in.

                    EMILY
          So her phone died, then. Probably
          she went into town to find some
          guy to fool around with. You know
          Vee.

                    LYDIA
               (worried)
          I don't think so. The cars are
          both here. Besides, since when
          does Vee let her phone die?

     Emily takes a deep breath. Her hands grip
     the edge of the counter.

                    EMILY
          What are you saying, Lydia?

                    LYDIA
          I'm saying . . . I think some-
          thing might have happened to Van-
          essa. Something bad.

2

I TRIED TO GO BACK TO MY WORK—I COULD feel myself staring too intently, if the woman at the counter turned she'd probably be creeped out, besides I owed everyone a revision by tomorrow—but I couldn't help myself. The details were different—wrong hair color, cheekbones higher and broader, outfit far too polished and prim for the seductive, sharp-edged girl I remembered—but the resemblance was strong enough to knock the wind out of me.

There was a time when she was the most important person in my life—not that I would have admitted it to myself then, how much I wanted her approval, how much we all did, really. The pain when she disappeared had actually turned physical, a sharp rock at the pit of my stomach that weighed me down all day, little shards of guilt breaking off any time some well-meaning classmate or professor would ask after her. Vanessa had been the girl who drew every eye in the room, the friend that you felt absurdly lucky to have found, her glamour so palpable it rubbed off on the select few of us she'd chosen for her inner circle. Before we met I'd had friends, obviously, but I'd never experienced the sense of connection she could give you, the intense intimacy I felt when we were together, like we'd cracked some secret code no one else even knew existed.

For months after she disappeared, I vacillated between

complete conviction that I could never have done anything to hurt her—this person who made me feel more alive, brighter, more *authentic,* as though she'd pulled back a veil over the real me I hadn't even realized was there—and a fuzzy, pervasive fear of the part of me that had always been a little jealous of Vanessa. Not just of her effect on the world around her, but of the times she turned her light away from me and onto someone else, a more frequent occurrence than I liked to admit to myself back then. Could that jealous goblin version of me, buried deep most days, have bubbled up on a groundswell of wine the night that, try for the life of me, I'd never been able to piece together? I didn't *think* so. I'd never been a violent person, and when I got drunk I tended to get either too friendly or nonspecifically weepy. But I couldn't be *sure,* and that nagged at me, the voice growing dimmer as the years passed, but never totally fading away.

The woman turned back to the counter, the resemblance fading slightly as she paid for her drink, then strode out of the shop, eyes slipping over me with zero recognition, her long, confident strides both familiar and foreign. Had Vanessa walked like that? In my memory, she'd been more sinuous, the atmosphere in a room seeming to caress her as she moved through it.

But how would I know? It had been almost fifteen years since she'd gone missing. If Vanessa was out there somewhere—and even I, the Midwestern Pollyanna of our little college cohort, wasn't naïve enough to believe *that*—how could I possibly begin to guess the ways that she'd changed?

I forced my eyes back to my laptop again, but I couldn't focus, my thoughts drifting every few sentences to the ghost the woman had so sharply evoked. I hadn't paid attention in years to the high-water line of long-receded fear that still marked my insides, but it was always there, a reminder that it was possible that even if I couldn't remember the night she'd gone missing, I'd somehow played a part in it.

I'd been turning Vanessa over in my mind ever since that weekend, worn the edges down on that eerily prescient conversation we'd had the evening before she'd disappeared, until I could barely be sure the shape of the thing was the same as how it actually happened. I'd dredged the muck of Friday night more times than I could count, trying to recall meeting Vanessa—trying to remember even a single one of the texts she'd sent and I'd apparently responded to—but there was nothing. I was desperate to uncover the tiny detail, previously unnoticed, that would unlock the puzzle box of what had happened to her, what I might have done to save her.

What I might have done *to* her.

But those hours remained a blank, a thick velvet curtain drawn over one of the most important nights in my entire life. I'd never even managed to peek beneath a corner.

Lately, with the fifteenth anniversary approaching, I found myself thinking of her more often than I had in a long time. A song would come on the radio, one I'd heard thousands of times before, but for some reason *this* time it would evoke a visceral memory of the five of us dancing around Brittany's apartment, drunk on cheap wine and our own youth, Vanessa always somehow at the center of things, even when she was standing to one side, sipping her drink with a knowing smirk as she watched the rest of us scream out the lyrics. Or I'd be waiting for a table at a favorite restaurant and someone's slightly woodsy perfume would waft over me and suddenly I was back in the bathroom of Vanessa's freshman dorm, watching her tap balsam oil on all her pressure points, eyelids lowering as she gazed at me through the mirror, *We can play around with my essential oils set until we find something that works on you, Emily.*

Or I'd spot a woman in the coffee shop—*my* coffee shop—who looked so much like Vanessa it literally took my breath away.

Maybe it was because Vanessa's story—our story too, the ones who were left behind—was the one I'd always wanted to tell. It was a fundamental turning point in my life, the one inarguably dramatic thing that had happened, if not to me, then in my vicinity. How could I not keep returning to it, trying to sort the threads into a tapestry that made some sort of sense? I'd tried to put the story on paper more than once, even made it to the end of the first act a few times, but inevitably I'd run up against the same wall: I had no idea what had actually *happened*. No one did, not really.

The disappearance had caused a stir at the time—girls as beautiful and "promising" as Vanessa don't go missing all that often, especially in the more remote regions of coastal Oregon. The local police had quickly been overwhelmed and called in the big guns to help with the search, and all of us had been grilled about the spring break trip, Vanessa's character, and our movements over the previous few days, a blur of questions that covered so much ground that I came away from them half-convinced they legitimately suspected me. Eventually the investigators landed on "tragic accident." There was no physical evidence to speak of, no body, and no indication that anyone else had had access to the remote winery. There were, however, the gigantic cliffs just yards from the house, the insatiable ocean nipping at their feet, and Vanessa's known predilection for risk taking, especially when drunk. The assumption was that she'd gone over the edge somehow, been pulled out to sea before any of us even realized she was missing. Even Topper and Mitzi's wildly expensive private investigators couldn't come up with a likelier scenario. And just like that, the world moved on, the silence in the wake of all that buzz deafening, and absolute.

The thing that had always bothered me most was that no one could explain *why* Vanessa would have been traipsing along the cliffs at night, what might have prompted her to leave the safety of her bed, of her friends, and risk her life in the pitch dark. As careless as she was when it came to self-preservation—sometimes her attitude of invincibility, pronounced even among her fellow college students, almost felt like a provocation—I had never been able to answer that question at the center of it all. And of course I held one vital clue—the texts asking me to join her, implying that maybe I had?—but that just confirmed the presumed *what* of her vanishing without any meaningful trace, leaving the more fundamental *why* flickering overhead like a faulty neon sign. It was one of the dozens of questions I still had about that weekend— had I really gone down to her, or had she seen someone else? (Please, *please* let it have been someone else . . .) I'd checked all my shoes inside and out that morning and couldn't find any traces of sand or damp, had peered at every inch of my body for unexplained scrapes or bruises, some sign that I'd stumbled down to the beach, and there was nothing . . . but what did that absence really prove?

And why had she asked to meet on the beach in the first place? There were plenty of private spots around the winery. Hell, why had she wanted a conversation with me, full stop? Vanessa knew, and I knew, that the secret I'd been keeping was as much hers as mine, maybe more so. Why would she risk it coming out?

Until I had answers for all those questions—real answers,

not just the cobbled-together clichés and jump scares any hack could employ to tie off a mystery plot—I didn't feel I could finish the story. Until then, it wouldn't do her justice. Or help me sleep at night.

It didn't help that lately *Back of House* seemed to have shifted from simply stultifying into something I actively dreaded. I'd worked my way up the credits ladder from staff writer to script supervisor to producer, my paychecks and residuals steadily growing larger each time the show was renewed. We'd even hit syndication after the last season, which was probably why my agent, Lucy, was *very* keen on my reviewing the new contract the studio had sent over, promising another extremely gilded year of indentured servitude. Yes, I could sign the contract. Hell, I could probably negotiate even better terms—as one of the few writers who'd been there since the beginning, I was the living repository of "No, we've already done that episode." I could probably keep writing on the show for another few years, keep inflating the ostrich-sized nest egg the show had helped me build, but just the idea of it almost made me want to cry. I didn't need another fancy vacation, or a bigger house, or a better car—I didn't even care about cars (I know, a sin against LA itself). The idea of diving back into that morass of tired plotlines and cardboard cutout characters now, when the story I'd been turning over in my mind for so long had just appeared in front of me as if by magic, made my skin crawl.

With a determined sniff, I stuffed the rest of the brownie into my mouth, slid my computer into my large, expensive (but not Birkin expensive) tote, and headed out, blinking in the midafternoon sunshine. One thing was very clear: These script notes were *not* happening. Not in the course of this afternoon, at least.

By the evening I'd managed to edit half of a single scene . . . and turn over half a dozen possible openings to a feature that told the story of Vanessa's disappearance. The story had been percolating in me for so long—fifteen years now—but something about seeing the doppelganger had flipped some vital switch inside me, turned the dial up from simmer to overwhelming, boiling *need*. I'd been executing Chip's vision of spectacular mediocrity for years now, wasn't it past time I create a vision of my own? Hell, it might be just as mediocre in the end, but at least it would be *my* mediocre.

But I'd been here before. I had an entire graveyard of previous attempts—the draft dates carved into the file names their epitaphs—to prove it. If I wanted to do this right, find the answers that would satisfy not only the demands of a screenplay, but me—the person who had never really gotten over the loss of the woman I'd once thought of as my best friend—I knew what I had to do. Frankly, I'd been psyching myself up to it all afternoon. I pulled out my phone, scrolling through the contacts until I found the number I needed.

"Hey, Brittany?"

"Ohmygod, *Emily Fischer*? Talk about a blast from the past. How *are* you, babe?" A metallic clatter in the background. "*Mason*," she hissed, "Mommy is *on the phone*. Can you deal with him, Rosaline?" Some shuffling and piercing whines, then eventually a door slam and silence. "Sorry, it's like kids have some sort of radar that makes them turn into little monsters *only* when you're busy with something else. Thank god for au pairs, right?"

"Oh. Totally . . ." Brittany's socials made her two-kids-under-five, wealthy-husband, sprawling-Greenwich-house, stay-at-home life look like something out of a catalog, but I had a feeling most of it was more like the tiny glimpse I'd just caught.

"So? Why are you calling?"

"Can't I just call an old friend?" I tucked my auburn hair tightly behind my ear, grimacing. I'd forgotten how blunt Brittany could be.

"You *can*. But we haven't talked on the phone in, like . . . five years? So, you know. Why?"

"I thought I saw Vanessa." I exhaled sharply, anxiety pooling in the pit of my stomach as I waited to hear what she'd say.

"No, you didn't," Brittany said, voice sharp. The response was so automatic it startled me a little. Sure, we all *assumed* Vanessa was dead, but still . . .

"I did. Trust me, if you'd seen this woman . . ."

"Okay, I have to ask this, sweetie . . . have you been drinking?" Brittany's sharpness disappeared, replaced by gentle, padded pity.

"Brittany, it's barely five o'clock here."

"Everyone has bad days sometimes. You can tell me, you know I don't judge on that stuff *at* all."

"I'm not drinking, Brittany."

"Okaaay." She dragged out the word carefully. "I know you know this Emily, but . . . Vanessa's *gone*."

"I know that. Obviously I know that. But you should have seen this woman, Brittany, they could have been sisters." They could have been *one person,* I almost added.

"I'm sure that was weird," Brittany said slowly, "but I still don't get why you're calling me about it." It had been years since we'd been in the same room, but I could almost see her eyes narrowing under the blunt bangs she'd worn since before college, her narrow chin tucking back in a way that blurred her already soft jawline.

Here goes.

"I'm calling because . . . I want us to go back there. All of us."

"Are you serious? Why?" Her voice had taken on that glassy edge I remembered so well. Of all of us, Brittany had always been most used to getting her own way. And least good about dealing with the times that she didn't. I had a feeling the actual answer—*So I can finally write the screenplay that has been trying to get out of me for almost fifteen years now, and also no big deal but it's possible I had something to do with what happened to her?*—wasn't the tack to take.

"Because I need answers." Almost the truth. "I think we all need them."

"What *answers,* Emily?" Brittany sniffed. "Don't you think if there was any sign of what happened to Vanessa, all those cops would have found it? Or the private detectives my grandparents hired? They spent a *fortune* trying to track Vanessa down. There was nothing then, and there sure as shit isn't going to be anything now."

I'd almost forgotten that Vanessa and Brittany shared a set of grandparents. They'd both always seemed so keen to downplay that information at the time. I pinched my nose, feeling this conversation slipping away from me.

"That was the wrong word, okay? But . . . don't you feel it too, Brittany? I know how much you feel things." My voice was a little pleading, and I realized I'd subconsciously fallen into the same peacemaker tones—and predilection for white-lie flattery—that I'd used back in college, when the more . . . *volatile* members of our circle's hackles started inching up. The sense of stepping back into some previous version of myself was briefly vertiginous, and I had to glance out my window, registering the traffic skimming down Franklin Street, the Gelson's, the Scientology Celebrity Center I knew was hulking behind the wall of massive trees that patrolled its perimeter, to ground myself in the moment again.

"It's like there's this . . . *hole* there. This gap in our lives that never got filled in. I'm not saying we're going to solve this," Christ on a cracker did I want to be wrong about that, "but I do think we could all get some closure."

There was silence on the line. If I had any chance of convincing her, now was the moment. So I went straight for the jugular—something I might have felt bad about if I hadn't been dealing with Brittany Chisholm. The only person I'd ever known who was better at immediately locating someone's pressure points was Vanessa herself, but Brittany had always been more willing to *use* that knowledge. Maybe it was a family trait.

"Brittany . . . the fifteen-year anniversary is coming up in a few months. I think Vanessa deserves a proper goodbye."

"There was the vigil . . ."

"But that was when everyone thought she still might turn up." It had been a few weeks after Vanessa disappeared, back on campus, and even at the time it felt like we were acting out a montage scene, a show of aesthetically appropriate worry, letting ourselves believe it was just a stop on our way to a happy ending. At least the other students all seemed to feel that way—I'd been working overtime to convince myself that even if I had seen Vanessa that night, I couldn't have done anything to her.

"We never really gave her a proper sendoff, and it just feels *wrong*. I mean . . . what would people think if they knew that?" That was the one-two punch. Brittany might not give two fucks about closure, or even about Vanessa, but if I knew anything about her, she cared *deeply* about being seen as the sort of person who did.

The silence drew out for several long seconds. I could feel my stomach tensing in anticipation.

"I know," Brittany finally murmured, her voice lower and more solemn than before. "Trust me, Em, I know that better than anyone."

My breath hitched in my throat.

"I've actually been meaning to visit the property," Brittany said with a heavy exhale. In the background, the squeaky sighs of a body settling into leather furniture. I could picture her in some dark-walled office, plaid accent pillows, chunky knit afghans, and a gigantic faux sheepskin rug giving it a modern horsey-set flair. Had I seen her post a room like that on her socials, or did Brittany's entire persona just exude that much country club? "They finally sorted out Mitzi's will, she left the winery to me like she always planned. But there's a lot to sift through. Markus and I need to decide whether we're going to try to keep it as passive income or just sell the whole thing, but we've just been too busy to get out there." A pause. I could hear the little flicking sound of Brittany picking the polish off her fingernails with her thumb, her nervous tic since forever. "It *would* be a good time of year to visit, it's the off-season, the tasting room wouldn't even be open unless someone booked it privately. I'd just have to let them know we were coming and we'd have the place to ourselves."

"It should be *we*, don't you think?" *Tread lightly, Emily.* "I have to believe Paige and Lydia would appreciate a chance to really deal with this too." And one of them might know something I didn't, remember a detail that hadn't seemed important at the time . . .

"Paige could probably write the whole trip off, actually," Brittany mused. I knew vaguely that our former friend worked in wine and liquor sales, but we hadn't been in proper touch for years. Without Vanessa exerting her gravitational pull, it had become clear that the rest of us didn't have all that much in common. Or maybe it was just too painful to go on without her. Whatever the reason, we'd all more or less gone our separate ways the last year of college—Brittany had continued to hold dominion over the boat shoe set she'd always been inclined toward, Paige had spent more time with the rest of the track team, Lydia wound up hitting a delayed rebellious phase and falling in with the club kid scene on campus, and I'd finally gathered up the courage to try out for a staff writer's spot on the campus soap opera. I kept in sporadic touch with Brittany, and Lydia and I had a brief stint of rekindled . . . *friendship* was too strong, but occasional-hanging-out, for the few years she lived in LA in our late twenties, but Paige had quickly wound up on the pile of social-media-only friends, and eventually the algorithms agreed we just weren't that invested in each other. "I have no *idea* how to reach Lydia, though," Brittany added with barely disguised distaste. "We're not exactly close."

"I can get in touch with Lydia." I fought to keep the eagerness out of my voice. "I don't think she's on social media anymore, but she and I talk every once in a while."

"I don't know . . ." Brittany's tone turned nose-wrinkling. "I'm still not sure how this is going to help anything."

"It's at least worth a try, though, right? Vanessa deserves better. And we all need this. *Closure*." I put extra weight on the word. Brittany seemed the type to be neck-deep in buzzword psychology these days. "Absolute worst case, we all get a little girls' weekend at a stunning winery."

"Lydia and girls' trip are not ideas that mesh."

"Trust me, she's grown into herself since college. And she's fun when she gets a few glasses of wine in her. When she was living here she took me to a puppet burlesque show."

"Oh my god, she's always been so *weird*."

"But good weird." I flung around for something else—Brittany wasn't a big believer in the existence of good weird. "Besides, she might hex you if she found out we all went back and didn't invite her."

"Good point." Brittany sniffed out a laugh. "I mean . . . a weekend away would be nice. I honestly can't remember the last time I've been able to sleep in after a big night. My kids are absolutely the center of my *world*, but they have no respect for a hangover."

"So . . . does that mean you're on board?"

"Ughhh, *fine*. Yes. But I do not have time for negative energy. If Lydia's a giant rain cloud the whole weekend I *will* throw her over the cliffs."

"I'd expect no less."

"I should go. Mason and Missy's bedtime is soon, it takes *forever* if I don't help Rosaline handle it. I'll talk to Markus when he gets home from work and we can sort out details."

"Sounds good. And thank you, Brittany. This means more to me than you know."

She was quiet for a moment.

"It's fine. I think you're right. It's time I went back there."

And with that, she hung up.

Anticipation started buzzing through me and I paced around my condo, wriggling my fingers as though that could expel the static. Even just the prospect of finding the answers I'd been waiting for the last fifteen years seemed to loosen something inside me.

Admitting defeat on the *Back of House* revisions—extensions had been granted before—I poured myself a glass of wine, took it into my office, and opened a new file in Final Draft.

The words started flowing, more effortlessly than they ever had in all the other versions of the story I'd tried to tell: the schlocky horror version, the excruciatingly self-serious coming-of-age version, the Important Movie tragedy version, all of them and half a dozen other false starts gathering dust in the Bottom Drawer file on my desktop.

This time I was going to find out how the story ended.

EXT. OREGON COAST—DAY (PRESENT DAY)

A more zoomed-out view of the large glass-fronted stone and timber home perched on the edge of the cliffs, the sheer rocks giving way to a strip of beach ribboning around the base. The rickety set of stairs zigzagging down the cliff face ends in a weathered wooden dock, the curve of the coastline sheltering it slightly from the rougher waves farther out to sea. It's clear from the water marks on the pilings that the tide is out.

PAN UP AND ZOOM IN to the northern side of the house, where a tall midthirties woman in a sleek button-down and fitted black pants, her office wear at odds with the wildness around her, picks her way along an overgrown flagstone footpath toward the viewer. This is PAIGE CRESSEY. The wind ruffles her light brown pixie cut, her eyes unreadable as she gazes out along the cliffs.

> PAIGE (V.O.)
> I never thought I'd come back to this place. It was beautiful, obviously, but so are tigers. And volcanoes. Something can be stunning and still be really fucking *dangerous*.

Paige makes her way to the edge of the cliff, craning her neck to peer down to the beach below. Eventually she pulls back, folding her arms across her chest and shivering.

> PAIGE (V.O.) (CONT'D)
> It was Maggie that finally con-
> vinced me to say yes. She's al-
> ways been good at that. We both
> pretend I'm the bad influence in
> our relationship, but really, I
> just get up to more trouble. Mag-
> gie's the one with all the influ-
> ence, period.

The camera pulls out, and we glimpse a figure
approaching from behind, body silhouetted
by the sun. Paige clearly doesn't sense the
dark figure's presence.

> PAIGE (V.O.) (CONT'D)
> I'd protested. Obviously. Tried
> to make her believe I was over
> what happened that weekend. But
> Maggie knows me too well to buy
> my bullshit. And she's been there
> for too many of the one-drink-
> too-many nights where I can't
> help but talk about Vanessa.

The figure is nearer now, a hunched woman
dressed all in black, a shock of pitch-
black hair sweeping across her forehead,
obscuring her features.

> PAIGE (V.O.) (CONT'D)
> She'd insisted I needed to work
> through this. Let myself *feel* my
> feelings. And eventually, I had
> to give in. Otherwise I'd have
> had to tell her the real reason I
> didn't want to be here.

> LYDIA
Paige?

Paige startles, stumbling forward a little,
and Lydia grabs her arm from behind, a re-
flexive gesture of protection. Lydia's large,
slightly bulbous brown eyes stand out
against her pale complexion, made paler by
her years working as a game developer. Not
that Lydia's the type to tan, regardless.

> PAIGE
Holy *shit,* Lydia. I nearly went
over the edge just now.

> LYDIA
Sorry. I wasn't sure it was you
until I got closer.
>> (beat)
> I like the hair, by the way.

She gestures to the top of her head. The
fact that Paige's pixie is new to her shows
just how long it's been since the two women
have been face to face. Paige, the former
athlete, shuffles from foot to foot, the
sense of awkwardness apparent in her need
for movement. Lydia stays very still.

> PAIGE
Thanks. Uh . . . you too. Did you
just get here?

Lydia nods, moving to one side to get a better view of the water.

                    LYDIA
          Traffic wasn't as bad as I ex-
          pected. What were you looking at?

                    PAIGE
                (sharp)
          What?

                    LYDIA
                (surprised)
          Down below? Was there something
          on the beach?

                    PAIGE
          Oh . . . no. Just an impulse, I
          guess.

Lydia raises an eyebrow but doesn't pursue
the topic any further.

                    PAIGE (CONT'D)
          I'm surprised you came, actually.

                    LYDIA
          Really? What reason could I pos-
          sibly have not to want to see all
          of you again?

                    PAIGE
          Seriously?

Paige snorts out a little laugh but quiets
when she catches Lydia's calm, expectant
look. She swallows hard, blinking, clearly
trying to find a socially acceptable way to
put into words what she'd assumed was obvious: because Lydia never really got along

with Paige and Brittany. Then the sound of
a door slamming draws both women's attention back toward the house.

> BRITTANY (O.S.)
> I swear to god, whoever's in
> charge of maintenance for this
> place is getting fired tomorrow. I
> read through the budget, we pay
> to repave that road *every year*.

> EMILY (O.S.)
> It has been weirdly cold up here
> the last couple months. Maybe
> they want to wait until winter's
> over before doing it?

> BRITTANY (O.S.)
> That's no excuse.

The two women emerge along the side of the
house, onto the same footpath Paige walked
down. BRITTANY (CHISHOLM) DEWITT's long
light brown hair shines in the late afternoon sun, and her oversized windowpane
blazer and leather leggings only accentuate
her trim figure. Next to her, Emily, in a
slouchy sweater, jeans, and slip-on shoes
clearly chosen for comfort during travel,
looks rather rumpled. She still has the
soft, curvy figure of her youth.

> BRITTANY
> Ohmygod you *made* it! I'd come to
> you, but the lawn will absolutely
> destroy these shoes.

She gestures at her suede ankle boots, which
do sport ludicrously high, narrow heels.
Lydia turns to Paige, holding her gaze a moment longer, then starts back to the gigantic house, the windows reflecting her slow
progress away from the cliff. Paige lingers
at its edge, watching the women.

>   BRITTANY
> They should have already stocked
> the house. I *totally* overordered,
> so you bitches had better be
> ready to destroy some cheese
> plates. I know Emily's down.

Brittany flashes a pert smile as her eyes
quickly run over Emily's curves. Emily
forces a smile in return.

>   EMILY
> Always am.

>   BRITTANY
> Hello? Paige? Are you coming or
> what?

Paige sucks in a deep breath, turns to
glance down from the cliff top one last time,
then makes her way back across the lawn, her
long, athletic strides quickly closing the
distance between herself and the other
women.

>   PAIGE
> Jeez, Bee, impatient much? I saw
> you like . . . last week.

                    BRITTANY
          That was in New York. This is
          here. Anyway, I need you to get
          my luggage, it's super awkward.

As they disappear inside, the camera pulls
down the stairs along the cliffside to the
dock, late-afternoon shadows starting to
streak the graying wood.

                    PAIGE (V.O.)
          We could all pretend we were here
          to celebrate our long-lost
          friend. That we were searching
          for . . . what had Brittany
          called it? *Closure*. But I knew
          the truth. The one I couldn't
          tell Maggie. We were all really
          here because of our secrets. And
          I, for one, needed to make sure
          mine were truly safe . . .

*NOTE: Is Paige the best entry point? Plausible for her to
have this sort of relationship with her wife? Revisit setup
here . . . —EF*

3

"FIRST THINGS FIRST: WE NEED *ALL* THE WINE. I told the staff to pull a few special bottles for us." Brittany pushed open the driver's side door of the gigantic SUV and hopped down onto the gravel driveway. Our flights had landed at the Portland airport around the same time, and she'd suggested we split the rental car, *It's easier that way, plus way more fun to road trip together, right?*

She had *not* mentioned that she would insist on renting a ridiculous Range Rover, but then, I probably should have expected it. Brittany had many millions more ways to fund her champagne tastes these days.

I pushed open my own door and shivered, pulling my cardigan tighter around me. Our impromptu parking spot was just far enough down the drive to catch the breeze coming off the ocean; I hadn't really considered how much colder it would be on the coast when I'd packed for the trip. A minor burst of shame spread across the rather large corner of my soul that would always identify as Minnesotan, despite more than ten years in LA at this point.

Luckily, the house itself—a behemoth in timber, stone, and glass, its multiple peaked, wood-shingled roofs giving off modern-day ski lodge vibes—served as an excellent wind-break. Fat manicured fir trees and deep green waxy-leaved hedges studded with bright berries had been planted around the edges of the patio and driveway, and even at this time of year they lent the gigantic building a specifically Pacific Northwestern hominess. Brittany tapped a code into the panel beside the double-height hardwood doors and swept them open, flourishing her hand toward the dim interior.

"Welcome back to Cliff's Edge Winery."

I'd hoped walking through the doors would be a revelatory moment—visions of Vanessa wafting out from the corners as soon as I set foot across the threshold, the memory gold I'd been hoping to spin by returning here helpfully piling itself at my feet. But while I'm sure the space hadn't changed all that much since we'd been there last—it all felt vaguely familiar—after nearly fifteen years, I felt like I was seeing it for the first time.

The room we'd stepped into was gigantic, its two-story cathedral ceiling crisscrossed with weighty square beams in a dark stain. Directly across from the entrance, floor-to-ceiling windows offered expansive views of the cliffs the lodge was perched on, the sheer drop down to the ocean visible at either edge of the panorama, where the shoreline curved inward, forming the small inlet that sheltered the waters just beneath the property. A large semicircular wooden bar dominated the left side of the room, tasteful built-ins behind it displaying precisely arranged phalanxes of wine bottles. A massive rough stone fireplace served as a focal point on the right-hand wall, and an eclectic mix of seating clusters subdivided the rest of the space—a handful of high-top tables surrounded by rough wooden stools had been sprinkled around the room; a low coffee table, the tortured whorls of its driftwood base visible through the glass top, fixed the gravity of a cluster of recliners near the windows; a pair of oversized leather chairs with an end table between them filled in a gap near the fireplace, their cousins tucking into all the other empty corners. Simple shelves piled with artfully worn books, wooden versions of a dozen kinds of board games, and wine paraphernalia added *just* that amount of quirk, and oversized, faux-aged maps of the Oregon coast and various growing regions in the state dotted the walls. Top it all off with the massive, conspicuously tasteful Art Deco light fixtures suspended from vanishingly slender supports, their copper accents gleaming in the late-afternoon sun coming in through the windows, and the "Ralph Lauren does a winery" picture was complete.

I was ninety-nine percent sure Brittany had nothing to do with decorating the place, but clearly the Chisholms had handed down their aesthetic alongside their various luxury properties. I made a mental note to find a time to sneak in here alone and snap some photos. You couldn't have asked for better set design.

A dim bell started chiming, the sound getting louder and louder.

"Okay, I *hear* you." Brittany bent to tug open her purse, pulling out her phone and tapping at it until the sound stopped.

"Everything okay?"

"Oh, it's nothing. We have the security system set up to send a notification if anyone enters the house or the winery during the off-season. It sits empty for days sometimes, and it's a solid twenty minutes from town."

"Have people broken in before?" Suddenly the sweeping views of the sea felt less charmingly remote and more just . . . *remote*.

"Not that I'm aware of. But you'd be shocked how many employees think no one will notice if they pop into the cellar and swipe a case or two when no one's around." Brittany rolled her eyes at the perfidies of the working class. "They all have alarm codes to the parts of the winery we open to the public, obviously. This ensures Markus and I have a real sense of what's going on here, especially during the slow season."

"Got it." There was something vaguely Orwellian about the notion, but then Brittany would hardly be the first upper-class individual to erect a ring of smart home devices as a sort of digital border wall around her demesne. She took a few steps into the room, gaze drifting upward.

"God, it's been so long." Brittany inhaled deeply, taking in the space, before turning back to me, eyes sparkly. "The tasting room still looks just like I remember." She hugged herself with both arms, gazing around the room a few moments longer, then shook her head, crossing behind the bar to pull out a bottle. "Down to start with pinot gris?"

"I'm just down for a drink," I said, making my way to one of the stools dotting the other side. Brittany smirked and uncorked the wine. While she poured, I glanced at the stack of paper placemats that detailed the winery's history in sepia-toned prose. Apparently during Prohibition, decades before anyone had thought to age wine in them, the natural caves and tunnels that pocked the sandstone cliffs had been a favorite stash for rumrunners. The detail made the several sentences devoted to the Chisholms' "stewardship" of the winery since 1992 that much duller by comparison.

Brittany was just passing me my glass when the front door opened again. It took me a second to recognize the tall, professional-looking woman with the pixie cut.

"There she is!" Brittany squealed, darting out from behind the bar to wrap Paige in a hug. Paige rolled her eyes but indulged it. I turned back to my glass, trying to hide my surprise. I knew they were in touch but I hadn't realized they were still close. Though I suppose it made sense; back in college, Paige had been Brittany's sidekick. Brittany would make the pronouncements—who was cool, which parties were worth our time, which guys were hot enough to even *consider*—and Paige would drive them home with a snide joke, eager to please both Brittany and anyone else in earshot at the time. She'd tried something similar with Vanessa early on, but Vee had called her *right* out. I remembered Vanessa telling me later how she *liked* Paige but in her opinion Paige needed to grow a spine. *You and I are way more alike, Emily. We're our own people, you know?* I could still remember the glowy feeling the private affirmation of our bond, and my place of preference on Vanessa's very exclusive list of friends, had given me.

The phone alarm started up in Brittany's bag again.

"Yes, yes, I *know*," Brittany said with an eye roll, pulling her phone out to stop the alert. "Sorry, I'd change the security settings but I'm worried I'd forget to put them back before we left. But enough boring stuff, you are going to *love* this pinot gris, Paige." Brittany strode back to the counter and pulled out another glass. "And you have to try the dry riesling, it's ridiculous." Once she had a glass, Paige twirled it vigorously, thrust her nose deep inside, then pulled it out and repeated the process before finally taking a sip, which she pulled back and forth through her teeth for several seconds before swallowing. A vision of her from years ago—then trademark long ponytail hanging down her back, dressed in her college uniform of an Under Armour T-shirt and the Queen Mary branded sweats all the athletes wore, slapping the side of a silvery boxed wine bladder, then popping the nozzle and chugging as much as she could before spluttering purple liquid all over the floor—floated into my head. Clearly I wasn't the only one who'd changed since college.

"So, Emily . . . you're in LA, right?" Paige sipped the wine, taking me in.

"Get this, Paige, she writes for *Back of House*." Brittany raised her eyebrows, miming surprise. Annoyance gripped me. Brittany had always known that—she sent me flowers when I first got the job—but she'd never told Paige, when they were obviously still so close? *Deep breaths, Emily. Think calming thoughts.* I couldn't let weird chips on my shoulder from forever ago get in the way of learning what I needed to now. *That* was what this weekend was about. Not whether someone I didn't even keep in touch with followed my career.

"Seriously? I *love* that show." Paige looked genuinely impressed, and I forced a smile onto my face. Somehow, that fact did not surprise me—Paige had always been a person who both played to a crowd and took her cues from it, which made her pretty much the dead center of our target demo— but it was gratifying, in a small way at least.

"Since the very beginning, actually. Though I'm thinking it might be time for a change. I have a lot of stories to tell."

"If you say so. Not sure what you could do that's cooler than *that*." Paige flashed a disbelieving face at Brittany, who shrugged, their private communication fully intact. I was starting to realize how odd-man-out I was—I probably never would have met Paige if it hadn't been for Vanessa, and clearly the loose atomic bonds that had once existed between us simply by virtue of our orbiting the same nuclear center that was Vanessa hadn't gotten any *stronger* over the years—when the door opened again. I slumped a bit in relief.

"Lyds, you made it." I raised my glass to her. "I was starting to worry."

Actually, I'd been worried ever since I got off the phone with Lydia a few weeks ago. The acerbic dismissal of Brittany when I'd proposed the idea of this weekend—she'd not only said that Brit had "always been destined for a Stepford life," she referred to Markus as "Wall Street Ken, but without the looks" (brutal, but I'd laughed)—had poured out of Lydia more quickly, and with a lot more sharpness than I'd expected, reminding me just how little the two women cared for one another. I suppose over the years I'd reformulated their relationship as the relatively benign classic, oil and water. Really, they'd been a tiger and a bear in a cage match over the same haunch. Lydia was just so much subtler than Brittany—a fan of the carefully planned deep cut, precisely targeted on the most vital organ, whereas Brittany went straight for the jugular, all her viciousness in plain sight—that you occasionally forgot the battle was being waged from both sides. Still, Lydia had admitted to being interested in seeing where everyone had wound up, had agreed that we all needed closure. I just hadn't fully trusted that she'd actually show until she walked through the door.

"I made it," Lydia confirmed, flashing one of her trademark sly, private smiles at me, pausing for a moment to take in the space before she made her way over to the bar.

"Wow, long time, Lyds," Paige said, offering a superficial smile. "What have you been up to?"

Lydia raised an eyebrow.

"Little of this, little of that. I'll give you the Cliff's Notes version after a few glasses of wine. You always had a ton of those lying around the apartment, right?"

"Then we're all here," Brit said with a tight smile that didn't reach her eyes. "Good for you for making the trip, Lydia. I wasn't sure you'd be interested. Since it's been so long since we've heard from you, I mean." Lydia looked amused as she settled onto her stool, feet dangling several inches above the floor, but she didn't take the bait. Lydia and I hadn't been exactly close back in the day; I'd always loved her wry, dark-leaning sense of humor, but she never seemed to really let anyone in. Except maybe Vanessa. But then, Vanessa had always been able to crack just about anyone. Still, it felt like Lydia and I were on the same team, if only because neither of us had been drafted by the Brittany-Paige franchise.

"I don't think I thought to ask the last time we came," Lydia said, toying with the stem of the glass Brittany had set in front of her. "Where are the actual *vineyards*? I didn't see any driving in."

"You can't ripen wine on the Oregon coast. *Way* too fucking cold." Paige sniffed, raising her eyebrows exaggeratedly at Brittany as she reached over the bar for a silver spit bucket. Paige's clothes and haircut might have changed, but clearly her almost pathological bluntness had not.

"I didn't realize that," Lydia said tightly, posture stiffening. "Believe it or not, most of us don't have encyclopedic knowledge of viniculture."

"I mean . . . clearly," Paige said with another snorting laugh. Brittany's lips curled in a small smile as she caught Paige's eyes.

"What can I say. Not all of us are lucky enough to find a way to turn blackout drinking every weekend into an entire career path," Lydia said lightly, shrugging. "I'm sure you're past that phase, though," she added, eyes dropping to Paige's near-empty glass. "After all, even in the wine industry, being *too* big a lush has to be a liability . . . no?"

"I wouldn't know," Paige snapped, making a point of spitting her sip into the bucket.

Had Lydia and Paige gotten along back in college? I couldn't remember anymore. I knew Brittany and Lydia had never jelled, and wherever Brittany led, Paige tended to follow.

"Paige is right," Brittany said as she poured. "About the winery, that is. We purchase our fruit. This is where the wines are blended and aged, but you could never grow grapes *here*."

"At least not until climate change cranks up another notch, right?" I took a big swig of the wine, feigning obliviousness to the tension. "This is really tasty, Brittany. I'd love to try the reds, though. I don't know about you ladies, but I always drink white wine way too fast."

"Of course. Actually, I made them pull a special bottle of pinot noir. It's got fifteen years of age on it; you're going to *love* it."

The focus on dumping, pouring, and smelling seemed to allow some of the tension to dissipate.

"Man, this could *still* take another few years of age," Paige said, raising her glass to the light and tilting it back and forth. "I never realized your grandparents actually made *decent* wine, Brit."

"Ummm, *rude*." Brittany rolled her eyes, laughing.

"Have you thought any more about whether you're going to keep the place?" I said, eager to find a more neutral track of conversation. I couldn't remember if the lines between us had always felt this sharply drawn, but I felt an almost visceral need to smooth them away as quickly as possible. We had a whole weekend ahead of us, after all. And I needed everyone to open up about topics much more personal than wine preferences if this whole trip was going to be worth the effort.

"Were you thinking of selling?" Lydia asked, sharp little frown lines appearing between her large eyes. Something about her newly jet-black bob (or maybe not-so-newly, how would I know?) seemed to intensify their effect.

"Maybe? The winery's profitable, but just barely," Brittany said. "It's not the only thing Mitzi left to me, but it's definitely the biggest chunk of the inheritance."

"You know what they say. If you want to make a small fortune in winemaking, start with a large one." Paige waggled her eyebrows and took a long sip.

"You're not wrong. From a purely fiscal standpoint, selling would make the most sense." Brittany shrugged, twisting the stem of her glass back and forth between her fingers. "But my grandfather loved this place. I remember a few years after he bought it, once renovations on the main house were finally done, he convinced my parents to send me out here with him and Mitzi for the entire summer. He'd let me run tastings sometimes, he thought it was hilarious to see all these old men get taught wine by a ten-year-old. I actually got great tips." She laughed softly at the memory. "Plus, it's not like we really need the cash at the moment."

"I envy your problems, Brittany," Paige said.

"Markus has been very successful in the markets," she conceded. Of course, it helped that both Brittany and her husband had trust funds to play the markets with at a time when most of us had only just been realizing how much debt we'd taken on to get our degrees. But I wasn't anywhere near tipsy enough to make that observation aloud. Fortunately for our fragile detente, Lydia contented herself with a smirk my way that spoke volumes.

"Enough about that, I just want to enjoy this weekend with you ladies," Brittany said. "Lydia, how long has it even been since we've hung out?"

"If I had to guess, I'd say nearly fifteen years," Lydia said, gazing at Brittany over the top of her glass. Brittany blinked at her, then flashed a broad smile that didn't reach her eyes.

"Gosh, time flies, huh? Faster every day now that my two babies are starting to grow up. I can't *believe* Mason's almost ready for kindergarten."

"Does that mean you're planning to go back to work soon?" Lydia's tone was casual, offhand even, but Brittany's eyes narrowed. "You must be so bored in that gigantic house with nothing to fill your days. I think my mind would turn to mush."

"Not anytime soon, no. They still need me at home. And trust me, once you have kids, you'll realize it's *never* boring. Anyway, Markus and I are more than comfortable. I'd hate to miss out on this time in their lives just to prove some point."

"That's totally the way to do it. I don't hate my job or anything, but, like . . . what's the rush to get back to it?" Paige said. "It's not like any of us are curing cancer or anything."

Had Paige meant to throw that in Lydia's face, or had she just forgotten that Lydia had, once upon a time, hoped to do something startlingly close to that? It didn't seem like her kind of dig—Paige was all about broadsides, not shivs between the ribs. Still, that wouldn't take the sting out any. I glanced over at Lydia, biting the inside of my cheek, but if Paige's remark had hit home, she wasn't showing it. *Maybe it would be okay.*

"Of course," Lydia murmured. "You always were comfortable, though, weren't you Brittany? I mean . . . all of this is your inheritance just from your *grandparents,*" she added, spreading her arms wide. "Must be nice to have such a capacious safety net. No wonder you never bothered to build a career."

Or maybe Lydia just knew the power was *on* the throne in this instance, not behind it.

Brittany considered Lydia for a long moment, then turned

away to straighten all the items behind the bar, her flawless pale manicure catching the light. I could feel any brief shoots of camaraderie the wine had sprouted withering.

I'd known none of us were all that close anymore—we hadn't been a *group* since Vanessa disappeared—but it was only now dawning on me how thin the threads were that tied us to each other; in some cases, they'd never really existed. Functionally, these women were strangers now, except maybe Brittany and Paige, who still had that Queen Bee / sycophantic sidekick dynamic I remembered from college.

We were worse than strangers, actually; strangers don't have old resentments to dig up. Which I suppose I could have guessed, if I'd stopped to think about it, but I was only now realizing I didn't really know any of them that well anymore either—who was this version of Lydia willing to throw shade at Brittany just to see if she'd get upset? The Lydia I remembered hadn't liked Brittany, that much had always been obvious, but she'd been more watchful, waiting for the moment to throw a snide remark hiding in a casual aside, almost giving the impression that engaging with Brittany was beneath her. Of course that had infuriated Brittany, and she'd made an even bigger point of picking at Lydia whenever Vanessa wasn't around. Generally, though—with notable exceptions—Lydia seemed to take it in eye-rolling stride. Now, though . . . I coughed loudly, sliding off my stool.

"Before we start really catching up, do you mind if we drop stuff off in our rooms? I'd love to freshen up from the trip. And I should probably get into one of those cheese plates you mentioned if we're going to open more wine."

"Ohmygod, of *course*." Brittany widened her eyes in faux dismay. "I'm such a terrible hostess, you're probably all desperate to just unwind for a minute."

"Wine helps with that," Paige quipped.

"The entrance to the main house is just through here," Brittany said, pointing to a door behind the bar. "Why don't we all grab our things and I'll show you to your rooms, then we can pick up where we left off." With that, Brittany strode out from behind the bar to the doors, waiting for the rest of us to follow. I exhaled, relieved to have something to focus on besides each other.

Twenty minutes later, after some car shuffling by Lydia and Paige, Brittany led us down a hallway just behind the bar—a private conference-room-type affair and a small office fanning out to the right—and through another keypad-locked doorway that opened into a massive, well-appointed kitchen. It felt a bit dated—there were flourishes of Tuscanesque scrollwork along the tops of the cabinets, and the whole room, including the marble countertops, was in shades of terra-cotta that very clearly time-stamped Brittany's grandparents' remodel of the property—but it was obviously expensive, and every surface gleamed. On the far side of the massive breakfast bar, a large living room expanded around another gigantic stone fireplace, this one surrounded by a homier array of overstuffed leather furniture, split-log stairs rising from just to the right of the hearth up to the second level. A long dining table dominated the right half of the open concept space, presumably positioned to take advantage of the views through a second array of plate glass windows, tinted darker than the ones in the tasting room, hinting at the mirrored effect on the opposite side of the glass. Another modern-lodge cathedral ceiling shot up from behind our heads, its dramatic slope cut short on the far side by the narrow walkway that overlooked the space, the entire length of it hung with the sort of hunting-y oil paintings you'd expect a wealthy Connecticut winery buyer to favor in his woodsy lodge retreat. A double-wide opening at the left-hand side of the walkway led onto a dim hallway, a mirror opening on the first floor hinting at just how many rooms the building held.

"We're the only ones here, but you'll probably want rooms at the far end of the house," Brittany said, pointing down the hallway. "The second-floor suite just over the living room is great, but you can hear everything happening down here if you're sleeping there."

"Works for me," Paige said, making her way around the counters and across the living room, her rolling luggage clicking against the hard wood. "Do we have room assignments, or is it just first come, first served?"

"I'll be in the master at the far end of the upstairs hallway," Brittany said, lips pinching slightly. "You're free to pick your rooms beyond that. They all have ocean views and en suites."

"Sweet. Dibs on not hauling this up the stairs, then." Without another word, Paige strode down the downstairs hallway, flicking on lights and opening doors as she went. One by one, we started after her, awkwardly maneuvering our luggage around rustic end tables topped with what were probably genuine Tiffany lamps. I crossed to the stairs, then stopped halfway up, frowning back at Brittany. She was trailing Lydia down the first-floor hallway.

"Sorry, didn't you say your master was on the second floor?"

"It is, but I could *never* carry this myself. Here, I'll show you a secret." I followed her down the hall and into a laundry room on the left. She opened a closet at the back, revealing . . .

"Wait . . . this place has an *elevator*? But . . . there are only two floors."

"They added this after Topper's hip replacement. This was the only place they could steal the space from." She shrugged, twisting an old-fashioned key in a circular hole at the bottom of another security panel, tapping a code in, and finally pressing the up button. "It really is more convenient when you have a lot of guests staying. And they ran it down to the cellars so Topper could stay involved with that side of things. There was already an elevator on the tasting room side, obviously, but it was easier for him to pop down from here." Brittany stepped inside, tugging her gigantic suitcase in with her. There was just enough room left for me to squeeze in with my carry-on.

The elevator opened in a small room one floor up, presumably another former closet, depositing us near the end of the long upstairs hallway.

"This is me at the end," Brittany said, tilting her head to the left. "Anything else is fair game."

She took a left down the hallway, so I turned back toward the main room, intending to give her some space, and opened a door to my right. It opened onto a simple staircase leading down past the first floor, presumably all the way into the cellars. The door opposite revealed a gigantic bedroom. I rolled my eyes at myself—*She told you all the bedrooms were ocean-facing, Emily.* But I always got flustered when people were getting tense with each other.

The decor in the bedroom was in keeping with the upscale ski lodge vibe of the rest of the house, the wide-plank knotty pine floors covered with a braided rug, the fluffy whipped cream of the down comforter accented with forest-green and plaid throw pillows featuring animal and tree silhouettes. An antique Shaker-style rocker nestled in the near corner, next to the closet doors, which were flanked by built-ins holding an assortment of books clearly *not* chosen for their visual value. There were dozens of paperback mysteries, a handful of "big idea" books from the last decade or two, and a smattering of novels I'd meant to get around to reading when they'd come out—the literary detritus of vacations and long, lazy summers. I tugged open the drawer on the nearest nightstand, idly curious, and found a paper coaster, the edges curling, and a weighty-looking corkscrew, *Cliff's Edge* emblazoned along the side. I picked it up, flicking the foil knife in and out with a thumbnail, then dropped it back into the drawer and pushed it closed. Neither the other nightstand nor any of the dresser drawers held anything more interesting than liner papers. When was the last time someone had *lived* in this room, not just visited it? As soon as the question formed in my mind, the answer followed: probably fifteen years ago. Had Topper and Mitzi ever even come back after our fateful spring break?

I crossed to the windows and tugged aside the blackout curtains and the gauzier set behind. The sun had fully dipped behind the far cliffs, so that the molten gold ocean rolling in seemed to dissolve into the shadows swathing the strip of beach below the house. Already the sand was disappearing beneath the creep of the tide. Eventually it would kiss the cliff's edge, each wave splashing up over the last few stairs that led down to the dock.

"What happened to you, Vanessa?" I murmured as the light slipped through pinks and bruised purples on its way to full dark. Sighing, I turned away from the window, the vastness suddenly overwhelming. If the answer was out there somewhere, buried beneath the relentless, unfeeling movement of the tides, there was no way I, or anyone else, would ever find it.

An hour or so later, freshly showered and dressed in clothes that didn't seem to exhale other people's trapped plane breath, I made my way down the long hallway and down the split log stairs to the living room—something about the bare-walled, narrow featurelessness of the stairwell I'd accidentally discovered prickled the hairs at the nape of my neck—to find Lydia moving silently around the kitchen, pulling open cup-boards and drawers, a truly spectacular-looking spread of meats, cheeses, nuts, and fruit taking shape behind her on the massive central island. I made my way to the edge and plucked a long cracker from the bowl she'd splayed them in, a mouth-watering fan of baked-in herbs and coarse-grained salt. All the residuals in the world would never be enough for me to stop thinking of them as the *fancy* crackers.

"Okay, are you starting a side hustle in food porn? Because this is beautiful. Were you this fancy when you were living in LA?"

Lydia laughed, glancing at me over her shoulder with a mischievous close-lipped smile that I'd forgotten felt so *her*.

"I figured we could all use some sustenance. Why not make it appealing?"

"Truly, you contain multitudes. May I?" My hand was al-ready hovering over a wheel of goat's cheese, the kind that had one texture around the outside and another in the center and all of which tasted like heaven.

"Please. The true meaning of this artwork is only clear in its destruction."

"Edible mandalas, huh? I could definitely get behind that." I cut a thick wedge of the cheese and smeared it along one of the long, thin crackers, biting into it with a little sigh of plea-sure. I hadn't realized how hungry I was until that very mo-ment.

"What are you guys talking about, that game with the

rocks?" Paige was scrunching up her nose in a trademark expression of confusion, one hand flicking through her pixie cut to shake off the lingering damp. In the oversized Queen Mary Track sweatshirt and slouchy joggers she'd changed into, she seemed much less distant from the girl I'd spent so much time with back in the day.

"No. Buddhism, actually," Lydia said, eyes flicking to mine with mild amusement. She clearly enjoyed the opportunity to highlight Paige's ignorance. But if she'd been hoping to get a reaction, she was disappointed. Subtle insults had always just rolled right over Paige; it was probably why she fitted so well with Brittany.

"Are you a Buddhist, Emily? Since when?" Paige crossed to the wine rack alongside the chef's-sized fridge, pulling out bottles and inspecting their labels, eventually settling on two.

"Since never. It was one of those had-to-be-here jokes. The headline is I'm very psyched on this cheese plate."

True to form, Paige shrugged and tugged out another bottle of wine, turning it over to see the back label.

"See, I *told* you Emily would be leading the charge on the cheese plates." Brittany's voice rang out from the landing. She'd also changed, but the high-waisted yoga pants striped at just the right angle to accentuate the slimness of her thighs, cropped tank, and long, flowing sweater in something like mohair or angora, so delicate you could see the last bits of the sunset shining through the knit, hardly looked relaxed. But then, I was generally against anything with a waistband after six P.M.

I popped a dried cherry into my mouth and sliced off a hunk of what looked like aged cheddar.

"Brit, do you mind if I open this cab franc?" Paige flashed the bottle.

"Please. Anything in the wine rack is fair game. And we have an entire cellar to dig into if there's nothing there that appeals." Brittany flicked her long hair over her shoulder and plucked a single almond off the board. "Lydia, was this you?" She pointed at the tray, slightly less composed than when I'd arrived but still beautiful. Lydia glanced up from where she was slicing vegetables near the sink and nodded once. "I'm impressed. It's like something out of a photo shoot. But then, you always were artsy."

"Was I? I never really thought of myself that way. Especially with the whole 'attempted career in science' thing." Lydia's shoulders dropped a hair, the tiniest flicker of a smile playing over her lips as she returned to her slicing.

"I mean, you did always dress like someone out of the *Addams Family*," Paige said, not looking over from the wine rack. "And you listened to the weirdest music. I'm with Brittany, you were totally the artsy one."

"And yet Emily's the only one with a career in the arts," Lydia murmured.

"Does *Back of House* count as art?" Paige scoffed. She glanced over at me, presumably mugging for Brittany's benefit. "Like, it's funny and all, but . . . you know. There was that whole episode about Maria having gas when the food critic came . . ." Paige chuckled at the memory of what had to rank in my top five least favorite episodes, which was saying something. "Man, my wife and I were *crying*, we were laughing so hard. But art?" She widened her eyes at Brittany, once again looking to her for approval, the way she always had. "I mean. It was *farts*."

Paige tugged the cork out of the bottle as she laughed at her own . . . was that a joke? Probably good enough for *Back of House*.

"Trust me, I get it," I said, holding my glass out for Paige to pour me some wine. "It's definitely not Shakespeare."

The rest of the evening was much less fraught, the crackling fire and ample wine filling in the cracks between us. Somehow we slid into a familiar rhythm, laughing over college memories of theme parties, walks of shame, regrettable style choices that felt so *chic* at the time, each of us falling into our old roles: Brittany throwing out subtly snide comments here and there, faux prissy but actually relishing the idea of her past social triumphs; Paige brash and blunt, willing to rag on anyone, including herself, to get the audience's approval; Lydia watchful, her sharpness from earlier in the evening seemingly tucked away for now, the better to allow her to get a read on all of us; and me, trying to preemptively smooth down ruffled feathers, steer the conversation away from problematic topics, desperate for everyone to just get *along*. Thankfully, my peacemaker instincts weren't getting too much play. We seemed to have managed to target the exact amount of alcohol that allowed everyone to just . . . go with it. Even Lydia was participating in the general nostalgia fest, an unexpected turn. She'd always been the type that you'd call a good listener at first blush; it was only after long acquaintance that you realized she rarely offered up her own inner life in return.

"I'm sorry, you did *what*?" Paige stared at Lydia, mouth agape.

"I pulled back the covers, sprinkled them all over the middle of the mattress, and pulled the sheets back up." Lydia took a slow sip of her wine.

"Where did you even *get* pubic lice?" I asked, feeling as shocked as Paige, though presumably for very different reasons. The careful, somewhat twisted administration of justice felt completely in keeping with Lydia's general "loyal until you cross me" ethos, but it was hard to believe none of us had ever heard about this particular eye-for-an-eye moment. It was the kind of story you'd think even *Lydia* would want to gloat over.

"One of my TAs that semester was mapping their genome as part of his thesis, something about their evolution across different human populations. He had thousands of them in the lab. It's not exactly hard to pocket a test tube after you finish your lab hours." Lydia shrugged. "The hard part was getting out of Bryce's room. I could hear the guys in the room next door come back from dinner while I was in there, and of course his door was at the very end of the hall, so there was no way I'd make it back to the main staircase and downstairs with no one seeing me. And considering what Bryce had told me in his little breakup speech about this new girl he was see-ing that he '*actually* liked,' I had a feeling his frat brothers would be . . . suspicious, to say the least, if they saw me com-ing out of his room. Not that the new girl was in the picture for long after that," Lydia said, mouth twisted with smirking satisfaction as she sipped her wine again.

"How did I never know you did this?" Paige said between barks of laughter. "That's totally *epic*."

"The same reason you never knew much of anything about me, Paige, you never bothered to ask," Lydia said. Her face had gone very still, like she'd been carved from stone. But Paige, even more heavily armored against subtlety than usual thanks to the wine, just threw out her hands, completely oblivious to the sliver of annoyance in Lydia's voice.

"Okay, but that's the kind of story you, like . . . shout from the *rooftops*. Seriously, I would still be dining out on that if it had been me."

"I'm sure you would," Lydia said, eyebrow quirking up ever

so slightly. "You probably would have then if I'd told you. Which is why I didn't. Knowing Bryce got what was coming to him was enough for me. Honestly, him not knowing how it happened felt even more . . . apt. Like the universe was generally punishing him for being a douche."

"So how did you?" Brittany said, eyes narrowed as she watched Lydia. It was Brittany's mention of some party at Tau Zeta that had led us here. I think she'd expected to embarrass Lydia by bringing up her brief infatuation with Bryce Colby; picking at Lydia had always been one of her favorite boredom relief tactics. But instead we'd all been surprised to learn that even if that relationship had ended a bit ignominiously for Lydia, things had presumably gone *much* worse after the fact for Bryce.

"How'd I what?" Lydia said.

"Get out," Brittany replied.

Lydia considered Brittany for a moment, then seemed to decide there was no point hiding that detail.

"Vanessa was waiting for me outside, she helped me find out which window let out onto a fire escape. I wound up crawling through it and meeting her in the bushes."

"No." I could feel my eyes and mouth making mirror *o*'s. "So wait, Vee *knew* you were doing this?" I'd always known Lydia and Vanessa had their own *thing*—Vanessa had this way of singling people out one by one, creating little pockets of rarefied air around the two of you that left you feeling like only you were special enough to see the *real* her. Which of course wasn't "real" at all, it was nothing more than a week or two's worth of in-jokes and stories that *you had to be there* for. Obvious in retrospect, but so effective at the time. She'd done it with me, and Paige. Never Brittany, but then, as first cousins, their relationship actually *was* different.

Still, I couldn't remember us ever undertaking elaborate capers together. And usually, once Vanessa was ready to swap you out on the ever-rotating wheel of her favor, she'd open up a window on whatever intimacy you'd been nurturing, giving everyone else a glimpse into the moments you'd thought were just between the two of you. She'd do it in a way that was impossible to object to—*We can trust Paige, obviously*—but which always managed to emphasize the fact that you weren't as special as you'd let yourself believe. Which of course made you want to get back in her favor that much more.

And yet, for Lydia, at least some of those secrets had *stayed* secret. Somewhere deep down, in a part of me that I hadn't realized still existed, I couldn't help but feel a little . . . well, jealous.

"Vanessa encouraged it," Lydia responded. "She was absolutely livid about how Bryce treated me. Actually, she was the one who swiped Aaron Mankey's keycard and got me into the frat house in the first place."

I took a big gulp of wine, trying to douse the inexplicable spark of hurt. *You're not here to decide the ultimate friend rankings, Emily*. Which reminded me, there was an *actual* reason we were here.

"Looking back, it's astonishing to me none of us ever got jail time for some of the shit we pulled in college," I said lightly. "Especially Vanessa."

"She always could wiggle her way out of anything," Brittany said, face fading into thoughtfulness.

"Well, almost anything," Paige murmured, eyes turning to the wine in her hand.

Just like that the mood flickered out and died, right as I'd been gearing up to launch into my *Let's talk about Vanessa together, find some of that* closure *we're all looking for* shtick.

I'd planned to work things around to her disappearance eventually—it was the elephant in the room, particularly *this* room, one of the last anyone had seen her alive in—but the abruptness of the atmospheric shift seemed to have left us all vaguely motion sick.

"I, uh . . . I think I'm gonna head to bed," Lydia said, rising swiftly. Her eyes looked slightly dewy in the firelight. "Brittany, thank you for ordering all the food."

"Of course," Brittany said absently, stare fixed on a random knot in the hardwood as she blinked slowly.

"Me too. See you all in the morning," Paige said, pouring another large glass of wine and moving swiftly after Lydia down the hallway, not making eye contact with anyone.

"Do you need help cleaning up?" I finally said after it was clear Brittany had no immediate intention of moving. "Or honestly, we should just leave it for the morning."

"Hmm?" Brittany started as though she was surprised to find me there.

"I was just saying we can clean up later."

"Oh, right. Yes." Brittany rose slowly, still not quite seeming to see the room, and sucked in a heavy breath. "That's probably best."

"Walk you upstairs?"

"Sure. Or . . ." Her eyes narrowed as she took me in more fully. "I'll just turn off the lights. I'll be right behind you."

I couldn't remember ever seeing this version of Brittany, simultaneously distracted and wary, even when we had been spending more time together. Brittany had always cast her own habit of saying whatever was on her mind, including the catty digs, as a virtue, her constant refrain of *I'm just telling the truth* the cover-up she'd apply to the livid emotional bruises she occasionally inflicted. Unsure what else to do, I made my way upstairs to my bedroom, keeping my ears cocked until I heard her steps passing by in the hallway, her door opening and closing.

I sat and listened a few moments longer, but there was nothing. Sighing, I pulled out my phone, scrolling through the emails I'd been avoiding all day. Class signups at my gym, *deleted,* an invite to a premiere party for a colleague's new series, the text so spiky with exclamation points that you could practically catch a whiff of the cocaine she'd almost *definitely* be passing around freely, *deleted . . .*

An email from Lucy. With a PDF attached. *Fuck.*

I opened it.

> *Hey, lady!*
>
> *I know you're on a well-deserved girls' trip this weekend, but wanted to make sure this didn't fall through the cracks. The studio was willing to sweeten the pot if you agree to a two-year stint on BoH—take a look at the new episode fees we've wrangled—but they want an answer by Monday.*
>
> *Happy to hop on the phone if you want to talk through any of this, or if you want to talk about what else might be out there. I've heard they're looking for a new showrunner on Marley and the Men, maybe a better fit?*
>
> *xoxo,*
> *Lucy*

I groaned. Lucy didn't mean to guilt-trip me—I genuinely believed she'd understand if I decided to just walk away from *Back of House* tomorrow without anything lined up—but I still *felt* guilty. Part of that was just dyed in the wool at this point—you don't make it out of Minnesota without a lot of vague, unspecified guilt around letting people down—but part of it was Lucy-specific.

She'd stuck with me for almost three years before I finally got staffed on a show—*no one* had agents stick around that long while they continued to not work—and she genuinely seemed to care about my well-being. Of course caring—or seeming to—was her *job,* but I couldn't help but feel like I owed her. Maybe not more years of servitude on *BoH,* or a jump to *Marley*—an equally insipid network offering *But look everyone it's set at a construction company run by a LADY?!?!?*— but if I *wasn't* going to commit, I at least owed her a reason.

Lip curling up toward my nose, I closed my email app. I'd figure out a way to hopefully buy some time—if not with the studio, at least with Lucy—when I was more sober.

I was just settling into bed when I caught it out of the corner of my eye. A flicker of movement along the darkened cliff face, shadows insinuating themselves over the edges of the protective circle the exterior lights cast around the house.

There was something outside.

Carefully, I pulled back the covers and moved to the window, tucking myself behind the heavy curtains I'd forgotten to tug closed. I scanned the ground between the house and the cliff, searching for whatever it was I'd seen. Could it be an animal? Maybe a bear? Surely if there were bears around, Brittany would have warned us. I scanned the area again, eyes stinging from the effort not to blink. Was it just some weird reflection from inside the room? I had a sudden sense of déjà vu as I peered across the darkened landscape, as though I'd been here, at this window, looking out over this scene, before.

I was just turning away when I caught it again, something peeling away from the house toward the cliffs, tall and moving fast. It looked weirdly . . . *human,* but in that misproportioned way people described in alien encounter stories. I stared at the space, breath held, for ten seconds, twenty. It had to be a trick of the light, didn't it?

Then a short, tight scream pulled my attention away from the window.

I hurried out into the hallway, turning right on instinct—the sound seemed to have come from the far end of the house, where Brittany was staying.

"Brittany?" I tapped on the door. "Brit, are you okay? What's going on?"

When there was no answer after a few seconds I twisted the knob.

Brittany was standing at the foot of the massive California king in an oversized T-shirt. Her hair was pushed back from her forehead with a little fabric headband, like she'd just finished washing off her makeup, which made it easy to see how pale she'd gone. She was breathing rapidly, hand trembling next to her cheek as she stared at the center of the bed.

"Brit? Talk to me."

She stared at me, eyes wide with horror, then turned back to the bed, unable to speak. I followed her gaze to the tiny indent in the center.

The thin gold chain had pooled in a fold of the fabric, but the ring it held sat right on top, the diamond in the center winking as I leaned toward it, two small rubies at either side like drops of blood against the stark white of the comforter.

"But that's . . ."

Brittany simply blinked, swallowing hard. We both recognized Vanessa's ring.

"Brittany . . . why is this here?" Dread started to spool out from my center like smoke, pluming into my chest, turning my limbs leaden as my body continued to suck in its poisonous fumes. "Didn't she have it with her when she . . ." I didn't need to finish the thought, and we both knew the answer. It was Vanessa's mother's engagement ring, one of the only things of any value she'd managed to keep after her parents died. Vanessa *never* took it off.

"It's . . . I guess . . ." Brittany's tongue moved over her lips, eyes fixed on the ring. Finally, she turned to me, mouth pinched. "It's nothing. We should all just go to sleep."

"Brittany, if someone has Vanessa's things . . . if they're leaving them here . . ."

"It's nothing, Emily. It must be something of my grandmother's that's . . . *like* Vanessa's ring. It was a family heirloom, after all. Just leave it. I'm fine, I promise."

"I don't mind if you want me to stay. Or you could sleep in my room?"

"Really, I'm *fine*. I just need to get some sleep."

The words were a command. Nodding, I turned and stepped back into the hall, stealing one last look at the ring before I pulled the door closed behind me and drifted back to my room, feeling strangely detached from my body, as if it were moving without my will or say-so. I forced myself not to look at all the doors I was passing, leading to so many empty rooms, with so many unseen nooks and corners.

I pulled the curtains tight and settled into bed, dutifully closing my eyes and running through my nighttime meditation, as though that would have any effect.

It *was* Vanessa's ring, I knew it. And Brittany clearly knew it too. Of course she would be spooked to see it. My entire body had crawled when I realized what I was looking at.

But then, slowly, the feeling had been replaced by a muscle-dissolving wash of relief. If the ring was here now, I *couldn't* have done anything to Vanessa, could I? It had always been hard to believe I'd somehow stumbled down the cliff face in the dark, turned inexplicably violent, and made it back into my own bed without a trace of what had happened on me, not even a grain of sand clinging to my skin, but the guilt of not knowing what *had* happened had made it impossible to let go of the possibility.

But even in the unlikely world where I somehow managed that, without tipping anyone off, without a scratch on me from a stumble or a struggle, how could I—drunk enough that my mind had simply stopped recording the night—have thought to retrieve Vanessa's necklace and then . . . what, hide it? Pass it off to someone else? *I* hadn't left it in Brittany's room just now, that much was certain, which meant there were whole constellations of dots not connecting here.

I exhaled shakily, muscles actually wobbly with the relief of it: Whatever had happened between me and Vanessa that night, I really *couldn't* have done anything to her. It just didn't make any sense.

But even if one of my biggest lingering questions about that weekend was, if not fully explained, at least neutered, there were still so many more swimming around inside me, all flickers of scales and flat eyes and slick skin brushing against an ankle.

Who could have possibly gotten their hands on Vanessa's necklace? Why would they have left it in Brittany's room?

And why would Brittany try to lie about it?

BEGIN FLASHBACK

INT. PRECIPICE WINERY PRIVATE
QUARTERS—NIGHT (15 YEARS AGO)

Late-aughts pop music blares from a speaker
perched on the edge of the counter. The rest
of the large farmhouse-style kitchen is in
disarray, a half-eaten plate of microwave
nachos fighting for space with open chip
bags, empty wine bottles, a tray of pre-
sliced cheese, the remnants sweaty and waxy,
a torn sleeve of water crackers, and other
detritus of a drunken food raid surrounded
by grisly splatters of spilled red wine.

The girls in the living room don't seem to
care, though. Brittany is swinging her hair
back and forth as she writhes in front of
the fireplace, her skimpy club outfit out of
place in the lodgy setting. Paige has jumped
up onto the couch cushions and is run-
dancing to the song, pointing at Brittany
whenever a favorite lyric comes up. Emily
twirls without much rhythm, but with great
enthusiasm, next to the coffee table. Lydia,
tucked into one of the large armchairs,
watches them all with flat, glazed eyes—she
seems to have been overserved.

                    BRITTANY
          Oh my god, Lydia, how drunk did
          you *get*? Talk about amateur hour.

                    PAIGE
          Should we get a bucket?

BRITTANY
God, gross.

Paige and Brittany cackle, but Lydia just shoots Brittany an angry glare, reaching for the glass at her elbow and taking a sip. It's water. Without a reaction from Lydia, the girls quickly return to lip-syncing the next song together. It's clear Paige doesn't actually know the words, but whenever Brittany looks at her, she *watermelon-rutabaga-walla-walla-rhubarbs* with her mouth, clearly eager to appear as enamored by the song as her friend is.

Vanessa, however, misses the entire interaction. She's standing apart, staring out the windows at the cliffs, their silhouettes made nearly invisible by the glare of lights inside the house. She has the sharp features and willowy slenderness of a runway model. Her choppy dyed-blond hair has faded to a brassy shade, but even mussed after a night of partying, it still accentuates her high cheekbones and large, vulpine eyes. She fingers a ring at her neck, turning it over and over on the chain it's strung from, pensive.

EMILY (O.S.)
Hey, everything okay?

VANESSA
(startled)
Hmm? Oh, yeah, I'm fine.

EMILY
Really? I'm pretty sure it's im-

possible to be fine and not dance
to "Party in the USA," Vee.

                    VANESSA
Lydia's not dancing.

                    EMILY
Lydia's wasted. She weighs
like . . . ten pounds. Besides,
when does Lydia ever dance?

                    VANESSA
Fair. But I promise, I'm fine.
Just . . . thinking.

                    EMILY
About anything in particular?

Vanessa's eyes narrow, and she seems to
make a decision before turning to Emily.
She leans in slightly, lowering her voice.

                    VANESSA
You haven't told anyone about me
and Alden, have you?

                    EMILY
What? No, of course I haven't.
     (whispering)
I would *never*, not after what you
pulled with the photo shoot.

                    VANESSA
Yeah . . . that might have been a
mistake.

Emily frowns, her hissed whispers gaining
intensity.

                    EMILY
          You think? You could have at
          least told me what you were plan-
          ning to do.

                    VANESSA
          But if I'd told you, you wouldn't
          have helped.

Emily's face contorts with annoyance bordering on fury, but it seems to roll right
off Vanessa, whose eyes dart down to the ring
she's still fingering.

                    VANESSA (CONT'D)
          You promise, though? No one?

                    BRITTANY (O.S.)
          Emily! Oh my god, *it's our song!*

Emily glances over at Brittany, face lighting up as she recognizes the tune. She turns
back to Vanessa, her annoyance lingering.

                    EMILY
          I told you I didn't say anything.
          Even though I probably *should*
          have. I could get in serious
          trouble for that.

                    VANESSA
          There's trouble and there's trou-
          ble, Em.

Emily's eyes narrow as she takes Vanessa
in. It's dawning on her how strange it is to
be having this conversation in the middle
of a dance party . . .

> EMILY
> Vanessa . . . is everything okay
> with you? You've been acting
> weird since we got here.

> VANESSA
> You've always been so good at
> reading people.

She rests a hand on Emily's upper arm, a
gesture of intimacy that almost immediately
softens Emily, who leans in closer, any
lingering annoyance quickly subsumed by
worry.

> EMILY
> What is it, Vanessa? You can tell
> me, you know.

> VANESSA
> You know . . . I almost believe
> that? And I would if I thought
> you could help. But . . . I don't
> think you can. I don't think any-
> one can. I've gotten myself in so
> deep. I thought I finally had peo-
> ple in my corner, people who
> would protect me if the worst
> happened, but maybe I was just
> kidding myself . . .

NOTE: Too melodramatic too soon? Or do we need more
details about outside threats she's facing? Revisit / send
out for notes. —EF

                    EMILY
               (really worried now)
          I'm in your corner. We all are,
          you know that, right?

                    VANESSA
          Are you, though? Are any of you
          really? Because I've started
          wondering—

Emily's startled look stops Vanessa short.
Vanessa shakes her head and takes a sip of
her wine, stepping away from Emily.

                    EMILY
          Wondering what?
               (beat)
          What have you been wondering?

                    VANESSA
          Nothing. It doesn't matter.

                    EMILY
          Vanessa . . . just tell me what's
          going on.

                    VANESSA
          There's nothing to tell. Go,
          enjoy the dance party. One of us
          should be able to.

Emily glances over her shoulder, lowering
her voice as she leans closer, anxious to
catch Vanessa's eye, to reach her.

                    EMILY
          If something really bad is going
          on, we can always talk to someone

at school. Oh, or your grandparents? They know all sorts of—

                VANESSA
Nothing's going on, Emily, okay?
At least nothing *you* could possibly understand. Just . . .
leave it.

Emily blinks, clearly stung by Vanessa's
sharp tone, then, when it's clear Vanessa
has no intention of saying any more, reluctantly turns away, letting Brittany pull
her back into the dance. Vanessa watches
them, nibbling the corner of her lip, eyes
glistening. None of the girls notice it,
but her face is drawn with real fear. She
sucks in a sharp breath and turns back to
the blank, empty space outside, hands trembling slightly as they turn the ring at her
neck again, and again, and again . . .

4

SOMETHING RUMBLED TO LIFE, THE HEAVY
mechanical sound jerking me out of the fitful sleep I'd fallen
into. It took me a moment to realize where I was, my heart
beating wildly in my throat with the vague wrongness of wak-
ing up in an unfamiliar space.

By the time I pieced it together, I was fully awake. I frowned,
sitting up in bed. The sound was still going, a low electric
hum.

The elevator.

I reached for my phone on the nightstand. It was three-
thirty in the morning. Why would anyone be using the elevator *now?*

It had to be Brittany. No one else even knew about it.

I sat there for a moment, debating whether to get up. *It's
none of your business, Emily. Brittany's probably just sick, or hungry, or—*

Or that ring had turned up in her bedroom fifteen years
after Vanessa had gone missing and she was as freaked out by
it as I'd ever seen her.

I'd lain awake in the darkened bedroom for over an hour
after I left her, trying to sort out how it could have happened.
Even if I really had seen someone skulking around the
grounds, they couldn't have made it into Brittany's room to
drop the ring off without alerting her to their presence. Her

app had pinged the second Paige and Lydia walked in, even though she'd unlocked the door at the security panel just minutes before. And if someone was already in the house—a thought that was more effective than an ab workout, it made my body clench so tightly—why would they toy with Brittany, specifically, the one person who would have had to know they were there?

Most important, how would anyone have gotten their hands on Vanessa's ring in the first place, unless they'd . . . well, *killed* her? And if they had, why come back fifteen years later? Why *tell* us all they were still out there? There was the possibility that the ring was a replica . . . but what would be the point of making one? I kept trying to sort through it the way I would a script I was giving notes on—find the logic behind the thing, the explanation that would come out later, the hints of which were already there, if only you knew what to look for—but I couldn't seem to make it add up. The wine wasn't helping.

Still, even through the fog of sleep, I was very clear on a few important details: Something was going on, I was almost certain it had to do with what happened fifteen years ago, and it was enough to make Brittany sneak through the house in the middle of the night alone. Whatever would drive her to do that was information I wanted—needed—to have if I was ever going to untangle the feature we were all starring in and what, precisely, my role in the production was.

Before I even realized what I was doing, I had thrown my feet over the side of the bed, my curiosity too strong to ignore. I crept out into the hallway, where soft running lights along the baseboards just barely illuminated the doors that lined it. I pulled open the one directly across from my room, carefully closing it behind me, and tiptoed down the stairs I'd discovered earlier, hardly daring to breathe.

The staircase was cramped and industrial, clearly more function than form, unlike the one in the main room. Tall, narrow windows at the landings let in spills of moonlight, rustling tree branches outside filtering it so that it seemed to skitter, insect-like, along the dull concrete and metal of the stairs. I could feel my shoulders hitching up around my neck as I made my way down the first flight, then the second, in a futile effort to protect my blind side from whatever might be creeping along in the shadows behind me.

I crept past the door that opened out to the first floor hallway and continued down. If Brittany *had* just wanted a midnight snack, and I was being ridiculous, so be it, but if I wasn't . . . I had to find out what she was doing before she finished up and slipped back into bed.

Almost immediately, the air turned colder and damper, clamming the skin of my bare arms. What little moonlight made it through the thicket of landscaping outside the first-floor windows seemed to catch on the rough surfaces of the cinder block walls, leaving nothing but the low phosphorescent glow of the running lights as I made my way to the bottom of the stairs. I flipped the deadbolt, then tugged on the handle of the industrial-looking door . . . but it didn't budge. I ran my eyes along the seam and quickly spotted the simple barrel locks at the top and bottom, a slightly heavier-duty version of the kind you found in a million restroom stalls. I slid them open and tried the door again. This time it opened, the hinges creaking slightly as I pulled it toward me. I could just make out the track it left in the dust on the landing by the light coming in from the cellars. I dropped the door and pulled again. Nothing seemed to have locked. Still, I didn't want to get stuck down here. I slipped through, then shook off my slippers, stuffing first one, then the other between the door and the frame, grateful that I'd worn my thickest socks to bed for warmth.

Inside, the cellars spread out in every direction, rows of wine barrels hugging the rough sandstone walls, little pyramids of additional barrels stacked on pallets splitting up the larger spaces like stacks in a library. The floor underfoot was unfinished, the earth packed hard by years of traffic, both human and barrel-based. I had a vague memory of the story on the tasting room placemats: the first winemaker on the property expanding a large natural cave he'd entered from the cliffside, the opening there just large enough for him to shuffle through if he hunched . . . though first he'd had to find a way to reach it, fifty feet down from the top of the cliff and fifty feet up from the shore. There was a hatch over that entrance now, but you could still access it from the staircase that wound down the cliff face, though no one had used it regularly in decades. Over the years, various winery owners had tunneled between the other caves in the cliffside, expanding the cellars into a spidery network of rooms, some larger than others, all shooting off from the main cellar space that I now found myself in.

The rows and stacks of barrels to the right were swathed in shadow, but flickering fluorescents illuminated the section of the room to my left. *If the lights are on, it means she has to have come down here.* Sucking in a deep breath, I set out, hugging the near wall as I picked my way past the little tributaries that ran between the barrel stacks.

A double door at the far end of the room was open, the

wide hallway that extended beyond it sloping downward steadily.

"Brittany?" I whispered, so low I could barely hear myself, the heavy stone on all sides quickly absorbing the small sound as I made my way deeper and deeper into the cliff, gripping tight to the handrail that ran along the left-hand wall, bracketed into the rock. Occasionally, a room would open up to the right, some of them barely more than alcoves, others large enough to house a few dozen barrels, stacked from floor to ceiling along the walls. The hall itself was regular, tool marks clearly visible in the curved ceiling overhead, but it still felt like something out of a fairy tale, the moment when the hero plunges into the dark tunnel beneath the mountain, uncertain if he'll ever see the light of day again. I couldn't tell if the small sounds I was hearing—tiny scrapes of friction, a rock skittering along the packed earth—were coming from up ahead or just my own footsteps, distorted by the late hour and the claustrophobic dim of the regular pendant lights overhead, glowing breadcrumbs marking my descent. I hugged my free arm around my body, but I couldn't get rid of the goose bumps prickling over me in waves.

After a few minutes of walking, I reached another, more expansive room, a pair of forklifts parked just inside the entrance. The ceiling swooped and dipped irregularly, and even the large modernist chandelier mounted in the right half of the space—faceted crystals dripping down from the giant silver circle at varying lengths like a rainstorm in motion—couldn't reach into the pockets of shadow overhead. The room itself was shaped like a teardrop clinging to the wall at my left hand; that was more or less straight, and the rest of the space narrowed, then widened outward from it, racks and barrels curving around the edges to meet at its swollen bottom. The walls I could see were somehow both rougher and smoother than the ones in the tunnel, the surfaces free of the telltale drill marks along its walls and ceiling. In this room, they undulated irregularly, and the barrels were all pushed out at least a foot to accommodate their subtle in-out motion, like ocean waves rippling along the surface of the stone. *It must be one of the natural caves.*

I stepped into the more open portion of the room, where a long wooden table with elegant high-backed chairs was positioned directly under the chandelier, pausing to run my finger over its surface. It left a narrow line in the thin film of dust there. They must not use it often. Which . . . yeah, no surprise there. Why have your fancy private dinner in the bowels of a mountainside when you could look out over an ocean painted pastel by the sun setting behind the rocks?

But the room, like every other room I'd passed so far, was definitively empty. *Had I imagined the elevator sounds? But no, all the lights so far had been on. That couldn't just be a coincidence . . .*

If Brittany had come this way, though . . . why? And where had she gone?

Suddenly, I was glad she hadn't heard me call her name before. Anything that would drag her out of bed into the middle of a mountain couldn't be *good*. And anything she was this intent on hiding from the rest of us had to be important.

There was a gap between the barrels at the corner opposite the entrance, almost hidden by the sharper angles of the cave walls there. When I got to the opening, I found a narrow spiral staircase, the bottom not quite visible when I craned my neck over the edge. *This is stupid. This is eminently stupid. Do not follow someone into the hole in a cliff in the middle of the night, Emily. You don't even know for sure it's Brittany down there.*

But then I thought of that last, mostly missing night, the film of it still clinging to me even as I told myself that, logically, it couldn't have been me. I thought of Vanessa's face the last time I'd seen her, taut with fear—and what it would look like now, after a decade and a half beneath the ocean's relentless waves, or moldering somewhere beneath a claustrophobic carpet of fir needles. And then I thought of the last round of notes I'd gotten on my *Back of House* script—*What if they have a* Ratatouille *moment and befriend a mouse that's been bugging them in the restaurant before finding a way out of the bathroom?*—and I remembered that email Lucy had sent, the two-year sentence to lowest-common-denominator monotony it threatened, and the idea of *not* finding out what the hell had happened here so long ago, was maybe happening here now, became much more terrifying than the stone and metal oubliette below me. Sucking in a deep breath, stomach clenching against the anxiety pulsing through me, I started down.

The staircase was clearly older than any of the fixtures inside the cellar I'd come through, its spindly metal corkscrew clinging so closely to the narrow chute it filled that I couldn't run my hand along the rail without scraping my knuckles against the rough stone of the wall. Within seconds I was dizzy from its tight spin, the wine from earlier turning sour in my stomach, and I gripped the central pole hard to keep my balance as it descended farther and farther into the cliff. Eventually it let out on a small stone enclosure facing a large, heavy-looking metal door.

I moved up to it slowly, a sudden bloom of dampness between my toes reminding me I'd hurried down here in my stocking feet. Shivering, I reached for the handle.

Locked.

I was trying to decide whether to try the door again when I heard the noises on the other side. Soft murmurs, possibly voices, interrupted every so often by a sharp cutting sound, like metal sparking against metal. I leaned toward the door, frozen by the proximity of something . . . someone . . .

Then something icy wrapped around my ankles, and, too terrified even to scream, I stumbled backward, rushing up the spiral staircase at a sprint, barreling back up the steep hallway, ignoring the fire in my lungs.

It was around the time I was slamming the cellar door closed and dragging myself up the interior staircase that I realized the ghostly touch had been a surge of seawater from under the door.

But I didn't slow down until I was back in my room, the door locked tight behind me. Whatever Brittany was doing on the beach in the middle of the night, I wasn't brave enough to uncover it.

INT. SEASIDE CAVE—NIGHT (PRESENT DAY)

A trickle of water flows in through the narrow, low entrance to the beach cave, stopping just a few feet from the mouth. We PAN
UP to take in the space that opens up beyond
the cave entrance, about the size of a walk-
in closet. Coarse sand dotted with large,
jagged rocks covers most of the ground, but
a large flat shelf of stone, darkened by
damp, forms the floor at the back. It's clear
that the walls have been smoothed by centu-
ries of ocean waves flowing in and out with
the tides. An industrial caged light is
bracketed to the ceiling near a heavy-
looking metal door at the very back. It's
unclear where it leads, and the light doesn't
do much to illuminate the subterranean
space.

Brittany is intent as she scans the ground
beneath her slowly with the aid of the flashlight of a new-model iPhone.

                    BRITTANY
          What else did you leave here,
          Vanessa? It *had* to have come from
          here . . .

The light briefly glints on the surface of
the rock and she sucks in a sharp breath,
bending to get a closer look, but when she
turns the rock over, she realizes it's just
a fleck of quartz in the stone.

                    BRITTANY (CONT'D)
          Dammit!

She picks up the rock and throws it against the cave wall so hard a piece chips off. Brittany doesn't seem to notice. She's poring over the stones again, jaw set.

> BRITTANY (CONT'D)
> What I don't get is how you even got the ring to me. Though I will say, solid way to fuck with me, Vee. Just like old times!
> (flips over another stone)
> You always thought you were so *clever*, didn't you?

> BEGIN FLASHBACK

INT. SEASIDE CAVE—DAY (15 YEARS AGO)

The same cave. The Brittany ducking through the low mouth is much younger, in a North Face and skinny jeans, and the tide hasn't started to make its way inside yet. Vanessa comes in behind her. She looks drawn.

> VANESSA
> Okay, we can talk here.

> BRITTANY
> Seriously, Vanessa, the cave? Dramatic much?

> VANESSA
> Oh for fuck's—do you *ever* stop, Brittany? I know your life is all garden parties and spending Topper and Mitzi's trust fund, but can you just take a step back for *once*?

> BRITTANY
> (indignant)
> I don't even have access to the
> trust fund until next year.

> VANESSA
> And I don't even *have* one. The
> trust fund's not the *point*.

Vanessa tugs her hands through her hair,
jaw clenching. Brittany's expression turns
sour.

> BRITTANY
> Then what is the point? Did you
> just drag me down here to yell
> about how mean Grandma and
> Grandpa are to you? Because I've
> seen that show already, Vanessa.

> VANESSA
> Brittany, they're going to cut me
> off. And no, I didn't really want
> to share that with fucking *Paige*
> so the whole track team can know
> about it by Monday.

> BRITTANY
> (prim)
> If they're really going to cut
> you off it's probably your fault.
> They did warn you, Vanessa.

> VANESSA
> Seriously? You're really okay —
> with them pushing me out on the
> street while you get to go back
> and play queen of the campus in

that ridiculous apartment they're
paying for?

> BRITTANY
> They're helping with your rent
> too. Anyway, I didn't say I *agree*
> with it, just that they have
> their reasons. I mean . . . if
> you're really flunking out . . .

Vanessa's eyes narrow and she takes a step
toward Brittany, thrusting a long finger at
the shorter girl's chest.

> VANESSA
> They would *never* do that to you.

Brittany backs up, frowning incredulously.

> BRITTANY
> I would never flunk out.

> VANESSA
> But if you did, they'd fucking be
> there to catch you. Even before
> your parents, probably. The whole
> family would come together to
> pick precious princess Brittany
> up, and dust her off, and give her
> a new Gucci purse to make it all
> better.

> BRITTANY
> Shut up, Vanessa.

> VANESSA
> Don't pretend you don't know it's

true, Brittany. You're the golden
child. If I get one bad grade, or
miss curfew, or fucking dare to
get a summer job where their
fancy fucking friends can see
me . . .
    (mincing)
What will people think, *Vanessa?*
    (normal voice)
. . . then they threaten to put
me out on the street. You wrap a
car around a lamppost *wasted* last
year and you *get a new fucking
car.*

          BRITTANY
That was an *accident*.

Vanessa punctuates her speech with more
jabs at Brittany, each one a bit harder than
the last.

          VANESSA
That's the *point*! You're allowed
to have an accident. You're allowed to screw up. I'm always one
step away from being out on my
ass, all because they're still
mad at my mom. My *dead* mom.

Brittany pushes Vanessa's hands off more
forcefully than she needs to. Vanessa stumbles back.

          BRITTANY
Fine, Vanessa. Do you want me to
admit that our grandparents like

me more? Would that make you feel
better?

           VANESSA
I want you to fucking do something, Brittany. For once in your
life stop being the spoiled little bitch you've always been and
do something!

She jabs her again. Brittany bares her
teeth.

           BRITTANY
Don't call me that.

           VANESSA
         (disdainful)
Why not? It's true. The only reason any of our friends even tol-
erate you is me. They know it,
just like I know it. You're. A.
Bitch.

           BRITTANY
That's not *true*! And I said don't
call me that!

Brittany pushes Vanessa again, hard, but
this time Vanessa's heel catches. Her eyes
widen as she falls backward.

                      CUT TO

Brittany's face, horror contorting her features . . .

                              END FLASHBACK.

INT. SEASIDE CAVE—NIGHT (PRESENT DAY)

Brittany flips over another rock, gasping
when she spots something long, slender, and
ivory-colored beneath it, but water is already beginning to pool in the indentation
it left. She drops to her knees, digging at
the sand with one hand, phone gripped tight
in the other, but the water seeps in faster
than her progress. Eventually, with a frustrated snort, she tosses the phone onto a
nearby pile of rocks and starts digging
with both hands.

                    BRITTANY
          Lot of good all that *cleverness*
          did you, hmm?
                  (digging faster)
          I just don't get . . . how you
          did it . . . now?

She finally gets to the bottom of the hole
and finds . . . a salt-bleached stick. Brittany shrieks, picks up a rock and throws it
at the wall in frustration, then another.
Sparks flare in the dark of the cave. She
sinks to her knees in the sand, tears of
frustration pouring down her face as the
tide washes over her knees, the waves creeping up almost to the top of the cave.

                    BRITTANY (CONT'D)
          It's not possible. It's not *pos-
          sible.*

She throws another rock, feebly this time,
the fight gone out of her.

                    BRITTANY (CONT'D)
          How are you still doing this to
          me, Vanessa? I *killed* you.

5

I WOKE UP WITH A START, THE MENTAL STAIN
of the previous night spiking my heart rate before I could
fully recall the contours of what had happened.

Then I spotted the balled-up socks on the floor next to the
bed, stiff with dried saltwater and cellar dirt, and my breath
started coming a bit easier. At least I hadn't imagined the
creepy descent into the viscera of the cliffside, even if it had
all felt a bit like a fever dream.

I stared at the timbered ceiling, trying to sort my thoughts
now that the wine had receded to a general wooliness in my
mouth, and the undulating shadows beneath the earth had
been replaced by a bright clear day, the sun sparkling on the
ocean through the windows to my left.

Brittany—I'd never actually seen her, but it had to have
been Brittany, didn't it? The screenwriter in me couldn't even
come up with another possibility. Anyway, she must have had
something very important to do if it dragged her out of bed,
through a maze of cellars, and down to the base of the cliffs
in the middle of the night. Vanessa's ring must have set it off—
was she handing it off to someone? Throwing it into the sea?
Burying it as some sort of cleansing ritual? That last was . . .
extremely un-Brittany. I could see her paying someone to lay
crystals on her during a massage, but I had a hard time be-

lieving a house witch was hiding under all the modern-prep paraphernalia.

Blame the hangover, but I couldn't for the life of me imagine a single thing that could have felt vital enough to inspire last night. Clearly Brittany wanted to keep whatever it was hidden from the rest of us. Which still felt important, but now, with a sliver of bright blue sky peeking in cheerily between the curtains, didn't quite reach the level of *sinister*.

Sighing, I dragged myself out of bed and slipped into some clothes. I wasn't going to figure anything out lying here alone, and besides, I was starving.

Downstairs, Lydia was perched on one of the stools at the island, flipping through the pages of a novel as she sipped her coffee, looking unfairly put together, given the hour and the amount of wine we'd all consumed. On the kitchen side, Paige was scraping almond butter across a piece of toast, face slack as she stared at the singed bread with the grim focus of the supremely hungover. I poured myself a large mug of coffee, wrapping both hands around it and leaning against the far counter, the awkwardness in the room coming more clearly into focus with every sip.

"Did everyone sleep well?" I finally ventured.

"Well enough," Lydia said, closing her book around her thumb and glancing up at me. "Ocean sounds always make it easier to sleep."

"What about you, Paige?"

"What?" She frowned at me, toast suspended in midair.

"I was just asking if you slept well?"

"Oh, uh . . . no. Not really." She gave a minute shake of her head, then turned back to the toast, raising it to her lips to take a tiny bite, grimacing as she forced herself to chew it. With a shudder, she dropped the toast back onto her plate, rubbing her hands vigorously against each other as though to remove any trace of the hideous offense. "I'm gonna go for a run. Clear my head."

Without another word, she strode around the peninsula of the island, not even slowing when her hip caught the corner of the counter. *So much for picking up the "Let's work through that weekend" thread.*

Stomach growling, I squeezed two pieces of the mostly-seeds, banish-all-carbs "bread" Brittany had ordered into the toaster, crossing to the fridge with vague thoughts of slathering triple crème cheese over the top. It was vacation. When I turned away, I found Lydia watching me, thumb between the pages of her book. I'd forgotten how penetrating her gaze could feel—it was some combination of how still she could be, body perfectly motionless, like a sitter for a portrait, and the large, somewhat bulbous eyes that dominated her face. I laughed awkwardly as I carried my cheese haul to the counter.

"Penny for your thoughts?" I said as I smeared my toast.

"Honestly? I was just thinking it was strange that Brittany invited us all back here." Lydia slid a playing card into the book and set it softly on the counter, glancing over her shoulder at the staircase to the upper level. "It's not like any of us have much in common anymore. *Maybe* Brittany and Paige do, they clearly keep in touch, but Paige would probably rather be . . . I don't know, out on a fishing charter all day, or hiking up the side of some volcano." Lydia rolled her eyes, clearly baffled by the idea. "I'm not putting it right."

"No, I know what you mean. Paige has always . . . needed a lot of external stimulation."

"Exactly. No wonder we never really jelled." Lydia smiled softly and took a sip of her coffee.

"You and I always were the indoor kids of the group," I said. "Are, actually. I live in LA, and this is me *tan*." I flipped an arm over to show Lydia the consumptive pallor I'd maintained via years huddled over computer screens.

"And here I thought I was the only one who got all her vitamin D through blue light," Lydia said. I smiled. Lydia's general air of silent watchfulness made her flashes of cleverness all the more fun when she decided to reveal them to you.

Brittany had always hated that. Moreso because Lydia's knowing asides clearly delighted Vanessa. But then, Brittany and Lydia had never really found much to like about each other.

"Speaking of, what have you been up to lately? Are you still working at . . ." I struggled to remember the name of the tech firm Lydia had been with during her time in LA, the one that had eventually moved her to a higher-up-the-food-chain position in their Bay Area offices. I'm sure she must have mentioned it, but honestly, thinking back to the handful of times we'd hung out during her LA stint, I couldn't remember her talking much about her work, or herself, at all.

"Agilvation? No, I left . . . maybe five years ago now?"

"Oh." Man, it really *had* been a long time since we'd talked. "Any reason?"

"The usual. I know scrum-training module design isn't world-changing work, but getting overlooked for a promotion three years running when you're functionally the only person keeping the ship afloat?" She shook her head, eyes narrowing at the memory.

"God, that's the worst," I commiserated, clutching eagerly at the brief moment of connection. "Did you at least get to tell them off in the exit interview?"

"No point, they're hard-wired to take advantage of anyone

with talent. Well, they were." Her lips curled at the side in a gleeful smirk. "The backdoor I *accidentally* left in their most popular module made it pretty easy for even the baby hackers to sweep up all their IP. I've heard they're filing for bankruptcy soon."

"Seriously?"

She shrugged.

"I told them for *years* that we needed to hire dedicated digital security staff, but they preferred to leave it on the devs' plates and pay them exactly the same amount as they were already getting paid. It's not my fault if they were too cheap to protect their own IP."

I took a sip of my coffee, dropping my eyes to the mug until I could control my expression. If there was any hint of judgment there—because seriously, bankrupting an *entire company* because of a missed promotion might be slight overkill, Lyds—it was better that she didn't catch it. The weekend was tense enough as it was.

"Where are you now?" I said, blowing on the surface of the liquid to buy myself a couple more seconds of cover.

"A mobile gaming company up near Redwood City. They mostly focus on puzzle games for female gamers. Solve this visual puzzle to get the next clue in the mystery narrative, stuff like that."

"Wow, that's so cool."

Lydia shrugged.

"I guess. Code is still just code, no matter what you're building with it." She turned back to her book, flipping it open to the marked page, a bright-red signal that she had no intention of digging into her work life any further.

I was casting around for some new topic of conversation—it only just now struck me how little I knew about what Lydia's life looked like these days, whether she had a partner, liked the Bay Area, had a regular board games night or a book club or any other hobbies. Paige and I hadn't been in touch practically since graduation, and yet I could rattle off a dozen conversation starters for her—the Brooklyn condo she and her pretty wife had bought a few years back, a recent vacation they'd taken to hike glaciers and see the northern lights in Iceland, her title at the wine importing company she worked for, what she actually *did* at all those "tough mudder" style runs she posted about—thanks to a single social media scan prior to the trip. But Lydia wasn't on socials, which meant that even now, she was at a certain remove from the rest of us, the texture of her life since college unknowable if you didn't actually, well . . . *know* her.

Luckily, I was saved from the increasing atmospheric pressure of awkward silence by Brittany clacking across the landing to the top of the stairs. She was dressed in a form-fitting turtleneck sweater dress, patterned tights, and a second pair of heeled booties, wedged this time, and crisscrossed with tiny, bondagey leather straps.

"Is Paige still not up? I would have thought she could hold her booze better. It is her job, after all." Brittany flashed a tight smile as she crossed to the kitchen. It emphasized the ample powder settling into the fine lines around her eyes and mouth. Even a full face of makeup couldn't fully hide the slightly hollow, bruised look around her eyes.

"She was planning to go for a run," Lydia murmured, not looking up from her book.

"Really? That seems a little obsessive." Brittany widened her eyes meaningfully as she poured a coffee.

"Don't feel guilty, neither of us is running either," Lydia said, still not looking up. Brittany's jaw tightened, and once again I tried to map this Lydia onto the girl I remembered. Yes, she and Brittany had always had their backs up around each other, but would she ever have taken the first swipe back in college? Lydia's sharp tongue and clever, cutting retorts weren't new, but they felt . . . unsheathed.

"Why would I feel guilty? We're here on a girls' weekend. Honestly, I'm all for fitness, but there's keeping healthy and there's being a total psycho, you know?"

"Still throwing that word around pretty recklessly, huh, Brit?" Lydia finally met Brittany's eyes, her face totally motionless, unreadable. "Bit classless."

Brittany reared back slightly, jawline disappearing with the motion.

"It's just a turn of phrase, Lydia. Don't get all worked up."

"What a privilege to think of it that way." Lydia held Brittany's eyes a few seconds longer, then turned back to her book.

Anxiety and coffee blended into a pool of acid at the pit of my stomach. The abrupt end to last night's reminiscences was frustrating, but understandable. Diving into painful memories of what had happened to our long-lost friend was never going to be *easy*. But if Lydia and Brittany were going to needle each other all day, we might never get there, and then this whole weekend would have been for nothing. I'd still have the sticky coating of guilt that had clung to me since that forgotten night, and almost as bad, I'd be seventy-two hours closer to being forced to give Lucy a decision on the *Back of House* contract renewal; if my screenplay was still as stalled out by the time I got home as it had been for the past decade, I'd never be able to justify making my escape. After all, that writers' room might be stale and airless, all of us growing weaker and fuzzier as the always-limited supply of mental oxygen depleted with every passing episode, but it was a *very* well-appointed place to wither and die.

"All right, clearly *everyone* needs a reset from the booze, hmm? Maybe a change of scenery?" Brittany turned to me, clearly expecting me to help her smooth over the prickly exchange. Emily Fischer, designated safe space. For a moment, resentment coiled through me, squeezing tight. We all knew that Lydia's brother had some pretty serious mental health issues back in college—Brittany *should* be more sensitive to the words she threw around all the time, and if she wasn't going to do that, she could at least rein it in for the *three days* she was spending with Lydia. So why did I always have to play peacemaker? Just so Brittany never had to own the shit she said to people?

No, it wasn't that. Conflict had always felt like an overtight wool sweater, full-body irritation that I'd do anything to shed. A fact that Brittany had likely sniffed out the very first night we'd met, the smell of my need even more pungent than the cheap vodka we were drinking in Vanessa's freshman dorm.

"That'd probably be good," I conceded, hating myself for making it so easy for her so quickly. Lydia might have shed some of the "keep me out of it" tendencies that wrapped around her like a second skin in college, but I couldn't seem to help falling right back into my longtime position in the group. Even when I didn't particularly agree with her, it had always been easier to give in to Brittany. Or at the very least not get in her way. But as it happened, this time, I actually did agree with her, at least mostly. I could almost *see* the tension between Lydia and Brittany, a taut, fraying cord threatening to snap at any moment. If they got into a real standoff, I wasn't going to learn anything about the weekend Vanessa went missing. A destination might at least distract them briefly from the effort of pulling against each other. They might even chalk up any questions I had about that time to me trying to keep the conversation going, to give us that closure we'd all claimed we wanted to find, *Good old Emily just doing her best to move past the awkwardness.*

"A change of scenery, and something greasy to soak it all up," I said.

"You always loved a hangover feast." Brittany's eyes darted over me again and I had to force myself not to suck in my stomach. I didn't want a life of counting every calorie and snipping at friends for working out when I didn't feel like it. But watching her mentally weigh me still wasn't *fun.* "But food is probably a good idea. We can head into town for brunch. There's a great diner there, nothing fancy but all the locals love it. And there are lots of cute shops, we could make a morning of it."

"That sounds perfect," I said, stomach already growling at the prospect of eggs, hash browns, and toast sogging under a lake of butter. I felt tired more than hungover—the adrenaline in the middle of the night seemed to have burned off most of the booziness—but an escape from the tense fug of the winery would be *very* welcome, whether or not it loosened any tongues.

Paige emerged from the hallway swathed in spandex, tilting her head to one side as she worked an earbud into place.

"Paige, brunch? I promise it'll be even better for your hangover than running," Brittany said.

"Pass," Paige replied, not even looking over. Brittany's nostrils flared.

"Are you sure? We were just saying we could all use a reset. As a *group.*"

"Yup." Paige started stretching one hamstring, then the other. "Have fun."

And before Brittany could look for a new pressure point, she strode out the front door, appearing half a minute later through the floor-to-ceiling windows, jogging along the cliff's edge and out of sight. Brittany's eyes narrowed as she followed her progress. Clearly Lydia wasn't the only one who had changed. Paige still played second fiddle to Brittany most of the time, still clearly fished for approval with every rough-edged "joke," but she wasn't *totally* under her thumb anymore.

"Welp, just the three of us, I guess," I said, voice chirrupy. "Let me just run upstairs and grab my coat."

"Actually, I think I'll beg off too," Lydia said, slipping the dog-eared playing card between the pages of her book again and laying it down on the counter. A faded jester's head peeked out over the top.

"Oh come *on*, Lydia. Don't be that way." Brittany rolled her eyes. "I'm sorry I said psycho, okay? But you know I didn't mean anything by it."

"Thanks for that. But go on without me. I recharge best with alone time."

"Suit yourself," Brittany snipped, turning to me. "Well? Were you going to get your coat?"

Ten minutes later, I was tucked into the front seat of the ginormous Land Rover that Brittany had rented at the airport, the mood far less buoyant than it had been on our long drive to the winery. To think I'd thought I was feeling the strain of making conversation *then*.

Brittany huffed out a heavy breath as she whipped the car around the hairpin curves of the private road leading away from the winery, eyes perma-narrowed.

Part of me wished Lydia had been willing to join—the

standoff was only going to be that much more intense when we got back, and even if she hadn't contributed much to the conversation, at least the weight of the silence wouldn't have felt like it was *entirely* on my shoulders.

But a tiny spark of excitement lit beneath my rib cage as we crunched our way down the gravel drive. Whatever answers I was looking for on this weekend, I was certain now that Brittany would play a part in finding them. And the more I thought about it, the more I realized I had a much better chance of digging them up without Lydia around. When Brittany had her back up, she mistrusted everyone, saw shadowy alliances against her if you dared to so much as *hint* that her opponent might have a point, or even just a right to a differing opinion. But in the moments after a standoff she could be expansive, her need to detail her injuries and their flaws, to bind herself to whoever she was talking to with the cords of mutual disdain, spilling over into a general willingness to babble. It was like a video game character who packed a supercharged punch, but throwing it completely wiped their defense score for a certain amount of time, left them vulnerable to all manner of attacks.

Not that I was attacking. I just wanted some straight answers. And if that was a *titch* selfishly motivated, well . . . Brittany clearly had her secrets from the rest of us, too.

"Lydia seems to have gotten up on the wrong side of the bed," I ventured, gazing out the window at the towering firs, pines, and cedars huddling against the edges of the road that led into Verdana, the resort town in the valley that concentrated both the wine and woodsy tourism in this part of the state. Every so often a narrow path would shoot off between the trees, their thick, bushy boughs obscuring all but the briefest glimpse of what it led to. Considering the concentration of wealth in the area, odds were good it was a gorgeous lodge, a million-dollar (or more likely multi-million-dollar) backdrop to postcard-perfect family holidays and summer vacations.

"God, *right*?" Brittany rolled her eyes dramatically. "I know she's always been sensitive but like . . . maybe stop *trying* to find reasons to be offended all the time?"

I bit the inside of my cheek in an effort to keep my face neutral.

"Or at the very least realize that this weekend is bringing up a lot of stuff for *everybody,*" I offered. Brittany nodded vigorously.

"Seriously. Like . . . we all have bigger things to worry about than word policing. Lydia always makes everything about her."

"Speaking of, how are *you* doing?" I turned to Brittany, tenting my eyebrows in a show of concern. "I know you said you were okay last night, but . . . it was really weird seeing Vanessa's ring. I couldn't sleep for hours afterward thinking about it."

"Thanks . . ." Brittany's voice turned a bit vague, forehead clouding over as she stared through the windshield. I had to tread very, very carefully here.

"I mean, obviously it might not have been the same ring. It just looked *so* similar, don't you think?"

"Vanessa never took that necklace off," Brittany murmured. I couldn't help but notice that she hadn't denied the ring's provenance.

"It was her mom's, right?"

Brittany nodded.

"Family heirloom. Mitzi always said she shouldn't have given it to Lauren when she did."

"Oh? I thought it was Lauren's engagement ring."

"Not by *Mitzi's* choice." Brittany's eyes went wide. "Lauren and David sort of turned it into that after they ran off. His divorce was messy, I'm guessing his finances were tied up?" She shrugged. "If the guy can't even buy a ring, that *should* be a sign, you know? But yeah, the ring was in the family first. A great-great something on Mitzi's side."

"Was Mitzi not a fan of Vanessa's dad?"

"Oh, she *was* a fan. Back when he was married to her *dear* friend Bunny on the town beautification committee." She sniffed. "But after David decided to blow up a however many years' marriage by running off with her twenty-year-old daughter, the shine wore off for Mitzi. And for Bunny, his ex. God, you should have seen the looks that woman would give my grandmother at social functions."

I made a vaguely sympathetic sound, wheels turning in my head as the denser woods gave way to a straggle of smaller homes, dingy sixties-era motels, and convenience stores on the outskirts of town. Vanessa had alluded to the rift her mom had caused in the family by marrying her father, but she'd never mentioned that he'd previously been a family friend . . . of her grandparents. From what I could gather Mitzi and Topper were *very* set on the "right way" of doing things, in that claustrophobic old-money way that it was still hard for my deeply Midwestern brain to fully comprehend. There had been snobs where I'd grown up, sure, but that specific variety didn't seem to thrive in Minnesotan soils.

I could imagine their daughter not only causing a scandal, but spraying that shit *exactly* where they ate—defiling the *beautification committee* with it, no less—had not gone over well. I had a vague memory of some party in college, Vanessa past tipsy, verging on sloppy, just before some holiday break.

I'd pressed water on her, tried to cheer her up with the prospect of heading back home soon. She'd just laughed. *Not home, Mitzi and Topper's house. I haven't had a home since the crash.* She'd been so matter-of-fact about it, like she was talking about the weather, that I couldn't think what else to say. I'd filed it away as normal grief, part of losing her parents—of course nothing would feel like home again—but maybe it was more than that.

The motels lining the road were starting to shed a degree of shabbiness, charmingly woodsy storefronts replacing the tired-looking aluminum-sided convenience stores. I had a sense that once we parked the car and moved on to the pedestrian tasks of finding seats, looking at menus, sipping coffee, the flow of conversation between us would end, a tap twisted tight once more. But if I was ever going to understand what had happened to Vanessa—or even what might have—I needed to know more about her. She'd always been so . . . opaque, especially about her past. And the only person who could clear up that portion of the picture now was Brittany. It was now or never.

"I always got the sense that Vanessa didn't have much from her mom," I said, careful to keep my tone light. "But I don't think I ever asked her why."

"Because there was no money," Brittany said simply, starting to scan the streets for parking as we approached the center of town.

"What do you mean?"

"David and Lauren were *hugely* in debt. Lauren was cut off after what she did, obviously, but she just kept spending like it was all Monopoly money. At least that's how Topper told it. I remember him telling my dad at Sunday dinner that he'd have been on the line for the helicopter ride, too, if it hadn't crashed." Brittany glanced over at me. I was trying to keep the horror off my face, but clearly I was failing. "Trust me, I know. Topper had a *very* dark sense of humor." Brittany sighed heavily. "Anyway, I think most of their stuff got sold to help with the debts. I'm sure there were a few things here and there, a favorite book or some clothes or whatever, but by and large it all went. Vanessa used to say she had to steal the ring off her mom's body at the mortuary and hide it in her bra to make sure they wouldn't sell that too. Though I'm not sure there was actually any truth in that, I think she just said it to mess with me. She really only trotted it out after lights out at Montrose. The dorms there made these sounds at night, you know how old buildings settle? I swear it was exactly like footsteps above your head." Brittany shivered at the recollection of the boarding school she and Vanessa had both attended.

"God, that's so sad," I said, a tiny ache of sorrow squeezing my throat at the thought of Vanessa then, just a kid—she was only fourteen or fifteen when her parents died—with nothing to remember them by but a ring, shuttled off to live with grandparents she'd never met, and who, by all accounts, had made an active effort to ignore her existence up until that point. By the time we all met in college, she'd managed to reshape the tragedy, wearing it like some especially daring accessory, just one of the many proofs of Vanessa's interestingness, her depth. I'd been so young, self-absorbed in the way only near-adults can be, that I'd bought it. Hadn't even seen that this polished bit of dark beauty was actually just layer upon layer of scar tissue. The tragedy was always deliberately on display, in what I could now guess was Vanessa's heartbreaking attempt to control it, to make it something she got to wield instead of something that had happened *to* her.

Brittany angled the car into a space at the end of a long row, extra-wide to accommodate all the other ridiculously oversized SUVs I was starting to realize were de rigueur in Verdana. Her eyes dropped to her lap, hands still gripping the wheel as the car idled.

"It was sad. It *is* sad," she said, turning to me. Brittany looked troubled in a way I couldn't remember ever seeing her. Something about being back here—or seeing that ring—seemed to have put a hairline fracture in her polished shell.

"Back then I didn't see it—you know how Vanessa was, it was hard to ever feel *bad* for her. She made it impossible, really. And she was just so much, suddenly she was everywhere, living at my grandparents' house, going to my schools, taking tennis lessons with me at the club, and always somehow just *better* at all of it." Brittany shook her head, eyes fixing on a point on the horizon. "I didn't realize then how hard it all must have been for her. Mitzi and Topper stepped up, obviously, gave her a home, and an education, but . . . I don't think they ever loved her. I'm not sure they even liked her. She was just so much like Lauren, you know?"

"I don't think I ever learned much about Lauren, honestly."

Brittany flashed me a look of grim acknowledgment. *Of course you didn't.*

"I looked her up in one of my dad's yearbooks once, Mitzi and Topper didn't have *any* pictures of her around. She and Vanessa could have been twins." She huffed out a little laugh. "If you'd known Lauren, it would have been impossible to look at Vanessa and not see her mom." She paused a moment, nibbling at her lower lip. "Vanessa never wanted for anything, I know that, but . . . they weren't kind to her. When I think about something happening to Markus and me, the idea of Mason and Missy being treated that way, by *family* no less . . ." She shook her head, eyes glistening slightly, then sucked in a deep breath. "Anyway . . . they should have been better to her. But I'm getting maudlin. We're here for brunch, right?"

"Oh my god, give me *all* of it," I said, playing up the need. I recognized the punctuation Brittany was putting on the conversation, her heady need to disclose receding; trying to wrench the tap back open now would only put me on Brittany's list of possible enemies. We hopped down from the car and made our way to the diner, filling the next hour with eggs, home fries, and the sort of surface-level chatter you might make just as easily with a perfect stranger as a very old friend. Still, I couldn't shake off that tenderized ache at my center. Brittany was right, it had always been hard to feel sorry for Vanessa—the glib way she'd rattle off her own problems made pity seem faintly ridiculous. It was a defense mechanism, obviously, but at the time it had come across as so evolved, throwing your own worries into stark relief. If Vanessa could shrug off the death of both her parents, didn't your concerns about a midterm, sibling rivalries, a friend's catty remark seem a bit overblown, childish even?

But I'd met Mitzi and Topper back in the day. We all had—they hosted a homecoming tailgate outside the stadium every year, complete with a full top-shelf bar and trays and trays of "game day food" kept piping hot by a small catering staff. They were unflappably polite, Mitzi able to hold a conversation with anyone . . . except Vanessa. She'd toss off some sarcastic reply to one of Mitzi's seemingly endless conversation lubricators, or refill her own drink at the bar, or start flirting with a grad student hovering around the alum tailgates (everyone knew they were the far superior road to getting day drunk), and Mitzi's entire face would tighten just a fraction, so her eyes and cheekbones seemed to pop forward. Topper's annoyance was easier to read, all thunderous barks and opera buffa frowns. And all—only—for Vanessa. Brittany, just a few feet away, chatting easily with friends of her parents or grandparents, shrugging off her dad's mock scolds about drinking her bloody mary too fast, singing the school song along with Topper and friends, badly, got nothing but doting smiles and tender squeezes. She so clearly *fit* there, the third-gen update on the model that Mitzi and Topper had first improved upon with Brittany's father, Brian, that it was easy to forget that Vanessa came from the same source code. The lovelessness, the obvious sense that Vanessa was a duty that couldn't be avoided—what would people *think?*—must have been hard enough. But watching Brittany soak up all the sunshine while she withered in the cold shade of her family's affection . . . it must have eaten away at Vanessa, no matter how blasé she might act about it.

Brittany was drumming her manicured nails on the formica tabletop, shoulders down as she craned to spot our server, just over half of the egg white omelet she'd ordered congealing in front of her, when the deep voice, slightly roughened by age, boomed out behind me.

"That isn't Brittany Chisholm, is it?"

We both turned to look at the man picking his way around a gleaming chrome-and-pleather chair, beaming at Brittany. He had that perma-tanned, windblown look men sometimes get after fifty, his silver hair sweeping back from his wrinkled forehead in a leonine pompadour. His elbow-patched sweater and wide-waled corduroys were both a bit tatty with age, but the scarf around his neck was Burberry, and the giant watch hanging over his large hand was clearly expensive—together, it all screamed "old money on holiday." His broad chest and shoulders, and his light paunch, gave him the look of a man just nearing his golden years, still ruddy with health, but the cautious way he moved around the chairs, steps slow and small, hinted that he might be more advanced in age than he looked at first glance. I frowned as I took in the small circular wire-rimmed glasses, the wry curve of his fleshy lips. I couldn't place the man, but there was something extremely familiar about him. I was about to say as much when a wave of nausea washed over me, flooding my mouth with too much saliva. Hands shaking a bit, I reached for my water. Maybe I was more hungover than I'd realized. Luckily, Brittany was more than covering for me, bouncing out of the bench seat and moving to hug the old man at my shoulder.

"Niko? Oh my *god*!" She gave him a genuinely warm squeeze and he laughed, tottering slightly and gripping the top of the booth for support when she finally released him. "Dad didn't tell me you'd be in town!"

"We are here much more these days," he said with a dry chuckle. "I'm 'out to pasture,' as they say."

"That's not true, dear. You're only semiretired, more's the pity," a small voice behind him said. I only then noticed the petite woman in the puffer vest at his shoulder, neat white bob grazing her chin. Her skin had gone a bit crepey all over, but seeing them side by side, it was clear she was at least ten years younger than her husband.

"Are you still teaching at Queen Mary's?" Brittany asked, tilting her head to one side and blinking pleasantly at Niko. I recognized the gesture as Mitzi's, one of the dozens of tiny social cues she had in her arsenal to draw out whoever she was talking to.

"Just one class in the fall. They wouldn't let me go." He shrugged with mock modesty.

"He wouldn't have let them if they tried," his wife noted, a small smile curling her lips.

"Well, I think that's fantastic," Brittany said. "And clearly it's keeping you young."

"I don't know about *that*." He laughed, waving a hand through the air, but the sparkle in his eyes made it clear how much her comment had delighted him. "And what has brought you all the way out to Verdana at this time of year? Without your children?"

"Actually, I'm here to take stock at the winery," Brittany said, face falling a degree. "I'm not sure if you knew, Mitzi left it to me."

"Ahhh, of course. I'm so sorry for your loss, Mitzi was a fine woman," the man said, bushy brows lowering over his eyes.

"Thank you, Niko. She really was. Betsy, I know my dad so appreciated the flowers you two sent," she added. The petite woman nodded gently. "And I have my friends with me as a support system, thankfully." Her eyes flitted briefly to me and I forced a wan smile, stomach still churning.

"And will you keep it? The winery?"

"Well, that's what we're deciding. But knowing you're here more often these days is definitely a tick in the pro column," Brittany said, squeezing his shoulder. He gave another booming bass laugh.

"You are a flatterer. And of course we academics love flattery," he said with a wry little smile. "But I'm being rude," he said, turning to take me in. His eyes glittered with interest and intelligence, and that shock of familiarity went through me again. He thrust out a meaty hand. "Niko Stavros. I am an old friend of Brittany's grandparents."

"You remember Professor Stavros, don't you, Emily? He's

actually the one who tipped Mitzi and Topper off to Verdana in the first place."

I blinked, too shocked for a moment to take his hand, nausea surging again. I swallowed hard. *Don't vomit on the elderly professor, Emily.*

"Of course. I think I shopped one of your courses my sophomore year," I finally managed.

"But you did not take it?" He raised a bushy eyebrow.

"English major," I said, patting my chest. It did nothing to still the fluttering of my heart. "I realized pretty quickly that cellular biology was way over my head. But you might remember our friend Lydia Kehoe?"

God, what if Lydia had actually *been* at brunch with us? The thought brought on a new wave of anxiety. I could feel clammy sweat oozing through the pores of my back.

He frowned, then shook his head.

"No, that does not sound familiar. But then I'm an old man, bits of memory leak out when I'm not looking."

"I don't believe *that* for a second," Brittany said, tone mock scolding. "Anyway, there's no reason you'd remember Lydia. Wasn't she in the chemistry department? Or . . . what *did* Lydia major in?"

I blinked at Brittany, not quite believing that she'd so thoroughly erased the incident from her memory. I had been just a bystander, and thinking of it still brought a flood of shameful heat to my cheeks. The professor must not have noticed, though. He smiled avuncularly at Brittany. Behind him, his wife took his arm, squeezing lightly. He turned to her and nodded slightly.

"But we should leave you to get on with your day. It was so lovely to see you, my dear. Please send my best to your father."

"Of course. So good to see you, Niko. Next time I'm out here let's get dinner, yeah?"

"That would be lovely."

With one last squeeze of Brittany's hand, he tottered out, his wife subtly keeping hold of his elbow as they navigated the narrow corridor between the booths and tables.

"God, it's been years since I've seen Niko. Topper always got such a kick out of him. I think he pushed the rest of the board of overseers to give him tenure back in the day just because he enjoyed his company so much." Brittany blinked, then turned to me. "Anyway, what next? There's a great gift shop down the street, they sell the most adorable tea towels. And I wouldn't mind getting my manicure touched up, the spa in town is actually completely decent. And they do facials. I'm sure your skin is feeling dry from the plane?"

"Hmm?" Brittany was gazing pointedly at my chin, and I felt my hand drifting up reflexively. "Oh, umm . . . actually, there was a used book store I wanted to check out." It was a gamble. Judging from what I'd seen of this town so far, "used" might just be a euphemism for "priceless rare antiques," which Brittany would be far less likely to avoid. But I was breaking out in a clammy, nauseous sweat, and it was the only thing I could grasp at quickly that might scare her off.

Thankfully, her nose crinkled up exactly like I'd hoped it would.

"Why don't I catch up with you in half an hour or so? I can poke around all the dusty stacks while you get your manicure touched up, and we can find each other after?"

Brittany tilted her head back and forth, considering, then nodded.

"Okay, but if you change your mind, the spa is just at the end of the block. My treat!"

I smiled blandly, we finished paying the bill, and then I popped into the bathroom, the better to let Brittany sweep out the door without me.

Inside the narrow headshot-plastered stall I sucked in deep breaths, shaking my hands out to get rid of the nervous energy.

Niko Stavros. *Professor* Stavros. No wonder he'd looked so familiar.

And no wonder I was feeling so queasy. Guilt always did that to me.

BEGIN FLASHBACK

INT. VANESSA'S COLLEGE APARTMENT—DAY
(15 YEARS AGO)

The apartment is spacious, but a bit dingy,
the furniture in the common room clearly
secondhand. The walls are covered in eclectic junk-shop art, vintage hats and acces-
sories hanging between the paintings;
floating shelves bursting with quirky knick-
knacks, china, even a retro toaster that
somehow manages to come off bohemian chic
rather than cluttered or random; and an
array of Polaroid photos, broken up occasionally by larger, moodier prints. There's
a haphazard element to the decor that
shouldn't work but does, somehow. Overall,
it screams Vanessa.

Emily is on her back on the faded princess-
style sofa, the cushions upholstered in a
garish oversized hibiscus print, reading
Tristram Shandy, while Lydia sits on the
floor nearby, staring intently at the laptop
on the gigantic baroque coffee table domi-
nating the center of the room.

> LYDIA
> (visibly frustrated)
> Dammit . . . how are all of these
> already filled?

Emily closes the book and turns to Lydia,
clearly welcoming the break from her home-
work.

                    EMILY
          All of what?

                    LYDIA
          The med school internships. And
          all the chem department research
          assistant positions. Those only
          got posted *Wednesday*.

                    EMILY
          Oh, I meant to tell you, I heard
          the radio station is looking for
          interns.

Lydia flashes Emily an annoyed look.

                    LYDIA
          They're credit-only. I need some-
          thing *paid*.
                    (lowers voice)
          My mom has to start a new round
          of chemo in a few weeks, and
          she's already maxed out her in-
          surance for the year.

                    EMILY
                    (surprised)
          But *you're* not going to pay for
          all her treatment . . . ?

Lydia glares at Emily with a look approaching disgust. The camera frames them in a way
that makes the differences between the girls
more obvious: Lydia's scratched-up laptop,
several years old and wheezing under the
strain of prolonged use; the careless way
Emily tosses her book (clearly bought new)
to the ground; Emily's giant Coach tote,

gaping open at her elbow to reveal a riot of
items; Lydia's choppy, at-home haircut vs.
Emily's layered, highlighted strands.

> LYDIA
> I have to at least try to help
> out. It's not like she has anyone
> else. Plus, my scholarships don't
> totally cover tuition.

> EMILY
> Right . . .

Emily flushes, clearly embarrassed to have
been so obtuse. She's aware that Lydia
didn't have the same comfortably middle-
class upbringing that she did, but in an
abstract way. Emily's eyes light up as she
thinks of another option—she's clearly hoping to smooth over the awkwardness.

> EMILY (CONT'D)
> I could ask Alden if he and So-
> phie have found anyone to help
> out over the summer yet? I only
> just told him I'll be back in
> Minnesota.

Lydia sighs, pinching her eyes closed, then
shrugs. She's choosing to accept the olive
branch.

> LYDIA
> I mean . . . maybe if I can't find
> anything else. The fellowship I'm
> trying for requires academic work
> experience.

                    EMILY
          He *is* a professor.

                    LYDIA
          Of English. Besides, I don't
          think nannying is really what
          they're talking about.

Emily nods and turns back to her book as
Lydia hunches lower over the screen, clicking listing after listing on the college's
career portal site. Eventually she lets out
a strangled scream.

                    LYDIA
               (near tears)
          Dammit, I *knew* I should have
          started this earlier. I'm going
          to wind up working at fucking
          McDonald's.

Emily drops the book again and moves onto
the floor next to Lydia, sitting cross-legged
beside her and gently easing the computer
out from in front of her.

                    EMILY
          I don't think it's gonna come to
          that, but even if it did, would
          that be the worst thing? The pay
          isn't terrible. And not everyone
          gets internships.

                    LYDIA
          Everyone applying for the Miller
          fellowship does. You have to show
          "clear interest in contributing
          to Queen Mary College's ongoing

mission of advancing the borders
of academic discovery." Which the
counselor said means internships
or research assistant positions
on campus. But there are
like . . . five research assistant
positions for undergrads *total*.

> EMILY
> Okay, so then . . . the radio
> station maybe? I know it doesn't
> pay, but Vanessa's letting you
> stay here over the summer, right?
> You could do, like . . . two days
> a week and get another job to
> cover costs? Maybe save up a lit-
> tle for tuition?

Lydia shakes her head sharply.

> LYDIA
> I need to make more than that.

> EMILY
> Right. Okay, so . . . we keep
> looking, then.

She refreshes the page on the laptop, scrolls
for a moment, then squints at the screen.

> EMILY (CONT'D)
> Have you seen this one? It looks
> like it just posted an hour ago.

> LYDIA
> Which one?

                    EMILY
        "Research Assistant to Niko Stav-
        ros, Steptoe-Edwards Professor of
        Sciences . . ." It looks like
        it's in cellular biology?

Lydia snatches the laptop away. We hear a
door opening offscreen.

                    PAIGE (O.S.)
        Seriously? Chip's a total douche.

                    BRITTANY (O.S.)
        We could just avoid him. It's a
        big boat.

                    LYDIA
        Oh my god, this would be per-
        fect . . .

                    BRITTANY
        Is Vee here? I need to borrow one
        of her shirts.

She notices Lydia, eyes narrowing. She's
ninety-five percent sure that Lydia had something to do with the disappearance of her
new designer top. Brittany's never been
careful with her things, but lately, the
most expensive, newest items just seem to
vanish when she's not looking . . .

                    BRITTANY (CONT'D)
        The one I'd been planning to wear
        went missing in my last laundry
        pickup. You wouldn't know any-
        thing about that, would you,
        Lydia?

LYDIA
Hmm? Oh, uhh . . . no, sorry. Why
would I?

BRITTANY
Hmm.
(sucks in her lips)
So? Where's Vee?

EMILY
(distracted)
I think she went out.

Brittany crosses to a door in the far wall,
then frowns when she finds it locked. She
turns back to the room, obviously frustrated, as Lydia's forehead crumples.

LYDIA
It's too perfect. There are gonna
be so many people applying, I'll
never get it.

BRITTANY
Never get what?

EMILY
This research assistant position
in the biology department. But I
think you totally have a chance,
Lyds.

She squeezes Lydia's knee absently as Brittany crosses the room, bending to look over
Lydia's shoulder at the screen. Lydia's
eyes dart back to Brittany, body tensing a
little to find her there. The missing top,

along with a Chanel handbag and a handful of
other items, are all folded into a pile of
sweaters in her closet at the moment.

> BRITTANY
> Wait . . . *this* is the job you
> want? It's with Professor Stav-
> ros.

Brittany starts laughing. Lydia's jaw juts
defiantly.

> LYDIA
> What's wrong with that?

> BRITTANY
> There's nothing *wrong* with it.
> It's just weird to imagine you
> working for him. He's over at
> Mitzi and Topper's like . . .
> every other week.

Lydia's whole body goes alert, eyes wide
with barely repressed hope. She licks her
lips slowly. She's not used to asking people for help, or asking Brittany for *anything*.

> LYDIA
> You know him?

> BRITTANY
> Yeah, since like . . . forever.

> LYDIA
> Do you . . . think you could in-
> troduce me?

Brittany considers for a long moment. She's still convinced Lydia's been fucking with her recently. But this could be a chance to gain the upper hand in their ongoing mostly cold war . . .

>   BRITTANY
> I mean, sure, I guess. He'll
> probably be at their garden party
> this weekend.

>   LYDIA
> Perfect. That's perfect. I can
> put in my application now,
> there's no way he'll have picked
> someone before the weekend . . .

You can see the wheels turning, her eyes shiny, a half smile cracking her stoic features for the first time.

>   BRITTANY
> You want us to go to my grandpar-
> ents' garden party just so you
> can meet *Niko*?

Lydia closes her eyes, swallowing hard. Her hands are in tight fists at her side, the struggle to keep her composure evident.

>   LYDIA
> Please, Brittany. I know it's a
> lot to ask but . . . it would
> mean a lot to me.

>   BRITTANY
> I mean, I hadn't planned to

> go . . . And there's this booze
> cruise that night . . .

Brittany folds her arms across her chest.
Lydia's practically vibrating with need.
Brittany's lips twist triumphantly as she
watches the other girl—it's clear she's enjoying being the one who holds the cards.
Emily catches Brittany's eye, raising an
eyebrow in a signal to get on with it. Brittany sighs and spreads her arms wide.

>   BRITTANY (CONT'D)
> *Fine*. I guess there are worse
> places to pregame. We can go if
> it's like . . . *that* important to
> you.

Lydia's relief is palpable. She nods rapidly. Just then the door opens again and
Vanessa enters, looking artfully dishev-
eled.

>   LYDIA
> That's awesome. Thank you so
> much. I'll make it up to you, I
> swear.

>   VANESSA
> What's awesome?

>   PAIGE
> I guess we're pregaming at your
> grandparents' garden party this
> weekend.

Vanessa tilts her head back and forth, considering, then shrugs. Why not?

> VANESSA
> Lyds, are you okay? You look a
> little tense.

> LYDIA
> No, I'm fine. Just busy.

Vanessa absently squeezes her shoulder as she makes her way to her bedroom. Emily looks up, clearly hoping to be acknowledged herself, but Vanessa breezes past. A whisper of hurt passes over Emily's face. Brittany rolls her eyes as Vanessa unlocks the bedroom door.

> BRITTANY
> You seriously lock the door when
> you're gone?

> PAIGE
> (snickering, watching Brittany)
> What do you expect, burglars
> after your old T-shirts or some-
> thing?

> VANESSA
> The fact that you know I lock it
> is exactly *why* I lock it.

Brittany's lips purse. She's fuming but can't come up with a retort.

> VANESSA (CONT'D)
> Was there something you wanted,
> Brittany?

> BRITTANY
> To borrow a shirt.

Brittany barely gets the words past her pinched lips. Vanessa assesses her, face twisting into a wince.

> VANESSA
> Mmm . . . yeah, that's gonna be a no.

> BRITTANY
> Seriously? Why?

> VANESSA
> You treat your own things like crap. Weren't you just bitching about some Comme des Garçons top you lost? Why would I let you do that to mine?

Brittany's forehead clouds, eyes narrowing to slits. She glances around the room, fixing on Lydia.

> BRITTANY
> You know what? I don't think the garden party's going to work out after all.

> LYDIA
>   (distraught)
> What? Why?

Vanessa's eyes dart back and forth between Lydia and Brittany. She's not clear *why* this party matters to Lydia, only that it clearly does.

                    BRITTANY
          Paige and I already have plans
          that night.

                    PAIGE
          Seriously, who wants to miss a
          booze cruise to hang out with a
          bunch of olds?

                    VANESSA
          So push your plans a little
          later. You're usually all about
          being fashionably late.

                    BRITTANY
          Did you not hear Paige? It's a
          cruise, you *can't* show up late.

                    PAIGE
          Right? What would we do, swim out
          to the boat?

Paige snickers while Vanessa and Brittany
stare at each other, locked in a battle of
wills. Then Vanessa's eyes dart back to
Lydia, whose face is sliding toward despair.

                    VANESSA
          What shirt did you want, Brit?

                    BRITTANY
          The French Connection wrap top.

                    VANESSA
          I think that's clean. Let me
          check.

She moves toward the door, fiddling with the lock as she continues to talk, eyes fixed on Brittany's. It's clear from the look on both their faces that this is a negotiation.

> VANESSA (CONT'D)
> For what it's worth, I think we should go to the garden party. Free booze, free food. Plus, Mitzi will love showing you off. She'll probably give you a shopping spree out of gratitude.

> BRITTANY
> I don't know. It would be tight to make the booze cruise after.

> VANESSA
> Isn't Chip's frat hosting that? He's such a creep.

Paige's eyes dart between Brittany and Vanessa. Though she's usually reliably in Brittany's corner, she's definitely not immune to Vanessa's influence. And Brittany is clearly considering Vanessa's words.

> PAIGE
> He is kinda gropey . . . but he won't be the only guy there.

> VANESSA
> Still, it's not like there's anywhere to go on a boat.

Brittany considers her for a long moment, then raises an eyebrow, tilting her head to the side with a tiny shrug. "Fine."

> BRITTANY
> I suppose if we pregame at Mitzi
> and Topper's the booze cruise
> isn't as important. And they *will*
> have better liquor.

> VANESSA
> Miles better. Plus, it's usually
> a cash bar on a booze cruise.

Paige is clearly relieved to be able to see which way the wind's blowing again. She sniffs exaggeratedly.

> PAIGE
> Seriously? Fuck that.

> BRITTANY
> Mitzi and Topper's it is, then.
> So? Is the top clean or not?

Brittany pushes past Vanessa through the open bedroom door, crossing to a clothing rack and rifling through it. Before she follows, Vanessa turns to Lydia and flashes her a quick thumbs-up. Lydia, blinking against a film of tears, mouths *Thank you* at Vanessa before she disappears into the bedroom, Paige trailing behind. Lydia's eyes linger on the door frame for a moment, a dazed, hero-worshipping look on her face as she fights to get her emotions under control. Finally she turns back to the laptop and starts typing furiously. Emily reaches over to give Lydia's shoulder a reassuring squeeze.

                    EMILY
          See? It's all gonna work out.
          That fellowship is as good as
          yours.

Lydia allows herself a tiny smile. Emily
returns to the couch, picking up her book
again, and the other girls' voices are
barely audible from Vanessa's room, so no
one seems to notice the intensity of Lydia's feeling.

                    LYDIA
               (under her breath)
          Maybe you're right . . . maybe
          for once things will work
          out . . .

6

"SO ARE YOU GOING TO TELL ME WHAT'S UP?"

I startled, turning away from the blur of dense foliage rolling steadily past the car window.

"What do you mean?" I did my best to make my voice light, digging my fingernails into the side of my far thigh in an attempt to gain some equilibrium. My entire body felt like it had been switched to static, skin buzzing, a dull roar filling my ears. But until I knew more, I couldn't let Brittany see that. I couldn't let *anyone* see it.

"You've been weird since brunch, Em." Brittany tilted her chin down, eyes darting over to me behind her oversized sunglasses, the tiny gold letters spelling out CHRISTIAN DIOR along the sidebar winking in the dappled sunlight filtering into the car.

"Sorry, just . . . a blast from the past, you know?" I swallowed hard, searching for the right words, trying to ignore the siren blare of *danger, danger, danger*. But from whom? My mouth flooded with saliva and I swallowed again, closing my eyes as I tested out the true—but deeply inadequate— statement: "This weekend is bringing up a lot of stuff I didn't expect."

Brittany stuck out her lower lip, reaching over with one hand to pat my leg. Through sheer effort of will I managed not to flinch.

"I hear you. Do you want to talk about it?"

"No." The word bulleted out before I could stop it. I winced, fear spiking through me again. Hopefully the expression would come off as apologetic. "I don't even know what I'd talk about. Honestly, it's probably just the hangover making me feel maudlin."

Brittany nodded and pulled her hand away.

I pulled out my phone, fingers autopiloting me to *Deadline*. I at least ought to *look* busy. If Brittany tried another conversation with me, she'd probably notice that I was far too twitchy for the hangover mauds to explain away. And if she started asking about what had happened while we'd split up . . . I considered myself a passable liar, but Brittany had an Olympic-level ability to sniff out bullshit. And I was too unsettled to pretend I was anywhere near top form right now. Hopefully she was focused enough on the road that she couldn't see my hands shaking.

I clicked over to the acquisitions section of the industry news website, scrolling idly through the announcements of various production companies' "new" book options that had to be months old already, streamers purchasing the distribution rights to this or that festival darling, plans to attach so-and-so to the remake of such-and-such. All of it was blurring past, an undifferentiated mass of other people's achievements, my mind still stuck in that café, on who I'd seen there. I was already scrolling past when the name in one of the headlines caught my eye.

I blinked, moving back up the page. There it was, in black and white:

Flickpix Orders 13-Episode Series of "Monkey See," Twisty Thriller from Lark Weeks

Lark. One of the handful of writers originally staffed on *Back of House* with me, her openly hungry brand of networking grating from minute one. Still, we'd bonded over being the two token women (not coincidentally both at the very bottom of the writing ladder) in an otherwise all-male room, moaning about how little respect we got over happy hour drinks, spinning each other fantasies of the features we'd sell and the shows we'd run someday. She'd managed to claw out a script supervisor credit before me, and she'd jumped ship after season two for a story lead job on *Clans,* a medieval melodrama that had seemed like a guaranteed loser at the time—I could still remember the catty conversations I'd had with all my other writer friends about how her naked ambition was finally going to bite her in the ass—until the post-*Game of Thrones* vacuum seemed to raise the tide for all vaguely-epic-maybe-fantasy boats.

Since then, she'd always been a step ahead of me—maybe because I'd continued marching in place at *BoH* while she'd skipped from show to show—and while not all of her moves had been successes, enough had that she'd managed to cobble together a reputation as a bit of a wunderkind.

I clicked open the article, jaw pulsing it was clamped so tight.

. . . new series is a brilliant puzzle box mystery set in a research laboratory . . .

. . . executive producer Marco Cisneros won a bidding war to bring the project to Flickpix . . .

. . . creator Weeks has previously struck gold with Parsed, a soapy limited series set in the world of academia. Cisneros told

*Deadline he was certain this series "would be an even bigger
success, the kind of show everyone's talking about for years to
come."*

Not just a pilot, an entire series order for *Lark*. A woman
whose episodes of the schlocky sitcom we'd both started at *I'd*
had to polish for her, not that she'd ever thanked me, or god
forbid owned up to the pre-revision-notes revision to the rest
of the room. A fucking hack who had managed to turn white
male levels of confidence into . . . well, a white-male-level career.

"*Fuck.*"

"Bad news?"

I startled, momentarily having forgotten where I was. Still,
the acid burn of Lark's success seemed to have cut through
some of the jittery fog I'd been suspended in since the startling encounter in the café.

"Just work stuff."

Brittany nodded, accepting my explanation as I turned to
the article again, hate-reading it a second time, a third, fingers curling into claws as the news of Lark's continued success sank deeper and deeper into my psyche.

That should be me.

But it never would be if I just kept hacking away at *Back of
House*. Even Lucy only ever offered up similarly insipid sit-
coms as alternate paths at this point. I mean, a showrunner
gig would be impressive, but *Marley and the Men*? Really?

I had to finish this script.

The thought had never landed with such feral desperation
before. But it was true. I needed to find a way out—now—
needed to make something better, smarter, *mine*. The alternative . . . well, it was rapidly becoming unthinkable.

Which meant I had to shake off the anxiety of the last few hours—after all, it was only that intense because I *was* finding things under the rocks I was turning over, creepy, skittering things I'd told myself I was ready to see but whose touch I still dreaded viscerally—and focus on what I came here for. I knew now that *I* hadn't done anything to Vanessa—*Try to capture the feeling of calm that brings you, channel it into the tips of your fingers, let it spread up to the roots of your hair.*

All that was left was finding out what had happened, what everyone else was hiding. Simple, right?

Before long, we were crunching to a stop outside the entrance to the tasting room. I took my time getting out of the car, sucking in a few deep breaths before opening the door. I couldn't let the encounter in town throw me, at least not visibly. It had left me more certain than ever that one of these women—maybe all of them—were holding on to past resentments, long-buried secrets that might help unravel the mystery of what had really happened fifteen years ago. And if I didn't find those answers now, I might never finish this story. Fuck, I might wind up stuck on *BoH* until the end of its run, a prospect that actually made me shudder. I couldn't let what was happening here get me so rattled that I lost track of what was at stake.

Inside, Lydia had migrated to one of the cavernous over-stuffed leather chairs near the wall of windows, their spare, crisp lines framing a moodier landscape than we'd left behind that morning. Clouds were starting to roll in from over the ocean, like a thick woolen blanket slowly but inexorably being drawn up over the land, dragging the sea with it. They had sieved out the golden quality of the light from earlier in the day, turning the whole scene steely and harsh, as though some otherworldly director had slipped a bleakness filter over the lens. You could practically see static in the air.

On the opposite side of the room, Paige was leaning on the breakfast bar, clicking regularly at her phone, one stockinged foot tapping a muffled rhythm against the wide planks of the floor. She had showered and changed into faded jeans and an oversized cable-knit sweater, a soft-edged flannel peeking out at the collar and hem, but the quintessential cabin coziness of her sartorial choices only highlighted the barely restrained nervous energy radiating off her. Her eyes darted up as we walked in and she dropped the phone, drumming her fingers rapidly along the edge of the marble countertop.

"You're back," Paige said. Lydia looked up at that, slipping a playing card into the pages of her book and laying it on a nearby table. The chair was so large, and she'd folded her petite frame up so completely, legs tucked up beneath her, that she looked almost surreal, like she was halfway through the process of slipping through the cushions to some alternate Alice in Wonderland dimension.

"I was starting to think you'd gotten lost," Paige added. She moved around the edge of the counter with tight, quick steps, filling a glass at the sink, drinking about a quarter of it, then dumping the rest before returning to her previous position, clicking the phone to life for a moment, then clicking it dark just as fast. I had to force my shoulders not to rise to my ears as she started tapping her foot again, faster this time, covertly dancing her own private tarantella, though to exorcise what, I couldn't guess.

"We asked if you wanted to come," Brittany said, the slightest hint of annoyance creeping into her tone. True to form, though, it seemed to roll right off Paige. She'd always had especially thick armor against the passive aggression that was practically a native tongue for Brittany.

"What took so long?"

"We were just poking around. I got a manicure, Emily wanted to drop into the Goodwill."

"Verdana has a Goodwill?" Lydia raised an eyebrow, incredulous.

"I don't know. Isn't that where you said you were going, Emily?"

It took me a beat to realize Brittany was expecting an answer from me.

"Oh, umm . . ." I blinked, trying to order my thoughts. *Stop worrying the encounter like a sore fucking tooth and focus. You only have* more *questions that need answers now.* Easier said than done. "She means the used book shop."

Brittany shrugged it off, *same difference,* and crossed to the fridge, carefully selecting a kombucha. It was my chance to steer things away from town, away from the unexpected meeting that, try as I might to stifle it with the threat of more years of *BoH* writers' room misery, still had my brain sparking crazily.

"Where did you run, Paige?" I asked, bending over the island in what I hoped looked like a languid, unbothered pose. If I planted my elbows firmly, it stopped my hands from shaking.

"Just a couple miles along the coast and back. I was too hungover for a real run. Once I saw another house, I turned around." She turned to Brittany. "That reminds me, how big *is* the property? I don't think I ever asked before."

"Somewhere around three hundred acres?" Brittany scrunched her nose, thinking. "Maybe more. I know when Topper bought the winery back in the nineties, land nearby was cheap. Most people don't really want to build and maintain their own roads. And of course *he* wanted to make sure people couldn't start crowding in around us and ruin this." She gestured vaguely at the Wagnerian views through the windows.

"And they left all of that directly to *you*? Jesus." Paige pulled an exaggerated look of shock. "What did your dad do to piss them off?"

"He didn't *piss anyone off*," Brittany said tartly, propping herself up with a hand on the counter as she sipped her kombucha. "Most of the estate went to him. The family home, their portfolios, the condo in Palm Beach . . ." She ticked each chunk of however many millions off on her fingers, as though she were talking about a grocery list. I'd known Brittany grew up wealthy—we'd all been to garden parties at Mitzi and Topper's mansion, spotted the labels in the clothes Brittany left balled up on the floor of her stunning college apartment—but I don't think I'd ever really realized the *magnitude* of it. Back then, coming from my comfortably middle-class family in Minnesota, the gradations of wealth had been totally lost on me, my mind only capable of processing a single bright line over which the rich existed—and at Queen Mary, there were always plenty of people happy to let you know they'd made it over that line. The not-really-a-joke on campus was that each class was roughly half financial aid students of varying degrees, and half high-donor legacy admits, a delicate balance that always managed to tilt in the endowment's favor.

Now I knew better. There was rich and there was *rich*.

"So what, this is the token inheritance?" Paige said. "Because in that case I'm really gonna need you to set up a weekend at the Palm Beach place."

"It's not *token,* obviously." Brittany rolled her eyes in mild exasperation. "My family has just been lucky enough to do well for themselves, and the plan was always to spread that around. Mitzi always said she didn't want her grandchildren to have to struggle when they were young when there was always going to be an inheritance coming eventually. And my dad felt the same way."

A strangled snort came from the depths of the leather chair. Brittany's eyes narrowed as they darted over to Lydia, who was already reaching for a Kleenex I had a feeling she didn't really need.

"*Bless* you," Brittany said. Lydia murmured a thanks.

"Anyway, the winery was their way of ensuring that Markus and I—and the kids—had a nest egg. Though I think Topper hoped we'd never sell. He always loved the idea of leaving a legacy behind. And I think he felt like a winery that went back to your *grandfather* instead of your father was just . . . nicer." Brittany's gaze drifted to the windows, a small smile curling her lips. "Besides, he always said my dad's palate was abominable. He had us both do a blind tasting when I was maybe sixteen just to rag on Dad."

"But I thought you said you inherited this place alone," Lydia said, her expression unreadable.

"That's right," Brittany confirmed.

"Sorry, maybe I missed something." Lydia frowned, the confusion on her face very convincing . . . though I had a feeling I shouldn't quite believe it, especially since it was being directed toward Brittany. "You said they wanted to make sure their *grandchildren* had a good start in life, right? Were there other properties that went to the other grandkids?"

"There weren't any other grandkids," Brittany said simply. "I'm an only child. Vanessa was, too. And, well . . . it's not as though she's here to split this . . ."

I was trying to parse the exact nature of the clouds rolling over Brittany's forehead, but Paige's barking scream of frustration startled them away too quickly.

"Do we *have* to keep bringing up Vanessa? I mean *fuck,* isn't being here hard enough without constantly talking about her?"

"But . . . that's why we're here," I ventured, keeping my tone carefully neutral. "I thought we all wanted this. Some closure. A chance to really work through what happened back then."

"Yeah, well, constantly picking at the scab isn't really doing it for me," Paige spat. "Keep torturing yourselves all you want, but just . . . leave me out of it, okay?"

"Paige, I don't think anyone—" Brittany had that same wide-eyed hostage negotiation tone I'd heard her use on her kid, but Paige was clearly less susceptible to it. With a grunt, she snatched up her phone and stomped out the front door, its punctuating slam heavy enough to rattle the vases on the occasional table just inside. We were all still suspended in shocked silence when she appeared through the windows, walking fast toward the cliffs, then pacing along the edge jerkily, her whole body rigid with tension. I considered heading out after her, asking what was really going on. Paige had always been a very . . . *external* person, more than happy to air whatever was running through her mind, especially if there was a chance it would gain her points with her audience. It was like she was constitutionally incapable of turning over her thoughts and feelings inside her own head, only able to process them once they'd emerged into the world, and the more agitated she was, the truer that became. She was a discloser, which could be good from a friendship standpoint— Paige didn't deal in passive aggression, and there was never any doubt as to where you stood with her—but the flip side was that she treated other people's information with the same "better out than in" mentality as her own. If there was anything beyond simple grief behind her little outburst, it wouldn't take much to figure out the details, regardless of whose details they truly were.

After a few turns she stopped in front of the staircase, its spindly rails barely visible against the gloomy gray of the water beyond, hands on her hips, one leg jiggling rapidly, then, with a determined forward thrust of her shoulders, she stepped onto the platform, disappearing down the vertiginous switchback staircase that clung to the cliff. The idea of following her down it brought on an actual, physical shudder. If I was going to get more out of Paige, it would have to wait for the moment.

"Talk about an overreaction," Brittany muttered.

"Not everyone has to feel what you feel, Brittany," Lydia said, chin jutting defiantly as she stared at Brittany. Brittany's eyes narrowed, jaw tightening, as she decided how to respond.

If I didn't get this train back on the rails, everyone would change their flights and hightail it out of here before dinner. And all the strange things that had happened since we'd arrived had only whetted my need to find some sort of answer to the puzzle of Vanessa's disappearance. I needed to keep us all on track, and as important, *together*.

"Either way, I'm guessing Paige might be a while," I said, too fast, voice chirpy with the effort to blow aside the thick, curdling atmosphere in the room. I took a deep breath, steadying myself. "And she'd probably appreciate some space when she gets back."

"I think we're more likely to need the space," Brittany said.

"Paige can be such a time bomb sometimes, it's like zero to emotional explosion."

I could see Lydia's eyebrows dropping, lips parting slightly as she formulated her next riposte.

"Which is totally fine, people process differently," I said rapidly. "But it might be better for everyone if she just works through some of it on her own, right?" I turned to Lydia expectantly. "I'm sure no one wants a big blowout."

She sucked her upper lip between her teeth, eyes narrowing slightly as she considered the statement, then gave a small nod. I exhaled, shoulders dropping with relief. It would have been hard to argue *for* creating a powder keg, but still, it felt like a win.

"What are you suggesting?" Lydia said. "I'm not sure driving away and leaving her here is exactly better."

"No, for sure. I'm not saying we should all leave. But maybe we could . . ." I blinked, casting around for a plan, then my eyes caught on one of the several empty wine bottles, neatly lined up against the edge of the counter. "We could tour the cellars!"

Dial it down, Em, this isn't a children's show.

"I don't think we did when we were here last time, and they sound pretty incredible. They're natural caves, right?"

"That's right. Or at least mostly. There's been a lot of work over the years to expand and connect them all, obviously, but most of the caves were naturally formed," Brittany said.

"Lydia, are you in? I know this is hard for everyone—and you and Vanessa were so close," I added, cutting off her path to a quick refusal. "But it's okay to try to take our minds off all that, at least for a while. Honestly . . . I think it's a lot healthier. Working through all of this is a marathon, not a sprint, you know?"

I swallowed down the overwhelming hypocrisy of that statement, focusing on injecting the exact right level of let's-be-friends pleading that had always served me so well as the group's de facto mediator.

"It would be interesting to see the caves," Lydia finally conceded, eyes dropping to her knees. "We should shoot Paige a text, though. So she doesn't feel left out."

"Totally." I pulled out my phone, tapping rapidly. "Done and done."

"In that case, we should all grab layers. It's chilly down there." With a tight smile, Brittany strode off up the stairs, not turning to add, "I'll meet you in the tasting room."

Ten minutes later, we were clustered at the front corner of the tasting room, Lydia hanging back slightly as Brittany held on to the handle of the door helpfully labeled CELLAR ENTRANCE.

"Ready?"

"Yup!" I smiled as widely as I could muster. "Paige said to go on without her."

Brittany nodded, typed in a series of numbers on the keypad next to the door, and opened it onto a wide stairwell, its rubber-treaded stairs and gleaming, fire-code-approved handrails worlds away from the narrow flights I'd crept down last night. She flipped a series of switches just inside, pulled out her phone to silence the *Perimeters have been breached* notification, then stood back, ushering us forward with a hand. A miasma of cold, musty air enveloped me the moment I stepped onto the first stair, and I shivered slightly.

We emerged into a large room lined with barrels, a phalanx of floor-to-ceiling shelves just near the entrance filled with hundreds of bottles, each section labeled by varietal and vintage. A dingy laminated sign had been strung across the farthest cubby, DO NOT POUR WITHOUT MANAGER APPROVAL. Presumably the tasting room's stores, then.

Brittany emerged last, moving past us to stand between the entrance and the amoeba-like expanse of the cave opening up beyond it.

"Welcome to the Cliff's Edge cellars. Right now we're standing in the original cave on the property, first discovered by Phillip Rosemont in 1919." Brittany spread her arms game-show-hostess wide. "Today we use it as our main aging room for our larger-production wines. Which are still fairly exclusive, we only produce about four thousand cases of the flagship pinot each year, and the numbers for our single vineyard offerings go way down from there. If this were the real tour, I'd pull open a couple barrels and let you taste the vintages side by side with one we've already released, but . . ." Brittany shrugged. "You can use your imagination. Just imagine what we drank last night, but less complex and brighter."

Brittany tilted her head toward the wall—it must be the side of the cave that faced the sea, unless I'd gotten totally turned around—and started drifting backward, gesturing as she went.

"The cave system opens up from the eastern half of the room, but first I want to show you something just over here." She stopped about thirty feet away, folding her hands primly in front of her as she waited for Lydia and me to approach. It wasn't until I was almost on top of her that I saw the narrow opening between the barrels lining the western wall of the cave, just a few inches taller than Brittany in her heeled boots, the rock of the arch and the narrow corridor behind it full of small irregular angles, as though it had been chipped away by hand. Once we were in front of her, Brittany ducked down the passageway to a large, bank-vault-style metal door at the back.

"This is the original entrance to the caves. Not the door, obviously. That's been updated at least a couple times over the past century. But Rosemont's discovery of the entrance itself was the first step toward the winery we've built today."

Brittany turned to the door, flipping a series of deadbolts and turning a steampunk wheel at the center until a loud click echoed through the small passage. Standing back, she pulled it open, pressing herself against the stone wall and beckoning to us to move closer.

The door opened up on . . . nothing. For a moment, all I could see was the dingy batting of the clouds, stitched tight to the liquid steel of the ocean below at the very bottom of the frame. A cold sea breeze swept in through the door, ruffling the hair at the sides of my face, and my breath caught in my throat. Tentatively, I took a step forward, only then registering the strips of weathered wood that made up the handrail to the staircase Paige had scurried down earlier. It seemed to solidify as I crept forward, the platform beneath, half a foot below the opening in the rock, materializing with each shuffling step. It was at least six feet wide, the planks broad and obviously sturdy, but even the thought of stepping out onto them made my stomach do a tight little flip. I craned my neck ever so slightly, trying to get a sense of how far down it was to the beach, but I could only catch the tiniest glimpse of the far corner of the dock before the totally exposed view brought on a wave of dizziness and I had to pull back, breathing hard.

"Do people still . . . *use* this entrance?" I murmured, inching back a bit farther, arms pressed full length against the cave wall, my body needing physical reassurance that I was still on solid ground.

"Not really. You can't even unlock it from the outside. But the stairs are the fastest way to get down to the beach, so guests sometimes choose to open it during their stays."

"And it's safe?" Lydia moved past me to the opening, reaching through to run a hand along the side rail. "Doesn't wood rot this close to the ocean?"

"Inferior wood does, of course. But the staircase and dock are both made of *cumaru*." Brittany enunciated exaggeratedly, the way I imagined she spoke to non-native English speakers. "It's an extremely durable varietal. It costs more up front, of course, but long-term it's the better investment."

Lydia took a tentative step onto the platform and tested the rail with a harder press of her hand, scanning the horizon until her gaze hooked on something about halfway across the panorama. When she turned back to face us, her body briefly blocked the railings behind her, making it look like she was floating in midair.

"Wouldn't the police have spotted a staircase up from the beach?" she said. "During the rumrunning, I mean."

"Back then, they used a rope ladder and pulleys," Brittany said. "And eventually, Rosemont explored the cave system further. It actually runs through all the way down to the shoreline."

"Speaking of, should we ... get on with the tour?" I squeaked, sidestepping again, eager to give Lydia space to get inside. Her mouth twisted in a wry smile as she stepped back through the opening. Once Lydia was past her, Brittany pushed the weighty door closed, flipping and twisting with satisfying metallic clicks. I exhaled a shaky breath.

"Not big on heights?" Lydia murmured, still smiling softly.

"Yeah, no." I shook my head hard. "Very emphatic no."

"Don't worry, the rest of the tour is going to be very much indoors," Brittany said, swishing past us back into the main room. "This way."

We made our way around a natural rock divide to the eastern half of the large cavern, weaving between stacks of barrels until we'd arrived at the top of the tunnel that I'd crept down last night. I made a show of gazing around at the aging wines, the curves of the walls and ceilings, *Gosh what an interesting cave that I've definitely never been inside before.*

"Originally, the tunnel behind me was just a couple feet wide at the narrowest parts. In the early days, Rosemont and his fellow rumrunners molded a false wall out of plaster to slot into that section of the tunnel. They painted the ocean-facing side to match the surroundings; unless you had a very powerful light, and were *looking* for the seams, you'd never know it wasn't real."

"Innovative," Lydia murmured. "God, it still looks so . . . tight," she added, biting her lower lip as she gazed along its length.

"That's just compared to the room we're in. It's hard to tell underground, but the ceilings in here are nearly two stories tall." Brittany's smile didn't reach her eyes. "The tunnel has been widened over the years. It's tall enough for the equipment we need to move the barrels. It's also given us access to several additional smaller caves, I'll show you as we pass them—we can control the temperature more precisely in those, which lets us do some really interesting things during the aging process—and at the bottom, well . . . it's better if I just show you."

Brittany started off down the tunnel, me dutifully falling in

behind her, but when I turned around, Lydia was still standing at the entrance to the larger chamber, shoulders heaving
as she sucked in deep breaths.

"Lyds, are you coming?" I tilted my head down the tunnel.
Hearing me, Brittany stopped and turned back, jaw tightening at the sight of Lydia frozen in place.

"I thought I would be okay, but it's so long, and the walls
just look . . . I think . . ." She pinched her eyes tight, shaking
her head rapidly and folding her arms around her narrow
figure. "It's too . . ."

I hurried back along the tunnel, placing an arm on Lydia's
shoulder. Her face was screwed up painfully, breath coming
much too fast.

"Lydia, what's going on?"

"I think I'm having . . . maybe a panic attack?" She opened
her eyes the tiniest sliver. "It's just being under the ground . . .
everything pressing in on us from every side, I didn't realize it
would feel so . . . oh god, it's like something's squeezing my
lungs." Her eyes went wide with panic and she gripped my
arm, her legs seeming to go out from under her. "I have to get
out of here. I'm sorry, I have to get out of here."

"Come on, this way." I threaded my arm under her shoulders, half-lifting her tiny frame around the barrels and past
the hatch opening to the door we'd come through. Still supporting her, I tugged it open. When she saw the stairs behind,
the hint of daylight coming in through the door Brittany had
left open at the top, she heaved in a sob-shaky breath.

"Thank you. I'm sorry, I just . . ."

"Nothing to be sorry about, just go lie down. Do you need
me to walk you up?"

"No, I'll be okay." Determinedly, she untangled herself
from me, stumbling to the staircase and leaning heavily on

the railing. "It's already a little better. It's just like . . . it's like being buried alive, you know?"

I offered a weak smile. I hadn't particularly needed that image. I watched while Lydia hauled herself up to the first landing. At the top she turned, a bit of color returning to her face, and made a shooing motion.

"Go, I'm fine."

"Are you sure?"

A ghost of her wry smile flickered over her face.

"I'm sure. Go before Brittany loses her shit. That's the only thing either of us *really* needs to be afraid of, right?"

With that she turned the corner to continue her ascent into the tasting room, and I headed back to the top of the tunnel, where Brittany was waiting with narrowed eyes.

"What was that all about?"

"Claustrophobia, I guess. She just said she needed to get out of here."

I could see Brittany's eyes drifting toward the exit. I couldn't let her stop this now; between the encounter in town, and her strange behavior with the necklace last night, I was absolutely *certain* she knew something important. Something tied to these caves—why else would she have crept down here in the middle of the night, burrowed all the way through the hillside to the cave that opened onto the beach? Lydia's leaving was actually a gift—Brittany was always so primed for a battle with Lydia that it left her on permanent defense. With Lydia gone, Brittany might let her guard down slightly, let something slip that she didn't mean to. Especially if she saw me as her ally against the annoyance that shrouded Lydia in her mind. Brittany was a devout follower of the "Common enemies make us friends" belief system. Rag on the right person, at the right time, and she seemed to trust you implicitly.

"I don't know why she said she'd come when she clearly didn't want to be here," I said, trying to match the vocal fry women seemed to reserve for shit-talking one another. "Though I guess she *could* have just developed severe claustrophobia in the last half hour."

I tried to tamp down the immediate guilt I felt piling onto Lydia, even in this inconsequential way. *You have to remember why you're here, Emily.* Honestly, if she knew what I'd learned in the past twenty-four hours, Lydia would probably approve of the strategy to get Brittany talking . . . right?

Thankfully, my gambit worked. Brittany rolled her eyes, then shrugged.

"Honestly, it's probably better without her. Lydia can be such a pill even when she's *not* having a breakdown. C'mon, let me show you a couple of the single vineyard wines. There should be a thief in there—it's what we use to get samples straight from the barrels. It's wild how different the wines taste with just the tiniest shifts in terroir."

We tasted pipettes of a thisward-facing-slope wine versus a thatward section of the valley floor one, me nodding along as though I was impressed by Brittany's mentions of black pepper and leather and "rot, but the good kind, think forest floor"—none of which I could actually taste, mind—letting Brittany soothe herself with the sense of superiority it probably gave her. It didn't hurt that letting her talk gave me that much more time to focus on calming myself. If I was going to get any answers from Brittany, I couldn't come into things twitchy with anxiety. Finally we emerged back into the tunnel and she started making her way downward, pointing out various rooms along the way. Eventually we arrived in the large cave with the elaborate dining setup, simultaneously luxurious and eerie, like the grand ballroom in some dark netherworld castle, kept waiting in case its drow prince should appear.

"I suppose this is the final stop on the tour," Brittany said, glancing upward to take in the glissando swoops of the cave ceiling. "We throw winemaker's dinners here occasionally for ultra-VIP visitors."

"They don't prefer the views upstairs?"

"The appeal is the exclusivity. *Anyone* can spend time in the tasting room." Brittany rolled her eyes indulgently, a pitying smile on her face. "And there's something glamorous about it, don't you think?" She drifted over to the table, running a finger along the rough edge of the reclaimed wood top. "What's the word? *Gothic.*"

I turned to one of the bottle racks along the wall, trying to channel all the laid-back, offhand vibes I could muster. This was the moment.

"Vanessa probably loved it here, hmm?" I just barely glanced over my shoulder at her, *This is just your old friend Emily thinking aloud, no reason to get your guard up.* "She could be so dramatic."

"God, right?" Brittany exhaled a half laugh.

"I'm surprised she didn't force us to come down here and . . . I don't know, hold a séance or something. It feels like the kind of thing she would have done back then."

"I'm sure Lydia would have been down." I could practically hear the eye roll.

"I'd have probably gone along with it too, honestly. Vanessa was pretty persuasive when she wanted to be."

"Sure. When she wanted to be."

Brittany's tone had turned subdued. I risked a glance at her; she was staring at the bottle in her hand, clearly lost in some memory. If there was ever a time to slip in beneath her defenses, it was now.

"Well, I don't think she wanted to be with *me,* at least not that weekend." Brittany looked over at me, cocking an eyebrow slightly. "She was being cagey the whole time. Acting all mysterious, biting my head off for no reason at all . . ." I moved around the edge of the room, inching closer to where I knew the spiral staircase was tucked away. "I never said anything about it after, I think I felt too guilty, but honestly I was kinda pissed with her."

"Oh? What was going on?" Brittany was aiming for casual, but I could hear the edge of interest in her voice.

"No idea. What was ever going on with Vanessa? Any time I tried to ask she'd get all moody and distant. 'It's complicated, you wouldn't understand.'" I shrugged. "I always figured it was something I'd done, but I never had any idea *what.* She'd do that sometimes. Just, like . . . flip a switch, and for whatever reason you go from being her absolute best friend to this outsider looking in. And then one day the switch would flip back, and you're her favorite again, and you have no idea what's changed. In hindsight it's kind of obvious, but back then it was so effective, you know?"

"She always did that. Even back at Montrose." Brittany's gaze turned distant as she remembered their days at boarding school.

"Still . . ." I sighed, frowning a bit. "It felt different that weekend. Less . . . controlled, if that makes sense. That weekend it felt like *everyone* was on the outside. And she had this weird energy the whole time we were here. But maybe I'm just imagining it. It was so long ago . . ."

"No, I don't think you're wrong. I don't know what all was going on with her, but she was definitely . . . on edge."

I pulled one of the bottles from the racks on the wall that ended in the staircase, turning it over slowly before replacing it.

"In hindsight, it's hard not to feel like there must have been more to it, especially if it wasn't just with me." I moved a little further down the racks. "Did she say anything to you?"

"Nothing important, I don't think. If she did, I'm sure I told the investigators, but I can't remember it now."

"That makes sense. It was probably just regular drama. The kind of stuff that felt so significant back then, you know?"

"Mmm."

Another couple steps down the row. Now or never . . .

"Oh, where's this lead?" I turned to face Brittany, pointing at the spiral staircase with what I hoped looked like genuine surprise.

"Down to the shore. There's a little cave at the bottom."

"Right." I nodded slowly, as though the puzzle pieces were just now clicking together in my head, as though I hadn't trailed Brittany down to the entrance less than twelve hours before. Well . . . I'd assumed it was Brittany. I suppose I still didn't have any evidence of that. It made me wonder, would the script I'd been toying with in my mind work better if you couldn't see who was in the cave? Shadows and the echoes of a voice on the rocks could make the whole thing more menacing . . . But that was a "future Emily" question. "That's the one you and Vanessa met up in that weekend, isn't it?"

It was a shot in the . . . not quite dark, but definitely dim. But Brittany creeping down here specifically *had* to be because of the necklace; she hadn't just been surprised to find it on her bed, she'd been scared. Even if I didn't have answers yet, I was certain now that Vanessa's disappearance that weekend wasn't the random accident investigators had ruled it, it was tied to something that had happened here, tied to one of *us*. Brittany and Vanessa had always circled around each other, hackles up, teeth bared, even at the best of times. The more I turned it all over in my mind, the surer I became that something must have happened between the cousins that weekend, something Brittany had never told any of us. And that something was tied to this cave.

Brittany went very still, the color draining from her face. *Bingo.*

"I'm not sure what you're talking about. Vanessa and I didn't meet there."

"Really?"

"Why would you think that?"

"Vanessa must have told me." I shrugged, but Brittany's suspended disbelief in my nonchalant act was rapidly plummeting to earth. "I was so jealous at the time. I figured she was probably telling you whatever was too important and grown up to explain to me."

Brittany stared at me for a moment, unblinking.

"You must be getting mixed up," she finally said. "We used to go down there a lot when we were younger. But not that weekend."

"Are you sure? I swear Vanessa told me she met you—"

"I'm sure. It was too cold for that, anyway." I could see Brittany's tongue running over her teeth beneath her lip. "Speaking of, we should go up. I think my lips are probably starting to turn blue."

Brittany swept her arm toward the entryway.

"You go ahead, I'll turn the lights off along the way."

I flailed around for something else to say, something that

would keep her talking, but even through her forced, hostess's smile, Brittany's jaw was tight, eyes narrowed as she stared at me.

"Good idea. It's way past time for a glass of wine anyway, right?"

"Absolutely." Brittany gave a small laugh, but her entire body was still tense with wariness. *Dammit.*

Unsure what else to do, I started off up the passageway, forcing myself to resist the urge to glance back over my shoulder at Brittany, asking chipper, inane questions about who the winery had hosted—*Oh really, but he's so famous!*—to fill the silence. It wasn't enough to drown out the anxious voice in my head, though.

Something had definitely happened between Brittany and Vanessa in that cave. Something Brittany clearly believed no one knew about. That no one *could* know about.

I swallowed hard as we picked our way back up the tunnel, forcing myself not to glance over my shoulder at the woman just a few feet behind me, certain that I wouldn't be able to keep the mixture of triumph and anxiety off my face.

Whatever had happened at that final meeting between her and Vanessa, she was intent on keeping it a secret, even now.

And I'd just told her that I was on to her.

INT. PRECIPICE WINERY PRIVATE QUARTERS—DAY
(PRESENT DAY)

The front door opens and Paige slumps into
the room, all the anxious energy from before drained from her. She looks hag-
gard . . . and wet. The tips of her hair
are ropy with damp, and her jeans have a
Pollockesque pattern of dark splotches
across the front, denser near the hems. She
glances at the wine rack in the kitchen,
clearly tempted, then exhales, turning down
the hallway toward her bedroom.

                              JUMP TO

INT. PAIGE'S BEDROOM—DAY

Paige kicks the door shut, already starting
to unbutton her damp jeans. She bends over
her suitcase to pull out a pair of pants,
tossing them on the corner of the bed to
wriggle out of her jeans . . . then she
frowns, stopping.

                 PAIGE
          What the fuck?

Paige moves over to the bed. ZOOM IN on a
thin stack of paper in the middle of the
comforter. The title reads "Sensation and
Sensibility: The Subversive Role of Touch
in Austen's Work," with "Paige Cressey" on
the line beneath. ~~Scrawled beneath the typed
words in a sharp, spiky hand are the words
Worth killing for? -V~~

NOTE: Showing your cards too early, and maybe too over the top? Consider how to play things a little subtler throughout. -Lark

PULL BACK to Paige's face, which has gone a sickly gray. Her breath comes short as she flips through the typed pages. She grows more and more agitated, until she whips the papers across the room.

>   PAIGE
>   No. *No!*

Paige's groans of frustration don't quite cover the sound of a door in the hallway creaking open and closing heavily. Seconds later there's a timid tap on the door.

>   LYDIA (O.S.)
>   Paige? Is everything alright?

Paige goes rigid, head whipping around to the door, fear plain on her face.

>   LYDIA (O.S.) (CONT'D)
>   Paige? I'm coming in.

>   PAIGE
>   *No!* Or . . . just give me a sec-
>   ond, I'm getting dressed.

Paige hurriedly strips off the damp jeans and wiggles into the new pants. She stares at the paper for a moment, frozen, then slips it under the closet door before crossing to open the door. She plants one arm across the frame.

PAIGE (CONT'D)
Hey, what's up?

~~Emily~~ Lydia frowns, glancing over Paige's shoulder at the room. Paige doesn't shift.

LYDIA
Is everything okay? I heard a yell.

PAIGE
Oh, yeah. I . . . tripped myself trying to get out of my jeans. This hangover is destroying me.

LYDIA
Why were you changing? Did Brittany make dinner plans she didn't feel like telling me about?

PAIGE
Not that I know of. I just got wet. It started raining.

Lydia bites her lower lip, clearly still concerned. Paige blocks the doorway further.

PAIGE (CONT'D)
I thought you were going on that hike.

TO DO: hiking scene, shadowy figure in woods following Lydia back, as her fear reaches a high point, a woodland animal rustles out of the underbrush behind her. She's relieved, we see the shadow-figure behind a tree.

Or too melodramatic? Consider setup here? — EF

> LYDIA
> We were. I just came back early.
> The path was really remote, and I
> didn't bring the right boots.
> Plus . . .

She gestures at her stomach, grimacing.

> LYDIA (CONT'D)
> Let's just say you're not the
> only one still feeling last
> night's booze fest. I was genu-
> inely worried I was going to shit
> my pants.

Paige barks out a genuine laugh. She's
clearly not used to Lydia admitting the
sorts of things *she* would. After the laugh
subsides, Paige can't help but glance back
into the room. Lydia clearly clocks the motion.

> LYDIA (CONT'D)
> Are you sure you're okay?

> PAIGE
> Yes. I mean . . . no, obviously.
> All this stuff is . . . fucking
> with my head. But nothing *hap-
> pened,* if that's what you mean.
> Besides me not being able to
> dress myself.

> LYDIA
> Well . . . if you need anything,

let me know. I'll just be reading
in the living room.

                PAIGE
Will do. Thanks for checking.

Lydia smiles again, but her eyes and brow
are still heavy with concern as she turns
and walks off down the hall. Paige pushes the
door closed and twists the lock, leaning
against the solid wood for a moment, breathing heavily, before she crosses to the
closet. With an anxious glance at the locked
door, she slowly opens the closet, wincing
when it creaks. There on the floor is the
paper with her name on it. She bends to pick
it up, but when she touches the pages, she
jerks back, as though scalded. Hurriedly,
she slams the closet door again.

                            CUT TO BLACK

7

WHAT TIME DID YOU LAST SEE HER?

I could still remember the smell of the room at the police station they'd taken us to that weekend, cheap lemon cleaner and burnt coffee and the faint hint of pine that seemed to permeate the air in coastal Oregon. I'd been expecting *Law & Order*—harsh lighting and metal furniture specifically chosen to maximize discomfort—but the table I sat at was ring-stained oak, the chair incongruously ergonomic, some remnant from a desk job.

For the hundredth, maybe the thousandth time, I sifted through my memories of that weekend, trying to come up with some bright nugget of truth hidden in the slurry of grief and anxiety and guilt.

But there was nothing, just the same answer I'd given the kind-eyed, middle-aged officer sitting across from me, his mustache so thick and mobile it was practically sentient.

Some time Friday afternoon. I think she was going into town.

I'd known then that it was a lie, but I didn't have a better truth, didn't have the information that would help him get from A to B. "I texted with her last night, apparently, but I have no memory of it or of whether I saw her" didn't seem particularly useful, after all.

By Friday, we'd all been tense with each other over various perceived slights that had been steadily accumulating over the course of the week: hitting on some townie at the bar that another of us had already "claimed"; taking one friend shopping and not asking another; splitting the bill five ways when it was obvious *some* people owed way more than others; acting moody and distant for days with no explanation. Thursday night had been one of those where suddenly everyone was much drunker than they expected or planned, but the alcohol-induced flood of false warmth had congealed by morning, coating all the existing resentments in a greasy layer of disgust. I hadn't seen much of Vanessa on Friday, but then I hadn't seen much of *anyone*. We'd all been finding ways to avoid each other all day, the simmer of general annoyance unignorable, even when it was only you in the room. The only person I was sure *had* been at the house that evening was Brittany, and only because I scared the shit out of her when I emerged from my bedroom for a snack at the same time as she did.

I repositioned myself against the headboard of the bed, propping my laptop on my knees, eyes locked on the slow blink of the cursor on my script. Being here was supposed to make things clearer, show me at least a suggestion of the big picture, but now I just felt more confused than ever. There had been glimpses of things I hadn't known before, little pinpricks of light poking through the dark veil that had always hung over that weekend, but I couldn't seem to connect the dots, turn them into a constellation that made sense. If anything, I was only now realizing how vast the expanse was that I needed to illuminate.

With a frustrated sigh, I slapped the computer closed, tossing it to the foot of the bed. I wanted to spin something out of what had happened in town, but until I knew where it ended, I wasn't sure quite how to start. Worse, reading over it again, I wondered if that scene with Brittany in the cave was even worth keeping—how did that even *fit* in the story? Halfway through the trip and I'd barely managed a first act. Still, whatever I needed for this story to come unstuck, I hadn't found it yet, and I wasn't *going* to find it holed up in my bedroom staring at a blank screen.

I padded down the hallway toward the main room. From the balcony, I spotted Brittany in the kitchen, fussily arranging platters of food along the breakfast bar.

"Wait, did you cook? You should have said something, I'd have helped out."

"*God* no." Brittany nudged the corner of the central platter with one finger, bringing it parallel with those on either side, frowning at it for a second before pulling her hand away. "I ordered some stuff from the restaurant that caters the wine dinners here. There's spinach salad with cranberries and goat cheese, salmon with dill sauce, grilled broccolini, and butternut squash with tahini dressing." She pointed to each of the platters in turn. "I figured we could just do buffet style. Oh, and there's a baguette in the oven, it'll be ready in a few minutes."

"Can I Venmo you, or . . ."

Brittany scrunched up her nose.

"Of course not. My treat." She drifted over to the fridge and pulled out a bottle of wine, busying herself with opening it. I couldn't help but notice that she still hadn't *quite* made eye contact. "I chilled down some gewürztraminer, but feel free to open whatever."

"Do you think anyone would drink red? I know it's not right for salmon . . ." I flashed an apologetic smile at Brittany, who was intent on pouring herself a glass of the white.

"I would." I jumped a little at the voice coming from over

my shoulders. I hadn't noticed Lydia, back in her oversized chair near the window. She heaved herself out of it, crossing to join me. "We can be déclassé together."

I smiled at her, grateful for the save, and moved to the wine rack to find a bottle of something that didn't look *too* expensive, not that I'd really know. Eventually I settled on a Cliff's Edge pinot—if it was special, at least I knew they could replace it without much trouble—and poured glasses for Lydia and myself. Then we started grabbing plates and silverware, slicing bread, and moving through the gourmet cafeteria line to avoid additional conversation. We were just settling down at the table when Brittany raised a finger, *Oh I almost forgot.*

"Let me get Paige, I don't want her to think we're leaving her out."

She strode across the main room and disappeared down the hallway. It was a full minute before she emerged again, lips thin as she made her way back to the table.

"Is everything alright?" Lydia said.

"Well . . . you'll see," Brittany murmured.

Twenty seconds later a loud thud from the hallway, followed by a high, thin giggle, signaled Paige's progress.

"Sorry, were you waiting for me?" Her words were thick, eyes glassy as she wove across the living room to the table, plopping herself—and her very full wineglass—down at the foot.

"Don't you want to get something to eat?" Brittany said, staring pointedly at Paige's glass. Paige groaned.

"What are you, my mother?"

"No." A vein in Brittany's temple pulsed. "Just trying to help you avoid *another* epic hangover."

Paige rolled her eyes, but she stood, made her way to the breakfast bar, and heaped a plate indiscriminately. Once she was seated again, she bit off a giant chunk of bread, washed it down with even more wine, and raised her glass to Brittany.

"There. Better?"

"Not particularly." Brittany broke off a tiny bite of the flaky salmon, dipping it daintily in the pool of sauce on her plate.

My heart started beating faster—I could not waste another night on some stupid cold war over afternoon drinking. We didn't have much more time here, and I definitely had more questions about that weekend than when I arrived. And considering how *fabulously* we'd all gotten along . . . I had a strong feeling there wouldn't be another weekend like this in the future. Or even many returned phone calls.

Start a normal conversation, get people to open up, then steer things toward Vanessa. Ideally when everyone was tipsy enough not to hold back . . . though maybe not quite so far gone as Paige. Forcing a smile, I raised my eyes to Lydia.

"I meant to ask what you're reading, Lyds. It's been forever since I've found a book that I really couldn't put down."

"It's this new sci-fi book a lot of people in my office were talking about. But honestly, it's only okay."

"Really? You seemed pretty into it."

"That's just so she won't have to talk to anyone," Paige said with a snorting little laugh. "Didn't you used to bring books to parties back in college?"

"I don't think so," Lydia murmured, eyes on her plate. I could see the muscles in her neck tensing.

"Huh. I could have sworn you did. I guess that was just your vibe back then. And now, apparently." Paige widened her eyes and took another sip of wine.

"Not everyone's an extrovert, there's nothing wrong with that," I said, trying to catch Lydia's eye. "Honestly, I wish I read more, I always wind up watching the stupidest—"

"*God*, can you drop the saint act for like . . . five minutes, Emily?" Paige turned her sneer on me. "We get it, *everyone's* your friend."

"I don't know what you mean." My heart was in my throat now. Any conflict was bad, conflict I was forced to be an active participant in was panic-inducing.

"Sure, Pollyella. Don't you think people notice how you're always playing every side? You know it's okay to occasionally have your own opinion, even if it means people"—she gasped, lifting her hand to her mouth in faux shock, the movements exaggerated—"*disagree*."

"I think you mean Pollyanna," Lydia said quietly, her large eyes narrowed on Paige.

"You would care about that." Paige rolled her eyes, leaning back in the chair and spreading her legs. "The point is we all know Emily's a pushover."

"Paige, for god's sake, stop *talking*," Brittany said evenly, still focused on her plate. "You're embarrassing yourself."

"No, *they're* embarrassing themselves." Paige leaned forward, slamming the table with a fist. Brittany pulled back, eyes wide with shock, though whether that was at the noise or the rare sight of Paige openly disagreeing with her, I couldn't tell. "They're acting like we're all fucking friends, and this is just some . . . what, special reunion for our dear departed Vanessa? Like being here again is going to make anything better? It's a fucking *joke*." Paige turned to me, teeth bared. The ragged purple stain of wine on the inside of her lips, and the grayish tinge it had given her teeth, made her look like a zombie creature on the attack. "You all can pretend whatever you want, but the fact is Vanessa was a *bitch*."

"Paige." Brittany fixed her with a warning stare, eyebrows low, jaw tight.

"What? *You* know it's true, we used to talk about it all the time! And if Lydia and Emily don't, that's just because they were too fucking naïve to see her for who she really was. Do you have any idea how much shit Vanessa talked about you?" She sloshed her glass toward Lydia. "About both of you?" Toward me.

"Friends gossip about each other," I started. "That's normal, especially when you're young, it doesn't mean that they—" Paige cut me off with a barking laugh.

"Sure. Tell yourself that. Tell yourself you knew her at *all*."

"I did know Vanessa." Lydia's voice was low, each word enunciated. "And I knew you. Maybe Vanessa complained about us occasionally, I honestly don't know and I don't care. But she was *not* the person you're trying to make her out to be. She cared about me. And about Emily. She was a good friend."

"What a *joke*." Paige laughed shrilly, almost maniacally, running her hand through her short hair in a way that made it stick up at crazy angles. Lydia pushed back from the table suddenly, planting her hands on either side of her plate, as though to anchor herself.

"No. *No*." Lydia's cheeks were bright pink, her jaw pulsing in a way I'd never seen before. "*You're* the joke, Paige. I'm sorry you're unhappy, that your life has turned out so badly that you're like . . . *this*. Not that I'm surprised." Lydia gestured at Paige with a sneer of disgust. "But don't blame Vanessa for that. She didn't make you some sad, mean little drunk. And don't make things up about her when she's not here to defend herself. I know my friend. If there was a bully in this group it *wasn't* her."

"Wow. *Wow*. You actually believe that, don't you?" Paige shook her head slowly, wonder and disgust warring on her face, turning her strong jaw heavy and coarse. "I know you always had a whole hero worship thing going on with Vanessa, but I thought you were smarter than that, Lydia."

"I'm not going to sit here and listen to you make things up about—"

"I don't *have* to make anything up." Paige slammed the wineglass down so hard I thought it might crack. "Vanessa was a snake. She actually *tried* to find dirt on all of you. On all of *us*. I know you bought her whole 'poor little orphan' thing, but Vanessa was calculating as fuck."

Lydia sat back down heavily, arms tight across her narrow chest, shaking her head back and forth as she stared at her plate.

"What do you mean?" I finally ventured. Cold bloomed in the pit of my stomach. Whatever Paige was on about, it wasn't just drunken rambling, I could feel it in my gut. But as desperate as I was to know what she was going to say, I was also scared. So far, every new nugget of information I'd found had been as unnerving as it was revelatory, recasting everything I thought I knew about the women I was sharing this house with, and the one we'd all left behind. Was I really ready for all this?

"Vanessa was planning to get me expelled," Paige said, leaning back in her chair, mouth twisted with grim triumph. *Checkmate.*

"Oh for god's—no she wasn't," Lydia said, rolling her eyes.

"Yes, she was. She was planning to go to the board of overseers. She told me herself. She'd been holding it over me for months, just to fuck with me I guess, but while we were here, she *told* me. She was going to ruin my fucking life just because she *could.*"

"What was she holding over you?" I asked, curiosity coming out a nose ahead of anxiety. "It must have been major if it would have gotten you expelled."

Paige sighed heavily, the heated anger that had been puffing her up cooling and contracting all at once, leaving her deflated.

"You have to understand, I was coming back from an injury that season. *And* the coach put me on a fourth individual event. I was pulling two-a-days to get back to where I needed to be, meeting with the PT pretty much daily to make sure I didn't reinjure myself . . ."

"So . . . this was about track?" I squinted, trying to understand.

"No. Well . . . yes, sort of." Paige shook her head rapidly, like she was trying to clear the Etch A Sketch. "The point is, I was training all the time. I tried to load up on easy classes that semester, but I was still just barely scraping by. The track team would pull your scholarship if your GPA went below 2.6."

"So you cheated," Lydia said flatly. Paige's brow lowered as she turned to her. "That's where you're going with this, right?"

"It's not like I wanted to. But it was the week we were up against Corpus Christi, they were like . . . our *enemies*. And they had this new sophomore running the fifteen-hundred-meter who was just so fast . . ." Paige took a huge gulp of her wine, pinching her eyes closed. "I bought *one paper* to make sure I wouldn't lose my scholarship. That's *all*."

"And Vanessa found out about it," Brittany said. She was leaning forward, intent on Paige in a way that surprised me. It was clear from the avidity in her eyes that she'd never heard this story before, which was even more unexpected. "She threatened to tell."

"Yes, that's right." Paige nodded, tongue pinned between her lips, blinking rapidly against the tears starting to glisten in her eyes. "I don't know how she found out about it, but she did. Then she spent the whole spring semester, like . . . *toying* with me."

"But they wouldn't really have *expelled* you for that, would they?" Lydia's face was twisted with incredulity. "There was a kid in my sophomore seminar who got caught plagiarizing a paper, the only thing I remember happening is they gave him a fail in the class. I know they didn't kick him out, he was in one of my lecture courses the next year."

"Even if they didn't actually expel me, it would have been the same thing. The code of ethics for athletes was *super* strict. I'd have lost my spot on the team. And my scholarship." Paige's eyes were still twinkling with unshed tears, but her jaw was jutting out defiantly again, a hint of her earlier fury returning. "Vanessa *knew* that. I *told* her that. But then the next time she got annoyed with me, or just . . . I don't know, had her period or whatever, she'd dangle it over my head again."

"But what was different that weekend?" I asked. Vanessa using the paper for leverage I could imagine—I didn't have quite as harsh a view of her as Paige seemed to, but I knew from experience how she liked to hoard information, parceling it out in a way that felt intoxicating—*I must be special if she's sharing this with* me—but that, looking back, was clearly about control. Even if you were sharing *her* secret—and that was rare—the fact that it was just the two of you bound by this thing, that all her trust (and implicitly her friendship) was wrapped up in its staying hidden, gave her a sort of power.

"I don't *know*," Paige said, shaking her head back and forth, the tears starting to flow over her sharp cheekbones. "I'd thought it was all over, she hadn't brought it up in weeks, but that night she texted me to meet her . . . and she was just *different,* you know? Mean. Up in my face. And she said . . ." Paige sniffed wetly, rubbing her nose hard with the back of her hand. It came away glistening. "She was going to the board, she told me. I begged her but she wouldn't listen. And then . . . I didn't mean to, it was all so fast, and she was laughing at me, and I just . . ."

Paige's eyes suddenly shot wide open. Her gaze was glazed and distant, forehead corrugated with pain, and her hands slowly curled into claws on the tabletop. My skin seemed to tighten half a size, every part of me prickling with anticipation.

"What are you saying, Paige?" I kept my voice low, even.

"I did it," she said, her voice strangely childlike, eyes still fixed on some scene none of us could see. "I didn't mean to push her, I swear, but I just . . ." She blinked a few times, then turned to me. I repressed a shiver. "I killed her. I killed Vanessa."

EXT. DOCK—NIGHT (15 YEARS AGO)

It's clear and cold, the stars cut crystal
in the weighty mantle of the night sky, the
sharp scythe of the crescent moon carving
out the spectral circle of the whole. The
tide is high, splashing up over the sides of
the dock every so often, kissing the base of
the cliffs as each gentle wave rolls in. Between the bulk of the cliffs and the vast
expanse of steel-gray ocean, the dock and
the staircase leading down to it look especially flimsy, and the tall, slim girl standing at the end seems almost wraithlike, a
figure of smoke and shadow. This is Vanessa.

ZOOM IN on her. She looks determined, and
perhaps a bit frightened. A sound from the
cliff face startles her, and she glances
back anxiously at the stairs, creaking under
the weight of some unseen person's descent.
Vanessa closes her eyes tight, takes a gigantic swig from the bottle of wine she's
strangling, and murmurs something sound-
lessly to herself. When she turns to face
Paige, just stepping onto the landward end
of the dock, any hesitancy has been replaced with a look of sharp disdain.

                    VANESSA
          I was starting to think you
          weren't coming.

                    PAIGE
               (annoyed)
          It's not exactly easy getting
          down those stairs in the dark.

Why meet down here anyway?

> VANESSA
> I thought you'd appreciate the
> privacy. Unless you'd rather tell
> everyone about this? I bet Brit-
> tany would be interested to hear
> what her little sidekick is get-
> ting up to behind her back. Brit-
> tany and I have our differences,
> but one thing we both can't stand
> is a cheater.

She reaches into her back pocket and pulls
out a stapled stack of papers. As Vanessa
unfolds them with her thumb we see a portion
of a title, "Sensation and Sensibility . . ."

Paige sucks in a sharp breath, then her expression turns determined as she lunges
toward Vanessa. Vanessa just barely manages
to move to the side, stumbling slightly.
She laughs as she moves away, taking another swig from the bottle.

> VANESSA (CONT'D)
> Naughty, naughty. Didn't you
> learn to ask nicely?

Paige grits her teeth, chest heaving.

> PAIGE
> Give it back, Vanessa. *Please*.

> VANESSA
> You know, I don't think I will?

She strides along the edge of the dock, watching Paige through narrowed eyes, a predator toying with its prey.

>   VANESSA (CONT'D)
>   In fact, I don't think I can hold
>   on to this secret anymore, Paige.
>   What you did is *wrong*.

Vanessa stops near the end of the dock, staring at Paige with a look of exaggerated disappointment, gesturing with the paper.

>   VANESSA (CONT'D)
>   This is against everything our
>   storied alma mater stands for. If
>   I don't tell the disciplinary
>   committee what you've done, how
>   you've tarnished the college's
>   good name . . . I'm just as bad
>   as you are.

Paige lunges for the pages again, but Vanessa sidesteps, stumbling a bit more this time, the wine bottle serving as a counterweight as she rights herself.

>   VANESSA (CONT'D)
>   *Temper,* Paige. You'll want to
>   rein that in before you go in
>   front of the board.

>   PAIGE
>   Why are you doing this, Vanessa?
>   What the fuck does it matter to
>   you?

Vanessa swallows hard, turning to look out at the ocean, a pained expression flitting across her face. When she speaks, her voice is softer.

> VANESSA
> Because the world's unfair enough without people gaming the fucking system.

She turns back to Paige, the cold light from the moon turning her already sharp features stony.

> VANESSA (CONT'D)
> Just thought you'd like to know. I'm going in when we get back.

> PAIGE
> Just give me the paper, Vanessa. You know I'm never going to do it again.

> VANESSA
> I wish I could believe that, Paige.

Paige lunges again, and Vanessa moves away a little too late, barely managing to stay upright.

> VANESSA (CONT'D)
> (taunting)
> Do you really think you'll stop me even if you *do* manage to take this away? I can print another copy.

Paige lunges again, grunting. Vanessa side-steps again, but now she's right at the edge of the dock. Paige glares at her, breath coming in massive heaves.

> PAIGE
> Seriously, *why*? You told me how bad your grades were. You of all people should get that I had to do it!

> VANESSA
> I never cheated to try to fix it.

Vanessa shakes her head pityingly.

> VANESSA (CONT'D)
> Honestly, I think this will be *good* for you. Learning that actions have consequences.

> PAIGE
> Just . . . give it to me.

Paige moves sideways this time, hip-checking Vanessa, taking advantage of her unbalance to snatch the paper out from between her fingers. But Vanessa's stumbling step to the side is over empty air. She turns to Paige, eyes wide with horror, then plunges into the icy water. It's not until she hears the splash that Paige, panting, realizes what's happened.

> PAIGE (CONT'D)
> Vanessa? Vanessa!

Paige squints hard at the spot where Vanessa went under, but the dark makes it hard to make anything out on the surface of the waves. Her head darts around, looking for any sign of her friend—a ripple, a trail of bubbles, her hair breaking the surface—but there's nothing.

> PAIGE (CONT'D)
> For fuck's sake, Vanessa, stop fucking around!

She crouches down on the edge of the dock, trying to peer beneath the boards, but the water is too high, and the section beneath is all swirling shadows.

> PAIGE (CONT'D)
> (weakly)
> This isn't funny.

Paige stands, pacing the edge of the dock, increasingly anxious. The tide keeps rolling in, the roar of the waves crashing on the shore drowning out everything else.

~~Setting her jaw, she kicks off her shoes, sheds her sweater, and dives into the water smoothly. But when she surfaces several seconds later she's shivering and disoriented.~~

> ~~PAIGE~~
> ~~Vanessa?~~

~~She dives under again, blinks hard when she emerges. After several seconds staring~~

~~around her, she pushes out of the water onto the dock, teeth chattering as she shakes the water off, throwing her clothes back on as quickly as possible.~~

Note: give Paige less of an out, it muddies the water more if she stays in a moral gray zone. —Lark

She's biting her lip, starting to nudge off a shoe with one foot, when a light flickers on from the staircase. It's the flashlight of a phone; once it's wobbled its way down, we see it belongs to Lydia. She steps out onto the dock, frowning.

> LYDIA
> I thought I heard something. What are you doing down here? ~~Jesus, why are you all wet?~~

Paige's eyes dart to the water, scanning it rapidly. But there's still no sign of Vanessa. She swallows hard, then turns back to Lydia.

> PAIGE
> Nothing. I just . . . ~~thought I'd take a swim~~ needed some fresh air.

> LYDIA
> Have you got enough? Because Brittany wants to order food and she's getting all pissed that no one's answering her texts.

> PAIGE
> Oh. Right. Uhh . . .

Her whole body tenses, and we see her fight not to look at the water again.

> LYDIA
> Speaking of, have you seen Vanessa? No one's heard from her since before lunch.

Paige's face contorts with pain. She sucks in a few deep breaths, eyes pinched tight . . . then she seems to make a decision. Her shoulders lower. She forces the expression off her face before turning to walk past Lydia toward the stairs.

> PAIGE
> Nope. I thought she went into town.

> LYDIA
> That's what I said. I guess Brittany thought she'd be back by now.

Lydia glances up at the staircase, sighing.

> LYDIA (CONT'D)
> I guess we should go up, then. If the tide weren't so high, we could go back through the caves.

> PAIGE
> Yeah. It would be better if the tide weren't in.

>   LYDIA
>   I just wish Vanessa would come
>   back already. She's the only one
>   who can handle Brittany when
>   she's on the rampage.

Paige shrugs, not quite managing nonchalance. But Lydia's turning her flashlight toward the staircase, picking her way up the first few steps, and doesn't seem to notice.

>   PAIGE
>   You know Vee. No one tells her
>   what to do.

>   LYDIA
>   I just hope she doesn't bring
>   some rando home. If I walk into
>   the bathroom and there's a guy
>   I've never seen in there . . .

Their voices fade as they continue up the stairs. A flight up, Paige turns to look at the water, but there's nothing there. Just the waves, rolling in one after another, relentless.

8

"SO NOW YOU ALL KNOW," PAIGE SAID, VOICE ragged with the effort to hold back her tears. "I killed her. I killed Vanessa." She blinked rapidly, palming her wine and taking a big, shuddering sip. "God, it actually feels good to say, if you can believe it?"

Everyone sat in stunned silence as Paige sniffled. I had to stop myself from correcting her, *No, it was me,* the potency of guilt with fifteen years of age on it far stronger than any of the recent discoveries that proved, fairly definitively, that I hadn't hurt Vanessa.

I looked around the table. Lydia's eyes were wide with shock, hands trembling slightly against the tabletop. Brittany, however, was leaning forward, frowning hard. I watched her out of the corner of my eye, intrigued to see how she'd react to this revelation.

"And this was *Friday* night?" she said slowly. "You're sure."

"Of course I'm sure," Paige snapped. Spit arced out of her mouth onto the table. "I wouldn't exactly forget *that.*"

"Still, we were all drinking a lot that week." Brittany ran her tongue over her upper lip. "And people's memories are notoriously faulty."

"So what, you think I just . . . invented a memory where I fucking killed one of my best friends?"

"Of course not." Brittany rolled her eyes. "I'm just saying some of the details might have gotten mixed up."

I dug my fingernails into the tops of my thighs, trying to steady myself. I could almost glimpse the hint of a picture forming, the random scattering of points resolving into something larger.

"Why would you think Paige had this wrong, Brittany?"

Brittany turned to me, clearly startled. For a split second, something like fear tugged at the corners of her eyes. My heart started racing, cold sweat breaking out beneath my armpits, but I forced myself to stay still, just watching her.

"I'm not saying she *does* have it wrong, just that it's possible she mixed up some of the details." She reached for her wine, eyes dropping as she took a slow sip. "It was traumatic for all of us."

"Trust me, I'm pretty fucking solid on this one," Paige said dryly.

"But . . . you didn't *really* kill her," I said, wheels in my brain whirring with the effort to glimpse the shape of it. I still couldn't make it add up, but I could feel myself inching closer.

"How do you figure?"

"I think Emily means it wasn't planned. You said she slipped, right?" Lydia said, eyes finding mine. I couldn't read her expression.

"More or less, yeah. She was backing away from me when I reached for the paper . . . she just kinda . . . fell off the end of the dock." Paige worked her lips in and out between her teeth. "I think she was a little drunk," she finally added. She seemed to notice her wine, already halfway to her mouth again, and lowered it, frowning.

"So it was an accident, then." I reached for Paige's hand. "It was just a horrible accident."

Paige looked down at my hand resting atop hers, then up at me, desperate hope in her eyes. Then her face crumpled and she shook her head, yanking her hand away. Her chin jutted out stubbornly.

"Either way, it was my fault. I couldn't find her in the water, if I'd jumped in sooner . . . And then I didn't even tell anyone what happened. It was my fault."

"Even a trained search and rescue team might not have been able to save her, Paige. The water is freezing that time of year, people get disoriented quickly," Brittany said.

"Exactly. Yes," I said, nodding rapidly. "And even if you put that aside, I don't believe that's the whole story." After all, what about my part of the story, whatever it might be? Those texts came in after the incident Paige was remembering, or possibly misremembering. And what about whatever had happened in the cave between Vanessa and Brittany? Her immediate, firm belief that Paige had the details wrong, plus that ring, had to mean she knew more than she was letting on.

"It *is*. I know it, and Vee knows it."

"Vee . . . what are you talking about, Paige?" Brittany frowned, confused.

"I'm talking about this!"

Paige pushed back from the table so sharply her chair wobbled perilously on two legs. But she didn't notice, she was already striding across the living room, steps nearly straight with her determination. About a minute later, she emerged from the hallway and crossed back to the table, dropping some stapled sheets in the middle. It seemed like it should have landed with a decisive *thump* for effect, but the stack was just a few pages thick, and it spread across the table with a tiny *whoosh*. Lydia reached for it first, turning it gingerly with one finger so she could read the title at the top of the first page.

"What is this, a college paper?"

"It's *the* paper. The one Vanessa had on the dock. The one I bought online." Paige folded her arms across her chest, raising an eyebrow at Lydia. She pointed at the splayed pages, a featureless blur of Times New Roman. "When I came back up this afternoon, that was on my bed. Did one of you leave it there?" She fixed each of us with a hard stare, waiting until we each shook our heads. "Did any of you even *know* about the cheating? Did you know, Lydia?"

"No," she said.

"Emily? Brit?"

Both of us murmured no.

"That's what I thought." Paige slammed back into her chair heavily.

Everyone sat in silence for a moment. I couldn't tear my eyes from the pages. What would have made Vanessa decide to turn Paige in? And more important . . .

"But *someone* had to have the paper, right?" I was still focused on the pages in front of me, the intensity of my gaze blurring the words to Morse code.

"What do you mean?" Paige jutted her jaw out defiantly.

"I mean . . . unless you think a ghost left that on your bed this afternoon, it had to come from somewhere. Same with the ring, Brit."

Brittany's face tightened with annoyance.

"Sorry . . . what ring are we talking about?" Lydia glanced between Brittany and me. Brittany pinched the bridge of her nose, exhaling heavily, her other arm wrapped tight around her slim frame like a line of defense. Finally, she gave the barest hint of a nod.

"Vee's ring. The one she always wore on the chain around her neck," I said. Lydia's eyes widened with recognition. "Brittany found it on her bed last night."

"Her *mom's* ring? But . . . Vanessa never took that off, are you sure it was the same one?" I'd never really understood the subtle specifics of *gawping* before then, but the look on Paige's face was definitively a gawp.

Brittany nodded heavily.

"It was the same ring."

Lydia nibbled at her lip, heel tapping rapidly against the rung of her chair.

"I wasn't going to say anything, I thought maybe . . . well, I thought one of you was playing a trick," Lydia said, glancing first at Paige, then at Brittany. "But I got something too." Silently, she pushed back from the table, heading down the hallway to her room and returning with a small bundle of what looked like cards, a strip of red lace wrapped around the center. She tugged the lace off and dropped the pile onto the table.

They were photographs, three of them, different camera angles on the same set: an ornate four-poster bed, obviously antique, in the middle of a luxurious bedroom, creamy chair rails and crown moldings blocking off the rich navy of the walls. Built-in bookshelves on either side of the bed were stuffed with weighty-looking tomes, which had also spilled haphazardly onto the spindly bedside tables. You couldn't see it in the photos, but they were almost universally *Intellectual*: the collected writing of Walter Benjamin, the entirety of Proust's *Remembrance of Things Past* both in translation and the original French, a copy of *Ulysses* walled round with biographies and critiques and collected letters and every other possible take on Joyce. The smattering of recent novels tucked in between the Great Works almost felt accidental, like the set designer had scooped up a pile at random at some thrift shop just to fill things out, hoping no one would notice the difference.

And no one would. It was almost impossible to focus on anything but the central figure of the scene: Vanessa, draped over the bed in a variety of come-hither poses, body caged by the elaborate black lingerie she was wearing. The look in her eyes went beyond seductive; it was almost predatory. Her gaze reached through the frame and grabbed the viewer by the throat.

My heart started thudding even more heavily, each hammer blow pulse shuddering through my chest, threatening to stop my breath.

"I've never seen the pictures before, but I think I know where they're from." Lydia sighed, tilting one of the images toward herself with a fingertip. "I'm not sure whether Vanessa told any of you, but . . ." She raised her eyes to the ceiling, bracing herself with both hands on the table, exhaling her words in a rush: "She'd been having an affair with one of the professors in the English Department. It ended sometime just after winter break. At least she *told* me it had ended. But she clearly wasn't over it, even when we were all out here. She hinted that there'd been some new problem between them, that he wouldn't leave her alone. Looking back, I've always wondered if maybe he wasn't a little . . . *obsessed,* you know? But she was so adamant that no one know about any of it, and . . . well, I hid it for her, even though I knew I shouldn't. I never even told the investigators it had happened." Lydia's face scrunched tight, regret for the choice she'd made so many years ago written in every line. She took a deep breath, forcing herself to loosen, and opened her eyes, turning back to the photos on the table. "I'm guessing the professor must have taken these at some point in the fall semester? Vanessa never showed them to me."

She hadn't shown them to me, either. To anyone, as far as I knew—I'd only seen one of them printed out before. But I remembered all of them well.

I'd taken them, after all.

INT. PROFESSOR LAVOIE'S HOUSE—NIGHT (15 YEARS AGO)

Emily sits on a leather sofa in a large, elegant living room. The ornate hand-carved fireplace is flanked by built-in bookshelves stacked with a mix of recent literature, literary classics, tasteful *objets*, and a smattering of photos showing a handsome man in his late thirties—his long shock of silky light brown hair and narrow frame, accentuated by the slim cut of his clothing, giving him a vaguely Byronic aspect—with a beautiful brunette woman with high cheekbones and heavy-lidded eyes. A few of the photos show the couple with a chubby-cheeked toddler with long dark lashes and a thatch of dark curls. The man is ALDEN LAVOIE, the inhabitant of the stately Victorian home that's owned by Queen Mary College. He is an assistant professor of English literature at the college. He also happens to be Emily's employer.

A baby monitor at Emily's elbow crackles with sound, drawing her out of the novel whose margins she was scribbling in. She peers at the video screen, but within moments the toddler it shows rolls over, and the sounds fade. She's just starting to get back into her work when there's a sharp knock on the door. Clearly surprised, she crosses to the hallway, peering through the sidelight to catch a glimpse of the figure waiting on the front steps. She frowns, then quickly throws the locks to let them in.

                    EMILY
          Vanessa? What are you doing here?

                    VANESSA
          Thank god I had the right house.
          It is *freezing* out there.

She pushes past Emily into the foyer, shuddering dramatically and pulling her long
wool coat tighter around her body.

                    EMILY
          Is everything okay? Did something
          happen?

                    VANESSA
          Everything's fine. Why?

                    EMILY
          Because you're showing up at my
          work?

                    VANESSA
          I texted.

Emily squints, disbelieving. After a moment, Vanessa rolls her eyes and leans
closer, lowering her voice.

                    VANESSA (CONT'D)
          The truth is . . . there's some-
          thing I was hoping you could help
          me with but I wanted to keep it
          private, okay? And it would have
          taken too long to explain on text.

                    EMILY
          Okay. So . . . what's up?

> VANESSA
> I told you I was signing up for
> that dating site, didn't I?

Emily shakes her head, a hint of hurt creeping into her expression. Lately, Vanessa has been keeping her at arm's length, and this just proves it.

> VANESSA (CONT'D)
> I could swear I told you. At that
> party the lacrosse guys threw?

> EMILY
> I don't remember you saying any-
> thing about it.

> VANESSA
> I was just toying with the idea.
> I'm sure it didn't really regis-
> ter, especially with *Declan*
> around.

Vanessa elbows Emily conspiratorially and Emily smiles in spite of herself. It's hard to resist Vanessa's moments of intimacy.

> VANESSA (CONT'D)
> Anyway, I decided I want to do
> it. College guys are all such
> children, you know?

> EMILY
> I don't think they're *all* like
> that.

> VANESSA
> No, you're right. I mean Declan

> is totally a catch. I just need
> to try something new, I guess.
> I'm feeling stuck, and . . . hon-
> estly? It's starting to really
> get to me. I haven't felt excited
> about anything in so long . . .

She turns, not quite hiding her pained expression. Emily immediately moves to put a
hand on Vanessa's shoulder.

>   EMILY
> Then let's get you signed up,
> right?

She perks up as an idea occurs to her.

>   EMILY (CONT'D)
> I could help you make the profile!
> I've always thought it would be
> kinda fun, honestly.

>   VANESSA
> I knew you'd be there for me.
> Thank you.

She wraps Emily in a tight hug. Her eyes
dart up the staircase as she pulls away.

>   VANESSA (CONT'D)
> First things first, though, I need
> to get some good pictures. If I
> want to match with guys who are
> actually going to take me to din-
> ner, I can't have a ton of photos
> from my shitty apartment, you
> know?

EMILY
Your apartment's nice!

VANESSA
Maybe compared to other college
kids. But I'm trying to find *men*,
Emily. I need to look like a
grown-ass woman.

EMILY
I guess that makes sense. Maybe
there are some good ones from the
winter ball?

VANESSA
Actually, I thought we could do a
little photo shoot here?

She tugs open her coat just enough to reveal
the lingerie beneath. Emily's mouth drops
open.

EMILY
I'm . . . I'm not sure that's a
good idea . . .

VANESSA
I promise I'll be fast. I'm already dressed. And I even brought
my own camera!

She pulls it out of her pocket, waving it in
the air for emphasis, grinning goofily, then
her face collapses a bit.

VANESSA (CONT'D)
I know it's silly, but I just
want to feel sexy, you know?

> Like . . . more in control. Plus,
> I read that you need to have some
> sexy photos to send privately if
> you *do* hit it off. Ones to take
> things to the next level.

Vanessa flashes a knowing half smile. Emily
hesitates, looking at a mantel clock, then
the front door.

> EMILY
> Well . . . they're not supposed
> to be back for an hour still. I
> guess if you were *really*
> fast . . .

> VANESSA
> Oh my god, I'm going to be like
> *lightning*. I'm already gone.

With a bright smile, Vanessa hurries up the
stairs. Emily doesn't clock how confidently
she makes her way to the LaVoies' bedroom.

> VANESSA (CONT'D)
> Oooh, this would be *perfect*.
> Smart girl but with an edge,
> right?

> EMILY
> I mean, I guess . . .

Emily trails Vanessa inside, taking the
camera from her friend as Vanessa arranges
herself on the bed. After a couple seconds,
Vanessa finds a pose she likes.

> VANESSA
> Okay, how about this?

Emily starts snapping photos, and the two girls laugh as they get into it. Before long, Vanessa flips around to a cross-legged position, extending her hand for the camera. She reviews the photos slowly, nodding.

> VANESSA (CONT'D)
> These are perfect. Exactly what I need. Seriously, have you ever considered going into photography?

> EMILY
> They're nothing special.

> VANESSA
> They're *totally* special. You're special.

She rises to her knees, wrapping Emily in a tight hug.

> VANESSA (CONT'D)
> Thank you so much. You can't imagine how much this means to me.

Emily softens in her arms, yielding to the hug.

> EMILY
> Okay, I love you too, but . . .
> you really need to go.

> VANESSA
>
> Oh my god, can you imagine if the professor came back and found me here? His head would probably explode.

She laughs and hops off the bed to grab her coat, wrapping it tight around her again. The girls make their way out of the bedroom as the scene

> FADE TO BLACK

> JUMP TO

INT. PROFESSOR LAVOIE'S OFFICE—DAY

Emily knocks tentatively on the half-open door to the professor's office, a standard-issue space (built-in plain bookshelves, a featureless desk, one ancient-looking window, its view mostly obscured by tree branches) that Alden's attempted to inject some character into with framed posters of eighties punk bands, indie films, and a handful of moody landscape photos, presumably his own. Alden, bent over a stack of papers at his desk, looks up quickly. It's clear from the tension radiating off his entire body that he's been waiting for the knock.

> ALDEN
>
> Come in.

Emily walks inside and he tilts his head at the door.

ALDEN (CONT'D)
Close the door, please.

She does as she's told and takes a seat
across the desk from him, perching anxiously at the edge of the chair.

EMILY
What's going on? I came as soon
as I got your text. Is everything
okay with Aurelie? She was cough-
ing a little when I was there
last night, but I didn't think it
sounded—

ALDEN
I'm just going to get right to
it, Emily. Did you have anything
to do with this?

He hands her a photo. As Emily looks at it,
her eyes widen. She's too stunned to speak.

ALDEN (CONT'D)
You and Miss Morales are close,
aren't you?

EMILY
Yes.

ALDEN
(angry)
So the two of you set me up together, then, is that it? Figured
you'd just sneak her in while
you're babysitting my *child*?

                    EMILY
          Set you . . . I don't know what
          you're talking about!

                    ALDEN
          This was taken in my *home,* Emily.

                    EMILY
          Vanessa just wanted it for her
          dating profile, I swear!

                    ALDEN
          Her dating . . . ? Is that what
          she told you?

He laughs bitterly.

                    ALDEN (CONT'D)
          You really expect me to believe
          you had nothing to do with her
          plan to blackmail me? She didn't
          get into my bedroom on her own,
          Emily. And you're the only stu-
          dent who has a key to our home.

                    EMILY
          Blackmail you?

Emily blinks, trying to piece it together.
Slowly, realization dawns.

                    EMILY (CONT'D)
          Wait, you . . . and *Vanessa*?

The professor stares at her for a moment,
horror flashing across his face, then his
shoulders slump. He rests an elbow on the
desk, propping up his forehead on his hand.

                    ALDEN
          She hadn't told you.

                    EMILY
          Did Margot—

                    ALDEN
          Margot doesn't know about this,
          nor do I want her to find out.

His voice is sharp, but when he sees the
fear and confusion on Emily's face, he softens.

                    ALDEN (CONT'D)
          For the record, whatever . . .
          happened between myself and Van-
          essa, it's over now. It has been
          for some time. Or at least I
          thought that was the case . . .

                    EMILY
          Okay.

                    ALDEN
                 (pained)
          I know it's not fair of me to
          ask, but for now, would you
          please keep what you've learned
          to yourself? I know it might
          change your opinion of me, and
          that's . . . fair. But I need to
          deal with this privately. And
          Margot doesn't deserve the embar-
          rassment of this getting all
          around the campus.

                    EMILY
         Okay.

    She nods robotically, face slack with shock.
    The professor regards her warily.

                    ALDEN
         Thank you. And . . . I'm sorry
         for dragging you into this. I
         promise you, I *will* take care
         of it.

                              FADE TO BLACK

9

I'D GONE TO VANESSA FILLED WITH RIGHTEOUS anger—*You could have lost me my* job, *how dare you pull me into your sordid little* blah blah blah. It had all felt so scandalous, but if I was honest with myself, a not-small part of me was delighted to be a part of the drama instead of squinting through the gaps in the blinds Vanessa pulled down over so much of her life.

But she'd crumpled so quickly and completely, breaking down in heaving, ugly sobs almost the moment I'd brought it up, that it was hard to feel anything but pity. The story had come out in a flood—the flirting at office hours and at social events in the English Department suddenly shifting gears when Vanessa spotted Alden on the street in New York City, the coincidence so great that both of them forgot to keep the line as bright as they should have, the drink that had turned into drinks plural and then to a handhold across the table, and then suddenly it just *happened*. She'd seemed so vulnerable when she was hiccuping out the story, raw in a way she'd never let me see her before, that when she begged me *not to tell the other girls, especially Lydia, I don't think I can handle any of them knowing about this,* I'd immediately agreed. Vanessa almost *never* opened up that way; knowing that we shared this knowledge, that I'd been allowed to glimpse behind her armor, felt special, intoxicating even.

I knew it was ridiculous, but realizing Vanessa had beckoned Lydia to follow her past the same velvet rope, probably months before I'd even known it existed, stung even now. In fact . . . if Lydia had known all along, it had to mean Vanessa had been playing *me*. Even midbreakdown, she'd been raising the drawbridge, making sure Lydia and I couldn't compare stories, controlling what each of us knew, thought, felt about her secret. I swallowed hard as that sank in. *What does that mean for everything else that's coming out?*

"That just leaves you, Em." Paige pulled her eyes off the photos to look at me expectantly. "We showed you ours."

"Sorry, what do you mean?"

"What little *memento* turned up for you?" Brittany arched an eyebrow, taking a long sip of her wine. "You're the one who wanted us all to share, after all."

"Oh, umm . . ." I frowned, eyes darting between the women. "Actually, I haven't gotten anything."

"Oh, come *on*," Paige drawled. "I just told you I fucking *killed Vanessa*, you're going to play coy about whatever showed up to haunt you?"

Trust Paige to browbeat you with her own confession of manslaughter.

"No one's going to judge you for whatever it is," Lydia said, eyes soft as she gazed at me across the table. She reached a hand out toward mine. "All of this was a long time ago, we were kids. None of us could have known which decisions we made would wind up having real consequences."

I took her hand and squeezed, grateful to have an ally, but as our hands met across the table, my eyes were drawn once again to the photos in the center. I frowned at the images we'd thought were so sexy and adult at the time, but which now looked overblown, even a little desperate, a pantomime of adulthood.

The photos were meant for me.

The thought appeared suddenly, fully formed, and part of me wanted to resist it; Brittany's and Paige's items implicated them somehow—even if I still wasn't entirely sure what the ring meant or how it had turned up, I was sure that it pointed to something Brittany had done that she'd rather keep secret, something big.

But I *was* implicated in the photos. Lydia might have known about the affair, might have gossiped with Vanessa about Alden LaVoie's sexual achievements and shortcomings for all I knew, but I'd let Vanessa into his home when I was supposed to be caring for his child, staged the scene with her on the bed he and his wife shared. Of course I hadn't known she meant to use the photos for blackmail, but I was still an integral strand in the noose Vanessa had planned to pull tight around her ex's neck. All the objects were unearthing some part of the past that the recipient wouldn't want brought to light. Those photos . . . they were *my* secret.

So why would Lydia have them?

And considering what had happened in town, the giant gaping hole that had opened up under my feet, sucking away everything I thought I'd known about the night Vanessa went missing in a tidal rush, why would they have turned up at all?

INT. ROSIE'S DINER—DAY (PRESENT DAY)

The morning rush has started to clear out
from the diner, its chrome-legged tables,
leatherette-topped seats, and curated decor
(a chalk specials board, pie stands lining
the countertop, publicity shots of fifties-
era celebrities) giving it a standard-issue
retro vibe. The interior, however, is pristine, and the customers are all dressed a
little too well, their smiles a little too
universally straight and gleaming, to maintain the illusion of Anywhere, USA. This
isn't any old greasy spoon, it's *Green Valley*'s version.

Brittany is looking out the window near the
table she shares with Emily, watching PRO-
FESSOR NIKO STAVROS totter away on his
wife's arm. The smile is just starting to
fade from Brittany's face. Emily, however,
looks troubled, and a little queasy.

                    BRITTANY
         I'm so glad Niko's doing well. He
         was always one of my favorites of
         Mitzi and Topper's friends.

                    EMILY
         Mmm.

                    BRITTANY
         Alright, well I'm going to see if
         they can fit me in for a facial.
         Are you sure you won't let me
         treat you to one?

> EMILY
> No, that's okay. I'll just poke
> around town.

> BRITTANY
> I'll walk you to the bookstore,
> then. It's on the way.

> EMILY
> Actually . . . I'd like to use
> the restroom first. Go on with-
> out me.

Brittany gathers her things and makes for
the exit while Emily hurries over to the
bathroom. Inside, she leans heavily on the
porcelain pedestal sink, sucking in deep
breaths, the uneasiness she was tamping
down before evident on her face. After a few
moments, she turns on the tap, splashes
some water on her cheeks, and towels it off,
standing up to look in the mirror.

> EMILY (CONT'D)
>   (whispering)
> It wasn't your fault. It's a long
> time ago and it wasn't your
> fault.

She doesn't look particularly convinced,
but she tosses the towel and exits the bathroom with a sigh. She makes her way to the
counter, getting the attention of one of
the waitresses there.

> EMILY (CONT'D)
> Could I get a coffee to go? Black,
> please.

> WAITRESS
> Gimme two minutes.

We see a slim woman move up behind Emily as she waits for the waitress to help a customer at the counter, but the camera angle leaves the woman's face invisible, her form blurred. She clears her throat, but Emily doesn't notice.

> WOMAN (O.S.)
> (hesitant)
> Umm . . . Emily?

The camera stays tight on Emily as she turns, so we fully register her shift from mild interest at hearing her name to jaw-dropping shock. The color drains from her face as she stares, wide-eyed, at the speaker.

> EMILY
> What . . . what are you . . .

> WOMAN (O.S.)
> I know this must be really hard
> to take in, and I'm sorry, but I
> had to talk to you.

> EMILY
> But . . . you're *dead*.

The camera pulls back to show a tall, slender woman. The hair is shorter and darker, the lines of her face carved slightly more sharply by age (though if anything, it only makes her beauty more apparent), and her trademark insouciant "I dare you" vibe has been replaced by a quiet watchfulness, but it's immediately evident: it's Vanessa. She glances over her shoulder anxiously, sucks in a shuddering breath, and turns back to Emily, a hint of her old wryness twisting her lips.

> VANESSA
> Trust me, Em, if I were dead I sure as shit wouldn't spend my time haunting Green Valley.

> EMILY
> I don't . . .

She blinks, shaking her head, too stunned to form coherent thoughts. Her body starts to tremble, and she leans against the counter heavily, senses overwhelmed. Vanessa is dead. If she's not . . . Emily's breath comes short, and she shakes her head rapidly, as though she can will this away.

> EMILY (CONT'D)
> This doesn't make sense. What in the fuck is even *happening* right now?

> VANESSA
> (tight)
> I'm sorry, I know you have a lot of questions, but we don't have time for that now. I'll explain everything later, okay?

Vanessa leans in slightly, creating an intimate space between her and Emily, and rests her hand on the other woman's upper

arm. Emily jumps, eyes darting to Vanessa's
hand. But it's real. This isn't some spec-
ter, it's Vanessa. Vanessa's eyes are wide
and solemn. Almost in spite of herself,
half in a daze, Emily nods. Her mouth hangs
open, voice a thin, childlike whisper. Shock
has drained her ability to resist.

> EMILY
> Okay.
> (beat)
> What . . . what did you want to
> say to me?

> VANESSA
> I suppose it's more a request,
> really. I need your help.

The waitress returns with the coffee, and
Vanessa tilts her head toward the counter,
cueing Emily. She doesn't want any extra
attention pointed their way. It takes Emily
a minute to understand the gesture, then
she turns around, clearly startled to find
the rest of the real world continuing around
them. Robotically, Emily pays and takes the
cup. Once she has it, Vanessa draws her to
the far end of the breakfast bar. Vanessa's
eyes keep darting to the window every few
seconds, and her whole body is tense. Emily,
for her part, is moving as though she's
fallen into a dream . . . or a nightmare.

> VANESSA (CONT'D)
> It's about Brittany. The whole
> thing is . . . complicated, but
> the digest version is I need
> something from her that she's not

> going to be happy about giving
> to me.

Emily exhales heavily, pinching her eyes shut to take a few deep breaths. She needs to get a handle on herself. On what's happening. Finally she opens her eyes, anger creasing her brow. The shock of seeing Vanessa hasn't quite worn off, but it's starting to dawn on Emily that Vanessa's reappearance means nothing Emily thought she knew can be trusted. Least of all Vanessa. When Emily speaks, her voice is brittle and peevish.

> EMILY
> Are you *trying* to be all mysterious? Because I can't exactly help
> if I have no idea what's
> going on.

> VANESSA
> No, honestly, there's just a lot
> of . . .

She waves her hand in the air, swatting off an invisible worry, her anxiety clearly mounting.

> VANESSA (CONT'D)
> Stuff. Inside baseball shit. The
> point is, Brittany and I are
> going to need to work some big
> things out, but I'm afraid that
> if I confront her on my own . . .

Vanessa's tongue darts over her lips, real fear twisting her pretty features.

                    VANESSA (CONT'D)
          She's not going to like what I
          have to say. And when Brittany
          gets defensive, things . . .
          don't go well.

                    EMILY
                (voice rising)
          Vanessa, what are you saying? I'm
          sorry, I get that you're in some
          big rush here, but you just show
          up after fifteen years, everyone
          thought you were *dead*, I thought
          that maybe I . . . that we . . .

She shakes her head sharply, the guilt she'd
carried all those years ballooning into
anger. Vanessa had *let* her believe that.

                    EMILY (CONT'D)
          And now you're talking in riddles
          about Brittany, and I just—

Vanessa grips Emily's arm, her need to re-
gain control of this conversation evident
in the tension coursing through every muscle, every ligament.

                    VANESSA
          She gets violent, okay? She got
          violent before.

Vanessa raises an eyebrow, fixing Emily with
a sharp look, her alphaness shining through
the anxiety. Emily blinks, trying to take
this in, trying to understand *any* of what's
happening, and Vanessa sucks in a ragged
breath, pinching the bridge of her nose.

                    VANESSA (CONT'D)
          I know it's a lot to ask, espe-
          cially when I can't explain it
          all right now, but I wouldn't
          come to you if I didn't really
          need your help, Emily. I need to
          find out whether Brittany—

Her eyes dart to the window, then widen. She
squeezes Emily's arm with a hand, too tight.
Emily stares at it, frowning.

                    VANESSA
          Is your number the same?

                    EMILY
          What? Vanessa, what are you—

                    VANESSA
          Is your phone number the same?

                    EMILY
          Yes, it's the same! But—

Without another word, Vanessa drops Emily's
arm and hurries through the doorway that
leads to the bathroom. Emily stares after
her, scared and so confused she's having
trouble not swaying in her seat. She rubs
absently at the place where Vanessa death-
gripped her. We hear the bell of the diner
door ring. A few seconds later, another figure moves up behind Emily.

                    BRITTANY
          You're still here? You really
          must be feeling rough.

Emily jumps at the sound of her friend's voice.

> EMILY
> (terrified)
> What are you doing here?

Brittany sniffs dismissively.

> BRITTANY
> I forgot my *scarf*. I'd ask what
> *you're* doing here, but I'm guess-
> ing I know the answer. Should we
> try to find you an IV?

She gestures at Emily's pale face, the clammy sweat beading near her hairline. Emily's confused for a moment, then she shakes her head slowly, forcing herself to focus on Brittany.

> EMILY
> No, I'll be okay. I think one
> more cup of coffee and I'll have
> it out of my system.

Emily raises the to-go cup weakly, fear lingering in her eyes as she watches to see what Brittany will do. *Is* she violent? Will she be able to spot it on Emily somehow, the trace Vanessa has left? Fortunately, her anxiety is easily mistaken for run-of-the-mill nausea. Brittany frowns at her for a moment, lip curling in disgust, then shrugs.

> BRITTANY
> If you say so. Do you need to
> wait here longer, or . . . ?

Emily's eyes dart toward the doorway leading to the bathroom. We see her assessing
for just a fraction of a second. Who will
she choose? Then she shakes her head.

          EMILY
    No, I'm good. Fresh air will
    probably help.

The two women exit the diner together, and
we see them through the window walking down
the street. Brittany's chattering on, but
Emily's clearly shell-shocked, eyes wide
and unseeing. What did she just agree to?
And who can she trust?

10

"EMILY? *WAS* THERE SOMETHING FOR YOU?" Lydia pressed. Her face was still gentle, but her words were more forceful. I could feel everyone's eyes on me, waiting.

"No, there was nothing." I shook my head rapidly, dropping my eyes to the photos just to have something to focus on while my brain whirled crazily through the possibilities.

I'd had my suspicions after Brittany and I got back from our trip to town, and when Paige had slapped her college essay down on the table, they'd seemed to be confirmed—Vanessa must have been leaving the trinkets somehow, though how I couldn't guess. Brittany's phone would have pinged if she'd managed to get inside, wouldn't it? *But can you trust that Brittany would tell you if it did? Can you trust anything she's told you? Or anything Vanessa told you in the diner?*

I squeezed my eyes shut, trying to force my thoughts back into formation.

The photos had to be meant for me, I was the only person who remembered them firsthand. Lydia having them instead could just be a mistake—it's not like our room assignments were posted at the entry points—but it felt intentional. Was my *not* getting the photos, not having to share my own moment of guilt, some sort of signal?

Maybe even a threat?

"So, what, we're supposed to believe Saint Emily never had a single secret?" Paige rolled her eyes as she swigged her wine.

"I'm not saying that," I said. "For what it's worth, I knew about the affair with Professor LaVoie, too." Lydia turned to me, a vaguely startled look on her face. *Vanessa must have been just as convincing when she'd siloed her.* Which led to another, more unsettling thought: Had Vanessa's fit of mortified sobs all those years ago been *entirely* an act?

"Interesting. The only one of us not to receive anything. Which we wouldn't even have known if Paige hadn't gone full confessional." Brittany gestured at Paige with her wineglass. "It wouldn't have been hard for you to get into all our rooms, either." Brittany raised an eyebrow at me, swirling the wine slowly.

"You think *I* left those things for you?" I was genuinely stunned.

"You could have," Brittany replied with a tilt of her head.

"Actually . . . yeah." Paige's eyes widened and she nodded slowly. "You were the one who wanted us all to come here in the first place, too." Her eyes locked onto Brittany's. "Brit told me it was all your idea. That you called *her.* When you said you wanted closure, did you mean you wanted to torture us all?"

"I told you, I *knew* about the affair too! For all we know, those photos were meant for me!"

Brittany sniffed out her disbelief. Lydia's eyebrows tented in something between pity and fear.

"Emily . . . you know I'm your friend, but . . . that does seem a little convenient for you to say *now,*" Lydia said quietly.

"But why would I be doing all of this? What would be the

point?" I was starting to get frantic. If they all bought into this, I'd never get another word out of any of them. And the one trump card I held, the thing I could use to *prove* it wasn't me—*Vanessa never even died, guys, she's hanging around trying to find a way to get in touch with Brittany without Brittany going apeshit on her*—would only make me look more guilty.

"Have you been holding on to some old paper of mine all this time? Why wouldn't you have just said something?" Paige was shaking her head. I could feel the temperature in the room rising. Then, in a flash, I had it.

"I *couldn't* have done all this." I could feel their incredulous stares like brands on my skin. "Think about it. Even if I somehow managed to plant all this stuff—which doesn't make sense, we were all together all this time—how could I have gotten her *ring*, Brittany?"

Brittany narrowed her eyes at me, trying to find the hole in my argument. My held breath was practically pulsing in my lungs, threatening to burst them . . .

Then Brittany finally exhaled, leaning back in her chair.

"She's right. She couldn't have had the ring. In fact, if Paige really *did* see her when she says she did—you're absolutely sure about which night of the week we're talking about?" Brittany's eyes lasered into Paige with an intensity I hadn't seen there . . . maybe ever, something almost desperate in the tension of her jaw.

"I told you, Brittany, I didn't fucking misremember *killing* her."

Brittany exhaled shakily, her entire body slumping back. She almost looked relieved.

"Then the only person who could have had the ring is you, Paige."

"Wait . . . what?"

"Was she wearing it that night? When you . . . you know," Lydia murmured. Paige startled, eyes wide as she stared at Lydia. In her heavily inebriated state, it was taking her longer to maneuver through all the left turns. Plus, I'm guessing the idea of her beloved commandant openly turning on her would have been fairly hard to process even stone-cold sober. She blinked a few times, frowning with the effort to remember.

"I don't know. I . . . I didn't check. If she did, it would have gone into the water with her. I can tell you I didn't stop to swipe it, that's for sure."

Lydia nodded, looking away. I couldn't tell if she believed Paige, but I certainly did, and not only because of what I knew about Vanessa's current whereabouts. Paige's lack of a filter was very real, and no one had pressed for the confession. I had to believe she'd told us exactly what she remembered. For a few moments everyone sat in silence, the tension in the room not quite gone, none of us fully sure who we could trust.

"Okay, but then who's fucking with us?" Paige leaned on her forearms, eyes moving between us. "I had no idea about Vanessa's thing with the professor, you all didn't know about me cheating, and none of us could have had her ring. Vee never took it off."

"There is one thing," I said, frowning in concentration, thinking through my words very carefully. If it really was Vanessa who'd been leaving the objects around the house, if she was somehow getting inside without our knowing, then the person I had to be *most* wary of was her. But some instinct crouching at the back of my brain told me not to reveal that I'd seen her. Brittany still hadn't offered any explanation of why Vanessa might be afraid of *her*, for one thing—and Vanessa's fear in the diner had seemed very real, not that I could be certain anymore what was and wasn't an act with her. Still, while we were all trapped here together, showing anyone my entire hand felt dangerous. Vanessa's existence was the one card I was fairly certain no one else knew was in play. Once I threw it down, all hell would break loose.

But I could still try to learn something from their reactions if I tiptoed up *next* to the truth. Brittany's screams had pulled me away from the window last night, but before . . .

"I think I saw someone last night. On the grounds."

"What? Where?" Lydia's eyes darted to the window anxiously.

"Outside my room, beyond the back patio. I couldn't make out the details, but . . . something was moving out there, near the cliffs."

"Some*one*, you mean?" Paige said with a shudder. I nodded slowly.

"I'm sorry, but no." Brittany shook her head, face twisted with incredulity. "I know we're all freaked out right now, but that doesn't make any *sense*."

"Why not?" I folded my arms across my chest, feeling defiant. Sure, I hadn't been able to make out details, or like . . . the specific contours of a human body, but considering everything that had come since . . .

"For one thing, this place is *way* too remote." Brittany ticked the points on her fingers. "We're the only property on this access road, and it's two and a half miles of switchbacks to the highway. The nearest house along the coast is maybe a mile down? As the crow flies, that is. The path between here and there goes through woods, there are some rocky sections, a couple gaps you have to see to step over. It would be impossible to navigate at night."

"What about the house in the other direction?" Lydia asked.

"It's closer," Brittany conceded, "but the cliffs shear off about half a mile to the north. Either you'd have to bring climbing gear, or you'd have to double back almost to the highway to get from there to here."

"But someone who knew the area could manage it," I retorted.

"Okay, fine. Maybe they *could* manage it if they brought their crampons or whatever. But why would they *want* to?" Brittany scrunched her eyes tight. "Both those houses are just as remote as ours, it's not like there's a public campground down the road or whatever. So why would one of the neighbors risk breaking their ankle—or their neck—to fuck with a bunch of strangers? And how would they have all this stuff anyway?" Brittany flourished her arm at the paper and the photos. "Maybe you saw something, I can't really say, but—"

Brittany's ultimate dismissal was cut off by a loud blare, her look of vaguely scornful disbelief transforming into tense watchfulness.

"What the fuck is that?" Paige yelled over the sound, shrieking through the house every few seconds.

"It's . . ." Brittany shook her head, twisting around until she spotted her phone on the counter. She hurried over to it, tapping at the screen, her frown deepening with each passing moment. "Follow me. Hurry."

Her tone was too clipped to argue with, and we all pushed back from the table, trailing after her to the door that led to the corridor between the tasting room and the house, creeping through the no-man's-land of conference rooms and offices until we reached a closed door with an EMPLOYEES ONLY plaque in the center. As Brittany tapped anxiously at the keypad, I realized that the wood finish on its front, complete with irregular dark streaks of "graining," was painted on. Somehow that felt emblematic of everything that was happening here.

After one false start she managed to enter the code, and we followed her into a narrow room, the wraparound counter-top built in to support multiple monitors, another row mounted on the walls above, making the already small space cramped. Brittany pushed the door closed behind us, flipping a deadbolt and a hasp lock for good measure, then, with a shaky breath, moved over to the computer at the back of the room. The alarm blare was slightly muffled inside, but it was still unignorable, and my whole body tensed every time it swooped up to its peak.

"What's going on?" Lydia murmured, glancing from screen to screen, eyes wide.

"I'm sure it's just a system error," Brittany said, clicking through windows on the computer.

"Can't you control it from your phone?" I asked.

"The main security system is digitally enabled, but it was too difficult to run new wiring through the caves. They're all on the old system. Besides the entrance from the tasting room, obviously." Brittany clicked a few more keys, and the alarm cut off. Her shoulders dropped with relief. "I need to check a couple more things."

Brittany started typing again, and the oversized monitor mounted just above her head flicked to a new image, a view of the main entrance to the tasting room.

"Last time it was opened was yesterday, that's good . . ." she muttered, squinting at a time log on the screen. She continued through the patio entrance to the tasting room, the front and back entrances to the main house, the cellar entrance from the tasting room, the image on the screen swapping to each new location as she checked the logs to make sure all the entries and exits made sense. From what I could see over her shoulder, none was more recent than a few hours ago. But . . . these *were* the "digitally enabled" entrance points. Did that mean Brittany had been tracking our movements, however roughly? *Stop being paranoid, Emily, it's just the alarm getting to you. And Vanessa telling you Brittany gets violent when her back's against the wall. And the fact that you're isolated in this house with three women you don't really know at all, all of them holding on to major secrets.*

"Alright, that all looks good. Let me just take a quick peek at the cave entrances and we can go back to the house."

The image that flashed onto the screen next was distinctly grainier than the others, and it took me a moment to piece it together as a metal door, swoops of wrought iron in the foreground hinting at the spiral staircase that led down to it. *The beach cave entrance.* Brittany tapped her nail against the screen as she scrutinized each of the series of bolts and hasps that subdivided the length of the door.

"Okay, that all looks normal."

She jumped to a slightly sharper view of a room filled with barrels, the camera centered on the door at the far side. *The entrance from the house.*

"Good to go there. That one locks from the inside, anyway. And none of us has gone down to open it."

My whole body tensed. Was I imagining it, or did her eyes flick over to me for just a moment? *Did she know I'd followed her into the caves last night? But why wouldn't she have said anything?*

The image switched one last time, the view even fuzzier than the others. I squinted at the large, grainy circle in the center.

"What the . . ." Brittany leaned forward, clicking the mouse rapidly. The image zoomed in slightly, turning even more pixelated as it was blown up, but I was just able to make out the central wheel, the bars cutting across it.

"Is that . . . the hatch entrance?" Lydia frowned as she peered at the screen.

"Wait, the one in the cliff?" Paige took a step closer.

"Yes," Brittany said, staring. Her face was entirely slack.

The image moved jumpily.

"But . . . what's happening?" Lydia started.

"It's open," I said, cold blooming from the base of my spine. "The hatch is open."

11

"BUT . . . DOES THAT MEAN SOMEONE'S INSIDE?"
Paige said, her jaw so tight I could see tendons popping out
along her temples.

"I don't think so." Brittany's voice was small, childlike even.
"The system would tell me if they'd come into the house."

"But someone could be in the caves?" Lydia whispered.
Brittany just nodded.

"Wait . . . didn't you say the hatch can only be opened
from the inside?" I frowned, trying to remember. "When you
showed it to us earlier you said that, right?"

"That's right!" Brittany whipped around to face me, eyes
lighting up. "I probably just . . . didn't close it right before."
Her head darted up and down in little birdlike twitches of
self-assurance.

"We're still going to check, though, right?" Paige clenched
and unclenched her fists a few times, hopping back and forth
from one foot to the other like a runner about to start a race.
"I don't know about you guys, but I'd feel a lot better *seeing*
the door close."

Everyone went silent, looking from one another to the
screens. My heart rocketed up into my throat, each heavy
beat choking me from the inside, a blood balloon expanding
all the way to the walls.

"Paige is right," I finally said, swallowing the acid wave of anxiety the words brought with them. "We have to close the hatch. And check to see if anything is . . . *off* in the cellars."

"Right. Yes, right." Brittany nodded, brow low with worry. "Then . . . I guess let's get it over with, yeah?"

We all filed out into the hallway, glancing over our shoulders as Brittany locked the room, entered the code to the tasting room, and led us across to the main entrance to the cellars.

"Hold on to your butts," Paige muttered as Brittany tapped another code into the keypad there. Brittany pulled the door open slowly, glancing back at us briefly, and started down the stairs.

I sucked in a sharp breath, closing my eyes tight for a moment, *There's no one down there, it will be okay, you will be okay.* But would I? And what, exactly, should I be most afraid of? Running after Brittany in the middle of the night had been an impulse decision, my brain still sleep-fogged. Plus, it had been hard to imagine a real threat even if she'd caught me. Brittany was my old *friend,* after all. Now, though, things felt different. The isolation of the winery was really starting to sink in, the vast empty stretches around it giving me a perverse sense of claustrophobia. There was no way out of here; I hadn't even rented my own car. And despite Paige's wine-soaked confession, Vanessa had only mentioned being afraid of Brittany . . . and I had no idea whether all of us should really be afraid of Vanessa.

Paige started after Brittany, then Lydia. My lungs were beginning to ache with held breath. With one last glance over my shoulder, I forced myself to exhale and follow them into the cellar.

I trailed the other women past the supply shelves for the tasting room and into the large, amorphous aging room, each stack of barrels ominous now, just so many blocked sight lines and unseen hiding places. Everyone stopped at the entrance to the rough, narrow tunnel that led to the open door. I stared down it, the few yards to the hatch seeming to telescope out in front of me. A whoosh of cold sea air swept down its length, punctuated with the loud *crack* of the door slamming shut. Slowly it drifted open again, a few inches of darkness appearing around the edge.

"Who's going first?" Paige murmured, her skin sallow from the combination of fear and the dim cellar lights. The descent into the cellars seemed to have sobered her up slightly. For a moment, no one answered.

"I guess I can," Lydia said, taking a tentative step forward.

"No, I should," Brittany said, sucking her lips in and taking a deep breath to steel herself. "I know the winery best."

I hung back as Brittany inched along the tunnel, shoulders visibly tight, steps cautious. The door slammed to again and she jumped. After a few seconds, Lydia took a few tentative steps down the tunnel behind her, then Paige. I hung as close to the tunnel's entrance as I could, heart banging around my rib cage painfully, my breath growing shallow. The illusion of the door opening onto nothingness was much more effective at night.

After a taffy stretch of time, seconds that felt endless, Brittany reached the door. Positioning herself near the hinges, she steadied herself with a tight grip on the circular handle at the center, leaning forward to peer at the bolt as she twisted it back and forth slowly.

"The bolt looks worn, but it doesn't seem to be broken," she said, pushing the door closed and twisting the lock into place. The same *click* I remembered from the tour echoed through the silent cave. Brittany stood in front of the wheel, pushing and pulling in turns, her entire body moving with the effort, but the door didn't budge. Lydia moved up behind her, placed a hand on the wheel lightly, and twisted it a quarter turn before tugging again. When it didn't move, she twisted the wheel just an inch or so more. The door swung toward her at the first pull.

"Maybe the mechanism's a little worn from the salt?" she said, bending to get a closer look at the bolts. "If it wasn't totally closed, it might have just . . . come loose?"

"I guess." Brittany frowned at the door, then twisted the wheel back and forth again. "I could have sworn I checked it after I closed it up. You both remember me locking it, right?"

Lydia and I nodded agreement.

"Maybe that was enough to loosen it," Paige said, craning her neck to see past Lydia. She'd stopped about halfway down the tunnel, sticking near the wall. "Tugging, I mean. If the mechanism's a little faulty. Do you know when it was replaced last? Or serviced?"

Brittany shook her head, slowly peeling her eyes from the wheel that controlled the door lock to look at Paige.

"I don't think it's ever been replaced. At least not since I can remember."

"I think Paige is right," I said. Overhead, a lightbulb flickered, sending my heart ricocheting around my body again. "Salt can do a lot of damage. Maybe it wore away some . . . catch or something."

"Maybe," Brittany murmured.

"What other explanation is there?" Paige said. "It can't open from the outside, right?"

"Right," Brittany said, nodding slowly. "That must be it." She pushed it back into place, twisting the wheel to the right, then twisting hard again after the telltale click said—or at least claimed—it had locked securely.

"So now what?" Paige screwed her mouth up. "Do we check the caves to see if someone's hiding, or . . ." Her gaze darted over my shoulder to the aging room, the far side still swathed in shadow.

"If you really want to," Brittany said, starting down the tunnel, neck tight in a way that made me think she was resisting the urge to look back at the door. "But even if there was someone here—which I don't think is likely—they couldn't get into the main house. All the entrances have locks, and the tasting room entrance is connected to the digital security system, so I'd see if anyone tried to open the door." She moved past me into the aging room, smiling tightly. "Besides, if someone really wanted anything from the winery, this is where they'd find it." She gestured around at the barrels. "If we're in the middle of some cliffside wine heist, I say let them have it. It's insured to the hilt anyway."

"Frankly, I'd just be impressed," Paige quipped, forcing out a laugh. "Barrels of wine have to weigh at least five hundred pounds. If you're somehow sneaking that out through a hole in the middle of a cliff, hats off, right?"

No one quite managed a laugh.

"Then . . . is it alright if we go back upstairs? I'm getting a little . . ." Lydia licked her lips, sucking in a deep breath. "I don't like it down here."

"Yes, let's. I'm sure it was just a mix-up," Brittany said, eyes pulling back to the hatch door. "I should turn the alarm off on this entrance until we get the door checked. And I could use a glass of wine."

We all trooped upstairs, pausing only for the elaborate

door locking and security notification cross-checking procedures Brittany had mentioned, then made our way back into the main house. It was a little startling to see the spread of papers and photos in the middle of the dining room table. Some deep part of my brain started whirring again at the sight. *Why had Lydia had those pictures? What did that mean for me?* But the rest of me felt like a wrung-out rag, and I couldn't quite manage to direct my thoughts into any meaningful channel.

"I think I'm going to head to my room," Lydia said once we'd all poured wine. "All of that . . . I just need to decompress."

"Seriously," Paige said, lifting her glass in Lydia's general direction. "Plus, our rooms have locks on the doors."

"I *told* you, there's no way—"

"Settle the fuck down, Brit, I'm just joking." Paige rolled her eyes toward Lydia, who frowned at Paige's entirely out of character attempt at commiseration.

"Well . . . maybe it's for the best to call it a night," Brittany conceded. "I'm not sure I have the energy to try to untangle all that anyway," she added, gesturing vaguely at the spread on the table. "If you need anything . . . honestly, I'm probably gonna take a couple Xanax, so try to figure it out for yourselves."

With that, we all started filling wine and water, retrieving books and phones, giving each other unnecessarily wide berths as we prepared our individual retreats.

When I finally closed my bedroom door behind me, the tense energy that had been straining at my seams rushed out all at once. I leaned back against the door, eyes closed, breathing heavily, until I could reinflate enough to stumble the few feet to the bed.

I had just set my wine down on the dresser and was making my way to the window to pull the curtains closed—the vast expanse of steel-gray ocean, the surface flickering as the sickle moon emerged from behind a bank of clouds, was making my shoulders creep up around my ears—when I heard rapid steps coming up behind me. Before I could turn, a hand shot over my mouth, clamping down hard, another wrapping around my middle, pinning me tight. I tried to scream, but the sound died against the attacker's palm. They squeezed me tighter, leaning over my shoulder to hiss in my ear.

"Don't scream. Don't make a sound. If they find us, it's all over."

INT. EMILY'S BEDROOM—NIGHT

Start in CLOSE UP on Emily's face, her eyes
bulging with terror, the strong hand over
her mouth unyielding even as she attempts
to twist out of its grasp. Her attacker
leans forward to whisper.

                    VANESSA
          Emily, it's me. It's Vanessa.

Emily stops writhing, but her expression is
still extremely wary.

                    VANESSA (CONT'D)
          I'm going to let you go, but
          promise you won't scream. Yeah?

Emily nods once, and after a long moment,
Vanessa drops her hands, stepping back.
Emily spins around to face her, brow lowered. Her whole body is trembling; it's not
the first time she's seen Vanessa, but there's
still the vertiginous feeling of encounter-
ing a ghost. Is Vanessa here to hurt her, or
someone else? Can she trust anything her
former friend has said? With effort, Emily
turns her fear into an approximation of annoyance; Vanessa needs to *believe*, at least,
that Emily's on her side.

                    EMILY
          What the fuck, Vanessa? You
          scared the shit out of me.

Vanessa raises a finger to her lips, wincing
at the sound of Emily's voice.

> VANESSA
> I know. I'm sorry. I just . . .
> if you saw me in here and didn't
> realize who it was, you might
> have screamed, and then someone
> would have come running . . .

She shrugs, spreading her hands open in a
helpless gesture.

> VANESSA (CONT'D)
> I'm sorry, honestly.

> EMILY
> Fine, just . . . text next time,
> yeah?

Vanessa smirks.

> VANESSA
> Answer your texts next time.

Emily pulls her phone out from her back
pocket, frowns at it, then blinks, tilting
her head to one side to concede the point.
It's not completely reassuring, but it's
something. She turns back to Vanessa.

> EMILY
> Wait . . . so did you come
> through the beach cave?

Vanessa nods, moving to sit on the bed. The
small action reveals how exhausted she is.

> EMILY (CONT'D)
> Jesus, does that mean you went
> down the cliff stairs in the dark?

                    VANESSA
          I've done it a hundred times be-
          fore.

                    EMILY
          But how did you know the door
          would be open?
                    (beat)
          And how did you get into the
          house without setting off the se-
          curity system?

                    VANESSA
          I'll explain all that once we're
          somewhere more private.

She makes as if to stand, but Emily shakes
her head, folding her arms across her chest.
Vanessa pauses, perched on the very edge of
the bed.

                    EMILY
          Nope. No way. Vanessa, I need more
          information here. You can't just
          show up after fifteen years and ex-
          pect me not to have questions. How
          do I even know I can *trust* you?

                    VANESSA
          I get it. And I can explain it
          all, just . . . not here.

Vanessa glances at the door, body rigid.
Emily raises an eyebrow, waiting. Vanessa's
jaw tenses—she's not used to Emily pushing
back on her—but then she sighs, drops her
eyes to her hands, folded in her lap, and
starts speaking.

(

              VANESSA (CONT'D)
This wasn't how I planned things
for this weekend. I wouldn't have
even come into the house if I
didn't absolutely have to.
But . . . something's gone wrong,
I'm not sure what. And the fact
is . . . you're the only person I
can trust.

She laughs ruefully, pretty features clouding with pain as she turns to Emily.

              VANESSA (CONT'D)
Honestly, I probably should have
known that from the start. You
were the only one who never let
me down. But hindsight's twenty-
twenty, right?

              EMILY
Sorry, no. That's not going to
work, Vanessa.

              VANESSA
         (startled)
What's not going to work?

              EMILY
The whole "You're my favorite
one" routine you pull. I'm not
some naïve twenty-year-old anymore. I'm not just going to do
whatever you ask because you're
telling me I'm special.

              VANESSA
Emily . . . it's not like that.

                    EMILY
          Maybe it is, maybe it isn't. Ei-
          ther way, I need answers.

                    VANESSA
                (nodding)
          I get that. You're right. And for
          the record, I wasn't trying to
          manipulate you. But . . . I see
          how it probably seemed that way
          when we were younger.

She rolls her eyes skyward, dragging her
hands over her cheeks.

                    VANESSA (CONT'D)
          Fuck, it probably was that way
          when we were younger. No excuses,
          but I wasn't in the best place
          back then. And I wasn't doing it
          on *purpose.*

                    EMILY
          Well, we're all adults now. So?
          What the hell is going on?

                    VANESSA
          Emily, I know you don't trust me,
          but we can't do this here. It's
          too risky. If Brittany catches me
          now . . .

She shakes her head sharply.

                    VANESSA (CONT'D)
          Come to the cellars with me. I'll
          explain everything, I promise.

> EMILY
>
> Vanessa, come *on*. You must real-
> ize how creepy that sounds.

> VANESSA
>
> If you don't want to, I get it.
> If that's the case, could you
> just give me a couple hours to
> figure out what I'm going to do? I
> know you don't owe it to me, but
> it would mean more than you know.

Emily folds her arms, deliberating.

> VANESSA (CONT'D)
> Think about it. If I wanted to
> hurt any of you, I'd already have
> done it, right?

Something about this doesn't quite feel
right, but Emily can't put a finger on it.
She rolls her eyes, annoyed to be conced-
ing.

> EMILY
> Fine.

> VANESSA
> Thank you.

Without another word, Vanessa slips to the
door, carefully peering around the frame
before opening it fully. She pauses, looking back for just a moment.

> VANESSA (CONT'D)
> If you change your mind, I'll be

in the cellars. I . . . hope you
come.

With that, she steps out into the hallway,
leaving Emily alone in the room. Emily paces
for a moment, body taut with tension. Then,
with a sniff of exasperation, she hurries
over to the bedroom wall, where a shadow box
displays military paraphernalia . . . including a flip-knife with a jagged edge.
After a second of hesitation, Emily tugs it
off the wall, wraps her hand in a corner of
the blanket, and smashes the glass on the
front, gingerly pulling out the knife, folding it at the hinge in its handle and slipping it into her pocket. She quickly tucks
the mangled frame under the bed and hurries
out the door after Vanessa, hands fingering
the threat in her pocket, not entirely sure
she won't regret giving in to her curiosity . . .

12

THE HOUSE WAS COMPLETELY SILENT, DARK except for the running lights along the skirting boards and, if I turned toward the main room, the faint suggestion of the pendant lights over the kitchen island, dimmed to their lowest setting. I crept across the hallway, hair prickling on the back of my neck as I listened for movement from the other bedrooms. Vanessa had left the stairway door open the tiniest crack, and I quickly slipped through it, pulling it closed with exaggerated care, stopping when the edge of the door touched the frame, just before the latch could catch. Slowly I made my way down the stairs, leaning heavily on the railing to keep my footfalls on the concrete steps as light as possible. Apparently Vanessa's appearance had transported us to the set of *A Quiet Place*. I ran my thumb over the large, weighty corkscrew in my pocket, the only vaguely weapon-like object I'd been able to find in the bedroom on short notice. If things turned ugly, it wouldn't be much help, but I might be able to scare her back with it, at least. Or maybe I was just telling myself that because there was absolutely no way I would have been able to resist following her. Vanessa was the story I'd been trying to untangle for so many years. If anyone had the answers I needed, it was her.

Vanessa was waiting at the entrance to the cellar, the locks and latches on the door already thrown, hand on the handle as she stared over her shoulder, body tense. She loosened slightly as I appeared on the landing. Raising a finger to her lips, she turned the handle, so slowly I could barely hear the latch open, and we moved into the dark of the cellars.

At the back of the room, near the passage down through the cliff, a red light glowed faintly, providing just enough illumination to turn the humped rows of barrels monstrous and slice the irregular swoops of the ceiling with hundreds of still bloody wounds. I shivered as Vanessa fumbled along the wall, my whole body tensing as the scrabbling of her fingers echoed eerily around the cave.

"There. Fucking *finally*," Vanessa muttered.

I exhaled shakily as the lights flickered on overhead, the atmosphere immediately dialing down from horror film to merely creepy.

"Let's move around the wall, toward the winery entrance side," she said, gesturing with her head. "If anyone comes down, they won't see us right away." I nodded, and she flicked on another set of lights, waiting until I'd made it halfway across the amoebal room to turn off the set nearest the entrance we'd come through. With any luck, someone would assume that bank of lights had been left on when we checked the hatch door. Actually, with *any* luck, no one would come down at all, but still, better to plan for the worst.

"So?" I said, folding my arms across my chest. "What the hell is going on, Vanessa?"

"I suppose the best answer to that is this." She reached into her hip pocket and pulled out a thick wad of folded papers and passed them to me. I frowned as I started reading.

"Last Will and Testament of Margaret Chisholm?" I scanned the thicket of text below, but it was all legalese. "Is that Mitzi?" Vanessa nodded. "What's this got to do with anything?"

"This has to do with *everything*," Vanessa said, taking the papers back and flipping through them until she found what she was looking for. "Here, see what it says?"

"I give the home at 95 Roaming—"

"No, the one below."

"I give the Cliff's Edge Winery property to my husband, Christopher Chisholm. If he predeceases me, I give the property to my surviving grandchildren."

"There," Vanessa stabbed the paper with a finger, eyes lighting with grim triumph. "*Surviving grandchildren*. That's why I'm here. It's why I had to come now. I'd been thinking about it for a while, honestly, but there was never a good enough reason to risk the blowback. But this?" She took the winery in with a graceful turn of her head. "This was too important to let slip through my fingers."

"But does that mean . . . did Mitzi *know*? That you were still alive, I mean?" The picture was starting to form, but I could only see one corner at a time, a curve here, a sharp angle there, tantalizingly close to a shape I could recognize, if only I could sort out how this connected to that.

"I honestly don't know. I never heard from them. Or that private investigator they hired. She certainly had plausible deniability." Vanessa reached over to pluck the will from my hand, carefully folding it into quarters again and sliding it back in her pocket. "But I think some part of her knew all along. Frankly, I think she didn't *want* to dig too deep; she was probably just relieved to be rid of me. For all I know, she called the investigator off before he had a chance to track me down." Vanessa gave a one-shoulder shrug, eyes darting to the side, and my breath hitched at the intense familiarity of the gesture, which had always accompanied her most gut-wrenching declarations, always delivered in the same wry, almost flat manner: *But then they both died, so spring break wasn't really in the cards that year. Shrug.*

How did Vanessa know about the private investigator if he'd never reached her? The thought wriggled at the back of my brain, one of those loose threads in the story you'd point to when you discussed the show with friends later, armchair quarterbacking the reasons you could have done it better. *I mean really, it's just sloppy writing.*

But that wasn't really the answer I cared about, and asking her for it right now might derail things. Vanessa had always teased me for the way I got hung up on the details, my practical Midwestern brain craving order, resolution. In a way, I think she'd resented it, especially when it threatened the integrity of whatever dramatic narrative she was crafting. I still remembered one conversation, all of us sprawled around Vanessa's living room, idly sipping drinks before some night out, when she'd started talking about who we'd all be in ten years. *Lydia will run some mega-important lab and she'll probably have cured cancer. Paige, you'll be . . . the mayor of some random town in Ohio, just rocking pantsuits every day and taking names. Brittany will be married to some handsome rich guy with a kid on the way, and like, a golden retriever. And Emily . . . you'll be a stock analyst or something, one of those jobs where people make stupid amounts of money because they're so laser-focused on tiny details no one else cares about.*

On its surface, it had *almost* sounded like a compliment. If she hadn't known how much I wanted to write, how scared I was that I didn't have the talent to make it, or the guts to keep going when—though at the time I was naïve enough to hope for "if"—I failed, it might even have been one. Looking back, it's possible they'd all been digs, the knives so thin and sharp you could only see them if they were sliding between your own ribs. Brittany had been the one to snap back at Vanessa.

Really. And where will you be in this psychic vision?

You know me. I'll probably be traveling. Living with some Spanish lover for a year, then taking off to Thailand when the passion fades, then maybe Morocco. You'll all be total adults and I'll be the penniless friend who crashes on your couch when she's in town. But I'll pay for it in super-authentic paellas.

It had sounded so painfully romantic, which made her vision of me—pedantic, bourgeois, successful but somehow still pathetic—hurt that much more. But how could I even argue with it? If I had, she'd have flipped the switch immediately, *Oh my god, of course you'll be an amazing writer if that's what you want. All I'm saying is you're so smart and like . . . dedicated that you'll probably be a millionaire while I'll still be playing guitar in some metro station in Paris.*

And it would have worked. Vanessa had been so *alluring*, magnetic in a way I'd never encountered before I met her, and even working in the industry—that mecca of ineffable *it* factor—have only rarely encountered since. Even now in the cellars—knowing she was probably consciously turning it on for me, that roping me into this wasn't about some realization of who she could really *trust*, it was just about her getting what she wanted—it was still hard to resist.

Brittany, though, never seemed to worry about losing Vanessa's favor. Honestly, I think they never really liked each other; they'd probably banded together by instinct at boarding school and stuck with it out of habit. I think it was part of why I always respected Brittany, even if I wasn't always sure I *liked* her. Brittany could be harsh, her "honesty" bordering on cruelty, but she said the things that deep down I wished I had the guts to say, too.

So, a string of sugar daddies, then? Pass. It had taken every ounce of willpower not to snort with laughter at the pissy look Brittany's words had brought to Vanessa's face. *Not so glamorous when you think of it that way.*

Vanessa took a few steps down the row of barrels, tracing her long, elegant fingers through the dust on top, one arm wrapped around her flat stomach, flimsy armor against the chill in the cellars.

"She never loved me, you know. Mitzi. I think she might have hated me a little."

"I'm sure that's not true," I said automatically. Though of course Brittany had told me the same thing earlier that day.

"No, it is. And honestly, it's okay. I mean it's fucked up, obviously, but it was a long time ago. Topper loved me, I think. But Mitzi wore the pants. She was the one that cut my mom off. I honestly think my mom *dying* was just more proof to Mitzi that she was an embarrassment to the Chisholm name. I mean, helicopter crash? So tacky." Vanessa rolled her eyes. I forced myself not to react to the glib dismissal of her mother's sudden death, her grandmother's cruelty in the wake of it. Trying to convince Vanessa that Mitzi cared was not only futile, it wasn't the point.

"But Mitzi never changed the will," I said instead.

"She didn't. I think, deep down, she knew she owed me at least this much."

"But how did you even find out about it? The will, I mean."

"Wills are public record. At least if the estate goes to probate, which any estate as big as Mitzi and Topper's is pretty much guaranteed to do." Vanessa flipped her hand through the air, trying to brush a veneer of casual over the statement, as though we didn't both know how deeply she was invested in all this. Even knowing that Mitzi had died was a serious tell. "I've asked friends about the situation, and it seems pretty clear, the will doesn't exclude me. It was probably drafted that way specifically to ensure I *could* get my fair share. It does make you wonder if she knew all along I wasn't really gone."

"Then can't you just . . . I don't know, go to a judge and get this all sorted out?" Vanessa scrunched up her face in a look bordering on disgust. I raised both hands, desperate not to turn her against me now, when I was so close. "Sorry, I'm not trying to be thick, I swear. I'm just new to all this stuff."

I turned to a barrel next to me, pretending to focus deeply on the handwritten label so that Vanessa couldn't catch my eyes. This wasn't the whole story, I could *feel* it, but Vanessa's familiar sharpness had taken on a distinctly brittle quality since she'd appeared in my bedroom; if I tapped the fragile globe she'd dropped over us in the wrong place, the whole thing might shatter. I needed to let her get there on her own if I had any hope of unraveling the knotty tangle of what had happened then, and in between, and what was happening right this very second, in a cave carved out of thousands of tons of stone.

"I'll go to a judge eventually, if I absolutely have to. But for any of it to matter, I'll need to prove who I am." She sighed heavily, crumpling slightly against one of the racks. "When I left, I didn't think I'd ever want to come back, and . . . well, I made it pretty fucking hard for myself to do it. Not on purpose, but that doesn't make much difference, really." She darted her eyes over to me, mouth twisting wryly. "Fun fact, if you spend fifteen years living under a false identity, it's actually pretty complicated proving you're someone else. Especially when that someone's presumed dead."

"A false . . ." I blinked, biting down against the rest of the question, even though my brain was practically itching with the need to get to the bottom of it. The *how* of her disappearance—how someone as unforgettable as Vanessa could vanish into thin air so completely the whole world took her for dead—was exactly what the scriptwriter inside me was desperate to understand. It was why I was here in the first place. Vanessa smirked knowingly at me.

"As far as the state of California knows, I'm Christine Silva. I even pay her taxes every year."

"Who is she?"

"Who knows? She's never asked for her name back."

"But Vanessa . . . where did you even *go*?"

"LA. Mostly." She sighed heavily, gaze going distant. "It was the only place I could think of that I might stay lost."

FLASHBACK TO

INT. WEST HOLLYWOOD BAR—NIGHT (15 YEARS AGO)

The bar is extravagant, a mix of rococo decor flourishes, velvet-upholstered lounging areas, and mirrors: on the walls, above the bar, even slotted into several of the painted tin tiles of the ceiling. Everywhere you look, trendy young Angelenos sip delicately from their coupes and cut crystal tumblers, bodies held precisely, as though they believe they're being watched, even photographed. Most of them aren't—they're here trying to be discovered, either by an industry insider or a similarly attractive individual, ideally with more funds than they possess—but the scene has the crackling energy of an audition, all of it lubricated with extremely expensive drinks.

Vanessa is behind the bar, wearing the same skimpy black halter dress as all the other female employees, though it seems like it's been tailored for her elongated, angular frame. She moves up to a man in his thirties, dressed trendily, sitting alone, eyes roving the room as he finishes his martini. This is TODD STONE. He's not quite handsome, but he's distinctly charismatic, enough so that you almost forget the fact.

> VANESSA
> Ready for something else?

                    TODD
         I am . . . but not to drink.
         What's your name?

He flashes a vulpine grin at her, and Vanessa
tenses for what's coming next. It's not the
first—or the fiftieth—time she's been hit on
at work.

                    VANESSA
         Whitney. But if you're not drink-
         ing I'm not sure I can help you.

                    TODD
         Oh, I think you can. The thing
         is . . . *you're* what I want,
         Whitney.

                    VANESSA
         That's flattering, but I'm already
         taken.

                    TODD
         But are you *signed*?

Vanessa's head tilts to one side, her polished "Sorry but no" face slipping a bit.
This is a proposition she hasn't received
before.

                    VANESSA
         Sorry, what do you mean?

                    TODD
         I can't be the first person to try
         to scout you.

She laughs, shrugging out a yes, and his
eyes go wide in exaggerated surprise.

> TODD (CONT'D)
> Really? How are you not already
> modeling? Your look is *perfect*.
> Are you new in town? Honestly,
> that's the only reason I can
> think of that you wouldn't al-
> ready have representation.

She's wary but excited. Vanessa's young
enough to think big breaks happen this way
all the time.

> VANESSA
> Pretty new, I guess . . .

> TODD
> Then I must just be lucky. I'm
> Todd Stone, I'm an agent. Here,
> take my card. And put it some-
> where you won't lose it, I'll be
> back here to hunt you down if I
> don't hear from you.

> VANESSA
> You really think I could model?

> TODD
> I *know* you could model. I *think*
> you could be the next Miranda
> Kerr. That is, if we work to-
> gether.

Vanessa half-laughs, her delight making her
look younger. She takes the card from him,

tucking it carefully into her bra, the only
safe spot on her body, eyes still lingering
on him as she responds to a yell for service
farther down the bar.

FADE TO

INT. TODD'S APARTMENT, HOLLYWOOD
HILLS—DAY (SIX MONTHS LATER)

Vanessa's lying on a gigantic king-sized
bed in a flimsy silk pajama set. She winces
as her alarm goes off, reaching to snooze it
blindly. Eventually, with a sigh, she half-
sits up, reaches for Tylenol on the mirrored nightstand, and washes down several
with the bottle of Fiji water nearby. She's
taking a few deep breaths to steady herself
as Todd enters. He moves up next to her,
draping an arm around her slim body and offering a cup of coffee.

                    TODD
          I thought you might need this.

                    VANESSA
          God, yes.

She takes a sip, eyes closed. Her hands are
slightly shaky. She turns to Todd, anxious.

                    VANESSA (CONT'D)
          How did we get home?

                    TODD
          I called my driver. Don't worry,
          babe, you just fell asleep.

She nods slowly. On the nightstand, her phone alarm goes off again.

> TODD (CONT'D)
> Do you have somewhere to be?

> VANESSA
> (grimacing)
> I have a shift at two.

> TODD
> Why are you still working there? I told you, I *want* to take care of you.

> VANESSA
> I know. But I don't want to quit until I at least book some real jobs. Not just rich people's parties and trade shows, like . . . *campaigns*.

> TODD
> I'm never going to be able to book you those sorts of gigs if you're not available for castings.

> VANESSA
> I make it to most of them! And besides—

> TODD
> Besides nothing. Babe, you have to trust me. This is what I *do*.

> VANESSA
> You really think I'll start book-
> ing if I quit?

> TODD
> Absolutely. And regardless, I'm
> sick of sharing you.

He wraps his arms around her, nuzzling his
face into her neck in a way that makes her
giggle.

> VANESSA
> Todd! I'll spill my coffee.

> TODD
> Good. Fuck knows I pay the maid
> enough. She can earn it for once.

His hands slip around her body and he draws
her in for a kiss as she fumblingly sets the
coffee mug on his nightstand, then gives in
to his advance.

> FADE TO

INT. LOFT PARTY—NIGHT (SIX MONTHS
LATER)

Vanessa stands in the corner of the party,
slim and elegant in a slip dress, occasionally sipping the drink she's holding. Next
to her, an intense, anemic-looking man is
chattering away, but she barely hears him.

> PARTYGOER
> I'm pretty sure the pilot will be

picked up any day now. It's exactly what everyone's looking
for.

> VANESSA
> Mmm. That's great.

It's clear Vanessa's planning her escape
from this conversation. The PARTYGOER looks
around, movements turning a little darty,
then leans in closer.

> PARTYGOER
> Any interest in party favors?

He reaches into his breast pocket just far
enough to tug out a small vial of white powder. Vanessa's interest is clearly piqued—
which is exactly what he'd been hoping for.

> PARTYGOER (CONT'D)
> Bathroom?

> VANESSA
> Sure.

As they make their way across the party, her
eyes hook on Todd, leaning against the
kitchen island, deep in conversation with a
very pretty girl around Vanessa's age. As
they pass by, she picks up just a hint of
his voice.

> TODD
> . . . can't believe no one's
> scouted you yet.

Her mouth drops open, eyes tightening, but she continues into the bathroom, where the man starts tapping the drugs out onto the counter. Once he's prepared them, Vanessa bends to sniff a thin white line, her stare as she stands a thousand yards long.

                                        FADE TO

INT. DTLA BAR—NIGHT (SEVERAL MONTHS LATER)

Vanessa's waiting on a trio of middle-aged men in suits, pouring expensive scotches and smiling coyly at them whenever she passes, clearly spending more time on them than on the customers closer to her own age. The bar has a clubby feel—all dark wood, elaborate stained glass light fixtures, and brass accents—and the crowd is more subdued than at her last job. After a few minutes, two of the three men stand, making their way toward the bathrooms in the dim interior of the restaurant. One of the men is clearly supporting the other. The third man, ARI, turns to Vanessa as she approaches. He's a little paunchy, his features a bit too rough to qualify as good-looking, but he has the whitened, easy smile (and extremely expensive suit) of a man who's done well for himself.

                    VANESSA
          Can I get you anything?

                    ARI
          Maybe a muzzle for Frank?

He tips his head after the two men, grinning
slyly. Vanessa mirrors his smile.

> ARI (CONT'D)
> Seriously, sorry if he's been a
> little out of line. We're cele-
> brating, and he's never been able
> to hold his liquor.

> VANESSA
> Don't worry, I've dealt with way
> worse.

> ARI
> Not sure that's a high recommen-
> dation.

> VANESSA
> He's fine, really.

She picks up a glass from the bar to polish.

> VANESSA (CONT'D)
> What are you celebrating, if you
> don't mind my asking?

> ARI
> We just closed a deal on a major
> development project downtown.

> VANESSA
> Like film, or TV . . . ?

> ARI
> I'm in luxury real estate.

> VANESSA
> That sounds interesting.

                    ARI
          You sure about that?

She laughs, the motion showing off her slim
throat.

                    VANESSA
          Honestly? It's just nice to meet
          someone who's not trying to brag
          about how important they are in
          "the industry."

                    ARI
          Let me guess, they come in claim-
          ing they want to "scout" you.

Her eyes tighten, but she manages to hold on
to her smile.

                    VANESSA
          It's been known to happen. I had
          a guy a few weeks ago who talked
          at me for an hour about his re-
          cent production with "*actor* James
          Franco." He said it that way
          every time.

                    ARI
          In case what, you confused him
          with lauded poet James Franco?

                    VANESSA
          I guess?

They laugh. Vanessa clearly notices the man
leaning toward her across the bar, but she
doesn't pull away. She also doesn't respond

to the hipster raising two fingers at the other end of the bar.

>ARI
>
>I, on the other hand, have nothing to offer besides a very, *very* good dinner.

>VANESSA
>
>Oh? How good are we talking?

>ARI
>
>Phones aren't allowed in the restaurant to protect the patrons' privacy good.

>VANESSA
>
>In case *actor* James Franco wants to get handsy with some aspiring actress?

>ARI
>
>Something like that.

His smirk gives his features more appeal. Vanessa signals to the increasingly annoyed patron, then leans on the bar on both elbows, biting the corner of her lower lip.

>VANESSA
>
>I suppose I *might* be interested in that. At least if I got to enjoy it with the right person.

>ARI
>
>Perfect. I'll tell Frank to book a table for you two.

She laughs easily, pushing up, but still angled toward the middle-aged man, their flirtatious chatter sucked up into the heavy, dark interior of the bar. As we pull out, we can finally see the ceiling, an intricate coffered affair created out of narrow strips of the same dark wood lining the walls, the sections they're framing painted to resemble a summer sky, as though the bar and everyone in it has been trapped inside a large, luxurious cage.

FADE TO BLACK

13

WAS THAT RIGHT?

As Vanessa flitted over the details of her life, conveniently eliding years at a time, offering zero explanation of how she'd been able to fund the luxe lifestyle she glancingly referred to—*And of course I had to start over after spending so much time abroad; the thing about living in Bel-Air is it's so isolating, it meant losing everything, but I had to get out of there*—I found myself smoothing out the details, beating out the scripted version in my head. I could *imagine* it happening the way I was mentally drafting it—a string of men promising her the world, and actually giving it to her, at least temporarily; the thrill of potential stardom blinding her to the infinitesimal odds of anyone, even someone as stunning as her, managing to achieve it; the creeping misery and desperation each time the rug was pulled out from under her, leading her to vow to do things differently . . . until the next man came in offering the next easy way out, a too-good-to-be-true vision of the good life she couldn't figure out how to string together for herself, but which she convinced herself was real simply because the alternative was too dreary to stomach for another minute.

It felt plausible. Like the version of LA someone like Vanessa *might* experience. But was I gravitating toward it because it was the best way to move the script along, or just because it was the most obvious option? It's not like she'd mentioned modeling, or acting, or any of the myriad *Look at me* careers young, beautiful people came to LA for. Hell, she hadn't even mentioned any exes. It was the version you'd expect to see during the big-screen montage of the years she'd been hiding in plain sight—but was that a good thing?

Fuck, had all the years at *Back of House* completely eroded my ability to tell a unique, interesting story? I'd been mentally deriding the show as hacky pap for longer than I could remember, but had it turned *me* into a hack? Or was this one of the few things it had actually taught me—when it's okay to rely on shorthand, to give people the expected contours of a story so the details you change will resonate that much more?

"So . . . yeah. That's the digest version, I guess." Vanessa flicked her hair away from her face, affecting indifference. She hadn't said much—just suggested the vague outlines of various dead ends, too much time invested in this opportunity or that person, and when it didn't pan out, the sobering realization that she'd cut herself off from any easy path to a different option the day she walked out on her old life. But knowing Vanessa, it must have felt like tearing open her chest for me to peer inside. She had always been stingy with information about herself, and she was especially reluctant to flaunt her failures. My hands were curling around my need to get more out of her . . . but digging now, when she probably felt she'd been painfully honest, would only shut her up entirely. And besides, if I couldn't come up with a satisfyingly specific version for the script on my own, that wasn't any fault of Vanessa's. *Time to move on, Emily.*

I nodded slowly, as though I was simply taking it all in.

"No one ever came looking for Christine?"

Vanessa's face clouded and she turned away from me. "A lot of teenagers run away, you know. Most of them don't get found. But all of them have Social Security numbers. If you're willing to pay, of course." She sucked in a deep breath, closing her eyes, throat working hard against whatever memory was resurfacing. After a few long beats, she lowered her shoulders, physically forcing away whatever thoughts were troubling her. When she turned back to me, any hint of pain was covered by her knowing smirk. "For the record, I go by Coco. I mean, would *you* buy me as a Chrissy?"

"So . . . is that why you need me? To help prove you're really you?"

"That's part of it," Vanessa said. "But what I really need is for *Brittany* to admit to it. The whole process of legally recovering my identity could take a while. If the estate closes in the meantime, I might never get my share of the winery. At the very least I'd have to fight it out in court, which is basically the same thing. It's not like I have piles of cash lying around to pay for two rounds of lawyer's fees."

That shrugging side-glance—it pained Vanessa, on some level, to admit to that. For the first time since she'd appeared so suddenly in the diner, I really examined her. She was dressed chicly—a creamy sweater so lightweight you could see through to the shadow of her bra; high-waisted black jeans that clung to her, emphasizing her otherworldly proportions; a pair of black ankle boots that looked expensive—but all of it was a bit faded, the toes of the shoes scuffed visibly, the jeans bagging at the knees. At first glance, it passed for affluence— her looks certainly helped complete the picture—but the sheen was starting to wear off. Whenever she'd last had money to spend on fancy clothes, it wasn't recently.

"I guess I figured Brittany would have a harder time wriggling out of it if I came to her with someone in my corner," Vanessa said, lips twisting in a mirthless smile. "She's a lot like Mitzi, you know. Acting like an absolute asshole isn't a problem for Brit, but if it became *public knowledge,* the world might end."

"I guess that makes sense, but—"

Vanessa raised a finger. "Pause for a sec, there's something I need to do before we get into any more of this." She swept past me, chin slightly up in a way that elongated her slender neck even further, and crossed to the racks just inside the entrance from the tasting room. After a few seconds skimming the labels, she pulled a bottle out, then looked around until she found a corkscrew tucked into one of the cubbies. *So much for being able to fight her off.* What were we going to do if she *did* suddenly turn threatening, corkscrew-duel? I ran my thumb along the spine of the corkscrew in my pocket. I might at least be able to throw it at her head and stun her.

She opened the bottle cleanly, taking a long drink before crossing the room again and holding it out to me. "Needs to open up a little, but beggars and choosers, right?"

I took a long sip of the wine, the alcohol moving through me hotly, trying and failing to loosen the muscles of my shoulders.

"So? I'm guessing that's not enough for you," Vanessa said with a sharp eyebrow raise. Something twisted in my gut, the ghost of the need for her approval that had always hovered over our friendship. An "I'm sorry" geysered up my gullet of its own accord.

But I managed to choke it down. We weren't those people anymore. And judging by the furtive meetings, the skittish demeanor, even just the state of her elegant but worn ensemble, Vanessa needed me even more than she was willing to let on. My breath caught behind my ribs as the realization finally dawned on me: Vanessa wasn't the one in charge here, *I* was.

"It's a good start," I said, using a sip of wine to buy myself a bit more time before I handed the bottle back to Vanessa. "But that only explains why you're willing to come back from the dead. It doesn't explain why you decided to disappear in the first place."

"Em, it was all so long ago. I was going through a lot . . ." Her forehead crumpled prettily, distress somehow more appealing on her than serenity.

Keeping her happy isn't the only thing that matters. She is not in charge of this.

"So were we all," I said, throwing my shoulders back, trying to reverse-engineer some confidence with the pose. "Especially after we thought our best friend had *died* and we were too busy getting wasted to notice. Did you ever think about that, Vee? Did you consider how everyone you left behind would feel when you decided to just waltz out of your life? What was so terrible that you were willing to make us all go through that?"

Vanessa's eyes closed slowly, the corners drawing tight as she took a few slow breaths. When she turned back to me, her shoulders slumped visibly, and her expression had that flat, wrung-out look you sometimes saw on the workers at remote highway truck stops, a mix of resentment, hopelessness, and simple exhaustion.

"Honestly? No. I was desperate, I needed a way out. I never really even thought through what it would mean for *me*. I definitely didn't worry about anyone else."

"Oh." I blinked at her, startled by the brutal honesty of the statement.

"I could bullshit you, but why bother?" Her half smile wasn't nearly strong enough to reach her eyes. "I've had a lot of time to think about it, and you know what? I was wrong.

About a lot of things. But at the time it all seemed so dire, I really thought this was the only way."

"*What* all seemed so dire, Vee?"

"You remember Alden LaVoie, right?"

"Of course I do."

"Well, he's as good a starting place as any."

BEGIN FLASHBACK

INT. ENGLISH DEPARTMENT FRONT OFFICE—
NIGHT (15 YEARS AGO)

It's after hours, and the English Department building is mostly dark, a handful of individual can lights at strategic intervals spotlighting randomly chosen patches of the gray industrial carpeting that lines the main thoroughfares through the building, strips of dark hardwood peeking out at the edges where undergrads can't easily trample them.

Vanessa stands near the entrance, clicking her nails across the blond wood registration desk, neat stacks of campus maps, course schedules, and departmental event flyers marching across its surface. Her posture is stiff, jaw working with annoyance as she taps aggressively at her phone with her other hand. After several seconds, the sound of a distant door opening echoes through the space, bringing her to attention. As Alden crosses the lobby to meet her, her tension transforms into a saucy, come-hither smirk.

> VANESSA
> Make a girl wait, why don't you.

> ALDEN
>   (tight)
> I couldn't get away earlier.

>   VANESSA
> Was Margot nagging you about—

>   ALDEN
> Actually, it was Aurelie's bed-
> time. And I'd appreciate it if
> you leave my family out of this.

Vanessa pulls back, startled by the curt tone, her face going entirely blank. Alden seems to notice the effect and sighs heavily.

>   ALDEN (CONT'D)
> Come on, let's go somewhere more
> private.

He leads her down a narrow hallway, frosted glass walls on either side modesty-screening a series of conference rooms, before arriving at a row of heavy wooden doors at the back of the building. Alden swipes a card over the panel at the side of one and pushes into a small, plain room dominated by a round oak table, the surface scuffed. A handful of flimsy metal-and-plastic chairs are arrayed around it. A single narrow window at the back shows a glimpse of a wrought iron fence hemming in a patch of snowy ground. He holds the door open for Vanessa, who stops just inside. She's breathing fast, entire body radiating tension as Alden slips in behind her, carefully closing the door so as not to make any sound.

>   ALDEN (CONT'D)
> We shouldn't be interrupted here.

                   VANESSA
        What is this, a classroom?

                   ALDEN
        A graduate seminar room. Occa-
        sionally we'll take meetings in
        here if the larger spaces are
        booked. Please, sit.

Vanessa swallows hard, pulling out the chair
nearest to where Alden is standing and
perching on the edge. A frown flits across
her forehead as he moves two seats away before sitting himself. Already this isn't
going the way she'd hoped . . .

                   VANESSA
        Why not just go to your office?

                   ALDEN
        All the department offices are on
        the same hallway. I wanted to
        make sure we weren't . . .

He sucks his lips under his teeth, one by
one, as he searches for the words.

                   ALDEN (CONT'D)
        What I mean is, I know this might
        be a difficult conversation. I
        thought you might want some more
        privacy.

                   VANESSA
              (cold)
        You weren't so worried about pri-
        vacy when you fucked me on your
        desk.

Alden's eyes pinch closed, jaw tightening.

> ALDEN
> Which was a mistake. I'm thinking
> more clearly now.

> VANESSA
> Wow. Okay.

She sneers, leaning back in the chair and
folding her arms across her chest.

> VANESSA (CONT'D)
> What, were you afraid I'd
> like . . . sex attack you? Start
> yelling *"Professor Alden LaVoie
> is fucking me and I'm an under-
> grad!"* when I came?

> ALDEN
>   (angering)
> Honestly? I have no idea *what*
> you're going to do anymore, Van-
> essa.

> VANESSA
> Now you're just being dramatic.

> ALDEN
> Really? You're going to call me
> dramatic after taking those pic-
> tures *in my bedroom*? What were
> you even trying to *accomplish,*
> Vanessa? We had already ended
> things!

                VANESSA
        No, *you* ended things. Without
        even bothering to give me an ex-
        planation, or tell me what had—

                ALDEN
        I'm genuinely trying to under-
        stand what you were after, Van-
        essa, and I just can't. I
        mean . . . what if Margot had
        seen one of those?

                VANESSA
        Then she'd have known you don't
        love her anymore!

Alden shakes his head in disbelief, running
both hands through his just-too-long shock
of hair. Vanessa leans forward, a pleading
look on her face. She's desperate to right
the ship.

                VANESSA (CONT'D)
        I swear, I wasn't trying to make
        things harder for you. I only
        sent the pictures to *you,* Alden,
        not to Margot. But if she had
        found one, would it have really
        been that bad?

                ALDEN
        What in the hell are you—*yes* it
        would have been "that bad." It
        would have been a fucking catas-
        trophe, Vanessa! How aren't you
        seeing that?

Vanessa's mouth falls open slightly, hope and confusion warring on her face. She looks younger, vulnerable in a way we've never seen her.

                    VANESSA
          But . . . we love each other.
          It's what you want, right? To be
          with me?

                    ALDEN
          Vanessa . . . it's not that sim-
          ple.

Vanessa stares at him, her expression shift-ing from bafflement to angry, intense hurt.

                    VANESSA
          That was all just a lie,
          wasn't it?

                    ALDEN
          It wasn't a *lie* . . .

                    VANESSA
          You just said it so you could
          fuck me. *God*, you must think I'm
          so fucking *stupid*!

                    ALDEN
          Vanessa . . .

                    VANESSA
          Which one am I, even? Number one?
          Or ten? Do you pick a few lucky
          idiots every semester, or is it
          more of a special treat to fuck
          your students?

ALDEN
I need you to calm down, Vanessa.

VANESSA
Or *what*?

She stands, slapping the table with a hand. Tight panic steals over Alden's face, and we can see the fight he has to make to keep his self-control.

ALDEN
Vanessa, what we had was real, and it was important to me. But right now, I think it's better for both of us to take a step back—

Vanessa lets out a bitter laugh.

VANESSA
Oh *fuck off*, Alden. It's better for *you*. Sleeping with me was better for you, and now getting rid of me before your precious fucking Margot finds out is better for you. This whole goddammed thing was better for *you*.

She blinks hard, eyes going wide.

VANESSA (CONT'D)
You want to know the pathetic part? I actually believed you. Just another naïve college girl who bought it. *Jesus.*

She's pacing in tight circles now, and Alden's starting to look genuinely concerned.

He stands, taking a step toward her and raising a hand, hovering it at the level of her shoulder.

> ALDEN
> Vanessa, I do care about you.
> That was always true, but—

She slaps the hand away fiercely.

> VANESSA
> *Don't* touch me.

> ALDEN
> I know this is hard for you. It's
> hard for me, too. But—

> VANESSA
> You don't have any idea what this
> is like for me. You don't know
> the first fucking *thing* about me.

> ALDEN
> If you just tried to calm—

> VANESSA
> No. You don't get to tell me what
> to do. Not anymore.

She reaches for the door and Alden rushes forward, physically pushing it closed, hand over hers.

> ALDEN
> What are you going to do?

> VANESSA
> Let me go.

                    ALDEN
          I need to know if you—

                    VANESSA
          Oh for fuck's *sake*, Alden, I'm
          not going to show up at your
          house, okay? Is that what you
          want to hear? Just . . . leave me
          alone.

He steps back just enough for her to wrench
the door open. She stops just inside the
frame, turning to him, face tight with rage.

                    VANESSA (CONT'D)
          For the record? I believed you. I
          believed I had finally found some-
          one who actually cared about me.
          Not just my vagina, *me*.

She storms out of the office, leaving Alden
behind, stricken, a sickly pallor creeping
over his face.

The camera follows Vanessa down the hallway. Within seconds tears start streaming
down her cheeks, and by the time she reaches
the lobby, she's choking back ugly, heaving
sobs.

                                        JUMP TO

INT. VANESSA'S BEDROOM—THAT SAME NIGHT

Lydia hovers over Vanessa, clearly unsure
what to do, tentatively stroking her back
as Vanessa continues to sob, curled up in a
ball on her twin bed, whole body heaving.

                    LYDIA
          Please, just tell me what's
          wrong.

                    VANESSA
          It's . . . over. It's all . . .
          over.

                    LYDIA
          Whatever it is, you can get
          through it. I know you can.

                    VANESSA
          But . . . what if . . . I
          don't . . . *want* to . . . ?

She dissolves into even more intense body-
racking sobs as Lydia tries to tend to her.
In the corner of the room, Vanessa's computer screen lights up with a reminder.
Lydia notices it, squinting to make out the
words of the calendar notification: *History
176b—midterm paper due tomorrow!* She bites
her lower lip, clearly unsure what the right
course of action is, but another gulping
choke from Vanessa steals her attention as
the screen fades to black again.

                                        FADE TO

INT. TOPPER CHISHOLM'S PRIVATE OFFICE—
NIGHT (SOME WEEKS LATER)

A well-groomed older gentleman sits behind
a massive mahogany desk, his body framed by
its ornate scrollwork and the built-in book-
cases behind him, stained to match. The
room has a clubby feel, and so does he, his

neat white hair, deep tan, and crisp resort wear pulling over a noticeable but not *too* sizable paunch, all pointing to the significant success he's achieved. This is TOPPER CHISHOLM, one of Queen Mary College's most significant donors, and Vanessa (and Brittany's) grandfather.

The door opens simultaneously with a light tap, and Vanessa darts her pretty face around it. We can't help but see the likeness to the woman in the silver frame on Topper's desk, Vanessa's mother, Lauren. He reaches for the frame, sliding it unobtrusively into a desk drawer as Vanessa moves into the room.

> VANESSA
> Ready for me? Because I'm happy
> to hit up the bar cart if you're
> not.

Topper's face softens. He gestures for her to sit. As she enters the room, we see she's looking more drawn than before, her cheeks and eyes a bit too hollowed for makeup to fully correct. Topper, however, doesn't seem to notice.

> TOPPER
> I invited *you*, remember?

> VANESSA
> And you're always so gracious
> about making sure guests are
> served.

> MITZI (O.S.)
> That glib attitude toward your
> responsibilities is precisely the
> reason we needed to see you, Van-
> essa. Please at least *pretend* to
> take this seriously.

MITZI CHISHOLM moves into the room behind
Vanessa in a swirl of pearls and Chanel. Her
platinum blond hair is perfectly coiffed,
held back with a velvet headband, and though
it's late in the evening and she's in her
own home, she looks ready to lead a meeting
of some local board in her pristine St.
John's knitwear. Distaste twists her still
handsome features as she moves past her
granddaughter to stand behind her husband.

> VANESSA
> I'm visiting my grandparents. I
> didn't realize it was an inquisi-
> tion.

> TOPPER
> It's not.

Mitzi lifts one slim hand, the ropiness revealing her age much more clearly than her
lightly lined face, and squeezes his shoulder once. Topper clears his throat, forcing
his features into a sterner expression.

> TOPPER (CONT'D)
> But your grandmother's right,
> it's nothing to take lightly.

Vanessa pulls a shocked face, focusing her attention entirely on Topper. Mitzi's eyes narrow as she follows Vanessa's movements.

> VANESSA
> Should I be worried?

> MITZI
> That's for you to tell us. Was there some sort of mistake here?

She reaches into her pocket to pull out a folded piece of paper, which she places on the desk, just far enough away that Vanessa has to stand to retrieve it. She glances over it, then frowns, jaw clenching as she glares up at her grandmother.

> VANESSA
> You're seriously pulling my grades? What the fuck?

> MITZI
> There's no need to speak like a dockworker, Vanessa.

Mitzi reaches across the desk to snatch the paper back, mouth pursed as she focuses on refolding it.

> MITZI (CONT'D)
> And for your information, no one *pulled* anything. One of our friends in the registrar's office was simply concerned. And from the looks of this, she was right to be.

Vanessa snorts loudly, disdain twisting her pretty, though somewhat wan, features into a much younger reflection of her grandmother's.

                    VANESSA
          I'd say they should be fired for
          violating basic privacy laws, but
          you probably sign their paychecks
          anyway.

                    TOPPER
                (gruff)
          Don't speak to your grandmother
          that way.

Vanessa grips the carved wooden arms of the chair she's sitting in, lips twitching with the effort of biting back a retort, then turns to her grandfather, focusing on him exclusively.

                    VANESSA
          I know my grades aren't great,
          but I can bring them up before
          the end of the semester.

                    MITZI
          Really? That *would* be impressive.
          Mathematically, that is.

                    VANESSA
                (tightly)
          Did you just invite me here to
          shit on me, or was there an ac-
          tual point?

Mitzi's eyes narrow at the vulgarity, but she decides not to take up the gauntlet.

> MITZI
> The *point* is that your grandfa-
> ther and I have no intention of
> paying for you to flunk out of
> school. If you can't get your
> grades up by the end of the se-
> mester, you'll have to find out
> how to provide for yourself.
> You'll no longer have access to
> the trust, either, so don't as-
> sume you can just coast on that.

> VANESSA
> Wait . . . are you serious?
> You're just going to what, throw
> me out on the street?

> MITZI
> This isn't our choice, Vanessa,
> it's yours. You're an adult now.
> If you have no interest in taking
> your education seriously, we
> won't force the issue.

> VANESSA
> But . . . what am I supposed
> to do?

> MITZI
> You could always try hard work
> for a change.

> VANESSA
> You've never even let me get a

job. God forbid a _Chisholm_ do
anything so grubby as that.

          MITZI
I'd say it was the right decision, since you can't even manage
a few simple courses, but perhaps
we should have. Clearly you're
destined for a brilliant career
in food service.

Vanessa reels back as though slapped. After
a beat to recover herself, she turns to her
grandfather again, eyes pleading.

          VANESSA
It's been a . . . rough patch, I
know, but I'll get through it.

He sighs heavily, face pained.

          TOPPER
I hope so. If you can't . . .
we'll have no other choice, Vanessa.

          VANESSA
Of _course_ you have another
choice. You have more money than
god! You could pay for me to go
to school for the rest of my
fucking _life_.

Mitzi sniffs, flashing Topper a look of grim
triumph. It's just what she expected from
their ne'er-do-well grandchild. Vanessa
rounds on her.

VANESSA (CONT'D)
And what the hell do you know
about hard work, *Mitzi*? All
you've ever done is marry rich.
Which clearly wasn't enough to
keep you from being a miserable
bitch.

MITZI
(shouts)
Enough!

Her face reddens, eyes bright with rage, as
she stares at her granddaughter. After a
few ragged breaths, she clenches her hands
into fists, closes her eyes, and regains her
composure, voice colder than before.

MITZI (CONT'D)
We won't make the same mistakes
we made with your mother. We're
sending you to that college to
earn a degree. If you'd rather
party and play the whore and generally waste the advantages we're
giving you, that's your choice.
But we will *not* support it.

It starts to dawn on Vanessa that Mitzi
is very, *very* serious about this . . .
and that she might not be able to talk—or
temper-tantrum—her way out of it.

VANESSA
Granddad . . . *please* don't do
this.

> TOPPER
> (heavily)
> You still have time to turn
> things around.

> VANESSA
> And if I can't?

> TOPPER
> (distinctly worn out)
> Then . . . you'll learn a hard
> lesson. I'm sorry, but this is
> how it has to be, Vanessa.

> FADE TO BLACK

14

"BY THE TIME WE GOT HERE THAT WEEK, IT WAS pretty clear there was no salvaging the semester. I went to sort of a . . . dark place after Alden fully ended things, I probably went to one class out of five that month? Paige was the only one who knew how bad my grades had gotten. Well, and Mitzi." Vanessa took a delicate sip from the bottle of wine, turning it over thoughtfully in her mouth before swallowing. "Of course Mitzi's response was to stop paying rent on my apartment—the *only* thing they ever helped me with, mind you—and tell me the winery was going to Brittany alone. As if I'd ever expected to inherit anything in the first place. It's not like they ever gave me a dime besides what I got from Mom's life insurance. Which they couldn't very well withhold."

Guilt twisted through me—had I known it was that bad for Vanessa? In my memory, she'd treated the breakup the same way she treated everything bad that had happened in her life, dismissing it with some flip statement—*That? It's beyond over, which thank god, sometimes he couldn't even get it up*—before moving on to what cocktails we should pregame with, which party was worth going to that weekend, any of the shallow, top-of-mind considerations that presented themselves at the time. I'd been so relieved that the secret I'd unwittingly become embroiled in seemed to have been defused that I hadn't wanted to dig any deeper.

And if I'd noticed she was drinking more, actually getting sloppy at parties and going home with guys she would have laughed off a month before, heading out on nights of the week that had previously been reserved for studying or *maybe* a movie night with the girls . . . honestly, I just felt wounded. That she seemed to be having all this fun when I wasn't around. That Lydia had vaulted over the rest of us in Vanessa's ever-shifting order of intimacy and wasn't being rotated out on schedule. That once again, when I held myself up to Vanessa, I came away feeling dowdy and timid by comparison, left wondering whether I was lacking some vital spark that would allow me to care less, follow fewer rules, enjoy the moment the way Vanessa did. Maybe she was right, maybe in my heart of hearts I was a pencil pusher in training, and she'd finally recognized it and decided to move on to someone worthy of her.

Vanessa poked her tongue into her cheek, worrying the memory.

"I tried to get Brittany to help me—she could do no wrong as far as Mitzi was concerned, if she'd come in all pouty and worried and begged for her cousin to be given another chance, I'm sure it would have happened. But there was nothing in that for Brittany. Not to mention I'd insulted her by implying that *maybe* she hadn't actually earned every single sparkly thing in her life. Have you ever noticed that about really rich people? How pissed they get if you tell them maybe they didn't hit a walk-off home run?" Vanessa turned to me with a wry, weary look and took one more sip before handing the bottle back. "Fuck, they really do make good wine. Somehow that feels like salt in the wound."

"Did you tell Brittany about the affair? Maybe she would have—"

"Oh, *fuck* no." Vanessa snorted out a little laugh. "That would have just given her one more reason to feel justified for doing nothing. Actually, she'd probably have gone straight to Mitzi with that one and then I wouldn't have just been on my own, they'd have . . ." Vanessa waved a hand through the air. "I dunno, branded me or something? They'd have found some way to give me a scarlet W to remind me that I couldn't escape my whore blood."

"Sorry, I'm not really following." I took the wine from Vanessa, raising the bottle to my lips but not drinking. Vanessa had never been a liar per se, at least not that I'd ever found out about, but she was very careful about how she parceled out the truth, handing out a slice of it here, a few crumbs of it there, making everyone believe they were feasting on the real her when all we'd gotten was a meager helping of some unimportant course. But wine loosened her lips too, and it was clear that finally sharing all this was intoxicating in itself. It must have been years since she'd been able to open this particular valve inside herself, release the thick slurry that just kept expanding, threatening to burst through the weak points. "Wouldn't a professor taking advantage of you have meant something to your grandparents? Especially when they held so much sway at the college, you'd think they would come in with pitchforks."

"Ahh, but you think the professor took advantage of *me*, when Mitzi would have known that I took advantage of *him* just to embarrass her," Vanessa said with a mirthless laugh. I frowned, tilting my head to one side as I handed the wine back.

Vanessa took another sip and sighed, rolling her hand through the air as she spoke, a transparent attempt to make the revelation seem less important.

"It's why they disowned my mom in the first place. My dad was Professor Morales before they got together."

"At Queen Mary?" My eyes went wide. This *was* new information. Vanessa just nodded, racing onward.

"Once he started the divorce proceedings, Mitzi and Topper more or less ran him off campus, and Dad eventually found a new line of work, not that he was ever very good at it. Hence the liquidating of everything we owned after they died." She glanced at me sideways. "Did you not know that before? I could have sworn I told you."

"I must have forgotten," I murmured, gears turning in my head, moving piece after piece into place. It struck me anew just how little any of us had known about Vanessa. Her parents' death in the helicopter crash had seemed so massive, a gigantic monolith of tragedy planted in the middle of her life, that it had never occurred to me, at least not at the time, to try to see what was behind it. "But your parents got married. They stayed together."

"Sure, but once a whore, always a whore. Especially if you dare to break up Mitzi's bridge group by winding up with one of their husbands." Vanessa shrugged, the motion jerky and stiff. The wine seemed to have stripped her veneer of nonchalance. "Frankly, Mitzi should have been thrilled by my little hot for teacher dalliance. I didn't actually manage to ruin Alden's marriage. No muss, no fuss, lesson learned."

I took a small sip of the wine, holding the bottle to my lips for much longer than necessary as I tried to sort through everything Vanessa was telling me. It explained why she felt trapped, assuming it was more or less true, but the rest of the scene was still too dim to see, the filter on the lens obscuring more than it showed.

"But if you just left all those years ago . . . why are you afraid of Brittany?"

"Who isn't afraid of Brittany?" An eyebrow raise, another swig.

"I'm serious. It sounds like something really bad happened between you two. You mentioned meeting her in the cave? And . . . violence?" It was basically all she'd managed to get out that morning before she scurried out of the diner with promises to be in touch, leaving me even more nauseated than I'd been before she appeared.

How had she guessed we'd be there in the first place?

I blinked, trying to find the answer—Verdana wasn't a large town by any means, but she could have been staying at any motel along the road in, could have been holed up in the library researching inheritance law. Her showing up there, at the precise moment that Brittany had sashayed away, leaving me alone, couldn't have just been *random.* But Vanessa was sighing, her face clouding as a shiver shook her thin frame, and I turned my attention to her, desperate not to miss a single thing.

"I did *try* to get her to help. I knew it was pointless, but hope springs eternal, right? It was that last day, actually. She'd always loved that cave as a kid, I thought if I brought her there maybe she'd be . . . I don't know, less shitty? Fat chance."

"But . . . Brittany told us you went into town after that." I frowned, trying to recall if that's why we'd all believed that particular element of the story. It *felt* right.

"Of course she said that. She had to cover her ass after leaving me for dead."

I blinked, and Vanessa's mouth twisted in a wry smile. This

truth, at least, she didn't mind telling in full. A distant part of my brain pinged. *Painting Brittany as the villain is important to her.* Notice *that*.

"I don't think she meant to knock me out, to be fair. Brittany's just . . . not able to stop herself, you know? She's like a house cat. Once you cross the line with her, she just keeps swatting until you back off. Or pushing, in this case. Onto a rock ledge in a remote cave no one knew we'd walked to." Vanessa took another big swig, eyes going glassy, though whether that was the memory or the wine, I couldn't tell. "If I hadn't woken up I would have drowned. That entire cave is underwater at high tide."

I squinted at Vanessa, still lost in thought with the bottle in her hand. If Brittany *had* turned violent, however briefly, it could explain why Vanessa wouldn't want to surprise her with major unwelcome news. Brittany wasn't exactly the type to take the intervening fifteen years to reflect on her own actions. More likely she'd found ways to progressively recast Vanessa as more in the wrong—lazy, mooching off their grandparents, deliberately provoking Brittany so she could say spiteful things—the same way she'd rewritten her and Markus's fortune as the result of good luck in the markets instead of good luck in family trees.

But then what about Paige's confession? Of all of us, she was the least capable of lying—every thought she had waterfalled straight over the edge of her brain and out her mouth. Whatever details she'd confused over time, it was clear Paige's feelings of guilt were real.

And what about those texts on my phone, that meeting on the beach that I was *almost* certain never happened? Vanessa hadn't mentioned Paige or me once in all this, but at some point she'd been angry enough to try to convince us we had a hand in her disappearance. Hell, she was apparently still holding on to enough bitterness to force Paige to relive her dark night of the soul as maximally as possible by leaving that essay on her bed.

I swallowed hard, sitting up straighter as the thought shot through me like an electric shock: *Why was I so sure Vanessa was the one who had left the paper? That my* lack *of a "souvenir" was a signal from* her?

I tried to recapture the look on Lydia's face as she'd laid the pictures down. She'd been staring straight at me. I'd thought it was because I was her ally, because she was hoping I wouldn't think less of her, but what if she was looking for something else . . .

Vanessa tucked the bottle between two barrels and heaved in a breath, clapping her hands in front of her.

"Alright, anything else you want to ask me is gonna have to wait. We need to figure out a way to get up to Brittany's room without freaking her out. If I use the elevator now, without the alarm going off to cover the noise, she'll hear it."

Of course, she'd come into the house via the elevator—Brittany hadn't even mentioned it in her list of entrances to check, because it not only required a code, it needed a *key*. Vanessa and Brittany had both spent time here before that visit in college. Vanessa had to either know where they kept a spare, or possibly she'd held on to her copy all these years. The revelation of *how* she'd wound up in my room didn't prove she was being honest, obviously. But the whole time, the storyteller part of my brain had been searching for missing pieces, and Vanessa had willingly just tossed one my way. Maybe I'd been looking in the wrong direction for the others . . .

But I needed to be sure.

"Before we go up, I have to ask. Why leave the tokens for us?"

"The . . . what now?"

"Paige's plagiarized paper, the photos we took at Alden's house, your mother's *ring*. I get if you're angry with us, but if you really came back so you could find a way to talk to Brittany, why toy with her first?"

"Just so I'm clear," she said, licking her lips slowly, her eyes tightening as she worked to process what I was saying. In the flickering fluorescent light of the cave, she looked older than I'd ever seen her. "*How* did you find all these things?"

"They just sort of . . . appeared in our rooms. I was there last night when Brittany found the ring on her bed, she was terrified. I was too, honestly. I mean . . . we all thought you were *dead*. It felt almost . . . supernatural for it to turn up that way."

Vanessa's nostrils flared, brow lowering.

"Of course," she murmured, shaking her head slowly. "I knew things weren't going the way we'd planned, but I couldn't figure out what was off."

"*We*? So you're saying it wasn't you leaving that stuff around?"

"No. Jesus, Brittany and I have . . . issues, but I'm not here to terrorize her. I need her on my *side*." Vanessa fixed me with a desperate stare. I took a step back, really nervous for the first time. Though I was starting to get the feeling Vanessa wasn't the person I needed to be worried about. My hand drifted into my pocket, thumb caressing the point at the end of the corkscrew's spiral, mouth suddenly dry as I murmured the words.

"But then who . . ."

Vanessa closed her eyes, entire face falling.

"Think about it, Em. Fucking with people's heads that way? That's always been—"

Just then the creak of door hinges echoed through the basement, and we both startled to attention, prey animals sensing danger. From where we were sitting behind the barrels, we couldn't see who had entered the large, irregular room. I glanced over at Vanessa. She was breathing fast, eyes wide, jaw tight, every muscle in her body tense.

"What were you going to say, Vee? Please, don't let me interrupt."

The speaker's voice echoed eerily around the caves. It wasn't until she'd emerged around the end of a row of barrels that I could make her out. Vanessa sucked her lips between her teeth, eyes narrowing as she stared at the other woman.

"Hello, Lydia."

FLASHBACK TO

INT. PRECIPICE WINERY CELLARS—DAY (15
YEARS AGO)

Lydia paces the narrow hallway just inside
the door to the cliffside entrance, brow
knitted with worry, hugging a gigantic beach
towel against her chest tightly. After a
few moments, the door creaks open and Vanessa stumbles in, wet and shivering, face
unnaturally pale. As she turns to close the
door, we see a trickle of blood winding
through her damp, matted hair and down the
nape of her neck. Lydia rushes to unfold the
towel and wrap it around Vanessa. She rubs
at Vanessa's arms through the terry.

               LYDIA
      What *happened*, Vanessa? When I
      got your text I was so wor-
      ried . . .

              VANESSA
      It was Brittany. I took her to
      the cave like we talked about, to
      ask her to help with Mitzi and
      Topper, but she was just so
      shitty. All smug, telling me I
      shouldn't have let myself fail
      out in the first place, that maybe
      this was the "lesson I
      needed . . ."

Vanessa shakes her head, face twisted with
disgust as angry tears spring to her eyes.

                    VANESSA (CONT'D)
          I mean fuck, I know we're not
          besties, but we're *family*. And
          she wouldn't even hear me out.

                    LYDIA
          Did you . . . get upset with her?

Vanessa frowns, confused, and Lydia gestures to the head wound.

                    VANESSA
          Oh. No. I mean . . . I told her
          how spoiled she was being, but
          she's the one who lost it. We
          were just talking, and then she
          was on top of me, and then every-
          thing went black . . .

She shakes her head, swallowing nauseously,
swaying slightly as she clutches the towel
around her body more tightly.

                    VANESSA (CONT'D)
          When I came to, she was gone and
          the water was up to my hips. I
          guess that must have been what
          woke me up . . .

Lydia's face tightens with fury.

                    LYDIA
          So you're saying she attacked
          you, then left you passed out in
          a cave while the tide came in?
          Vanessa . . . she left you to
          die.

Vanessa shakes her head, wincing at the motion.

                    VANESSA
          I don't think it was like that.
          I'm sure she just . . . freaked
          out.

                    LYDIA
          So what if she "freaked out"? The
          tide doesn't give a fuck if Brit-
          tany was having a meltdown. And
          what does she even have to freak
          out over? Just . . . what a com-
          plete monster she is? *Jesus*.

Lydia's pacing now, hands tight at her
sides. Vanessa lifts a hand to the back of
her head and winces when she finds the wound,
skin going ashen. She lowers herself awkwardly to the floor of the cave, eyes unfo-
cused as she leans heavily on the walls for
support. She's clearly concussed.

                    LYDIA (CONT'D)
          I shouldn't be surprised. When
          has Brittany ever done a nice
          thing for someone else? She
          spiked my chance at that research
          assistant position just because
          she *could*. It's not enough for
          her to be selfish and oblivious,
          she has to proactively try to
          fuck up other people's lives.

                    VANESSA
          I don't think she knows how bad

it is with your mom's medical
bills.

> LYDIA
> So what? She doesn't have to know
> the details of how much I'm send-
> ing home every month to be a de-
> cent fucking human being. I told
> her I needed the money, I told
> her I needed the *job,* that should
> have been enough!

Lydia's working herself up further and further. It's clear that her long-simmering
resentments with Brittany have reached a
boiling point.

> LYDIA (CONT'D)
> And today, she knew you needed
> her help, but even though it
> would cost her *nothing* to give
> it, instead she gets up on her
> high horse and then she . . . she
> *attacks* you!

> VANESSA
> (quiet)
> What do I do now?

Lydia stops short, startled by the despair
in Vanessa's voice.

> LYDIA
> What do you mean?

> VANESSA
> That was my last chance, Lyds.

                    Mitzi and Topper *told* me they
                    weren't going to support me if I
                    failed out. No access to the
                    trust . . . and I've never even
                    had a job. If Brittany won't try
                    to get them to change their
                    minds . . .

She blinks against the tears.

                         VANESSA (CONT'D)
                    I'm gonna flunk out of school, I
                    won't have anywhere to live after
                    my lease is up . . . and I'll be
                    a fucking laughingstock, Lydia.
                    Brittany will probably start
                    spreading rumors the minute we
                    get back, and Paige will be her
                    little henchman playing it
                    up . . . And meanwhile what, I
                    try to wait tables on campus? *If*
                    anyone will hire me? I mean,
                    fuck. Why even go back to that?

Vanessa gives in to the tears, but Lydia
goes still. We can see her working through
some puzzle in her mind.

                         LYDIA
                    What if you didn't go back?

                         VANESSA
                         (sniffs)
                    What? You're not serious.

                         LYDIA
                    No, think about it. You could
                    just . . . start over. You said

it yourself, there's nothing
there for you. If you're just
going to be getting some random
job, why come back at all?

> VANESSA
> Mitzi and Topper would probably
> cross the country and drag me
> back there just to punish me.

> LYDIA
> They wouldn't if they didn't know
> where you were.

Lydia starts pacing again, eyes shining.

> LYDIA (CONT'D)
> I mean . . . for all Brittany
> knows right this second, you're
> already gone. Dragged out to sea.
> Right?

> VANESSA
> I guess so . . .

> LYDIA
> If you never showed up again,
> she's not going to get back to
> school and start shit-talking
> you. Not when she's the *reason*
> you never came back.

> VANESSA
> So what . . . you're saying we
> try to convince her that she
> *killed* me? That's . . . seriously
> messed up.

                    LYDIA
        But we don't really have to con-
        vince her of anything. If she
        feels guilty for what she *actu-
        ally did*, then good. She *should*
        feel bad for attacking you. Es-
        pecially when you were only
        asking—no, *begging* her for help!

                    VANESSA
        I'm not trying to send her to
        jail, Lyds.

Lydia's face tightens briefly, then she turns
to Vanessa, shaking her head rapidly.

                    LYDIA
        Of course not. If things got that
        far, you'd come back. But seri-
        ously, Vanessa. Don't you think
        she should learn a lesson for
        once in her life? Why should she
        be allowed to just go around
        treating people like crap with no
        consequences?

Vanessa closes her eyes for a long time,
then opens them, fixing on Lydia, her stare
a bit glassy. She doesn't see the intensity
on Lydia's face. This clearly isn't just
about Vanessa for her . . . in fact, maybe
it's not about Vanessa at all.

                    VANESSA
        But what about Paige and Emily?
        Even if Brittany believes that,
        they're going to wonder where I
        went. And if they start asking

questions, Brittany will break
down and tell them about the
fight, and I'm back where I
started. Actually, I'm worse off,
Mitzi will probably put a hit out
on me if I dare to damage her favorite granddaughter.

                LYDIA
We could keep them quiet too.

                VANESSA
How? They both know . . . not everything that's been going on,
but enough. If I just ghost everyone, they'll put it together
pretty quick.

                LYDIA
But if they were worried that
they had something to do with
your disappearance . . .

                VANESSA
Why would they think that?

                LYDIA
I have a couple ideas that might
work.

                VANESSA
You're saying I convince everyone, all my friends, that they've
murdered me?

                LYDIA
If your friends are so awful that
they'd do something like leave

you passed out with the tide coming in, why are you worried about
their feelings?

                VANESSA
But Paige didn't do that.

                LYDIA
You said it yourself, Paige is
Brittany's henchman. She'd sell
you out just as fast if Brittany
told her to. And she never thinks
at *all*. I bet it would take all
of two minutes to get her worked
up enough to come at you the way
Brittany did.

                VANESSA
But what about Emily? She didn't
do anything to me at all, Lydia.
And she's not like that.

                LYDIA
Emily's not as innocent as she
likes to pretend.
        (beat, collecting herself)
Anyway, I'm not saying we stage
some scene where she stabs you.
We could just . . . put her in a
position where she's worried
about what she *might* have done.
Brittany brought her Xanax, it
wouldn't be hard to . . . I don't
know, get Emily loopy and then
mess with her texts or something.
And while they're worrying about
themselves, like always, you've

bought enough time to get out of
here and start fresh.

          VANESSA
You really think that will work?
What if everyone sees through it
right away?

Vanessa's frowning, still not believing it,
but there's desperation in her eyes as she
stares at her friend. We see Lydia see this,
the first time the power balance has shifted
to her in their entire relationship, and
the tiny smile she saves for the moment she
turns away from Vanessa reveals just how
much she's relishing it.

          LYDIA
What if they do? They still need
to answer for why they'd attack
you in the first place, why they'd
focus on saving their own skins
instead of tracking you down.
Worst case, you're back where you
started, but maybe at least *one*
of them thinks twice before they
treat people that way again. But
best case, you're free to do
whatever you want, and all the
stuff you were dealing with is
just . . . behind you.

          VANESSA
I don't know. Can I really just
walk out on my life?

                    LYDIA
          It's not really about whether you
          can, it's about whether you want
          to. Do you think there's anything
          there for you if you go back?
          Would Mitzi and Topper come
          around if you let them know how
          bad it's gotten?

Vanessa's defenses are down from the head
wound, and real pain crosses her face as she
considers the question. They're her only
family. She *wants* them to want to help
her . . . Finally she heaves out a shaky
sigh.

                    VANESSA
          No. But . . . I'm not sure that
          I'd know how to just start over.
          Alone.

Lydia swallows hard, carefully considering
her words. The idea of having Vanessa truly
to herself holds a visceral appeal.

                    LYDIA
          You wouldn't be alone, I'd be
          there. And I'll help you now. You
          know you can count on me, Van-
          essa, always. You focus on stay-
          ing out of sight and getting
          ready, I can handle the rest.

                    VANESSA
          I *would* want to take out some
          cash . . .

LYDIA
Exactly. And you'll need to pick
up a burner phone, just to use
for the next few days. In
fact . . . you'd better pull your
SIM card out as soon as you
leave, they can trace those
things. We can keep in touch with
the burner until you get a new
one without pointing your grandparents straight to you.

VANESSA
I hadn't even thought about
that . . .

LYDIA
That's what I'm here for.
So . . . why don't you head into
town and do that, I'll figure out
everything else?

Vanessa reaches up for Lydia's hand, grati-
tude softening her features.

VANESSA
Thanks, Lydia. Probably none of
this will work, but it's really
good to know you're in my corner.

LYDIA
Always.

FADE TO BLACK

CUT TO

INT. PRECIPICE WINERY CAVES—NIGHT
(PRESENT DAY)

Vanessa and Emily stand frozen behind the
racks of aging wine as Lydia steps out of
the deeper shadows in the far corners of the
cave. Though a small smile twists her lips,
her face is cold, eyes glittering with
anger. She holds a small handgun, but it
isn't trained on the women, her grip loose,
the weapon seemingly almost forgotten in
her hand. Vanessa sucks in a deep breath,
anxiety and rage warring on her features.
She runs her tongue over her teeth, eyes
never leaving Lydia's face.

> EMILY
> You're saying . . . *Lydia* planned
> all that?

> VANESSA
> Down to my lines on the dock with
> Paige. I should have realized
> then that she was just settling
> her own scores, but I was desper-
> ate. *And* concussed.

> LYDIA
> Oh, *spare* me, Vanessa. You were
> practically begging me to handle
> it. All I did was help you do
> what you wanted.

> VANESSA
> No, no way. It wasn't about me at
> all. Not then, not now.

EMILY
Oh my god, of course! *Lydia* has
been the one leaving things
around the house. But . . . why?

VANESSA
Good question. Why have you,
Lydia? It's not what we planned.
It's not what you promised me.

LYDIA
I promised I'd help you figure out
how to access the trust fund Topper and Mitzi set up for you.

VANESSA
And how is terrorizing everyone
helping me do that, Lydia? How is
it convincing Brittany to hear me
out?

LYDIA
        (deeply frustrated)
I wasn't trying to get her to
meet with you, I was trying to
get her to *leave*. You're so set
on barreling in right now that
you refuse to see reason. If we
just head home, and I call my
lawyer like I told you I would,
then I can help you—

VANESSA
That's not what I *want*.

LYDIA
Not everything is just about what

> *you* want, Vanessa! Jesus, how can
> you still be so fucking selfish?

She's taut with fury now. Emily takes a step
back, fear in her eyes.

> LYDIA (CONT'D)
> For fifteen years I've been help-
> ing you, giving you handouts when
> you needed them, letting you
> crash with me between jobs. Fuck,
> I even helped you track down a
> clean social on the dark web all
> those years ago. "Whitney Lauren-
> tis" would still just be a too-
> young car crash victim if I
> hadn't found her.

> VANESSA
> So what, you just decided to stop
> helping *now*?

> LYDIA
> I decided I didn't want to spend
> an entire weekend with the
> bitches who ruined my life just
> so things could play out exactly
> how you imagined them! Which, by
> the way, wouldn't have *worked*.

Lydia shakes her head, sighing. Her voice
turns pleading as she continues.

> LYDIA (CONT'D)
> There are other ways to do this,
> but you refuse to see them. To
> see *me*. If you don't get exactly
> what you want immediately, why

bother checking in with the only
real friend you have when you can
just use someone else, right?
Drag Emily into things even
though this has always been
about us.

> VANESSA
> This isn't about *us*, Lydia, it's
> about *me*. My life.

Vanessa sniffs in disgust.

> VANESSA (CONT'D)
> To think I really believed you
> were my friend.

> LYDIA
> I *was* your friend, Vanessa. I *am*
> your friend. It's them you can't
> trust.

She points at Emily, who raises her hands
defensively.

> LYDIA (CONT'D)
> Not one of them ever told anyone
> about the last time they'd seen
> you. About what they'd done. They
> didn't care about you, they only
> cared about saving themselves. I
> wasn't going to roll out the red
> carpet for them to hurt you
> again.

> VANESSA
> *Hurt* me? Newsflash, Lydia, *I never
> actually died.*

Vanessa's furious now, eyes narrowed to
slits, lips so tight they're almost white.
Lydia's face clouds with worry. She hadn't
planned for this. And she's clearly losing
the upper hand she's enjoyed for so many
years.

               LYDIA
     Listen, we can still make this
     right. I . . . miscalculated,
     okay? But it was only because I
     care about you. Let's just go
     home, and—

She steps toward Vanessa, laying a hand on
her arm, but Vanessa shakes her off angrily.

               VANESSA
     No. I didn't see you then, but I
     see you now, Lydia. You've never
     been looking out for me, you've
     been getting your own petty re-
     venge. Because you're still hang-
     ing on to shit from *fifteen years*
     ago. This is done. *We're* done.

She shakes her head, pity and disgust curling her lip.

               VANESSA (CONT'D)
     I just can't believe it took me
     so long to see it.

15

"WHAT ARE YOU SAYING?" LYDIA TOOK A STEP
back from Vanessa, eyes wide, mouth hanging open.

The idea that the two of them had planned this so many
years ago set off a swarm of bees in my brain. Jesus, how had
Lydia held this in since then? How had she watched Brittany's grandparents grieve Vanessa's death—because they had
grieved *deeply*, whatever Vanessa wanted to tell herself, especially Topper—knowing that she could have brought Vanessa
back to life at any moment? Watching Topper cry at that vigil
toward the end of the school year had set me off more than
my own grief had, this formidable man losing his dignity,
shrinking beneath the weight of pain. It had been the first
time I'd really let myself believe that maybe she wasn't coming
back.

Even that you *might* be able to chalk up to youth—things
must have spun out of control so fast, I can't even imagine
what I would have done if I'd been in Lydia's position, maybe
only realizing once Vanessa was gone the magnitude of what
they'd set in motion. But how had she come here this weekend, knowing that Vanessa had been alive all along, and chosen to spend the time twisting the screws on all of us? If she
really hated us all as much as she would have had to in order
to pull that off, how had she managed to keep that calm, wry
exterior for the last forty-eight hours?

And where did I stand in all this? Watching Lydia now, face pained as she advanced on the two of us, it suddenly seemed extremely vital that I find out.

She took another step forward.

"Vanessa, I care about you. I'm sorry if I screwed this up, but you have to see that." She spread her hands at her sides, almost like she was waiting for a hug. I stared at her fingers, then her pockets, looking for a weapon, but there was nothing. And why should there be? This was Lydia. The tiny, watchful, darkly funny woman I'd known for almost twenty years now.

But had I known her? Ever?

I'd always thought Lydia was the remaining friend in the group who I . . . not quite *understood* best. She'd always been intensely private, not in the way Vanessa was, trading penny-ante intimacy for something she needed in the moment, but truly closed off, her own pains and fears something none of us—or at least I—ever really had access to. But we'd stayed in touch, rekindled the friendship those few years she was living in LA. We'd smirked and side-eyed our way through this weekend with Paige and Brittany, tacitly acknowledging that we didn't have much in common with them anymore, but at least we both still had one ally at the table. Even as the threads of past and present had started to tangle and knot around us, I'd felt sure Lydia, at least, was someone I could count on.

And it had all been an act. Which reminded me.

"Lydia . . . are you okay?" Her head whipped toward me. She looked almost startled to find me there.

"What are you talking about?"

"Your claustrophobia," I murmured, doubt blooming through me the minute the word left my mouth.

"Her *what*?" Vanessa barked out a single hollow laugh. "You told them you were claustrophobic, Lydia? Why?"

She licked her lips, eyes fixed on Vanessa. You could almost see the gears in her head whirring as she searched for the right answer.

"You know what? Forget it. I know why. It was all part of you helping *me,* right? God, I've been such an idiot. You just want to keep me as your *toy.*"

"Don't say that . . ." Lydia took a step forward, hands out, and Vanessa pulled back dramatically, sneering. Lydia stared at her, stricken, expression flickering back and forth between hurt and shock. I took the opportunity to move closer to the far wall, the one formed by the cliff face, away from the two women. Lydia's bulbous eyes had taken on a peeled, desperate quality that I could only remember seeing one time before, and she'd had far less on the line then.

"You seemed happy last time I visited LA," Lydia murmured, eyebrows tenting with worry. I tried not to startle at the *"last time."* All these years, Vanessa had been flitting around just outside my field of vision, hiding in plain sight. And Lydia hadn't just known about it, she'd been participating. *It was probably the reason she spent those years in LA at all.*

"Of course I *seemed* happy!" Vanessa leaned forward, looming over Lydia, the tendons in her neck straining. "My *job* was to seem happy. I was a professional fucking *girlfriend,* Lydia." She exhaled a bitter laugh, turning her gaze to the shadowy roof of the cave, eyes glistening. "And not that it matters to you, but Randall fired me a few weeks ago. With a really shitty severance package."

"Okay, but you can pick yourself up. So Randall's too stupid to appreciate you, that doesn't mean—"

"You have no idea how hard it is to keep doing this." Vanessa was blinking rapidly now, lips trembling slightly. "This was supposed to be my way out. This was supposed to be how I was finally allowed to have my *own life* again."

The lights in the cave flickered again, and my throat tightened in the brief instant I couldn't pick out Lydia's small form, practically quivering with tension as she stood a few feet from Vanessa, arms outstretched toward her . . . *friend* didn't seem quite right. Was there a scientific word for mutually parasitic relationships?

"All this time I've just been barely holding on," Vanessa murmured, shoulders slumping with exhaustion. "I can't go back to working some temp job, hoping the right person starts flirting when I pick up the office coffee order."

"It's not your only option." Lydia laid her hand on Vanessa's shoulder and squeezed lightly. I expected Vanessa to shake her off, but she just heaved in a deep breath, resting her hand over Lydia's. I legitimately couldn't tell whether it was genuine or just a new tactic.

"I'm a dropout with a spotty-as-fuck résumé, zero savings, and zero real skills. Looking good next to your ancient producer boyfriend is *not* something they hire for."

Lydia licked her lips anxiously, totally focused on Vanessa. I took another step toward the wall. Maybe this was all going to be okay . . . or whatever version of okay we could wrestle out of our dead friend suddenly reappearing, and our . . . *whatever* Lydia had been to the rest of us having spent years lying to us all. Still, I wanted a clear path to the exit in case it didn't.

"I know it seems hard now, but you always land on your feet . . ."

"No, Lydia, I claw my way back up out of the fucking *mud*."

Vanessa shook her head, lips pinching so thin they went nearly white. "I never realized what it would *mean*."

"What . . . what would mean?" Lydia blinked.

"Us pulling it off! Making me disappear!" Vanessa shook her head, eyes tightening again, and brushed Lydia's hand off her shoulder. Lydia's flinch went through her entire body.

"It's what you wanted," Lydia murmured.

"Who knows what I wanted then. Honestly? I don't think I *did* want it to work. I mean, did you ever really believe everything would just . . . fall into place that way? That Paige wouldn't say anything, Brittany wouldn't break down about our fight in the cave, no one would check each other's stories at *all*?"

"It was a good plan."

"It was a fucking *temper tantrum* that we cooked up together in about an hour while I was dealing with what was definitely a concussion. It was *insane*. The only reason I even made it over the California border is that burner phones were barely even a *thing* then, at least if you weren't a dealer. Plus, the cops around here have never dealt with a mystery more involved than 'Where are the rich underage teenagers drinking this summer?'"

Vanessa ran both hands through her hair again, face taut with anger. She didn't notice the way Lydia's shoulders dropped, the coldness that had reentered her eyes. She took a step away from Vanessa.

"If that's how you felt, you always could have come forward. No one was stopping you."

"I was *scared*!" Vanessa blinked, stupefied. "For all I know, just paying that addict I met in the Mission for her social could have put me behind bars. And you must have told the police you hadn't seen me that day. That's obstruction, right?

I mean . . . seriously, you weren't even a little worried about what would happen to us if people realized what we'd done?"

"I was more worried about helping my friend get through the worst crisis of her life," Lydia hissed, jaw tense. "I was worried about *you,* not me."

"*Fuck,* Lydia! If that's true, why pull all this shit with Brittany and Paige?" Vanessa's voice was echoing around the cave walls now.

"Because they hurt me too, Vanessa! They should *pay* for how they hurt people!"

Vanessa actually pulled back from Lydia's venomous bark. For the first time, something like fear played at the corner of her eyes.

"Lydia, if I want to forgive them, that's my right." After half a beat, Vanessa leaned forward, face softening, eyes turning more liquid somehow. I'd seen that look before, over dozens of heartfelt conversations. Vanessa's "wise but caring friend" look. Even knowing that she was probably deploying it tactically, I could feel something in me pulled toward it, a desire to zoom in until her pained, wrung-out beauty filled the entire screen. "Honestly? They have just as much to forgive me for as I have to forgive them for. And I want to try. I want to see if we can all forgive each other."

"Well, I *don't,* Vanessa! I don't fucking '*forgive*' them for taking away my future just for fun. For making me choose between the career I'd been planning my entire *life* and making sure my mom got treatment for her cancer." Lydia's face was twisted tight with fury. "Jesus, I forgot how fucking self-centered you could be."

Vanessa took a step back from Lydia, unconsciously protecting herself. Lydia advanced on her, thrusting a finger toward Vanessa's narrow chest, and that same pulse of fear constricted Vanessa's features. I took another step in the direction of the exit, barely daring to breathe, trying to remain forgotten, an extra they didn't need for the scene. I was just twenty feet shy of the tunnel that led out to the cliff face now.

"Forgive whoever you fucking want, Vanessa, but I'm not letting them just forget about the things they've done, the harm they've caused. Not now, not *ever*."

FLASHBACK TO

EXT. CHISHOLM ESTATE REAR GARDEN—DAY
(15 YEARS AGO)

The grounds of Mitzi and Topper's mansion
are extensive and beautifully landscaped,
the large main patio that clings to the back
of the mansion giving way to planned flower
beds and carefully trimmed greenery, a series of smaller connected terraces like
bread crumbs leading guests toward the edge
of the thickly wooded area at the back of
the property. The entire place is only just
starting to bud with signs of spring.

The yard is buzzing with activity. A gigantic party tent has sprung up over the larg-
est section of the lawn, heat lamps scattered
through it casting a warm glow over the
smattering of high-top tables and lower,
larger options, spindly gold Chiavari chairs
perched primly around their perimeters.
Every table is decked out elaborately, with
creamy tablecloths, lush bouquets of rare
flowers, and a variety of faceted candle-
holders carefully arranged to appear casual.

Guests drift between the tables, the various seating areas, the gazebo, and the bars
and catering stations that dominate the
main patio, sipping drinks and chattering
with each other. Most (but not all) are in
late middle age, and they all have a well-
heeled look in their crisp springy dresses
and Nantucket red pants, heat lamps all

around the party allowing them to defy such plebeian inconveniences as the March weather in Connecticut. Brittany blends right in, but the other girls are varying degrees of sore thumbs: Paige is dressed too casually, Emily too formally, Lydia's plain black dress and tights look funereal against all the preppy summer wear, and Vanessa is in a pair of faux leather pants and a drapey silk camisole more suited for a club, and which is drawing more than a few stares from the older gentlemen at the party. Lydia's visibly nervous, gripping a sweating glass with both hands.

> PAIGE
> Is that Trip Wilkinson?

> EMILY
> Who's Trip Wilkinson?

> BRITTANY
> Uh, *duh,* the lacrosse captain?
> And yes, it definitely is. His
> dad's on the Board of Fellows
> with Topper.

> VANESSA
> See, Brit? And you thought pre-
> gaming at Grandma and Grandpa's
> would be *dull.* If you're lucky,
> you can slip in with King Bro for
> the night early enough that he'll
> fuck you in his frat's bathroom
> later out of sheer inertia.

> BRITTANY
> Ew, Vee. Why are you always
> so . . .

> VANESSA
> Right? Come on, you *wish* you
> could bone Trip.

Vanessa smiles slyly, as though the teasing
is playful. With anyone else in the group,
it might be received that way.

> PAIGE
> Uhh, of *course* she'd want to. I
> mean, look at him.

> VANESSA
> Really, you expect us all to be-
> lieve that *Trip's* your type?

Vanessa raises a skeptical eyebrow at Paige,
and Paige flushes. She's still a couple years
from coming out, but Vanessa's guessed
Paige's secret, and occasionally uses it to
her advantage . . . or just to toy with
Paige.

> VANESSA (CONT'D)
> I think he looks like he came out
> of a catalog. Back me up, Emily.

Vanessa tilts her head toward the boy in
question, Ken-doll perfect for the occasion
in his boat shoes and navy-sweater-and-
polo-over-faded-khakis look. He raises his
glass to Brittany when he catches her looking. She smiles, raising hers in return,
then turns back to the girls, looking a

little embarrassed. She narrows her eyes at
Vanessa.

> EMILY
> He's not my type. But I totally
> get it. I mean, he's definitely
> handsome.

> VANESSA
> Exactly. He's perfect for *Brittany*.

> BRITTANY
> It doesn't even matter. I'm *not*
> planning to sleep with Trip
> Wilkinson.

> VANESSA
> Really? He looks like every other
> guy you take home. Though to be
> fair, they do keep a *lot* of that
> model in stock at the warehouse.

> BRITTANY
> Stop being bitchy just 'coz
> you're in a dry spell.

> PAIGE
> Seriously. Jealous, much? When's
> the last time you even made out
> with anyone, Vee?

> VANESSA
> Not winding up with one of the
> children at the parties we go to
> is an *accomplishment,* not an em-
> barrassment. On that note, I'll
> let you two fight over the meat-

head. I want to talk to Professor
LaVoie about an assignment.

Brittany purses her lips at Vanessa's re-
treating form.

                    BRITTANY
          She's always so *crude*.

                    EMILY
          She's just in a bad mood lately.
          Don't let her get under your
          skin.

                    BRITTANY
          Trust me, I never do.

She's too casual, eyes narrowed as she
tracks Vanessa through the party . . . and
as she notices all the heads turning to follow Vanessa's progress. At the far side of
frame, we see Mitzi's look of real worry as
she sees Vanessa and Alden start chatting.

                    BRITTANY (CONT'D)
          In other news, who needs another
          drink?

                    PAIGE
          Me. We should come to more of
          these, Brit. I don't think I knew
          tequila could actually taste
          good.

                    EMILY
          It almost makes you want to work
          in finance or something, right?

The girls start off toward the bar, leaving
Lydia standing alone, clutching her drink.
After a moment, Emily turns back.

>   EMILY
>   Lyds, are you coming?

>   LYDIA
>   What? Oh, uh . . . no, I'm good.
>   I still have to finish this one.

With a shrug, the other girls walk off to the
nearer of the two bars, leaving Lydia on her
own. She sucks in a few deep breaths, pinching her eyes closed, whispering to herself.

>   LYDIA (CONT'D)
>   *You can do this . . . Mom needs*
>   *you to do this.*

After a few seconds, she opens her eyes,
clenches and unclenches a fist, and walks
over to a much younger Professor Stavros,
his wife smiling gently at his elbow as he
chats with a fellow party guest. Lydia hovers a few feet away until the guest departs,
then, seeing her opportunity, she swoops in.

>   LYDIA (CONT'D)
>   Uh . . . hi. Professor Stavros?

>   NIKO
>   Yes? I'm sorry, have we met?

>   LYDIA
>   Oh, umm . . . no. I mean, I took
>   your Intro to Cellular Biology

> class a couple years ago, but,
> you know . . . it's a really big
> class.

>   NIKO
> Are you a biology major?

>   LYDIA
> No, but biology really interests
> me. Actually, I'm really glad I
> caught you. The thing is . . .

>   BRITTANY (O.S.)
> Niko!

Brittany rushes up, the drink in her hand
already half gone, and folds the professor
into a hug. He laughs, hugging her back.

>   NIKO
> There's my favorite young
> scholar. How is life treating you
> these days, Miss Brittany?

>   BRITTANY
> Good! I just locked down an in-
> ternship at *Cosmo* for the summer,
> so that's exciting.

>   NIKO
> Impressive! But then I'm not sur-
> prised. You've always had your
> grandfather's work ethic.

She smiles and turns to gesture at Paige and
Emily in turn.

                    BRITTANY
          You remember my friend Paige. And
          this is Emily.

                    NIKO
          Nice to meet you, ladies.

They murmur hellos as Brittany turns to
Lydia, lips quirking into a subtle smirk.
She may have agreed to help to appease Vanessa, but she hasn't forgotten her never-
ending war with Lydia . . . and Vanessa's
not here right now . . .

                    BRITTANY
          It looks like you've already met
          Lydia. Sorry, Lyds, I forgot you
          wanted to talk to Niko. Did you
          do your pitch yet?

                    LYDIA
          Umm . . . no. Not yet.

                    PAIGE
          Oh, man, you've gotta work on
          your sales technique, Lyds.

She laughs and takes a swig of her drink as
Lydia flushes. The professor turns to Lydia,
a look of perfunctory interest on his broad,
wind-burned features.

                    NIKO
          Pitch? What for?

                    LYDIA
          I, uh . . . the thing is . . .

>   I applied for your research as-
>   sistant position, actually?

>   NIKO
>   Really? I thought you just said
>   you weren't studying biology.

>   LYDIA
>   Well, not exclusively, but I'd
>   like to learn more. I've always
>   found it fascinating.

Brittany laughs, face scrunching up in
amused disbelief.

>   BRITTANY
>   She's trying to be polite, Niko.
>   You don't even really like biol-
>   ogy, do you, Lydia?

>   PAIGE
>   Didn't you call it science lite
>   when I was looking at core re-
>   quirements?

The professor frowns and takes a sip of his
drink as Lydia's entire face and chest purple with embarrassment. Emily titters ner-
vously behind the other girls.

>   LYDIA
>   Well, that class, sure. But you
>   were looking for the easiest way
>   to get the credit . . .

>   NIKO
>   What branch of science *are* you
>   focusing on?

LYDIA
Chemistry. I'm still deciding between a focus on nanotechnology
and pharmacology.

He frowns.

NIKO
Perhaps I'm misunderstanding
something. Why would you apply
for a position in my lab when
your discipline is so different
from what I focus on?

LYDIA
I thought it would be a great opportunity to . . . broaden my
knowledge base. And your work's
so interesting, really . . .

BRITTANY
What *specifically* about Niko's
work interests you *most,* Lydia?

She smirks, raising an eyebrow as she watches
Lydia wriggle on the end of the hook, eyes
only darting away once to ensure Vanessa's
occupied. Per usual, Paige is backing Brittany's every play.

LYDIA
I . . . I hadn't really looked
into specifics of the work yet,
but . . .

PAIGE
I guess anything would be cooler
than going back home for the sum-

mer, right? I mean . . . *Buffalo*?
Pass.

Paige laughs and sips her drink again. Stavros's wife flashes her a disapproving glare,
but Paige, half-drunk, doesn't seem to notice. Professor Stavros, however, is bris-
tling with wounded academic ego.

> NIKO
> It sounds as though you wouldn't
> be a good fit for the work we do.
> I prefer assistants with passion
> for *my* work, not another field of
> science entirely. But I wish you
> the best of luck in *pharmacology,*
> Miss. If you'll excuse me . . .

With a quick nod, he peels away from the
girls, weaving through the party quickly,
his wife trailing from his elbow. Lydia
gapes after him, the color draining from
her face. She turns to the girls, eyes bulging with disbelief.

> LYDIA
> Why *do* that?

> BRITTANY
> Seriously? I just saved you from
> an entire summer of torture,
> Lydia. You would have *hated* that
> job. You heard him, it's nowhere
> near what you're interested in.

> LYDIA
> But I *told* you. I told you I
> needed it.

                    BRITTANY
          You'll find something else. Oh,
          maybe you can go back to Ohio
          with Paige. Your dad would give
          Lydia an internship, right?

                    PAIGE
          Sure, if I asked.

She turns to Lydia, mirroring Brittany's
look of nonchalance, either oblivious to or
uninterested in the devastation on Lydia's
face.

                    PAIGE (CONT'D)
          I know large equipment sales
          sounds boring, but it's actually
          way better than a lab, I worked
          there last year and some days all
          I did was watch movies in the
          main office. And he'll pay like
          eighteen dollars an hour.

                    LYDIA
          I . . . I don't . . .

                    PAIGE
          Let me know soon if you want it
          though, he might have other in-
          terns lined up, but he can cancel
          their offers if it's early enough.

                    BRITTANY
          Okay, Trip is texting me now.
          What do we think of this?

She holds up the phone to Paige, and they
drift over to a nearby seating arrangement,

whispering together. Emily lingers, wincing
at Lydia.

> EMILY
> They really didn't mean anything
> by it, you know. Brittany can
> just be . . .

> LYDIA
> Horrible?

Her eyes are starting to glisten. Emily
grimaces.

> EMILY
> Oblivious. But there are other
> jobs, right?

> LYDIA
> Sure.

Lydia's tone is completely dead. After staring at her for a moment longer, Emily walks
off as well, bypassing Paige and Brittany on
her way to Vanessa, leaving Lydia in the
middle of the party, alone, tears running
silently over her pale cheeks.

16

LYDIA WAS PACING NOW, HANDS BALLED INTO tight fists at her sides.

"They took away my future, just like that. Poof! They didn't even *blink*. It's the same thing they did to you, Vanessa. They just took everything from you and went on with their coddled, *easy* lives."

I was inching along the wall again, hand slipping into my pocket to get a better grip on the corkscrew. It seemed so flimsy now, barely more than a nail file . . . *If this* were *a movie, I'd at least have thought to grab a knife.* But then, if this were a movie, Lydia would have shown up carrying a gun.

"And of course Emily just sat there on the sidelines like always, too much of a fucking coward to stand up to anyone."

Lydia whipped around to me and I froze, every muscle in my body tightening. Against all reason, I'd been hoping she'd forgotten me.

"In a way, it's worse, you know?" Lydia cocked her head to the side sharply. "Brittany can't help lashing out if some-thing's bothering her. She's like a *child*. And Paige never met an original thought that she didn't just climb onto after it came out of someone else's head. Usually Brittany's. But *you* knew better, Emily. You knew how sick my mom was. And you saw what they did, you saw them constantly tear me down, and take swipes at Vanessa, and eventually *destroy my entire future*. And *still*, you were so fucking afraid of anyone ever having a conflict that you just let it happen."

Lydia pinned me with her stare, her too-wide eyes giving it a slightly unhinged quality. She was clearly waiting for an answer.

"But . . . things worked out in the end, right?" I cleared my throat. The sides were sticking together, choking off the words. I could hear that hint of pleading in my voice, the innate need to keep the peace blunting my words. It probably wasn't helping, but I didn't know how to stop it. Other people had fight or flight, my body seemed to default to a third option, mediation. "You have an incredible job. You make great money, and—"

"*Jesus,* you're *just like them!*" Lydia barked, the tendons in her neck standing out. "Life isn't only about *money*, Emily. Some people want more than *fucking money*."

She started pacing again, a tighter radius now, as though she was physically coiling a spring inside herself.

"I was supposed to be something more than just another code monkey. I had *plans*. I was going to get a PhD, then find work in one of the top labs, find the drug that would help people like my mother. I was going to make a *difference*. Until Brittany and Paige took that away from me while you just stood there trying to avoid a fight."

"Here's the thing," Vanessa said, raising one eyebrow in elegant disgust more cutting than anger would have been. "You still could have *done* all that without the internship." Lydia scoffed and Vanessa lowered her chin, lips twisting in a cruel smile. "I know you wanted that fellowship, but getting it *was* just about *fucking money*, wasn't it, Lydia?"

Lydia's entire face seemed to pull back, her eyes pressing

further forward as her tight lips seemed to draw everything else in. Clearly she hadn't expected this betrayal.

"Don't you fucking *dare*. I had to pay my mom's medical bills, my student loans. You have no *idea* the pressure I was under."

"Actually? I think I do. I know would-be PhD students have it *super* hard, but believe it or not, so do twenty-year-olds with a few hundred dollars to their names who don't technically fucking *exist*."

"Then you should *get* it!" Lydia spread her hands wide, eyebrows tenting. "You should understand why I wanted them to face the consequences for once. They did it to both of us, Vanessa. They ruined things for—"

"*No,* Lydia, *they* didn't do anything. I made the choice to leave. I'll never know if I had other options, because that's the one I took. And even if she was terrible, even if she scared the shit out of me that day, Brittany didn't make that choice for me. Paige didn't make it. *I* made it." Vanessa shook her head, exhaling heavily through her narrow nostrils. "I mean, *fuck,* Lydia. All Brittany did was push me when she got worked up. All Paige did was *watch me trip,* and even that was a setup. If anything, we ruined *their* lives. At the very least I think we can call it even on that front."

"They had choices too. They could have just told the truth." Lydia folded her arms across her chest, jaw jutting forward.

Vanessa regarded Lydia curiously, her movements feline as she made her way across the cave to stand nearer to me. This close, I could smell a hint of Chanel No. 5—she must still wear it—but it was almost totally overpowered by the acrid, oniony scent of her fear. Lydia's eyes followed Vanessa, two oversized camera lenses glimmering in the wavery light of the cave, sucking in every line, angle, movement.

"Why didn't they?"

"What?" That stopped Lydia short, her head actually jerking back on the slender stalk of her neck, the sudden cessation of her constant motion juddering through her.

"Why didn't they tell the truth? I mean . . . let's be real, it was barely a plan. *We need to make sure Brittany and Paige won't start gossiping the minute I'm gone.*" Vanessa threw up scare quotes, rolling her eyes as she recalled their long-ago thought process.

"We both agreed it was the best option, Vanessa."

"You're right. I agreed to that. While concussed, let me re-iterate." Lydia's jaw tightened, but Vanessa just kept going. "But I've had a lot of time to think about it since then. I get why I said yes to you that day. I even get why Paige might have panicked and clammed up at *first*. But I don't get why she *never* said anything. I mean shit, as far as she knew, it was only the two of us on the dock that night. She could have just told everyone it was an accident from minute one, that I slipped and by the time she realized what was going on it was too late. But she didn't." Vanessa tilted her head to one side, taking Lydia in. "We didn't talk about making sure they'd lie to the cops. Since, like I said, I'm pretty sure looking back that I *wanted* to be found. Some part of me actually wanted all that drama, I can admit that now."

You still do. But . . . not the time to voice that, Emily. Vanessa's eyelids went heavy, her gaze almost seductive.

"But even though they had every reason to, even though all it would have taken was one slip-up at the wrong moment, no one ever talked. Tell me, Lydia, since you've always been doing what *I* wanted you to do. Why was that?"

FLASHBACK TO

INT. PRECIPICE WINERY TASTING ROOM—DAY
(15 YEARS AGO)

The views through the floor-to-ceiling windows are breathtaking, sunshine sparkling
across the waves, as though some thought-
less god has strewn the silky surface of the
sea with thousands of tiny gems.

It only makes the girls inside, huddled
around one of the high-top tables in their
pajamas, look more insubstantial: dingy,
wispy refugees from some unknown conflict. A
pair of plainclothes officers is visible
through the windows, walking around the
grounds, and a uniformed officer stands near
the entrance to the winery, speaking into
the walkie at his shoulder.

                    EMILY
          They really think something hap-
          pened to Vanessa?

                    BRITTANY
          No, Emily, they're all searching
          the property for a game of hide
          and fucking seek.

                    EMILY
          I just meant . . . couldn't she
          have left on her own? There might
          be another explanation for it.

                    PAIGE
          Yeah, that makes sense.

                    LYDIA
          No, no way.

Paige's eyes dart to Lydia. She fiddles with
her fingers as the other girl shakes her head
emphatically.

                    LYDIA (CONT'D)
          Vanessa could be . . . reckless,
          but she never would have just
          disappeared and not said anything
          to *any* of us.

Emily thinks it over, then nods reluctantly.

                    EMILY
          She did leave all her things be-
          hind.

                    LYDIA
          Exactly. It makes no sense, un-
          less . . .

She swallows hard, squeezing her eyes tight
as a shudder runs through her. Brittany
looks especially hollowed out as she speaks,
voice flattened.

                    BRITTANY
          So you think something happened
          to her. Like . . . they're look-
          ing for her body.

                    PAIGE
          Jesus, Brittany.

                    EMILY
                (gently)
        I mean . . . we're all thinking
        it, right?

Paige shrugs, unable to meet anyone's gaze.
Lydia starts tapping the table, nervous energy practically pulsing through her.

                    LYDIA
        Well, if someone *did* do something
        to her, they'd better be prepared
        for their lives to get absolutely
        destroyed.

                    PAIGE
        What, are you going to go vigi-
        lante on them?

                    LYDIA
        I won't have to. The media are
        going to have a field day with
        this.

Emily's eyes widen as she cottons on to
Lydia's meaning.

                    EMILY
        I hadn't thought about that.

                    PAIGE
        What do you mean?

                    LYDIA
        Think about it. A girl that beau-
        tiful goes missing? We've all
        seen how stuff like that gets cov-
        ered. "Such a promising future,

> everyone loved her," then they
> show a picture of her laughing
> with her arms around us or what-
> ever.

Brittany leans forward, lowering her voice.
It's the first time she's looked genuinely
nervous. Lydia's meaning seems to be getting through to her, too.

BRITTANY

> Okay, but back it up . . . we
> don't even know anything *did* hap-
> pen to her. She could just be at
> some guy's house, or . . . I
> don't know, doing some manic
> pixie dream girl shit like hitch-
> hiking?

LYDIA

> I guess. But you'd think she
> would have said something to *one*
> of us. Or called. Her phone
> wasn't in her bedroom, and as far
> as anyone can tell it's been dead
> since last night. If she were
> just . . . *out* don't you think
> she'd find a way to call? Or even
> just come back for her charger?
> It's been a day since anyone's
> seen her, she wouldn't just be
> *totally* out of touch that long.
> And if they can't find any leads,
> they'll probably start looking
> into anyone who might have had a
> grudge . . .

                    EMILY
             (distant, almost dreamy)
       It does sorta seem like one of
       those made-for-TV movies, doesn't
       it? Someone that beautiful going
       missing, and her parents died
       that way, and her grandparents
       are millionaires?

                    LYDIA
       Totally. It's ready-made. The
       only thing that's missing is a
       villain.

                    PAIGE
       Who says there even *is* a villain?

                    LYDIA
       Maybe there's not. My point is
       that it won't matter what really
       happened if the whole world has
       already bought into some story
       that the media spun about Vanes-
       sa's disappearance. It's like
       that girl with the murdered room-
       mate in Italy. It doesn't matter
       what happened anymore, everyone
       believes she did it.

Lydia glances at the cop again, confirming
they won't be overheard, then leans forward, stretching her slight frame as far as
it will go in order to make sure her whisper
is heard.

                    LYDIA (CONT'D)
       All I'm saying is I'm definitely
       not going to bring up like . . .

arguments we were having or anything. Whatever ends up happening
with Vanessa, I don't want to be
the friend everyone believes is a
murderer.

BRITTANY
So what, you're going to lie?

LYDIA
Of course not. Why would I have
to? None of us know where she
went yesterday afternoon, or who
she talked to. I'm not withhold-
ing anything *important*. But I'm
not going to volunteer stuff that
will just get me crucified.
They're going to want to find
someone to pin this on. I don't
want it to be me. I'll tell them
what matters: I hadn't seen her
since the morning, and we all
think she went to meet up with
those guys.

PAIGE
But what if it was just an accident? Whatever happened to her, I
mean. If we don't tell them everything, won't it point them in
the wrong direction?

LYDIA
They'll be looking into that already. But trust me, they'll make
someone into the bad guy if they
can. We just need to make sure
it's not one of us.

As Emily surreptitiously opens her text
messages on her lap, clicking to delete the
thread, Paige swallows hard and Brittany
turns away, face going pale. Lydia's fingers
keep tap-tap-tapping at the table, the beat
slow and regular, seconds ticking away on a
clock.

FADE TO BLACK

17

GUILT SLITHERED THROUGH ME.

Nobody talked because of me.

Brittany's grandparents had sent a lawyer friend to whisk her away the moment the police informed them of Vanessa's disappearance, and the officers who'd driven the rest of us to the station had set us up in a spare conference room with cups of burnt-tasting coffee and a haul of random vending machine foods while they took us out to question one by one. Lydia had gone first, so it had just been me and Paige sitting across the table from each other, somehow embarrassed by eye contact. I can still remember the swoopy, geometric pattern of browns, taupes, and grays on the carpet tiles on the floor, the scratchy, industrial kind designed to hide all types of stains.

"Are you nervous?" I finally said, fiddling with the corner of a bag of Cheez-Its, unsure whether I wanted to open it. The texts from last night, and the gaps in my memory, had combined with my hangover into a swill of nauseous shame in my gut.

"Why would I be nervous? It's not like I did anything to her," Paige said, still not looking up. She was picking at the cuticle on her thumb over and over, long enough that the skin around the nail bed had turned an inflamed reddish-pink.

"I don't know. Just being here makes me feel . . . like they suspect me or something." My eyes darted up around the perimeter of the room again, not for the first time, trailing around the edges until they hooked on the blank gaze of the closed-circuit camera in the corner. It wouldn't be recording us now, would it? *Why was I even worried if it was?* Probably because it felt like we'd fallen into one of the many procedurals I'd watched over the years. Because even then, a few years away from starting my screenwriting career, I knew the next beat in the story was the police breaking one of us. Possibly *me.* I'd deleted the texts on the way to the station, but I couldn't get rid of the fear that somehow they'd find them. And then they'd fill in all the blanks in my brain with a horrible, unbearable truth.

"I guess," Paige said, running her tongue around her mouth, lip distending as it passed along the fronts of her teeth.

The silence in the room was broken only by the too-loud ticking of the clock on the wall. I started jiggling my leg, unable to stand the mounting tension.

"It's just . . . it feels like one of those movies of the week, you know?" I was already starting to think of what was unfolding around us as the story of itself. This giant shadow just below the surface, the details unknowable, but the monstrous size of it enough for your mind to start filling in details of razor teeth, rough skin, cold eyes.

"I mean . . . she probably just left, right?"

Without any of her clothes, or her laptop, or her toiletries? And Vanessa *never* let her phone die, which meant it had probably already been tossed into the woods or shattered on the rocks of the cliff face or shorted out under a hundred feet of seawater by now. Still . . . mentioning all that felt dangerous, somehow.

"Maybe. But people love stories like this."

"What do you mean?" Paige's eyes clamped on to mine, brows drawn down, her strong jaw clenched.

"Think about it, Vanessa is just so . . ." I shook my head, unable to find the words for her ineffable magnetism. "I mean she's gorgeous, for one thing. And all that stuff with her parents is kinda . . . like glamorous, right?"

"You think dead parents are glamorous?" Paige's face twisted in trademark lip-curling disbelief.

"Of course not. I just mean . . . it makes her feel sort of tragic already. She's the kind of person that the news will run updates on for weeks, you know?"

"I guess."

"And they'll want someone to blame."

Paige's eyes narrowed but she didn't say anything.

"Sorry, I'm being weird. It just feels like we need to be careful. I don't want to wind up like that girl who killed her roommate in Italy. What was her name?"

"Amanda something," Paige murmured. "But I thought they were saying now that she *didn't* do it."

"Yeah, but everyone will always *think* she did. It's how they'll remember her forever. I mean . . . you knew who I was talking about right away, right?" I ripped open the Cheez-Its, stuffing a few into my mouth just to give myself something to do. Tiny crumbs clung to my fingertips, and I brushed them rapidly against my leg, frantic to dislodge them for some reason, skin crawling at the thought of the greasy detritus sticking to me. "All I mean is people want someone to blame. And once everyone has latched on to someone, it doesn't really matter what the truth is anymore. The story is what they remember."

The door had opened then, and they'd ushered a shaky

Lydia back inside, pulling Paige out for her interview. Paige glanced over her shoulder at me as she left, her skin gray in the fluorescent tube lighting. At the time, I'd been so caught up in my own vague feelings of guilt, I hadn't thought about the effect my words might have on her.

But without knowing it, I'd convinced Paige not to say anything about what had happened between them that night. Convinced her that the only way *her* life didn't end alongside Vanessa's was hiding the details that might paint her as anything other than a loyal friend, unwittingly reinforcing the flimsy web Lydia and Vanessa had hastily spun. And now here we were, fifteen years later, circling each other in a cellar, none of us sure who we could trust anymore.

But this was not the time to volunteer as tribute. I bit down hard, blockading any errant mea culpas with the wall of my teeth.

Vanessa walked over to the next row of barrels, arms folded across her chest as she stared at Lydia.

"Well? Don't you have any answer for that, Lyds? What did you say to Paige to make sure she wouldn't talk? What did you *do*?"

"I didn't do *anything*, Vee, I swear." Lydia's eyes were wide, pleading. Vanessa sniffed loudly. "Besides . . . it's what you wanted, right? To make sure no one would follow you?"

"I wanted a fresh start . . ."

"And that's what you got!" Lydia nodded rapidly, a frenetic birdlike motion. "Whatever happened after you left, Vee, it was all just to make sure you got that fresh start. If I did say anything—and I'm not saying I did—it was only to protect you."

"*You're* the only person I need protecting from, Lydia." Vanessa whipped around, eyes narrow, lip curled into a snarl.

"I just can't believe I was too stupid to see it sooner. Though in my defense, you did a great job making sure you were my *only* connection to my past life. 'Don't sign up for any socials, Vanessa, it's too risky. Don't get in touch with Emily down in LA, Vanessa, she's still friends with Paige and Brittany, you don't know what she'll do.' " Vanessa singsonged the words venomously. "You were just like everyone else in my life. You were trying to keep me in a cage."

"It wasn't like that." Lydia looked absolutely miserable, her face like a wax doll melting. "I only wanted to help."

"If that were true, you would have helped me get my life back, Lydia, but you did everything you could to make sure that I couldn't. We're done. Fuck, we should have been done *years* ago."

Vanessa turned to me, throwing her shoulders back in a way that made her look like some sort of avenging demon.

"Come on, Emily. It's time I told Brittany everything. This is nowhere near how I'd hoped we'd do this, but it's now or never. And I need someone I can *trust* by my side."

With that, Vanessa started toward the door Lydia had come through, the one that led back through the winery, but Lydia darted over, blocking the narrow hallway through the tasting room's bottle storage with her body.

"Vanessa, I can't let you do this."

"Jesus, just . . . get out of my *way*, Lydia!" She pushed at Lydia's shoulder, but Lydia stayed firm, spreading her arms to either side to make a bigger obstacle. Then she leaned into one of the cubbies and pulled out . . .

"A knife? What the actual *fuck* are you doing?" Vanessa took a step back, allowing me to catch a glimpse. It was just a paring knife from the block upstairs, not likely to do real

damage, but it was a Wüsthof, sharp enough that I found myself backing away too.

"Protecting you! You're not thinking clearly, but I promise,
things will go better if we leave quietly and let the lawyers
handle this. You just have to trust me a little longer."

Lips pursed, Vanessa glanced at the far side of the room,
the darkness there so thick it practically had a texture. She bit
the corner of her lower lip, trying to decide whether we could
manage it.

"You can't get through that way," Lydia said, eyes following
Vanessa's. "I locked it before I came down. Anyway, Brittany's
not even awake! She took a Valium or something."

"What the *fuck*!" Vanessa's hands balled into fists. Lydia
flinched at the intensity of the hatred in her eyes.

Of course. It was the only way Lydia could have been confident coming through the winery-side door in the first
place—Brittany would have seen the notification by now if
she were anything less than drugged to the hilt. Which meant
no one knew we were here. And there was no way out except
through Lydia. Unless . . .

Breathing heavily, nostrils flaring, Vanessa's gaze moved
past me to the tunnel that led to the cliff. "Fine. We'll go out
the way I came in."

Before Lydia could fully take in Vanessa's meaning, Vanessa was striding past me down the tunnel. My heart jumped
into my throat as I gazed after her, the tunnel stretching to
infinite lengths as I stared at the hatch at the end. She wanted
me to go through it. To go *out there*. And unlike Lydia and her
"claustrophobia," my anxiety at the prospect was very real.

"Emily, come on!" Vanessa was already twisting the handle
that opened the hatch. I swallowed hard. Lydia was starting

after Vanessa, the knife gripped tightly in her hand. Could I make my way past her to the winery entrance? Would that make her follow me instead? My fingers closed around the corkscrew in my pocket, its cool, sleek shape growing less and less reassuring by the moment. I flicked open the twisted strip of metal, pressing the pad of my thumb to the end, testing its sharpness. The only pain I felt was from the pressure.

But before I could make a decision, the metal door had ground open. Cold night wind whipped into the cave, the opening a gaping maw into nothingness. Low clouds across the sky blotted out even the moonlight, turning the ocean into a tar-black void, the tiniest glimmers of light on the surface only making the waters seem thicker, deeper. But Vanessa was already stepping through, and Lydia was just a few feet behind her. I could feel an almost magnetic pull in the center of my chest—*Go the other way, get out through the winery, now's your* chance, *you idiot*—but the look in Lydia's eyes as she scrambled after Vanessa, pained and angry at the same time, like a kicked dog, stopped me in my tracks. She'd have Vanessa cornered out there. And if Vanessa kept pushing her away, who knew what she'd do? A wild slash through the air wouldn't have to hit home for someone to stumble away from it . . . on a platform barely clinging to a sheer cliff face . . .

Closing my eyes tight and sucking in a huge breath, I drew the corkscrew out of my pocket, pressed my back against the wall of the tunnel, and sidestepped my way along it, trying to let the bulk of it against my body steady me as I crept after them.

Lydia crawled through the porthole door after Vanessa, her scream of frustration nearly carried away by the wind whistling past the entrance to the cave.

"What are you *doing*, Vanessa? You're going to ruin everything!"

I inched closer. I could see both women framed in the giant circle of metal, the light spilling out from the cave slithering strangely over their skin, pooling in the orbs of Lydia's eyes. Lydia reached for Vanessa's hand and Vanessa jerked it away so hard she stumbled back on the rickety wooden platform. I almost choked on my heart, terror rocketing it up into my throat.

"Leave me *alone*, Lydia!" Vanessa bent to the opening, barking through it. "Emily, hurry up!"

"Coming," I whispered, swallowing hard, my entire body starting to tremble as I neared the door. I was just a few feet away now, and the platform had come into view. I tried to focus on the heavier support posts instead of the strips of oozing, endless black visible between each plank, each too-slim stair.

"I know you're mad, but trying to prove a point here will only hurt you. We can still fix this!" Lydia lowered the knife to her side, lifting her other hand to Vanessa—*See, not a threat*—but Vanessa's sneer just deepened, the dim light carving her face into something cruel and ugly.

"*We* can't fix anything. In fact *we* won't be doing anything together ever again."

"Don't say that! I'm your best friend!" Lydia's body jerked forward, arms moving puppetlike through the air, her need to hold on to Vanessa juddering through her.

"We were *never* friends!" Vanessa screamed, bending so close to Lydia's face that the other woman startled back. "You were just some freak who was obsessed with me. You *liked* that I didn't have anyone else. That only you knew I existed.

You're just like every other asshole I've dealt with since I left, you tell me you care while you're tightening the noose around my fucking *neck!*"

I was just inside the mouth of the tunnel now, sucking in deep breaths, trying to work up the nerve to follow Vanessa out the door and up the cliff face.

"We were friends when it helped *you!*" Lydia's hands balled into fists, body shaking and rigid with rage, the point of the knife jutting out of one hand like some physical shard of her pain. "We were friends when you needed money, or a place to stay . . ." She started toward Vanessa and Vanessa stumbled backward a step, eyes on the knife. The opening to the flight of stairs leading down to the next level was just a few feet behind her, their drop so precipitous I couldn't see to the bottom even this close to the door. "You ungrateful bitch! Do you think you can just throw me away after everything I've done for you? *You owe me, Vanessa!*"

Lydia took another step forward, thrusting the hand holding the knife at Vanessa's narrow chest, Vanessa stepped backward again to get away . . .

. . . and her boot met empty air.

I could see it happening in slow motion, Vanessa tumbling backward into nothingness, shock wiping all the anger off her features as her fingers scrabbled at the cliff face.

And then she disappeared from sight with a sickening series of thuds.

"Vanessa!"

The scream was mine. Lydia's head swiveled sharp to me, her fear turning her face young again, then she clattered out of sight, down the stairs after Vanessa.

My heart was beating so hard now I could feel it pulsing through every inch of me, fingers, stomach, throat all seeming to tense with each hammer blow of blood. Wind heavy with ocean spray flung my hair across my cheek and I reached up to scrape it away, craning my neck as far as I could, desperate to see something, *anything*.

But the angle was too sharp, the surface of the cliff too irregular. If I was going to help Vanessa, there was only one option.

Breath hitching in my throat, body seeming to hum I was shaking so hard, I stepped through the opening.

Outside, the cold, wet wind attacked me at a thousand points at once, a hail of tiny invisible arrows slicing straight through the flimsy armor of my sweater. I wrapped an arm across my stomach, the other gripping tight to the door frame, trying to anchor me against the immediate swirl of vertigo. My eyes darted out to the far edge of the platform, the ground and sea below barely visible beneath the thick shadows cast by the cliff. I gulped against a geyser of nauseous saliva and forced my eyes back to the platform's solid surface. Or . . . solid-adjacent. Hand still on the door frame, I took one shaky step forward, until the stairs came fully into sight.

Vanessa was sprawling at the bottom, one arm flung out between the rails that circled the lower landing, fingers trailing in the open air. Her legs were bent at crazy angles, and her head lolled back against the splintery wood, mouth hanging open, eyes closed. Lydia bent over her, pressing fingers to her throat, the smooth skin silvered by the hazy moonlight.

Dimly, part of me registered a glint of metal on one of the stairs.

"Vanessa?" Lydia's whisper was almost too quiet for me to hear. She moved her arms to Vanessa's shoulder, shaking it hard. Vanessa might have groaned—her face seemed to contract slightly—but it could have just been the wind, its keening wails as it swooped in and out of the pocked cliff face uncannily human.

I took another step forward, the flash flood of horror surging so fast even the terrifying precarity of the steps disappeared beneath its inky waters.

"Oh my god," I murmured, hand flying to my mouth as Lydia swung around to stare at me, eyes wide. "Lydia . . . what have you *done*?"

EXT. CLIFF FACE STAIRS—NIGHT (PRESENT DAY)

Lydia crouches over Vanessa's limp body at
the foot of the stairs, face slack with horror as she glances between Emily above her
and Vanessa below. Eyes fixed on the pair on
the lower landing, Emily reaches into her
pocket and pulls out the folding knife she'd
stowed on her way down to the cellars with
Vanessa. She flicks it open with her thumb,
revealing the surprisingly vicious-looking
jagged-edged blade. Her grip tightens around
the handle as she inches to the edge of the
stairs, but she holds it back from her body
slightly, keeping it out of Lydia's line of
sight for the time being.

                    EMILY
          Lydia . . . did you . . . ?

Lydia's tongue darts over her lips, eyebrows peaked with fear.

                    LYDIA
          I didn't mean to . . . I was just
          trying to talk to her, and
          then . . .

She shakes her head rapidly, unable to put
it into words: the violent push that sent
Vanessa tumbling down the stairs.

                    EMILY
          We have to go call the police.

She turns, making for the porthole door.
Over her shoulder we see Lydia's fear rap-

idly switch into savage, teeth-baring rage.
Before Emily can even take a step, Lydia's
bolting up the stairs. Emily glances over
her shoulder, startled.

                    LYDIA
          This is *your* fault!

She pushes Emily from behind, and Emily
stumbles forward. As she rights herself,
her hand grips the knife more tightly. When
she turns to face Lydia, she still tries to
conceal it at her side, desperate for this
to play out some other way. Her eyes can't
help but flick to the gun Lydia's thrusting
into her chest.

                    EMILY
          Lydia, I know you're upset right
          now, but we need to—

Lydia pushes Emily's shoulder, harder this
time, and Emily stumbles backward. She's
just inches from the railing around the
upper landing. Lydia's eyes are wild as she
advances on Emily.

                    EMILY (CONT'D)
          Lydia, what the fuck? We need to
          get Vanessa help!

                    LYDIA
          If you hadn't stuck your nose
          into all this, everything would
          have been okay! But you couldn't
          help yourself, could you? And now
          look what happened! Because of
          you!

She points down at Vanessa with the nose of
the gun, shaking with anger. For a moment,
Emily's too indignant to remember her fear.
She scoffs.

> EMILY
> Are you fucking kidding? *You*
> pushed her down the stairs,
> Lydia.

> LYDIA
> She was *provoking* me. Which
> wouldn't have happened if you'd
> just let us figure this out alone—

> EMILY
> Really? If I'd just stayed out of
> it you wouldn't have acted like a
> complete fucking psycho? Somehow
> I doubt that.

Lydia's eyes narrow and she takes another
step toward Emily, but Emily raises the
knife.

> EMILY (CONT'D)
> Back the fuck off, right now.

Lydia hesitates, but she doesn't move away.

> EMILY (CONT'D)
> I said get *back*! I'm going in
> there to call the police, and if
> you follow me, I swear I'll . . .

> LYDIA
> You'll *what*?

She takes a step forward, lips curling into a vulpine smirk. She raises the gun to point it at Emily's head, steadying it with her other hand.

> LYDIA (CONT'D)
> Are you going to *stab* me, Emily? Play the hero?

> EMILY
> I'm just going inside to call the police. That's all. No heroics.

Lydia takes another step forward. Emily raises the knife, edging toward the opening, but her arm is shaky.

> LYDIA
> You know what your problem is? You've always been a coward. You never stood up for me, you never stood up for *yourself,* and you sure as hell don't have it in you to save the day *now.*

Lydia steps forward again and Emily slashes at her feebly, eyes averted—Lydia's right, she's not ready to do this. Lydia easily grabs Emily's arm, gripping it tightly, and presses a thumb into a tendon in Emily's wrist until Emily drops the knife with a whimper of pain. Eyes never leaving Emily's, Lydia kicks the blade to the side, where it skitters over the edge and tumbles through space.

> LYDIA (CONT'D)
> And to think I thought I might
> need this.

She waves the gun for emphasis.

> LYDIA (CONT'D)
> Though I suppose it's still use-
> ful as a backup. Never can be too
> careful, right?

> EMILY
> Lydia . . . where did you even
> *get* a gun?

> LYDIA
> Oh for fuck's—stop pretending you
> know the first *thing* about me.

Lydia emphasizes her point with a gun poke
to the chest, and Emily jerks back. Lydia
smiles tightly at that, enjoying the control.

> LYDIA (CONT'D)
> Some fucking detective you were.
> Did you think I didn't notice you
> sneaking around the house all
> weekend, trying to trick everyone
> into saying something they didn't
> mean to when they were drunk?

She advances another step and Emily retreats. Her back just barely grazes the
railing of the platform. She glances toward
the stairs behind Lydia, desperate for some
escape route to materialize, but there's

nothing, just the night wind peeling past
the two of them, and empty space in every
direction.

> LYDIA (CONT'D)
> Did you really think you could
> swoop in here and steal her from
> me after *fifteen years*?

> EMILY
> I'm not trying to steal anything.
> I just want us to get Vanessa
> some help before it's too—

> LYDIA
> Get her some *help*? Where were you
> when she needed your help back
> then? Where were you when *I*
> needed your help?

Lydia advances on Emily, thrusting the nose
of the gun into Emily's chest again, hard.
Emily stumbles backward, but there's nowhere left to go. The railing catches her
near the hips, and it creaks beneath her
weight. Lydia affects a look of pity as she
presses the gun forward, forcing Emily to
lean back over the edge. Emily can't help
but look over her shoulder, swallowing nauseously at the sight of so much emptiness
behind her.

> LYDIA (CONT'D)
> It's too bad you've been holding
> on to such a terrible grudge
> against Vanessa for so long.

EMILY
What? What are you talking about?
Lydia, it doesn't have to go this
way.

LYDIA
You just couldn't get over how
she stole the one man you ever
cared about away from you. Professor LaVoie was supposed to be
your great love, not hers.

Horror dawns on Emily's face.

EMILY
No one will believe that.

LYDIA
Of course they will. You went
after her fifteen years ago, and
when you realized it hadn't
worked, you decided to finish what
you started. You would have managed to do it, too, if the wood
of this deck weren't so rotten.

Emily glances over her shoulder again. As
if in response, the wood creaks ominously.

EMILY
You don't need to do this, Lydia.

LYDIA
I'm not doing anything. You went
over in your struggle with Vanessa.

> EMILY
> This won't work, Lydia. Vanessa
> will never agree to—

> LYDIA
> If she wakes up, and you're gone,
> she'll agree to whatever she has
> to in order to get her hands on
> that money.

Lydia laughs as she watches that sink in.

> LYDIA (CONT'D)
> That's the thing, Emily. You
> never understood Vanessa. None of
> you did. But *I* did. I've always
> known who she is, and I've loved
> her anyway. That's what real
> friendship is. Loving someone no.
> Matter. What.

She thrusts the gun barrel into Emily's
chest to emphasize the words, teeth bared.
The wood behind Emily creaks menacingly,
then splinters. Emily grits her teeth, forcing herself not to give in to fear, her eyes
narrowing as she stares at Lydia.

> EMILY
> And if she doesn't wake up?

This catches Lydia off guard. Fear tugs at
the corners of her eyes.

> LYDIA
> She will.

                    EMILY
          I don't know, Lydia. Bodies
          aren't supposed to bend that way.

Emily stretches up to look over Lydia's
shoulder. Lydia has to check herself not to
follow Emily's gaze.

                    EMILY (CONT'D)
          I'm sure you'll come up with
          something to cover your tracks.
          But you'll always know deep down
          that *you* killed Vanessa. The only
          person you ever really cared
          about would still be alive if it
          weren't for you.

                    LYDIA
          That won't happen . . .

                    EMILY
          It's already done, Lydia. It's
          funny, really. All that talk about
          what all of us did to her, how we
          were so awful and deserved to be
          punished, and you're the monster
          who actually finished her off.

Lydia swallows spastically, forehead crumpling with pain and fear, and she can't resist it anymore, she has to turn to look.
It's the half-second that Emily needs to
chop at Lydia's wrist—the one holding the
gun. Lydia yelps, pulling her arm away reflexively to rub at the pain, and Emily takes
the opportunity to grip the other woman's
shoulders, wrestling her backward.

                    LYDIA
        No. *No!* This is *not* how it's
        going to happen!

She fights back, pushing Emily against the
railing again. Another piece of wood splinters and Emily almost loses her balance.
She kicks at Lydia's feet as she slips,
bringing the other woman to her knees. The
gun clatters across the landing and both
women scramble for it, but Lydia's faster.
She points it at Emily again, cruel triumph
lighting her face as she stands.

                    LYDIA (CONT'D)
        Where were we? Right. You were
        going to stumble to your death in
        your crazed need to get rid of
        Vanessa.

Emily's eyes widen as Vanessa appears over
Lydia's shoulder, limping and leaning heavily
on the railing, her plodding steps drowned
out by the wind.

                    VANESSA
        Really? I'm not sure I like that
        ending.

Shock, relief, and fear war on Lydia's features. She lowers the gun, turning to face
her friend.

                    LYDIA
        I'm so sorry. I didn't mean to
        hurt you. It was an accident, I
        just—

VANESSA
You meant it. And so do I. So
just to be very clear, this isn't
an accident. It was just a long
time coming.

She takes hold of both of Lydia's shoulders, gritting her teeth as she throws her
whole weight into Lydia, pushing the other
woman to the edge. Vanessa's leaning in
hard, unbalanced on one leg, using Lydia's
body to hold herself up. As they struggle,
the wood creaks beneath Lydia. Vanessa has
Lydia's back up against the railing, and
she's pushing with all her might, when,
with a final splintering crack, the railing
gives way. Lydia hovers on the edge, tee-
tering in space, then Vanessa pushes once
more and Lydia begins to fall . . . but as
she does, she grabs the other woman's shirt-
front with both hands. Before Vanessa can
get hold of anything, Lydia slips back, her
weight taking both women over the edge and
into the darkness beyond.

FADE TO BLACK

18

THE SUN WAS STARTING TO RISE, A PALE GRAY-pink bleeding into the sky, reflecting on the caps of the waves. I was turning the events of the night over in my mind for the hundredth time, imagining how the last moments on the ledge would need to play out in a movie version—there would have to be a gun, definitely, and Lydia would have to be more clearly a villain, obsessed with Vanessa, the kind of over-the-top unhinged that moviegoers sucked up like dew on desert sand—when I finally heard the wail of the ambulance approaching.

"Are you going to be okay for a few minutes? I need to point them in your direction."

Vanessa nodded, attempting a weak smile that immediately turned into a grimace. She'd managed to pull herself into a sitting position, and together we'd moved her up against the cliff. I'd grabbed a blanket off the couch when I ran inside to call the police, but she was still shivering, possibly from shock. I tried not to look at her leg beneath the blanket. It was twisted in a way that made my insides go crawly.

I took a deep breath, eyes half-closed as I scrambled up the staircase to the hatch door, all ideas of the script I'd been mentally drafting all weekend subsumed under a wave of shaky anxiety. Sitting motionless next to Vanessa the last few hours I'd somehow just managed, but with the surge of adrenaline definitively sucked back out to sea, ascending the entire staircase was beyond my capabilities at the moment.

I met the EMTs on the driveway, taking them across to the cliffside staircase to show them where Vanessa was waiting. She offered a weak wave as they clattered down to her to start assessing the situation. The staircase was solid—Brittany had been right about whatever extra-special wood they used to build it—but I couldn't help but shiver as I watched it judder under their heavy, booted feet. I wondered idly if they'd have to bring in a helicopter. Nice and dramatic. Though not part of the ending I was already planning in my head. We'd had plenty of time to talk that over as we sat on the platform, the heavy curtain of the night slowly lifting off the surface of the sea. Luckily, it hadn't taken much to convince Vanessa to go along with the version of events I was still fine-tuning in my mind.

I was just turning back toward the house when Brittany emerged onto the back patio, arms folded tight across her slim body. Paige stumbled out behind her, rubbing the back of her hand across her eyes blearily.

"What the fuck is happening?" Paige blurted, turning to Brittany for support with a look of exaggerated incredulity.

"It's kind of a long story," I said. Brittany moved up next to me, craning her neck to see down the steep flight of stairs.

"Wait . . . is that *Vanessa*?" Brittany's mouth went slack, entire body slumping under the weight of the revelation.

"Vanessa? What are you—" Paige stumbled over then stopped short next to Brittany, eyes going wide. She ran a hand through her short hair, making it spike in every direction. "Holy fuck."

"Like I said, it's a long story. Why don't I explain over coffee? It might take them a while to figure out how to get my friend Christine up safely."

"Christine? What are you—" Brittany's face scrunched up in disbelief but I just shook my head, eyes flashing a warning.

"We'll talk inside."

"AND THEN LYDIA just . . . fell?"

Paige was leaning forward on the gigantic dining table, hanging on my every word. The coffee in the mug abandoned between her elbows had long since gone cold.

"Sort of? Everything was happening so fast."

I pinched my eyes shut, Lydia's face flashing into my mind for maybe the thousandth time since the night before. Vanessa was screaming at me from the platform below, *Get the knife, Emily,* and then I was running down the stairs, moving on instinct, just a hair faster than Lydia, and then the shocking ease with which it went into her stomach, the expensive steel slipping into her body with only a hint of resistance. Horror on her face, her stumbling backward, tripping over Vanessa's outstretched body, Vanessa screaming at me as Lydia staggered sideways against the railing, unbalanced, Vanessa crawling over as I descended from above, both of us heaving against her . . .

"She was coming after me, I moved away at the last second, and she went into the railing way too fast. Lost her balance," I finally said. "If she hadn't, I don't know what would have happened. She was like a completely different person, it was . . . well, it was terrifying," I said, shuddering. That much, at least, was entirely true.

"Jesus," Paige murmured. Brittany nodded slowly, exhaling a sigh.

"I always said the handrails on the stairs weren't high enough."

They almost definitely were. At least for someone Lydia's height.

I didn't say that out loud. We all sat in silence for a moment, the only sound in the room the dim crash of the waves against the cliff.

"Will they . . . find her?" Paige finally said. "Her body, I mean?"

I bit my lower lip. It was the one thing Vanessa and I hadn't been sure of. Or at least the most important thing.

"Maybe?" I took a slow, steadying breath. "I couldn't tell last night, it was so dark, but . . . I think the tide was pretty high when she fell. And this morning, we looked at the beach, but . . ." I shook my head.

"The curve in the cliffs creates a weird undertow, Topper and Mitzi were always really strict about us swimming during high tide," Brittany said, eyes fixed on the surface of the table. "If it pulled her out . . ."

I nodded. She might never be found. And even if she was, the time in the salt water would degrade any but the most basic truth: She fell too far and it killed her. At least I *thought* that was true. I'd worked up enough versions of this story in my head before now to know not to risk searching that on my phone, no matter how much my fingers itched to type in the words.

"So she was leaving all that stuff around the house," Paige murmured. "Did Vanessa ask her to?"

"No, Lydia was trying to scare us all away, she was still so angry about what happened back in college that she couldn't stand being here with the rest of us. And she was probably more than happy to punish us all a little more." It wasn't exactly true, but it was close. She *had* said she wanted to make us leave. "Vanessa just wanted Lydia to help ease Brittany into a really weird conversation. She asked Lydia to tell you what had happened, Brit, and show you the necklace to back the story up. She knew it would be hard to accept that she'd been alive this whole time without some sort of proof."

I kept my eyes on Brittany, watching for any sign of guilt at that—if she had spent all these years believing Vanessa *wasn't* alive, it's because she knew she'd left her to die after their fight in the cave fifteen years ago. But of course . . . I didn't really know what had happened there. I only had Vanessa's vague references to a cliffside walk, Brittany turning violent, her persistent fear of her cousin . . . the rest I was just filling in the way I would in a screenplay. Brittany nodded slowly, the same thousand-yard stare that had been glazing her eyes throughout the entire conversation immobilizing her sharp features. In this light, with Brittany totally motionless, you could see a flicker of resemblance between the cousins.

"So my paper . . ."

"Lydia must have dug that up herself. And the pictures. I think they were meant for me, but after you told everyone about the paper, she had to improvise." It was a bold move, if a miscalculated one; if we'd bothered to compare notes about the objects turning up *before* Paige's tear-stained confession over dinner, Lydia must have known we'd suspect her. But . . . maybe she was banking on our not comparing notes, on all the secrets that had been festering in each of us for so long keeping us quiet, on our friendships—and our trust in one another—being weaker than our guilt. Whatever else she was, Lydia really was good at reading people.

The never-quite-turned-off section of my brain that wanted to know the end to every story wished I could ask her why she'd chosen that route, why she'd agreed to come along in the first place if she was so dead set against Vanessa's plan. Was she too much under Vanessa's sway to resist her even now? Or did she just like the idea of playing puppet master to the rest of us? But it was too late to ask that now.

"I think she couldn't handle the idea that she wouldn't have Vanessa to herself anymore," I added with a small shrug. True? Unclear. But it was definitely going into the script version, and planting the seed now with the only people who might spot the differences between the two Lydias—the one we'd all known, if never as well as she'd known us, and the one I was planning for the silver screen—could only help.

"Fuck that's twisted," Paige said, voice so low it was almost a whisper.

"I'm not surprised," Brittany said, mouth tightening in a way that aged her face at least ten years as she finally roused herself to look around the table. Whatever private reflection she'd been going through was clearly tucked away again, the lid snapped shut. "Lydia's always been off, if you ask me. And she blamed everyone else for her problems."

I thought back to that garden party, the look on Lydia's face then. *Sometimes other people deserved the blame.* But it wasn't worth getting into with Brittany. She had many, many tools in her arsenal, but self-examination wasn't among them. Besides, it served me far better for her to cement Lydia as the villain in her mind.

Brittany let out a sharp little laugh.

"And they really believed this would *work*?" She turned to me, eyebrow raised expectantly. "I hope you let Vanessa know that her plan was doomed from the start."

"What do you mean?"

"They thought they were going to waltz in here and extort

me for half of this place!" She rolled her eyes hugely. "Vanessa really must be desperate if she thinks I'm going to just bend over and give her a handout *now*."

"It's not a fucking *handout*, Brittany. Jesus." I scrunched up my face in open disdain. Brittany's chin drew back sharply, and she blinked several times, clearly trying to process the sight of me initiating the conflict for once.

"I'm not sure I take your meaning," she finally said.

"I saw the will, for one thing, so you don't really have a choice," I said. Not to mention that if Brittany hadn't been so needlessly cruel to Lydia, so deeply selfish, none of this ever would have happened. Brittany started to interject, but I raised a hand, speaking over her, carried along by indignation. It was mildly intoxicating—no wonder Brittany liked it so much. "And even if you did, don't you think you at least owe Vanessa that much?"

"*Owe* her? After the pain she's put us all through?"

"Yes, *owe* her. You attacking her in that cave is what started this whole thing, Brittany. It's what made her even think of running away in the first place. If you want to talk about *pain*, we should probably start there."

Brittany's mouth dropped open, and I had to fight to repress my smirk. Didn't know I had *that* trump card, did you? The version I was crafting might not be what had actually happened between the cousins, might not even be all that close, but it was near enough to get Brittany scared.

"Attack—what the fuck is she talking about?" Paige bit her lip, eyes darting between the two of us.

"I'll let Brittany explain. Unless she plans to stick to her guns on this one, in which case, I'm sure it will all come out in the news eventually. That is, if you *force* Vanessa to go public in order to claim what's rightfully hers. Seeing as I'd gladly testify that she is in fact who she says she is."

Was that even a thing? Either way, the threat seemed to be landing. Brittany stared at me for a few long moments, eyes narrowing, the muscles along her temples jumping. I decided to really drive it home. I'd probably feel guilty later—having it out with anyone went against my fundamental programming—but it was like being at a dessert buffet as a child. I couldn't seem to stop myself, even knowing it would probably make me sick. At that moment, I couldn't quite understand why I'd been resisting the temptation for so long.

"It would be messy, of course. We'd probably have to really dig into *why* Vanessa felt the need to disappear in order to clear up all the stuff around her using her friend's identity for all those years. But being afraid that you'd hurt her if you knew she was still alive feels pretty compelling to me." Paige's eyes kept ping-ponging from me to Brittany as I spoke, growing wider and wider until they practically looked like the balls themselves. "Even if the court doesn't see it that way, the public certainly will, especially when I contact all my friends in entertainment journalism to make sure they play up the story. Vanessa might have to pay some sort of fine for using someone else's identity, but I'm pretty sure that wouldn't negate the terms of Mitzi's will."

I stared at Brittany, clamping my teeth together to keep what I hoped was a stoic, fuck-if-I-care expression in place. I honestly couldn't tell if I believed my approach would help Vanessa's case—and by extension mine; this story only worked if certain details stayed deeply buried—or if I just wanted to watch Brittany squirm for once. After all, she wasn't the only one at that table who had to answer for what she'd done fifteen years ago. But she didn't need to be reminded of that right now.

Brittany exhaled a long breath, nostrils flaring with the force of it.

"Nothing actually *happened,* things just got . . . a little heated that day. Vanessa knows that." Her arms were still folded across her chest, gaze still defiant, but she was clearly standing down. Relief fizzed through me.

"*She* probably does. But I doubt everyone else will buy that quite as easily. I mean, you sat on that information for *fifteen years*. Lied to the police. Even if the statute of limitations is up on actually prosecuting you for any of it, people will love the story." I sucked both my lips between my teeth, widening my eyes meaningfully.

"If we go to court to . . . what, *revive* Vanessa? What do you even do to declare someone alive?" Brittany squeezed her eyes shut tight, shaking her head rapidly in frustration. "The point is, the story will come out anyway. There's no way to give Vanessa what she wants without it blowing up for *all* of us."

"Oh, I don't know about that. Mitzi's estate probably put a value on the property, and even if it didn't, a realtor would be more than happy to. If the spirit of the will were honored, I'm sure we could persuade Vanessa that it was easier for everyone if she just kept living her life as Christine, don't you think so, Paige?" Paige seemed startled to hear her name, then nodded rapidly.

"Totally. It just makes the most sense, right?"

I repressed a sardonic grin—it seemed like it wasn't Brittany to whom Paige had always been playing yes-woman, so much as it was the strongest person in the room.

"You're a smart woman, Brittany. I'm sure you could dream

up something that you need to hire my friend Christine for. Or a rare object you'd like to buy from her? Something where the fees just happen to come out to half the winery's value?"

She glared at me, knuckles turning white she was clenching her fists so hard. I could almost see her working it over in her brain—*Would Vanessa really come forward? If she did, would there be a way for it not to blow back on Brittany?*

But she was checkmated and she knew it. Vanessa had nothing to lose anymore—at least, not that anyone here knew about. Brittany, on the other hand, had *plenty.* Which she'd be happy to tell the world she'd earned fair and square.

"Tell her I'll have to talk to Markus first. We'll have to move some money around if we're going to work out a private transfer on that scale." Brittany forced the words out between gritted teeth.

"I'm sure she'll understand." I couldn't keep the triumphant smirk off my face. I didn't actually have skin in that part of the game, but the idea that Brittany might get away with Vanessa's inheritance—that she'd even try to—had really gotten under my skin. It almost made me understand why you might not want to do everything you could to avoid an argument, at least not *every* time.

Brittany's eyes narrowed further, and she pushed back from the table sharply.

"I think I need a shower. And you're going to need to sort out your own ride back to the airport, Emily, since *I* won't be driving you," Brittany said. Then, without a backward glance, she strode off across the living room and disappeared down the hallway to the elevator. Paige stared after her, frowning, tongue moving slowly over her lips as she tried to work out the puzzle. Finally she turned to me.

"Brittany really tried to hurt Vanessa?"

"I don't think she *tried* to," I finally said, shaking my head slowly. I *could* try to convince Paige otherwise—part of me felt a perverse pleasure at the idea of bringing her fully over to my side—but the fact of the matter was we all had plenty of things to atone for, me more than anyone at this point. Painting Brittany as some twenty-year-old monster just felt . . . unnecessary. "Things just got out of hand and she panicked. At least that's what Vanessa seems to think."

"But then . . . why does it matter if she didn't say anything about it back then? To the police, I mean?"

"She happened to panic while Vanessa was passed out in the beach cave. With the tide coming in." It may or may not have been true, but planting the idea in Paige's head felt like the smart route, especially since I was starting to really *like* that version for the script.

Paige's eyes went huge. After a few seconds, she tilted her head to the side, like a dog hearing a whistle beyond human range.

"But then . . . why?"

"Why what?"

"Why did they want to convince *me* I'd killed Vanessa? Or at least that I'd let her die?" Paige's face, always an open book, was scrunched with obvious pain. For the first time, it occurred to me just how large a role that night had played in her life. How heavily it must have weighed on her to hold something like that inside, where the dark and damp burrowed into it, rot blooming over every surface of the memory and turning it even more monstrous.

"I think the idea was that if you felt responsible, you wouldn't tell the investigators about Vanessa flunking out of school? It might have clued people into the fact that she *wanted* to disappear."

"But . . . why would I have ever told them that? What would flunking a couple classes even have to do with her going missing?" Paige squinted, genuinely trying to puzzle it out. "It's not like she ever seemed all that worried about it. Besides, Vanessa had trusted me with that, I wasn't going to start blabbing it around."

I swallowed hard, guilt that wasn't even mine welling up in my throat like some sort of sympathetic vomiting response. Had any of us ever really known each other?

Or maybe it was my guilt, just not for this particular conversation. Suddenly the all-you-can-eat dunk-fest felt not just unnecessary, but vicious. *They don't know what a hypocrite you are, but you do.*

"I think maybe . . . Lydia just wanted to punish you. Both you and Brittany. That research assistant job could have changed her entire future, let her help pay for her mother's treatment without giving up her own dreams. Brittany might not have known how much it mattered to Lydia, but she definitely knew *that* it mattered." Paige nodded, face drooping with shame. "After the fight in the cave, Brittany was already convinced she'd killed Vanessa. Honestly, if we'd been paying attention, we probably would have realized something was off with her." Had Brittany acted guilty that afternoon when she came back to the house? Try as I might, I couldn't dredge up any memory of it at all. "I think Lydia just . . . saw her chance with you and took it."

"Yeah, well, she really stuck the landing on that one," Paige muttered.

EPILOGUE

"I WONDER IF IT HAS TO BE AT A SKI LODGE— it's been done so many times before. What about an island? Oh, or a winery? I've never seen that before. And some of them are very remote, no?" The woman from the production company's forehead was preternaturally smooth, her cheeks plump and rosy, lips unlined in a way that I'd somehow stopped seeing as strange in the last several years in LA. Her hands, though, tendony as she flipped through my script and lightly speckled from years of sun damage, belied her carefully tended face. So did her name; you didn't meet a lot of Lindas under a certain age these days.

I kept my smile wide. I was very used to these sorts of "notes" at this stage in my career, the ones that didn't actually improve anything, just changed it, somehow proving in the note-giver's mind that they had *added* something. Beyond the financing, obviously.

"I could definitely rework the setting if that's what the team wants," I said. It was important that they realize I *would* take the note, and just as important for them not to realize how eager I was to take that note in particular. Not that the events at Brittany's family lodge at Lake Tahoe had garnered much attention—our names hadn't even appeared in the single article I'd found about Lydia tumbling over the cliff behind the vast property, the as-yet-unsuccessful efforts to recover her body from the remote ravine that kept the lodge that much more private than those of the other uber-wealthy vacationers that flocked to the area not worthy of coverage, apparently—but the more distance from my real life, the better.

"It's not a hard note, just something to consider. And of course it will all depend on who we attach to the production." Linda turned to the man sitting to her right around the gigantic conference room table, Perry. He was closer to my age, handsome in his fitted button-down, open at the throat, with a strong jaw and an impish smile. "Maurice would be perfect for this—he's been eager to take on a suspense story since he missed out on *Knives Out*—but he can be very particular about setting."

"I'd be more than happy to work with him on the next draft," I said, forcing myself not to react to the casual first-name-drop of one of the hottest directors working.

"And did I hear that it's a true story?" Perry said, not quite able to keep the eagerness out of his voice. He turned to Linda. "It could be a great marketing angle."

"Unfortunately it's not," I said, flashing an apologetic smile. *This* part I'd practiced in the mirror. Then later with an audience of one to hone the performance. "I did have a friend go missing in college, which definitely inspired me, but everything else is fiction."

"We can probably still use that," he said, jotting down something on a notepad at his elbow. After a moment he turned to Linda, raising an eyebrow sharply. She nodded. "I don't think there's any point in playing coy, we're very interested in partnering with you on this."

I nudged my agent's knee under the table. To her credit, Lucy didn't even roll her eyes.

"It would need to be a true partnership. This story's very

personal to Emily. She's going to need to be on all future drafts. Which isn't really a big ask, she's spent years in the trenches at *Back of House,* she's certainly proven she knows how to rework a script."

"Of course," Perry said, flicking his hand through the air. "We'd want to get moving on this immediately. It fits a couple of our mandates at the moment."

"I understand. Send me your offer today and we can start talking details." Lucy flashed her disarmingly open smile at the room of execs. We'd bonded immediately over our shared Midwestern roots when she'd signed me, over a decade ago now, and her "I'm just so genuinely glad to be here, feel free to take advantage" expression of aww-shucks excitement was one of my favorite weapons in her arsenal, specifically because I was the only one who ever seemed to recognize it had serious firepower. "I'm sure you understand we have to consider the other offers that have come in as well. But with the resources and connections at your disposal, I think we could turn this into an absolute blockbuster. I know Emily's eager to get this story out to the widest audience possible."

Specifically this *version* of the story. Even more so the soon-to-be-revised winery draft. Already I could see just how advantageous that telling would be, not only to the story—it could have *caves,* there was infinite thriller potential in caves, and if the winery were coastal, maybe one or both of the bodies could disappear into the ocean?—but to *me.* But . . . no one in the room needed to know that.

"Then we're all on the same page." Perry stood, extending a hand across the polished table, a single rough-edged slab of some sort of probably-now-illegal-to-harvest wood. I followed suit, taking it in mine and returning his wide smile. "We'll be in touch *very* soon."

With that, everyone started packing up, bustling out into the hallway, chatting about weekend plans and movies they had in the pipeline, and generally sucking up to one another in that way that would feel *extremely* unsubtle anywhere but LA. Lucy waited until we were across the lobby to turn to me, voice low.

"So?"

"So I want to see their offer," I said, glancing over my shoulder. "But assuming it's as good as I think it will be, it's definitely them."

"Oh my god, I'm *so* glad you said that, because I was getting such positive vibes through the entire meeting. Plus, Maurice Ripaldi? *Dream* director for this."

"Let's not count chickens," I said, biting my lower lip against the giddy grin threatening to consume my entire face.

"Of course. Unless you wanted to, because the offer from Martin and Rivers just came in, and it is for a *lot* of chickens." She squeezed my hand with a delighted little squeal. "Can I buy you lunch? I never let myself get Porto's, I can't resist their tres leches cake, but I think today is worth an exception."

"Let's rain check. I already promised a friend I'd meet up with her while I'm in the Valley. I always make her come to me."

"As it should be," Lucy said, widening her eyes meaningfully.

With that, we headed out into the acid-washed sunshine, cheek-kissing before we headed our separate ways along the broad streets of Burbank. I waited until she'd disappeared around the corner to send the text. Moments later, Vanessa drove up in the vintage Mustang convertible she'd been driving since we got back to town. She and Brittany were still working out their payment plan, but a *very* generous first installment had already come in.

"So?" Vanessa tugged off her gigantic sunglasses to fix me with an expectant stare as I slipped into the passenger seat. She'd wrapped an ivory headscarf over her dark hair and around her neck, and was giving off strong Audrey Hepburn vibes. Part of me wondered if she might get scouted right now, waiting outside the studio. Though in LA, beautiful women—even women as beautiful as she was—were a far less remarkable sight.

"They're going to offer. And from the sounds of it, it's pretty much a blank check."

"Oh my *god*!" She leaned across the car to wrap me in a Chanel-scented hug. I could feel myself melting into it physically, even if my brain was throwing up a bright red warning flag. I was still shocked by how strong her pull was, how much I wanted to just give in to the feeling she could still spark in me.

These days, though, I knew better than to trust it. I couldn't fully shed Vanessa—we were tied to each other now, by the story that we'd both lived, and the version I had carefully reshaped. Keeping up the act—that we were friends who cared deeply about each other, that she was "letting" me tell the story because she wanted me to succeed, that I was cutting her in because I cared about her too much to even *consider* not doing so—was clearly important to Vanessa. So I dutifully played my part in what she surely still believed was the Vanessa Show, both of us conveniently ignoring the fact that this "renewed friendship" was enforced less by love than by the terms of the contract I'd had drawn up *to keep us both safe*.

And it's not like it was all that hard to pretend. Vanessa was still *fun*. Being with her still conjured that same sparkly, anything-can-happen feeling I'd thought I'd left behind for good once I crossed the threshold of my thirties. I just knew now, in a way I'd never realized before, that liking someone's company was just one metric of friendship, possibly the least important one. All the others I used to think I had with Vanessa—intimacy, trust, vulnerability—had died the day she reappeared in that diner in Verdana. She might look the same, smell the same, share the same tics as the girl I'd loved fifteen years ago, but for all intents and purposes, I didn't know *this* Vanessa at all. Or that one, apparently. And I had zero intention of forgetting that.

Eventually I pulled back and Vanessa worked the car out into traffic. I'd told her she didn't need to chauffeur me to the meeting, but she'd been insistent, and I couldn't quite blame her. I had no intention of cutting her out of the deal, but if I were her, I wouldn't have trusted that promise either.

"So . . . if they *do* come through, how much would that work out to on my end?" Vanessa asked, eyes shielded by both her attention to the road and those massive sunglasses.

"Twenty percent of my earnings, like we talked about."

We'd signed the basic version of the contract at a tiny one-man law firm on the Nevada side of Lake Tahoe, where neither of us would be recognized. Vanessa proved it wasn't hard to get lost in LA, but in some ways—especially when it came to things like contracts over story rights—it was a *very* small town.

Vanessa nodded slowly.

"That goes away if you ever come forward, though," I said, eyes darting to her sharp profile. "Legally, I own the story. You can't ever try to take it back."

"Legally I don't exist."

"Vanessa . . ."

"I know, I know. Don't worry, if I'd been that intent on getting my fifteen minutes, I would have shown up to more castings back in the day." She flashed a sly smile at me. "Anyway, I have no reason to come forward. If Vanessa Morales ever makes an appearance on this earth again, Christine Silva's payments from Brittany are going to dry up fast. I am *very* confident the contract she sent is airtight."

"Good point. You stand to gain a hell of a lot more this way."

We smiled at each other, but the threat was visible, a hulking shadow beneath the still waters of our feigned camaraderie. I didn't have to say what both of us knew. If she talked about what had happened at the lodge either time, it wouldn't just be money she'd be losing. I had looked into it, and it seemed *fairly* certain that the statute of limitations was up on everything Vanessa had done to help herself disappear. But that night on the cliff face with Lydia, racing after her down the rickety stairs Brittany's family had installed to give them access to the off-piste trails that opened up at the bottom of the ravine, the entire structure creaking in the winter wind, shaky under our combined weight?

The moment flashed into my head again, Lydia lunging at me, Vanessa hauling herself up by the stair rail to stab at her from behind, Lydia stumbling around, mouth gaping, blood starting to soak through her shirt, then Vanessa scrambling on hands and knees to place herself in front of the railing, a human lever screaming at me to push her, *push her before she kills both of us* . . .

At least that was one version of how it played out in my head. It wasn't *exactly* the truth—none of the mental film reels I watched were—but soon, if I kept imagining all the different endings, the actual truth wouldn't matter so much. It would just become another one of the many possible stories of that night.

Of course, we both knew there were only a couple possible endings if either of us ever talked about it to the authorities; which one we wound up with would just come down to who they thought was more believable. I liked to think it was me—shaping events into something more satisfying was my vocation, after all—but Vanessa had a way of making you *want* to believe her, even when what she was saying didn't quite add up. I knew that better than anyone.

Basically, it was mutually assured destruction, and we both knew it. But with regular "girls' nights" at LA's trendiest cocktail bars.

"Honestly, Em, you have nothing to worry about. After this long? I know how to keep my head down when I need to." Vanessa reached across the console to squeeze my thigh quickly, and I decided to let myself be soothed by it. We both lived in the land of manifesting the reality you wanted, after all. "So? Where to?"

"How about Grandeur in Exile," I said. If I hadn't been watching closely, I wouldn't have caught the tiny twitch at the corner of Vanessa's mouth. Seeing her there however many months ago was what had set this whole thing off in the first place, after all.

"Grandeur in Exile, hmm? I've always loved that spot," she said, glancing over her shoulder as she merged onto the 101. "But then, you already knew that."

I closed my eyes, sucking in a deep breath as my hair whipped in the balmy wind of another perfect southern California day. There were still *t*'s to cross and *i*'s to dot, but it was all finally happening. The future was brighter than ever, and Vanessa and I were, if not exactly a team, at least after the same goal. If things hadn't unfolded *exactly* according to plan, the plan we'd cobbled together along the way was working even better.

And for the first time in our entire . . . *friendship* wasn't quite right anymore, but it was the best stand-in, I'd not only had the chance to truly peek behind the curtain, to glimpse the shape of the self Vanessa had always worked so hard to keep hidden, I had the upper hand. If it ever *did* come down to she-said, she-said, who would people be likelier to believe? The woman who had faked her own death, tortured her entire family, mooched off a string of unsuspecting men for over a decade . . . or the sweet Midwesterner who'd worked hard for years to finally make good, and who'd unwittingly found herself pulled into something dark and dangerous that she'd never asked for?

After all, Vanessa might have *it,* that ineffable quality everyone in this town was always hunting for, but I had something just as potent.

I knew how to tell the better story.

ACKNOWLEDGMENTS

The relationships in this book are mostly toxic, but I could never have brought them to life without the help of some truly incredible, life-affirming people, any of whom I'd trust to have my back on a rickety cliffside staircase.

First off, a huge thanks to Anne Speyer, the most incredible editor a girl could ever hope for. You invariably provide sharp insights and much-needed perspective, and I genuinely feel like the luckiest writer in the world to have you in my corner (especially when I come in with a probably-that's-one-step-too-far idea). Heartfelt thanks as well to Jesse Shuman and the entire editorial staff at Bantam: having all your brilliant brains working for my books feels like some sort of evil-genius trick I've managed to play on the universe.

Taylor Haggerty: you are an absolute wonder. This book in particular would never have come together without you. Our brainstorm sessions are one of my favorite perks of author-dom, and I trust you completely. Huge thanks to Jasmine Brown as well: every note you give is so undeniably dead-on I always wonder how I didn't spot it myself.

This book revolves around female friendship, and I'm incredibly lucky to count so many smart, funny, generous women as my lifelong friends. Your support, honesty, and willingness to discuss truly horrifying details of my personal life mean the world to me. Not only am I certain none of you would ever try to use me to enact your own perverse revenge, I know that if I asked you to do that for *me,* you wouldn't even blink . . . which should scare me but really just makes me love you that much more.

Thanks always to the brilliant writers whom I rely on for both honest critique and (regular) ego repair, particularly Lana Harper, Chelsea Sedoti, and Adriana Mather. You are the absolute best.

Mom: thank you for so much more than I could ever encapsulate here. Your endless love and support have made me the person I am. Claire and Janie: you're my best friends, and I wish everyone could be so lucky to have sisters like you.

And last, but most, thank you, Danny, for everything you do for me and for our family. Your belief in me means more than you can possibly know, and without your support I could never have followed this dream. I love you more than anything.

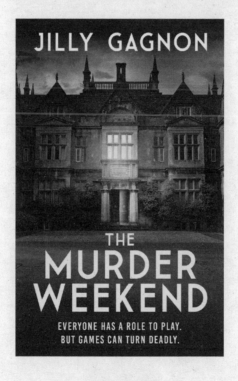